Praise for the charming Highlander series

A HIGHLANDER CHRISTMAS

"Romantic and magical. . . . Chapman dishes up all the passion and tender love she's known for."

—*Romantic Times*

"A humorous plotline, self-deprecating characters, and a decided dose of enchantment make this a warm read for the season."

—*BookPage*

"Filled with poignant realism interwoven with the enchanting magic of the holiday season. . . . Will charm and delight readers."

—Single Titles

"An extraordinary seasonal story full of laughter, romance, and magic."

—Fresh Fiction

SECRETS OF THE HIGHLANDER

"Liberally spiced with mystery, this story has warmth and genuine love that make it the perfect antidote for stress."

—*Romantic Times*

ONLY WITH A HIGHLANDER

"A mystical, magical book if there ever was one. . . . A perfect 10!"

—Romance Reviews Today

"Chapman's amazing ability to meld rich characterization with passion and romantic adventure is unmatched and unforgettable."

—*Romantic Times*

Also by Janet Chapman

JANET CHAPMAN

DRAGON WARRIOR

POCKET STAR BOOKS
New York London Toronto Sydney

Pocket Star Books
A Division of Simon & Schuster, Inc.
1230 Avenue of the Americas
New York, NY 10020

This book is a work of fiction. Names, characters, places, and incidents either are products of the author's imagination or are used fictitiously. Any resemblance to actual events or locales or persons, living or dead, is entirely coincidental.

First Pocket Star Books paperback edition February 2011

POCKET STAR BOOKS and colophon are registered trademarks of Simon & Schuster, Inc.

For information about special discounts for bulk purchases, please contact Simon & Schuster Special Sales at 1-866-506-1949 or business@simonandschuster.com.

The Simon & Schuster Speakers Bureau can bring authors to your live event. For more information or to book an event contact the Simon & Schuster Speakers Bureau at 1-866-248-3049 or visit our website at www.simonspeakers.com.

Cover design by Craig White

Manufactured in the United States of America

10 9 8 7 6 5 4 3 2 1

ISBN 978-1-4391-5989-7
ISBN 978-1-4391-9050-0 (ebook)

Chapter One

Fully aware that she was losing the argument from sheer absurdity, Maddy crossed her arms under her breasts and lifted her chin, determined to go down fighting. "You take that back right this minute! Refusing to have anything to do with another man named Billy does *not* make me a chicken."

Eve Gregor—her supposedly very best friend—rolled her eyes. "I'm not implying you're a chicken, he is. And his name is *William*." She suddenly shot Maddy an eager grin. "But I'll give you a manicure if you come over to supper tonight and call him Billy to his face. Or Bill. Or even Willy." Eve leaned on the counter, obviously warming to the idea. "And I'll throw in a pedicure if you wear your short shorts."

Maddy dropped her arms to her sides in surprise. "Are you forgetting that he threatened to *spank* me if I ever wore those shorts again? Right after he walked up, *stark naked*, and kissed me in front of half the men in town? I don't care if he is Kenzie's friend; William Killkenny is an uncouth, outrageous, lecherous brute."

Eve dismissed Maddy's concern with a laugh as she walked

from behind the counter. "William wouldn't really spank you; he was just blustering because your short shorts had been driving him crazy with lust all week."

"But I hadn't even *met* him before he walked out of that library carrying your mother, so how in hell could I have been driving him crazy with lust?"

Eve started rearranging the shrunken supply of bread and pastries on the table of her woodstove shop and bakery, and shrugged. "There must have been two dozen men who showed up to help rebuild our house and barn, so it's possible you simply didn't notice William." She glanced over her shoulder and smiled. "But the men all sure as hell noticed you and Susan."

Maddy pounced on the chance to change the subject. "Speaking of Susan, nobody's seen her since last Wednesday. I checked at the bank, but she never showed up for work on Monday, after her vacation. So I drove to her house last night, just to make sure she wasn't lying in a pool of blood at the bottom of her stairs, and the place looked as if she hadn't been there in days. All her plants were wilted, and there was a package from Victoria's Secret on her doorstep that was still soaked from the rainstorm we had three nights ago. I think we should file a missing person report or at least talk to the sheriff. What if something terrible happened to her?"

When Eve said nothing, Maddy straightened the sign on the banana bread with a frown, wondering why her friend didn't appear at all concerned about their friend. "I'm beginning to see why Susan feels so desperate to have a man of her own," Maddy continued. "She's been missing for six days, and nobody even noticed. Can you imagine being that alone in the world?" She nudged Eve with her hip. "I know she acted bitchy toward you when you moved back to Midnight Bay, but how can you not be worried about her?"

"Because not only do I know that Susan is on a mountain in

western Maine, I also happen to know that she's up there with Hamish MacKeage."

Maddy slapped her hand to her chest in surprise. "Susan ran off with *Hamish*?"

Eve nodded. "I guessed as much when they both turned up missing last Wednesday, so I asked Robbie MacBain to check it out when he went home. He called Thursday evening and told me to quit worrying, because he'd spotted the two of them at an old cabin he owns up on West Shoulder Ridge."

"Susan ran off with *Hamish*?" Maddy repeated, utterly shocked—and downright appalled. "Why, that no-good rotten witch! I can't believe she managed to hook her claws in one of those sexy, seemingly intelligent MacKeage men."

"Hey, two seconds ago you were feeling sorry for her."

"That was before I knew she actually had the nerve to run off with one of them." She shook her head. "Poor Hamish; by the time Susan lets him come up for air, he'll be ready to swear off women forever."

"It's more likely Susan is the one trying to come up for air," Eve said with a giggle. "Last Wednesday, just before we realized Mom was missing, Robbie MacBain warned me that he wouldn't put it past any of his MacKeage cousins to steal you or Susan away if one of them took a serious liking to either of you. And sure enough, Hamish stole Susan."

"Are you saying he *kidnapped* her?"

Eve's grin widened. "Kenzie assured me she wouldn't be protesting too long, once Hamish gets done with her."

Maddy snorted. "Does your husband think *all* Scots are God's gift to women?"

"I imagine Susan is thinking so right about now."

"So you've known about her running off with Hamish for five days, and you simply *forgot* to share that juicy bit of gossip with your very best friend?"

Eve's grin turned into a scowl. "It's hard to share juicy gossip with someone who's never around. I keep inviting you over to dinner, but you keep declining."

"That's because I wanted to give you newlyweds some privacy. You and Kenzie have only been married six days."

Eve rolled her eyes again. "Privacy? We have an old priest, my mother, and a boisterous Irishman living with us, not to mention a spoiled-rotten harbor seal pup that keeps trying to get into the house. What's one more? No, two more; I distinctly remember inviting Sarah, too."

"Yeah, like I'd expose my sweet, innocent child to Killkenny. He was *buck naked* when he walked out of the library, Eve. But instead of having the decency to ask the paramedics for a blanket, he was more interested in threatening me."

"Oh, will you get past that? I told you, William is *not* going to spank you." Eve arched a brow. "Likely because he knows you'd clean his clock if he tried."

"Damn right I would."

"So, will you please come to dinner tonight?"

"I don't know." Maddy crossed her arms under her breasts again, this time to ward off a sudden chill. "The man gives me the creeps. His hair is longer than mine, for crying out loud, and his beard pretty near suffocated me when he kissed me. The guy not only acts like a caveman, he looks like one, too."

"But he's such a *tall* caveman. Come on, you have to admit he's got one hell of a ripped body. And I have a feeling he really likes you."

Maddy glared at her. "That's the creepiest part. I'll have you know that I heard a noise outside our house Sunday night, and when I shut off my bedroom light and went to the window, I saw a man going into the woods. And the next morning I found a collection of seashells on my back porch."

"What makes you think William is the one who left them?"

"They were arranged to spell out *my bonny sweet lass*. And if that wasn't bad enough, yesterday I caught him outside the nursing home talking to one of our male residents in the garden. But when I went out to ask him what in hell he was doing, he scaled the six-foot fence as if it were knee-high and was gone."

Eve's eyes widened. "You think he's *stalking* you?"

Maddy was glad to see that her friend was finally taking her seriously. "You got a better definition for what he's doing?"

"Then all the more reason to come to supper tonight and confront him." Eve touched her arm. "That's what the Maddy Kimble I know and love would do."

Maddy balled her hands into fists at her sides. "You're right. Since when have I started letting some full-of-himself man scare me off?" She stormed to the door, but then stopped to look back at Eve. "And I will bring Sarah with me tonight, if only to let her see me in action." She shook her head. "She hasn't said anything, but I think Sarah is being bullied at summer rec. And seeing me stand up to Killkenny just might help her do the same for herself."

"She's being bullied? Then you need to talk to the head of the summer recreation program. They must have a policy for dealing with bullies."

Maddy sighed. "I'm sure they do. But if I make an issue out of it, Sarah will be mortified. And besides, I don't think it's any one kid in particular; I think a whole bunch of the little snots started teasing her after she got back from her trip with Billy's parents."

"Are they jealous that Sarah got to spend three weeks in a fancy motor home?"

Maddy smiled sadly. "What kid wouldn't be jealous, considering the farthest most of them have ever gone is Ellsworth? But I think they're really teasing her about the fact that her daddy knocked up an eighteen-year-old over in Oak Harbor."

"So it's true, then?" Eve whispered. "Billy got another woman pregnant?"

"An *eighteen*-year-old," Maddy repeated. She snorted. "Apparently my ex-husband's sperm only works on barely legal girls. Billy got me pregnant on my eighteenth birthday, but when we tried to give Sarah a brother or sister a couple of years later, he suddenly started shooting blanks."

Eve held her hands over her gaping mouth. "What are you going to do?"

Maddy shrugged. "Privately, I am sincerely praying that this marriage works out for him. And publicly, I'm telling everyone that Sarah is going to be a flower girl at their wedding."

"You want Sarah to be in the wedding?"

"Of course I do. She needs to be included, if only to know that she's just as important to her father as his new baby. Jeesh, you're acting as if you expect me to be embarrassed or something."

"What do you have to be embarrassed about?"

"Maybe that Billy replaced me with a younger woman?"

Eve was back to rolling her eyes. "Oh, for the love of— Everyone knows that *you* left him. And this woman can't be considered a replacement if it's been six years since your divorce. Hell, I had barely been divorced six *months* when I married Kenzie." She cupped her slightly bulging belly and grinned. "And I got knocked up before my wedding, too."

Maddy gave a dramatic sigh. "Sperm just runs rampant in Midnight Bay." She looked at her watch and then opened the door. "I have to get back to the nursing home. I'll pick up Sarah when I get off work, and we'll be on your doorstep in plenty of time to set the table." She started to step onto the sidewalk, but immediately scurried back inside and headed for the rear office. "Speaking of the devil," she muttered, rushing past Eve. "Kenzie and William just pulled up. I'm leaving the back way."

"Jeesh, come on," Eve said, running after her and grabbing her arm. "Now's your chance to confront him."

Maddy brushed down the front of her nursing scrubs and then tucked a stray lock of hair behind her ear. "I'm a mess."

"What do you care, if you're going to read him the riot act for stalking you?"

She took a deep breath and smiled tightly. "I promise I will tonight, right after supper. But instead of being covered in other people's body fluids and looking like something the cat dragged in when I do, I intend to be dressed like a woman he'll think twice about messing with."

"Omigod," Eve said, covering her mouth again. "So you *are* going to wear your short shorts tonight."

"No, I'm going to dress like a schoolteacher!" she said, poking fun at her friend. "And I'm going to waggle my finger in Killkenny's face just like old Mrs. Bean used to do, and tell him— Oh, shit!" Maddy cried when the bell over the front door gave a cheery tinkle. She immediately bolted out the back door, leaping a pile of old pallets as she made her escape.

"Cluck-cluck-cluck!" Eve called after her with a laugh, watching Maddy sprint down the back alleyway. The woman might be acting as though William Killkenny's far from subtle pursuit offended her, but Eve suspected Maddy was secretly thrilled.

Though probably not nearly as thrilled as she was. Maddy was her best friend, and it was important to Eve that she also find happily-ever-after.

Well, she was her best friend after Kenzie. But husbands didn't really count—especially when they were ancient enough to believe that a woman should be deliriously happy living on Old MacDonald's farm.

Which Eve was. Deliriously.

And she wanted Maddy to be deliriously happy, too.

Preferably with William.

Not only did William have the potential to be Maddy's desperately needed knight in shining armor, but Eve had a more selfish reason for wanting to see them become a couple. William was actually a ninth-century Irish nobleman whom some vindictive old witch had turned into a dragon twelve hundred years ago, and the poor guy could probably use some happiness of his own. He'd somehow managed to travel through time to this century in hopes that Kenzie could help him lift the curse, and now that he was a man again, keeping William's past a secret from Maddy was just about killing Eve.

She desperately needed someone to talk to about the strange things that had been happening in Midnight Bay over the last few months—not the least of which was that *she* was married to a time-traveling, eleventh-century highland warrior!

Maddy wasn't stupid, and would eventually figure out that it wasn't until Kenzie and Father Daar had moved to town that Midnight Bay had started experiencing scientifically unexplainable . . . stuff. Like the fact that several reputable people in town swore they saw a dragon walking down Main Street last Wednesday, and watched it carry Eve's mother into the library—only to have William Killkenny walk out carrying Mabel just after a flash of blinding white light had filled the building.

And really, Eve didn't know how Kenzie expected her to keep coming up with excuses as to why violent storms destroyed only *their* farm, why men suddenly stepped out of the ether buck naked, and why everyone on the farm was fawning over some silly harbor seal pup. And if she couldn't tell Maddy that the newest rumor about a *mermaid* being spotted just ten miles out in the Gulf of Maine was true, she was going to explode! What was the fun of knowing that magic truly existed if she couldn't share it with her very best friend?

"Is there a reason you're standing in the back door, clucking like a chicken?" her husband asked, sliding his arms around her from behind. "Wait, don't tell me," he whispered against her ear, his voice filled with amusement. "Ye have the urge to tell the world that you're hatching our son."

Eve turned in his embrace and smiled up at him. "I was clucking at Maddy for running away when she saw you and William drive up." She leaned sideways to look behind him. "Speaking of the devil, where is he?"

"Headed for the library with a list of books on modern home building Mabel suggested he get." His arms tightened when Eve gasped and tried to get free. "Ye needn't worry; your mother explained the library rules to him."

"It's not William I'm worried about, it's Maddy. She's headed back to work, and he's the last person she wants to run in to." She glared up at him. "Did you know he's been stalking her?"

Kenzie kissed the tip of her nose with a laugh. "Nay, wife, I believe he's courting her."

"Taking her on a date is courting; lurking outside her house at night and going to her place of work is *stalking*. He's overwhelming her, Kenzie. And if he doesn't back off, he's going to ruin any chance he might have of winning her heart." She patted his chest. "And since you did such a great job of winning *my* heart, I think you should have a talk with him about modern courtship."

"Oh, no, you don't," he said, setting her away with a fierce glare. "I am not getting involved in Killkenny's love life. And neither are you. If anyone has any chance of influencing that hardheaded bastard's behavior, it's Maddy."

Eve fought to hide her smile. Her husband was such a warrior, and talking to another warrior about matters of the heart appeared to be against some manly code. "So you don't have a problem with bailing William out of jail when he's arrested for stalking? And you've come up with a way to explain what he's doing here in America without a passport or any proof whatsoever that he existed before last Wednesday?"

"What are ye talking about, woman? What's a passport?"

"It's a document stating that William Killkenny is who he says he is and that he's here in America legally." She frowned at him. "Come to think of it, you don't have any documentation stating that *you* exist, either."

He pulled her back into his arms, his golden gaze locked on hers. "I believe the babe you're carrying is proof enough that I exist," he drawled.

"But how did you get your driver's license?"

"I showed them a copy of my birth certificate."

Eve arched a brow. "And they didn't have a problem that it said you were born in Scotland in the year 1047?"

"No, because it says I was born in 1977. And I have an immunization record, an entire set of school records—including something ye call a bachelor's degree—and even citizen papers."

She narrowed her eyes at him. "How did you get all those kinds of documents?"

He lowered his mouth to within inches of hers. "By magic," he whispered, just before he kissed her.

As soon as he finished—which was way too soon for her liking—Eve rested her head against his chest with a sigh. "Then you'd better have your brother the wizard conjure up some documents for William, too." She suddenly leaned back. "Wait, where is William getting the money to buy the land surrounding Dragon Cove and build his house? It's got to be costing a small fortune."

"Matt gave him the money." He sighed, hugging her to him again. "As it seems my brother has resigned himself to supporting the displaced souls I help return to their true natures."

"Yeah, well, I wish you'd hurry up and return that harbor

seal to *her* true nature," Eve muttered into his shirt. She tilted her head back to look up at him again. "How are all these displaced souls finding you, anyway? Did you staple pamphlets in every century or something?"

"Or something," he said with a chuckle.

Eve blinked up at him. "You actually *advertised*? Saying what: Need Help Lifting a Curse? Call 1–800–SOUL-WARRIOR? Kenzie, if we're going to keep having all these desperate . . . creatures showing up here, we're going to have to find a way to keep them contained."

"We?" he asked, lifting a brow. "And just when did you join my team?"

Eve arched a brow right back at him. "I believe I was drafted the night I rescued you from that cliff."

He hugged her to him again. "Aye, I remember that night quite well." He gently pulled her rounded belly into his. "It was the night ye not only saved my life but conceived my son."

"*Our* son," she said with a sigh, melting against him. "And you only remember our lovemaking as an erotic dream."

"A rather *vivid* erotic dream." He also sighed. "I'm finding the problem isn't breaking the curses of those who seek me out but what to do with the displaced souls once they become themselves again."

Eve looked up at him. "But I thought the plan was for William to help you fight the evil forces that keep following them here?"

He nodded. "That is the plan. And being a skilled warrior who relishes a good fight, Killkenny will be invaluable to me— that is, if I don't run him through with my sword first out of sheer frustration. I'm afraid he's embracing his new life a little too eagerly. *Everything* about this century fascinates him, and he's trying to experience it all at once. He's insisting I take him to buy a truck today. And are you aware that he and Mabel have eaten in just about every restaurant within fifty miles?"

Eve giggled. "William is Mom's new pet project, and she's having the time of her life explaining how everything works." She glanced up with a smile. "She's a born teacher, and . . . and I think helping William is actually keeping *her* in the here and now. She rarely has bouts of confusion anymore."

Kenzie kissed her forehead and stepped back with a grimace. "Aye, she's even offered to teach him to drive. And she has been a great help with our newest lost soul."

"Speaking of which, there are rumors going around town that someone saw a mermaid out in the Gulf—which means our harbor seal isn't always fur and whiskers when she's out of our sight. Can't you at least lock her in the barn during the day, before one of the local fishermen catches a spoiled-rotten *mermaid* in his net?"

"I can't, Eve," he said, his eyes turning pained. "She stops eating whenever I do. According to Fiona, the pup is running from an abusive man, and that's why she came looking for me. It's a wonder she even lets me near her, considering how much she fears men."

Eve snorted. "Personally, I think she's playing you. And I think she's playing your sister, too. She won't tell Fiona her name or where she came from or what century, yet she was pretty quick to say some evil man is chasing her just as soon as she learned Fiona isn't all that fond of men herself."

"The pup's not faking her desperation, and the energy searching for her sure as hell is real. As much as I hate to admit it, I'm thankful Killkenny will be living just across the cove. Which brings us back to him and Maddy. I want you to leave them to figure out their own courtship, like you and I did," he said, clasping his hands behind his back.

Eve felt a lecture coming on. She clasped her own hands behind her back, taking immediate, evasive action. "How much longer are you going to pretend that you love sleeping in my bed, *in the house?*"

That certainly did the trick; he dropped his hands to his sides and frowned at her.

Eve stepped into his arms and focused on toying with a button on his shirt so he wouldn't see her smile. "I bought a baby monitor today, so we can camp down by the ocean and still hear what's going on in the house. I know you're having a hard time adjusting to being a man again, and I don't want you fighting your old nature," she whispered, finally looking at him, her eyes shining with all her love. "And . . . well, I've discovered that I like sleeping under the stars with you."

Instead of a lecture, her husband kissed her again, this time quite thoroughly.

Chapter Two

William reclined on the knoll overlooking Madeline's home, watching the bonny lass hang out laundry as he munched on a loaf of bread. He wished he had some mead to go with his snack—and not some of that sissy ale the moderns called beer, either, that turned his stomach. Christ, but he yearned for a pint of the dark, sweet brew of his old homeland.

Maddy was working in almost complete darkness, the porch light not reaching the clothesline set near the woods. The interior of the house was black but for the soft light coming from the kitchen window, and she wouldn't be able to see what she was doing if there hadn't been a nearly full moon.

William washed down the bread with a swig of water pulled from the spring he'd found behind Maddy's house, and wondered why in hell the woman was still doing her chores at midnight. Especially considering that he knew she had to be up early to get her child fed and dressed, then get to her job at the nursing home by eight.

He'd only caught one side of the phone conversation Eve

had had with her earlier this evening, but it had been enough for him to realize that Maddy was backing out of yet another dinner invitation. So how in hell was he supposed to implement dear Mabel's suggestion that he ask Maddy to go on a picnic if he couldn't even get close enough to talk to her?

He admittedly may have come on a bit strong last Wednesday, but hell, he'd been lusting after the woman for nearly two months, since the first time she'd come to Kenzie's farm to visit Eve. And he'd been so excited the old hag's curse had finally been lifted, that when he saw Maddy standing there on the library lawn in the rain, he hadn't been able to restrain himself. He'd grabbed her beautiful face between his very human hands, pressed his very human lips to hers, and feasted on her sweetness.

Madeline Kimble was a startlingly beautiful woman, with long, wavy brown hair that refused to stay confined, skin that glowed with the kiss of the sun, and large, expressive brown eyes a man could drown in. As for below the neck, her full hips just begged to fill a man's palms, her lovely legs cried to wrap around a hard body, and her ample bosom all but screamed for a man's attention.

And William had decided that once the curse was lifted, *he* would be that man.

Only the lass didn't seem all that interested in him, which was vexing, considering the women of his old time had found him rather attractive. He tore off another bite of bread with a snort. More likely, they'd been attracted to his position of power. But he hadn't earned and then held his lands by sheer brawn alone, and any woman, of any century, would be lucky to catch his eye. He was legendary not only for his skills on the battlefield but also in the bedroom—or the hayloft, or the kitchen, or wherever else he happened to catch a handsome woman.

A lass had to be willing, though, as that was his one sacred rule when it came to dealing with the fairer sex. He'd been shoveling dirt over the bodies of his ravaged mother and sister when he'd given his vow never to force himself on a woman— right after he had hunted down, castrated, and then killed the plundering bastards who had murdered them.

William suddenly rolled to the side and sprang to a crouch in one swift motion, his dagger drawn. But just as swiftly as he'd prepared to defend himself, he sat down with a curse, slipped his weapon back into his boot, and picked up his bread again.

"Christ, Gregor, ye know better than to sneak up on a man like a goddamn cat."

Kenzie sat down beside him with a chuckle. "Old habits die hard, my friend."

"What are ye doing here?" William snorted. "Don't tell me your bride has had her fill of you already. Or did the pixie throw up on you again?"

"At least I *have* a woman willing to throw up on me; whereas you, Killkenny, have to sit up on a knoll in the dark to be near yours."

"Why are ye here, Gregor?"

"To find out your intentions."

"Toward Maddy?" he asked in surprise. "Why? What concern is she to you?"

"She's Eve's friend, which makes her my concern." Kenzie watched Maddy in silence for several seconds, and then looked at William again. "She's a good woman, Killkenny, and Eve told me Maddy is having a rough go of it right now, what with trying to rein in her strong-minded brother until he leaves for college in a few weeks. She doesn't need you adding to her problems, if all you're looking for is sport."

"Ye expect me to live the rest of my life like a monk in this century?"

"I expect you not to hurt her," Kenzie said softly. "Don't force my hand, William. Either tell me that your intentions are honorable, or give me your word that you'll leave her alone."

"How in hell can I tell you what my intentions are if I can't even get close to the woman? Christ, she could be a demanding bitch for all I know, or a tiresome nag or, even worse, a flaming shrew."

"She's a loving, sincere, compassionate, hardworking single parent and the sole support of her mother, daughter, and brother." Kenzie looked over at him, the moonlight revealing how deadly serious he was. "If that's more woman than you can handle, then ye need to walk away."

"I can't."

Kenzie blew out a heavy sigh. "Then at least back off a bit. Eve told me you went to the nursing home the other day, and she explained that if ye pester Maddy at her place of work, you could get her in trouble with her boss."

That surprised William. "Just by my talking to some old man who lives there?"

"Why do ye think they have a tall fence around the place? It's as much to keep the residents safe as it is to keep them from wandering away."

"But why are they locked away from everyone? They couldn't have committed any disturbing crimes; hell, half of them can barely walk. Have ye been to that place, Gregor? Everyone living there is positively ancient," he whispered in awe. "Some are ten, even twenty years older than Mabel."

Kenzie chuckled. "Fifty years old was considered ancient in your time, whereas today it's considered middle age. And we, my friend, are considered to be in the prime of our lives."

"But where are their families? Why aren't they living in their homes, watching their grandbabies grow up?"

"A good many of them have no families. And some are

infirm, and some have the minds of children—like Mabel's mind is getting."

William reared back. "You'll not be moving Mabel there, Gregor! As God is my witness, I'll steal her away if I have to."

"Nay, as long as I have breath in me, Mabel will remain with us. But Eve told me some of the residents choose to live there for the companionship." He grinned. "And because of the attention the workers like Maddy give them. Can ye not imagine how pleasant she's making their later years just by showing up to work every day?"

Only moderately mollified, William settled back on his elbow and watched Maddy carry her empty basket to the house. "I still don't understand the point of such a place. All that wisdom is being wasted," he muttered. When she disappeared inside, he looked over at Kenzie. "I spoke to an old man in the garden the day I went there, and he told me his name was Elbridge, and that he used to work in a mill that made paper. He was a warrior, too, and fought in what he called World War Two. He buried his wife ten years ago, and one of his sons came back in a pine box from a war in some country called Vietnam. He's been living in the nursing home for five years, having moved there when his only remaining child, a daughter, died of something called cancer." He shook his head. "And now he has practically no one."

"He has Maddy."

William grinned. "Aye. And when I happened to mention her name, Elbridge's eyes lit up. And then he told me that if he were my age, he sure as hell wouldn't be wasting his time talking to an old man in a garden."

Kenzie stood up. "Then maybe you should heed his words of wisdom. Instead of jumping fences in town and lurking in the shadows up here, ye could walk in the front door of the nursing home like a respectable citizen and offer to take Maddy to lunch on her noon break."

William laced his fingers behind his head and stared up at the night sky. "Maybe I'll do that."

"Oh, and William?"

"What else, Gregor?" he asked with a sigh.

"Shaving off your beard and getting a haircut might go a long way in convincing Maddy that you can at least *look* civilized."

William sat up and smoothed down his beard. "But I haven't shaved since my first whisker showed up when I was twelve."

Kenzie shrugged. "It was just a thought; Eve said something about Maddy calling you a caveman."

"The lass called me a caveman?"

"Among other things," Kenzie said with a chuckle.

"Like what?"

"I'm not playing 'he said, she said.'" Kenzie pointed at him. "And I was never here—you understand?"

William perked up. "The pixie *asked* you to follow me tonight? To what? To give me pointers on how to deal with Maddy?"

"The only point I intend to give you is the tip of my sword if Eve finds out I was here. This conversation never happened."

William reclined back on the grass with a snort, and Kenzie Gregor disappeared into the darkness as silently as the panther he'd once been.

Chapter Three

$\mathcal{O}$f the eight full-time residents and four day campers at the River Run Nursing Home, no less than six of them were waiting at the front door when Maddy showed up for work Monday morning. Some were sitting in wheelchairs, some stood clutching walkers, and all of them looked more excited than a squabble of seagulls at a clambake.

Eyeing them curiously as she pulled her hair forward over her left cheek, Maddy plastered a warm smile on her face and opened the door. But because she wasn't too steady on her own feet, she stubbed her toe on Samuel's walker and almost knocked Lois over when they all rushed forward, barely catching herself by grabbing the back of Charlotte's wheelchair.

Lois dodged Maddy's swinging purse and grabbed her arm. "You're late, young lady. Come on, let's get that hair of yours combed out," the spry octogenarian said, leading Maddy toward the nurses' station. "Of all the days for you to oversleep. He's going to be here any minute, and you look like you've been on a four-day bender."

"Who's going to be here?" Maddy asked, hiking her purse onto her shoulder as she tried to keep up without wincing. "Dr. Petty? Since when does everyone get excited over one of his visits?" she asked, glancing back to find everyone following them. She stopped walking and turned with a frown. "I told you people, I am not asking Paul Petty out on a date. He's old enough to be my *father.*"

"Not Petty," Lois said, tugging her arm to get her moving again. "Come on, we have to wash off that makeup, too." She made a *tsk*ing sound. "Gracious, Maddy, you slapped it on so thick this morning, William's going to mistake you for a hooker."

Maddy pulled to a halt again. "William who?

"William Killkenny," Charlotte said, beaming brightly.

"William Killkenny! He's coming here? *This morning!*" Maddy cried at the halted parade of people, who were all nodding excitedly.

"He's been visiting us every day since last Thursday," Elbridge said. "Which you would know if you hadn't called in sick the end of last week."

"He's been visiting you?" Maddy asked, this time in a strangled whisper.

Everyone nodded again.

"But *why?*"

Hiram puffed out his chest. "To get our advice, because we have . . . we have . . ." He frowned at Elbridge. "What did he say we have, Elby?"

"Several centuries' worth of combined wisdom," Elbridge said, straightening his own shoulders. He nodded to Maddy. "He claims we're more valuable than a whole library of books."

"And he needs our help," Charlotte interjected. "Because we know just what he should build and exactly where."

"Build what exactly where?" Maddy asked.

"His home."

"The one he's planning to put up over on Riley Cove," Hiram added.

"It's called Dragon Cove now," Elbridge corrected. "Remember? They changed the name of it after those kayakers saw that dragon."

"What in tarnation are kayakers?" Hiram asked.

"That's what you call people who paddle those covered sea canoes."

Lois made another *tsk*ing sound, shaking her head. "Land sakes, Maddy, did you go out for ladies' night last Wednesday and get roaring drunk again? You obviously still haven't recovered; you look like hell."

"Is that why you called in sick last Thursday *and* Friday?" Charlotte asked. "Oh, Madeline, you know drinking doesn't agree with you. Whatever possessed you to take another chance like that?"

"I did not go drinking last Wednesday. I fell off my porch and wrenched my knee. I couldn't come to work Thursday and Friday because I couldn't walk."

Charlotte immediately got out of her wheelchair and pushed it toward her. "I thought I saw you limping on your way across the parking lot. Here, use my chair."

Knowing that Charlotte would be insulted if she didn't, Maddy sat down with a sigh, setting her purse on her lap so she could maneuver the chair. "Thank you," she said, turning around to wheel backward down the hall.

Everyone started following again like a herd of excited turtles.

William Killkenny was coming here this morning?

"Hiram, why are you wearing your jacket?" she suddenly asked. "It must be seventy-five degrees in here."

Hiram fingered the zipper on his jacket. "Because it ain't

gonna be seventy-five degrees down on Riley—I mean, Dragon Cove," he said, shooting Elbridge a grin. "The water temperature probably ain't even fifty, and the breeze'll be chilly."

Maddy stopped wheeling. "What's the sea breeze got to do with anything?"

Hiram puffed up his chest again. "William and his friend, Mr. Gregor, are taking some of us to Dragon Cove to help him figure out where he wants to build his house."

"Elby and Hiram and I are going," Samuel piped up, catching his own jacket as it started to slide off the front bar of his walker.

Charlotte smoothed down her sweater. "And Lois and I are going with them to make sure they position the house so the kitchen has a good view."

"Because men never think about that sort of thing," Lois added, pulling Maddy's chair backward toward the nurses' station. "But no woman wants to look out her sink window at some silly old forest when there's an ocean around."

Maddy was so dumbfounded that she just let herself be dragged down the hall. William and Kenzie were taking some of her residents on a field trip? Because William had been coming here for the last four days, asking for their advice?

"Did Doris say it was okay for you to go?" she asked.

Elbridge snorted. "We don't need her permission; we're not exactly prisoners."

"We *told* Doris we were going," Lois explained.

Hiram made a harrumphing noise. "Her face got all screwed up again, in that look she gets whenever we tell her something we're planning."

"But after William turned on his charm," Charlotte interjected, "and assured her that he would personally make sure none of us got swept out to sea, Doris calmed down."

"His *charm*?" Maddy whispered, standing up when Lois stopped the chair.

"Oh, my, yes," Lois breathed. "William got that twinkle in his handsome blue eyes and smiled that crooked smile of his, and Doris literally melted."

"Are you sure he said his name is William Killkenny?" Maddy held her hand several inches over her head. "About six-two, wild dark hair down past his shoulders, and a beard that's bushy enough to hide a flock of birds in?"

"Not anymore," Charlotte said. "Well, he's definitely tall, but the beard and most of the hair is gone."

"The poor man actually flinched when Elvira started hacking away," Lois said, "and he broke into a sweat when she took the electric razor to his beard."

"Elvira barbered William? *Our* Elvira?

"She's the best stylist east of Ellsworth," Charlotte defended. "And unlike that little twit Doris hired from Oak Harbor, Elvira keeps up with the latest trends. She left William a goatee because all the sexy men are wearing them. And I must say, it certainly makes him look dashing."

"Especially now that he's wearing the fancy new watch Janice found for him on the Internet," Lois added. "We told William he simply *had* to have it to go with his new look. And we also talked him into letting Janice order a sporty leather jacket, too, for when it gets chilly at night."

Elbridge snorted. "There wasn't any need to pay extra to have it overnighted. But you all insisted William needed the watch *now*. Money doesn't grow on trees, you know. I don't know why you women can't wait even a few days for anything."

"Because we could be dead in a few days," Charlotte snapped. "And it was only an extra fifty-three bucks."

"It damn near maxed out Janice's credit card," Elbridge shot back.

"Omigod!" Maddy yelped. "Please don't tell me Janice paid for William's watch and jacket!" Honest to God, she would kill him. *Nobody* took advantage of her residents, especially not some caveman of a scam artist. "Wait. Janice has a thousand dollar limit on that card! Are you're saying she maxed it out?"

Lois patted her arm. "Now, calm down, Maddy. William gave her the cash to put toward her credit-card bill."

"In fact," Charlotte added, "he gave her extra to purchase a brooch he saw on the same website, that he claimed would bring out the green in her eyes. He said he wanted to buy it for her as a thank-you for shopping for him."

It was Hiram who snorted this time. "Apparently the boy not only has money to burn, but he's color-blind, too. Janice's eyes are as faded as her hair. Elby, where'd William say he got all his money? I can't remember what he told us he does for a living."

"He said something about making a killing over in Ireland," Elbridge said with a shrug. "He must have been talking about investing in the stock market before it tanked."

"He mentioned owning a bunch of land over there," Samuel offered. "It's more likely he's one of them land developers. That must be why he didn't mind paying Frank Riley a small fortune for Dragon Cove."

"Which means he's as smart as he is handsome," Lois said smugly. "He'll make a killing here, too, once the economy turns around. There's enough land on that cove that William could sell several oceanfront lots and still have plenty left over." She nudged Maddy and lowered her voice. "There was a little something else in the package that came Saturday, but I believe it's a surprise for . . . a certain someone. William asked Janice to add it to the order, because after we told him how pretty and kind and caring you are, I guess he wanted to thank a certain someone. So will you please go comb your hair and wash your face before he gets here? First impressions are very important."

Utterly dumbfounded again, Maddy plopped back down in Charlotte's chair. Jeesh, take a few days off and this place went to hell in a handbasket. Now what was she supposed to do, if William kept showing up here to get *advice* from her residents?

"Maddy, come on!" Lois cried, tugging on her arm to get her to stand. "Your hair looks like you've been up partying all night!"

"Personally, I like tousled hair on a lass."

Maddy snapped her head up at the sound of the deep, lilting voice and would have gasped if the marine-blue eyes locked on hers hadn't stolen her ability to *breathe*. It took her several thundering heartbeats to realize she was staring at . . . he was . . .

No, that couldn't be William. He didn't even come close to the Neanderthal who had kissed her on the library lawn in front of God and half the men in town, and he sure as hell didn't resemble the outrageous lech who had stood opposite her as best man at Kenzie and Eve's wedding.

This guy was . . . he was . . . hell, he actually looked *civilized*.

And so drop-dead gorgeous Maddy didn't think she'd ever breathe again.

It took her several more heartbeats to realize the residents had abandoned her in favor of crowding around William.

"Close your mouth, Maddy girl," Kenzie said with a chuckle, walking up and gently lifting her chin with his finger. "And tell me why you're sitting in a wheelchair."

It took some time—and a surprising amount of effort—but Maddy finally tore her gaze away from the imposingly tall, impeccably groomed, sexy *hunk* laughing at something Hiram had said. She blinked up at Kenzie "I . . . he . . ." She took a steadying breath. "William bought the land surrounding Dragon Cove? And he's going to be living here in Midnight Bay? *Permanently?*"

Kenzie nodded. "Why are ye sitting in the chair? Did ye hurt yourself?"

"Huh? Oh . . . I fell off my porch Wednesday night and wrenched my knee."

His eyes went from amused to concerned. "When on Wednesday night?"

She frowned up at him. "I don't remember. It was late." She levered out of the chair and hiked her purse over her shoulder. "It was more like early Thursday morning."

"It's not only your knee ye hurt," he said, gently brushing her hair off her cheek.

Maddy stepped away with a humorless laugh, and walked behind the nurses' station. "I guess I also smacked my head on the steps when I fell."

"You should have called Eve to come help out, if you couldn't walk. Or at least Sarah could have come to An Tearmann for the weekend, and played with the puppies while your knee mended."

Maddy stuffed her purse under the counter and straightened with a smile. "Sarah spent the weekend with her father. I just sprawled on the couch for four days, read a ton of books, and let Mom wait on me."

Seeing his gaze focus on her cheek again, Maddy went to the medicine cabinet, fished her keys out of her pocket, and unlocked the door. "Charlotte," she called out, turning to see everyone following William as he made his way to the nurses' station. "You're not going anywhere until I check your blood sugar."

"My blood is just fine," Charlotte said, lifting her chin defensively. "I checked it myself this morning."

"How? The monitor is locked up."

"Not anymore, it isn't."

Not seeing the monitor in the basket, Maddy moved the medications around in the cabinet, searching for it. She turned back to Charlotte with a sigh. "You're going to get our new weekend nurse in trouble. You know Valerie wasn't supposed to let you keep that monitor because it could get broken or lost again. If I have to replace it a fourth time, we're *all* going to get in trouble."

Charlotte's smug smile disappeared. "I didn't lose those other ones. Someone must have stolen them. And I'm not five years old; I can check my own blood sugar."

"Now, Charlotte, my sweet," William said, wrapping an arm around her frail shoulders. "Ye mustn't take this personally," he said, lowering his head next to her ear—though Maddy could still hear him. "This really has nothing to do with you. It has to do with not wanting Miss Kimble to worry about you. Did ye not spend these last few days telling me what a wonderful nurse she is and how lucky you all are to have her working here?"

"We are lucky," Charlotte whispered back, smiling up at him. "It would be quite gloomy around here without her."

"Aye, I can see how she brightens up the place. And ye said she's not shy about telling you bawdy jokes, which proves she knows you're not a child who needs coddling. So, would it not make her feel needed if ye simply let her take care of you?"

"I hadn't thought of it that way." Charlotte reached into her pocket, pulled out the small monitor, and set it on the counter. "Maybe you *should* keep it locked up, so it doesn't get stolen again."

His deep ocean-blue eyes locking on hers, William gave Maddy a wink.

And once again, she stopped breathing.

"So, people," he said, turning to the residents and rubbing his hands together. "Are ye ready to go have a look at my land? Mabel Bishop and Miss Kimble's mama, Patricia, kindly packed us a picnic."

Kenzie reached across the counter and gently lifted Maddy's gaping mouth again. "I take it ye like William's new look," he said.

"Huh? Um . . . but what's he doing here?" she whispered,

forcibly tearing her gaze away from William's broad shoulders. "Why is he suddenly hanging around my residents?"

"He's fascinated by all that these folks have seen and done in their lifetimes, and he feels there's much he can learn from them."

"Do either of you realize what taking a bunch of senior citizens on a field trip involves?" She waved toward the residents, where Elbridge was pointing at what looked like a small map William was holding as the others crowded around them. "Samuel can barely walk *indoors*; he'll never be able to maneuver his walker on uneven ground. And Charlotte's legs just suddenly give out on her, and she has to resort to using a wheelchair half the time. And old people get chilled easily, Kenzie, and they won't tell you they're cold because they won't want to spoil the field trip."

"We will take good care of your precious charges."

She didn't doubt they would, as she trusted Kenzie implicitly. She'd seen how well he took care of the old priest, Father Daar, who had moved to Midnight Bay with him five months ago, and how he kept a watchful eye on Eve's ailing mother. Maddy blew out a sigh, knowing she was being ridiculous. But dammit, seeing William this morning— looking so handsome—had rattled her more than her fall off the porch.

"Why don't ye call Eve to come have lunch with you?" Kenzie suggested.

Maddy forcibly tore her gaze away from William again. "I can't today. My cousin is stopping by to have lunch with me. I haven't seen Trace in over five years. He just got back from Afghanistan, and I'm looking forward to our visit."

"Afghanistan?"

"Trace is in the military." She frowned. "Or he was. We all thought he intended to make a career of it, but he suddenly came home a week ago, announced that he'd quit, and bought a fishing boat." She shrugged. "Mom's sister—Trace's mother— said she thought he might be burned out or something, because he's been acting sort of strange since he got back."

Kenzie's golden eyes filled with concern. "Aye, war does have a way of taking its toll on a man."

"Trace was in some special forces group. I don't know which one, though, because he refuses to talk to anyone about what he did."

"Well, he's home now," Kenzie said. "So, is your knee all better? I know ye have your mom and your brother to help with your chores, but I'm sure Eve would love to visit with you this evening. She says she hasn't seen very much of you since our wedding."

"I know," Maddy said with a sigh. "But I've had a lot of stuff going on lately."

"Maddy . . . ye know that if there's anything we can do to help lighten your load, all ye have to do is ask."

Maddy shot him a thankful smile. "Eve lending me her car until I can save up to get a new one has been more than enough help."

"When is your brother leaving for school?"

Maddy kicked her smile up another notch. "Rick heads out in two weeks."

Lois and Charlotte walked over to the counter. "We're going to ask Doris if you can come with us," Lois said. "I think we should have a nurse on our field trip."

Maddy shook her head. "I have meds to dispense and a couple of treatments to give. But I can see if Katy can go with you if you want."

"She's a CNA," Charlotte said. "What if Samuel's pacemaker suddenly quits or my blood sugar goes haywire after lunch? We need a *nurse*."

Maddy slid the monitor toward her. "If you start feeling

woozy, you can check your own sugar. And Samuel's pacemaker isn't suddenly going to quit. You'll be in good hands with Kenzie and William." She darted a look down the hall and immediately wished she hadn't.

Damn, the man was gorgeous. Now that his hair was shorter and he was clean-shaven—except for that sexy-as-hell goatee—she couldn't seem to stop staring at him. And he certainly filled out a pair of jeans rather nicely. But it was the crisp white shirt he was wearing, spanning unbelievably broad shoulders that really got her heart to thumping. He'd rolled the cuffs back, and for some unexplainable reason muscled forearms and powerful, masculine hands were Maddy's greatest weakness when it came to men.

And that fancy new watch glistening on his wrist definitely finished the look.

Damn, she was in trouble.

"Come on, you two," Elbridge called out. "We're not getting any younger standing around here."

"Ladies," Kenzie said, ushering the women ahead of him while giving Maddy an amused nod. "We'll have them back for dinner. Enjoy your lunch with your cousin."

Maddy leaned over the counter to watch the turtle parade shuffle down the hall and out the front door. She rushed limping into the sitting room to look out the window and saw them gather around Kenzie's large black SUV, where they immediately started arguing over who was going to sit where. She covered her mouth, laughing out loud when she saw William suddenly realize that getting any of them into the third-row seat was going to be about as easy as getting a newborn chick back in its egg.

She cracked open the window to listen.

"Charlotte and Lois," she heard William say. "Since the rear seat is smaller than the middle one, why don't ye let me pick up you two wee lassies and set ye inside?"

Lois's eyes widened. "I'm not *that* wee a lassie."

"Of course ye are, darling," he said, sweeping her off her feet, chuckling when she gasped. "Why, I've lifted kittens that weigh more than you do."

By the time he reappeared from settling Lois in the third seat, Charlotte was positively giddy with anticipation. Maddy fought but failed to hold in her laughter when the tiny woman all but threw herself into his arms. "Oh, William, you are *so* strong," Charlotte said, her arthritic hands clutching his broad shoulders.

"What's so funny?" Doris asked, coming to stand beside Maddy.

"How many strong men does it take to load a truck with senior citizens?"

Doris looked out the window and sighed. "I don't know if those two are saints, or if they're really sinners trying to worm their way into heaven. I can't imagine what possessed Mr. Kill-kenny to offer to take them on a picnic."

Maddy grinned at the thirty-year veteran of nursing-home administration. "Maybe we'll find out when they bring them home this afternoon."

"I know Kenzie Gregor married Eve Anderson a couple of weeks ago," Doris said. "And whenever I go to Mabel's shop to buy bread, she can't stop raving about her new son-in-law." Doris glanced at the nearly loaded SUV, then back at Maddy. "But I can't quite get a handle on William Killkenny. He walked in here last Thursday morning and asked if it would be okay for him to visit with the residents."

"Did he say why he wanted to visit with them?"

"He told me he was building a house down on Riley Cove and that he'd like to get their advice on how he should go about it. He said that if anyone knew what would work and what wouldn't in this climate, they would." Doris broke into a rare smile. "I have to say, my first instinct was to call the sheriff and have him removed from the premises. Lord," she said, shaking her head, "the man was scary to look at; big as a barn, strong enough to stop a freight train, and so hairy I thought Bigfoot was standing in my office."

"What stopped you from calling the sheriff?"

"Elbridge came in just then, and William's face—at least what I could see of it—immediately lit up. He shook Elbridge's hand, and I realized that very few of our visitors ever think to offer such a simple, respectful gesture. Just then Lois peeked into the office, and William's eyes turned . . . well . . . tender. He tucked his hands behind his back, gave her a slight bow, and formally introduced himself to her."

Doris shrugged. "I've been in this business long enough to know that just like dogs and children, seniors have a sixth sense about a person's character. So I told William I'd be willing to give him a chance, and in the four days he's been coming here, I can only say that the atmosphere has been nothing short of electric." She waved at the window. "Just look at them. They were up at the crack of dawn and waiting at the kitchen door for breakfast, dressed in their Sunday best. I haven't seen them this excited since I lost my mind and gave them permission to paint their own rooms whatever color they wanted."

"We're still scraping neon pink paint off of Janice's mirror and windows."

"Oh, thank God you're here!" Katy said, rushing into the sitting room. "Maddy, I need your help!"

"Why, what's wrong?" Maddy asked, going on full alert when she saw Katy's hands and scrubs were smeared red. "What happened?" she asked, rushing toward her. "Who's hurt?"

"No, this isn't blood," Katy said. "It's Passion Red nail polish!"

The young CNA thrust something toward her, and Maddy gasped so hard she actually hurt her chest.

"I was painting Mem's toenails," Katy continued in a rush, "when Janice asked me to go see if someone had accidentally unplugged the Wi-Fi again. I was only gone for a minute, I swear." Katy thrust her hand out again. "But when I came back, I found Mem painting her *dentures*! I tried cleaning them, but I can't get it off. And there's no more polish remover; Lois used the entire bottle to clean the pitch off Hiram's hands when he collected all those pine cones last week. What do I do? The polish is drying!"

"Relax, Katy," Maddy said calmly, trying her damnedest not to burst out laughing. She wrapped her arm around the teenager's shoulders and headed into the hallway. "We'll try denatured alcohol, and if that doesn't work, you can run to the drugstore and get more polish remover."

"Welcome back to the most exciting place in Midnight Bay, Ms. Kimble," Doris chortled, walking toward her office.

"I'm quite impressed by your restraint this morning, Killkenny," Kenzie said.

William finished stowing Charlotte's wheelchair and Samuel's walker in the back of the SUV, closed the hatch, and arched a questioning brow. "How so?"

"I half expected you to jump over that counter and demand that Maddy tell you who put that mark on her face."

"And if I had, do ye believe she would have told me?"

"No. There's a good chance she would have slapped *your* face," Kenzie said with a chuckle. But just as quickly, his features hardened. "She told me she fell off her porch, hitting her head and wrenching her knee, in the wee hours of *Thursday* morning. What time did ye leave there Wednesday night?"

"About twenty minutes after you did, when I saw the kitchen light go out and assumed she'd gone to bed."

"Then it seems we weren't the last people to see Maddy that night. A porch step doesn't leave a handprint on a woman's face."

William realized he must have looked somewhat lethal himself when he saw Kenzie stiffen. "Ye can't think to extract personal retribution, Killkenny," Kenzie growled. "That's not how things are done in this century."

"Then what do you suggest I do? Let some bastard get away with abusing her?"

"I can't answer that until we find out who the bastard is."

"Most likely it's her ex-husband."

Kenzie shook his head. "I have every reason to believe Maddy and Billy Kimble are on good terms with each other. In fact, Eve told me he's marrying a young woman from Oak Harbor who is carrying his child."

"Billy Kimble? Are ye saying Maddy still uses his name?"

"I asked Eve about that, and she said Maddy kept it out of concern for Sarah, so they wouldn't have different surnames." He shook his head again. "I haven't heard Eve or Maddy mention there being any other man in Maddy's life."

"There's her brother," William said with a frown. "And I recall seeing an old pickup truck as I was leaving there Wednesday night, a few miles from Maddy's house. It was speeding, and I remember thinking that whoever was driving must have a death wish, because it was weaving all over the road."

"It's possible it was Rick, as he has an old blue pickup," Kenzie offered. "And he could have been drunk. From what I've seen since moving to Midnight Bay, there's not much for the young men to do at night around here, other than drink and get into mischief. Word is it was a bunch of teenagers who painted that dragon on the front doors of the library."

William snorted. "They must have been drunk, if that was supposed to be a dragon. Do ye think Maddy's brother would actually strike her?"

"If he'd been drinking, he might, if she confronted him. It would certainly explain her not saying anything to anyone, including Eve. Maddy has been the head of their household since her papa died several years ago." He nudged William toward the passenger's side of the truck. "Come on, we better get going before these folks decide to drive off without us. We'll deal with this problem tonight. Maybe Eve can help us decide how to approach Maddy."

William walked up to the passenger's door, but stopped and looked toward the nursing home. Kenzie *should* be impressed by his restraint. Hell, it was a wonder he'd managed even to wink at her, when he'd really wanted to pull her into his arms, kiss that bruise off her face, then demand the name of the bastard who'd put it there.

William finally got into the truck and immediately turned to smile at the very people who could likely tell him about Maddy's brother. "Just to make the day truly interesting," he said, "I thought I'd offer a prize to anyone who spots the dragon living in my cove."

Chapter Four

$\mathcal{M}$addy was caught off guard a second time that day when a tall, rather imposing man silently walked up to her nurses' station at ten minutes to four. Apparently realizing that it took her a moment to recognize him, her cousin's mouth lifted in the beginning of a smile—only it disappeared when his sharp, piercing gray eyes suddenly narrowed on her face.

"Who in hell hit you?" he growled instead of the warm greeting she'd expected.

Maddy touched her cheek. "I, um, tripped and fell off my porch last week. And it's wonderful to see you, too, even if you *are* four hours late."

Instantly contrite, Trace stepped behind the counter, pulled her up out of her chair, and hugged her fiercely. "I'm sorry for growling at you like that, and for missing our lunch date." He blew out a sigh. "Damn, Peeps, I've missed you. Every time I caught a whiff of antiseptic in the last five years, I saw your beautiful face."

"My signature cologne," she said with a laugh, hugging him

back just as fiercely. She leaned away to look at him. "Oh, Trace, it's so good to see you. Are you really home for good?"

"I'm not leaving Midnight Bay ever again." His eyes crinkled at the corners with another hint of a smile. "Except to drive my two favorite girls over to Port Stone. Just as soon as you get off work, we'll strap Sarah's booster seat in my truck, and the three of us will go pig out on lobster down at the pier."

Maddy stepped away with a laugh. "Sarah hasn't used a booster seat in four years; she's nearly *ten,* Trace, and already quite a young lady. And I'm sorry, but old man Walsh died three years ago, and rumor is they buried him in his lobster shack."

Trace stared at her in disbelief, but then his gaze strayed to her cheek, and his eyes hardened again. Maddy laced her fingers through his and started down the hall, stopping to peek into the sitting room.

"Katy, I'm heading out back to the gazebo for a few minutes. If you need anything, just give me a holler."

Katy looked up from the newspaper she was reading to some of the residents, her eyes widening when she noticed the man holding Maddy's hand. "Oh. Sure. I'll give you a holler," the young girl stammered. "Um, shouldn't the others be back by now?" she asked—though Maddy wasn't sure if she was asking her or Trace, as the poor girl couldn't seem to stop staring at her cousin.

"They'll be here soon. When they arrive you should probably check them for sunburn, and if anyone's tired, tell them they can have supper in their rooms."

"I'll get them settled in for the evening," Katy promised.

Maddy gave her a nod and started down the hall again. "Instead of taking us out to eat, you can follow me home when I get off work in an hour, and *I'll* feed *you,*" she told Trace, leading him outside into the bright August sun. She stopped to make a face at him. "Mom said you bought a fishing boat.

Mind telling me what in hell possessed you to become a fisherman?"

"There's not much call for soldiering around here," he snapped. "And I'm sure as hell not going to work at the textile mill."

"That mill closed two years ago," Maddy whispered.

He gave her hand a squeeze. "I'm sorry, Peeps. That was an uncivilized response to a very reasonable question." He started them off again, and they walked across the lawn in companionable silence. "Do you have any plans for this Saturday?" he asked when they reached the gazebo overlooking the river.

"Nothing pressing. Why?"

"Can you get a babysitter for Sarah?"

"She stays with Billy most weekends. Why? What's up?"

He sat down on the gazebo step and stared out at the gently flowing water. "I'd like you to spend the day with me on my boat."

She snorted. "You know I love you to pieces, and that I'm dying for us to catch up, but you also know that the smell of bait makes me puke out my guts. Why don't we just take a ride to Acadia National Park? I'm sure we can find a lobster shack in Bar Harbor that's falling-down dirty like old man Walsh's."

Trace shot her a quick glance before looking away again, but it was long enough for Maddy to see the guarded look in his eyes. "Because what I want to show you is out on the water," he said quietly. "And because you're the only person I can trust to tell me the truth."

"The truth about what?"

"About whether or not I've gone insane."

"Excuse me?" She reached out to grasp his forearm. "Trace, what are you talking about?"

"Have you heard a rumor going around town about a . . . mermaid being spotted ten miles offshore early last week?"

"I've only heard bits and pieces."

"Well, I'm the one who started it."

Caught completely off guard again, Maddy could only gape at him.

He looked down at her hand on his arm, then took it between his callused palms and turned on the step to face her. "When I was out putting my new boat through its paces last Monday, I spotted something splashing in the distance off my port side, so I headed toward it. But when I reached where it should have been, whatever had been making those splashes had vanished. Only it reappeared not fifty yards off my stern, and I saw . . ." His hands tightened on hers. "I saw a woman in the water, watching me."

"A *woman*? Ten miles out? Were there any other boats around?"

He shook his head. "And when I shouted at her to hold on, that I'd throw her a buoy, she looked as startled as I was, and suddenly started swimming away. I dug around for a buoy, but when I went to throw it, she'd disappeared again. So I stripped down to just my jeans, and dove in."

"Trace! The ocean is freezing!"

"It sure as hell wasn't bathwater. But what else could I do? I had no idea how long she'd been out there. She was in a lot more danger of getting hypothermia than I was." He shook his head, dropping his gaze to her hand still clasped in his. "I dove again and again searching for her. I swear I'd catch a glimpse of something out of the corner of my eye, but when I swam toward it, there was never anything there."

He looked up at her, and if he'd been guarded before, he appeared positively haunted now. "One time when I came up for air, I found her treading water not twenty feet away from me and realized she was as naked as a newborn. And dammit, Maddy, she *smiled* at me," he growled, squeezing her hand. "I was so stunned I just bobbed there like flotsam, completely speechless. She suddenly laughed, and then dove under the surface again. I got my wits back just in time to put my face in the water and see her swim underneath me, so close she actually tugged on my toes. And then . . . then she simply vanished again."

"She *vanished*?"

Trace stood up, his hands balled into fists as he faced her. "I swam back to my boat and put out a Mayday to the Coast Guard and to any other boats in the area. I told them there was a woman in the water, gave the coordinates, and then started scanning the waves again."

"You broadcast a Mayday? Saying what . . . that there was a naked, laughing woman swimming in the Gulf of Maine?" she asked, hoping to make light of what he was saying, as she sure as hell couldn't comprehend it.

He glowered at her. "You of all people know the symptoms of hypothermia: mental confusion, the sensation of warmth, euphoria."

"But a person can't survive more than an hour—two hours tops—in water that cold, Trace." Maddy also stood up. "And you'd been swimming around in it for what? Half an hour yourself? Have you considered that maybe *you* were the one experiencing confusion? You probably mistook a seal or a porpoise for a person at first, and only thought it was a naked woman once the cold started getting to you."

"I'm trained not to let the cold get to me. I could have swum the ten miles to shore if I'd had to. Dammit, Maddy, I need you to believe me!" He started to say more, but suddenly turned away and stood rigid, staring at the river.

Maddy had no idea what to say, either.

Or do.

Or even think.

"And because of my Mayday," he said, his back still to her, "now there's a rumor going around town that poor Trace Huntsman must have snapped over in Afghanistan, because he called the Coast Guard to come rescue a mermaid."

"And did you snap in Afghanistan?" she asked softly. "Is that why you came home, Trace, because they sent you home?"

He turned to her, and Maddy nearly cried out at the pain in his eyes. "I took myself out of the game *before* I snapped." Apparently in an attempt to appear indifferent, he gave a shrug, though Maddy knew he was anything but. "If they chose to believe my beating a man nearly to death meant I was losing it, who was I to argue with them?"

She took a shuddering breath. "And did you . . . when you . . . had you reached some point of no return, Trace?"

"I beat the bastard because he deserved it." He slashed the air with his hand. "And that's all I'm saying on the subject, so let's get back to my mermaid."

"But—"

"I returned to the same spot the very next day," he continued, "and have gone there every day since, except today." His hands balled into fists again. "And I saw her three more times: last Thursday, again Friday, and then again yesterday." He reached into his pocket and pulled something out. "Yesterday she surfaced not ten feet from my boat and hit me square in the chest with this," he said, holding his hand toward her.

Maddy stared at the tiny metal object.

"I've decided it's a coin," he said, taking her wrist to lift her hand, and pressing the object into her palm. "An ancient coin made of some metal I don't recognize. I spent today at the library searching the stacks and online, but I wasn't able to find anything like it. I couldn't find anything resembling the symbol stamped on it, either."

When she still said nothing, he turned the coin over, leaving it sitting in her palm. "But I think the marking on the back is a word, and near as I can tell, it's Sanskrit."

She lifted her gaze to his. "Sanskrit?"

"It's an ancient Indic language used around twelve hundred to four hundred B.C."

"Indic?"

"It was spoken in India and is still used in some parts of it today. Sanskrit is supposedly as old as Latin and Greek."

She squinted down at the coin. "Do you know what the word is?"

He lifted it out of her hand and held it up to study the marking. "No. It's worn smooth in places, and I don't know jack about ancient languages."

"Do you know anyone who does?"

He shoved the coin back into his pocket and clasped both of her hands between his. "What's on the coin doesn't matter as much as the fact that it's real. And now I need you to confirm for me that the woman is also real."

Maddy felt a bit like flotsam, herself. "I-I don't know what to say, Trace."

"Say you'll come out on my boat with me Saturday. And once you see her, say you'll help me figure out how a woman can be swimming around in the Gulf of Maine as if it were a heated pool."

"And if I don't see her?"

"Then we go back out on Sunday."

"And if I go out there with you every day and I still don't see her?"

He took hold of her shoulders—more to anchor himself than hold her in place, Maddy suspected. "Then we concentrate on figuring out where that coin came from."

She pressed her palms to his chest, but instead of feeling a racing heartbeat like she'd expected, she felt a strong, steady, surprisingly slow thumping; and Maddy realized that Trace wasn't nearly as desperate to confirm his sanity as he was deadly serious about proving that the coin-throwing woman actually existed.

"You've been deployed to Afghanistan at least twice that I know of in the last five years," she said. "Which, if I remember my high school geography, is one country away from India. There's a good chance you came across the coin during one of your tours, forgot about it, and just found it again in the pocket of an old pair of your jeans."

"I came home with only the clothes on my back. I gave everything I owned to some kid and his mother in Kabul."

"Everything? But why?"

He shrugged again, and this time she knew he truly was indifferent. "I figured they needed it more than I did."

Maddy looked deep into his storm-gray eyes. "Oh, Trace. What happened to you over there? Where's the boy who chased me halfway home when he caught me watching him screwing Leslie Simpson in the woods and then threatened to cut off all my hair if I told anyone?"

"He left Midnight Bay ten years ago." He enveloped her in a heartbreakingly fierce embrace. "And for the last three years, he's been trying his damnedest to get back here in one piece."

Maddy felt him suddenly tense; his arms around her coiling with energy, every muscle in his body poised to respond.

"Ye'd best be telling me you're her *brother*," a deep, threatening voice said from directly behind her.

Maddy gasped and tried to step back, but Trace held her firmly, threading his fingers through her hair to hold her head pressed against his chest. "Are you the bastard who put that bruise on her face?" he asked far too softly.

"Well now, I was just about to ask you the same question."

Trace's grip slackened ever so slightly, though he continued to hold her facing him. "Is this your boyfriend, Peeps?" he asked—loud enough for William to hear.

Maddy tensed. Damn. Saying yes would only encourage William, but saying no might get him beat up. And with both men being equal in strength and stature, and apparently *temperament,* well . . . things could get really ugly real fast.

Trace gave a chuckle, though it lacked any humor. "Are you still hung up on jocks, Maddy? I would have thought you learned your lesson with Billy."

"Trust me, I did," she muttered into his shirt.

"Then why does this . . . gentleman look like he wants to rip out my throat if I don't get my hands off what he obviously considers his property?"

"Please don't antagonize him, Trace."

"Why? Because he might suddenly turn violent? Tell me who hit you."

"I fell off the porch."

"I don't doubt you did—right after someone slapped your face. Tell me who, Maddy. I promise I won't kill the bastard; I just want to have a little talk with him. Or," he said when she said nothing, "at least give me your word that this guy isn't the bastard."

"He isn't."

He suddenly opened his arms, but when she started to turn, Trace took hold of her shoulder to stop her. "Okay then, prove it to me."

She blinked at him. "Prove what?"

"That he's your boyfriend." He gave her a nudge. "Go on, prove it."

"How?" she growled, fully aware that William could hear every damn last word of their crazy conversation.

"By kissing him."

Maddy narrowed her eyes, trying to figure out what he was up to. "What in hell would that prove?"

Trace crossed his arms over his chest and relaxed his weight back on his hips. "Well for starters, it would prove you're not afraid of him, which would go a long way in convincing me that it's not his handprint on your face. And second, it would go an even longer way in convincing him that *I'm* not your boyfriend."

Dammit all to hell and back! If she knew anything about Trace, it was that once he went off on a tangent, nothing short of a nuclear explosion could make him change course. "I am so going to make you pay for this," she hissed, pivoting around and marching up to William. "I feel even a hint of your tongue, Killkenny, I will bite it off. You got that?"

"Yes, ma'am," William said, his eyes sparkling like sapphires in the sunlight. He held his arms out from his sides. "Give me your best shot, lass."

She so wanted to punch him in the stomach, if for no other reason than to wipe that grin off his face. Honest to God, *all* men were trouble, every damn last one of them. Maddy clapped her hands on William's clean-shaven cheeks and yanked his head down; and with her lips pursed as tight as a clam hanging over a pot of boiling water, she pressed her mouth against his—all while trying her damnedest not to notice how really nice he smelled.

Or how really good he tasted.

Or how badly she wanted to stick her tongue in *his* mouth.

She tried stepping away the moment she felt his arms start to wrap around her, but she wasn't fast enough. William canted her head into the crook of his arm and kissed her so soundly that a herd of bumblebees started buzzing around in her belly. Only before she could even think about poking him in the ribs he suddenly set her away, but then had to grab hold of her shoulders when her knees started to buckle.

"No wonder you're still single after six years," Trace said with a chuckle from right behind her. "That wasn't a kiss, Peeps, that was an assault. Good thing at least one of you knows what you're doing." He extended his hand to William. "Trace Huntsman, Maddy's cousin."

"William Killkenny, Maddy's *boyfriend*," William said, tucking her against his side to return Trace's handshake.

It was as she was trying to figure out just how much trouble that kiss was going to cause her that Maddy suddenly noticed something more than a handshake was happening. Apparently in some secret code only men knew, they reached some sort of unspoken agreement as their eyes locked and they both nodded ever so slightly.

Wonderful. Now there would be no dealing with either one of them.

Only semiconfident that her knees wouldn't buckle again— seeing how that herd of bumblebees was still buzzing inside her—Maddy glanced toward the nursing home so neither of them would see her licking her lips. But she stopped in mid-lick when she spotted several sets of eyes staring out the window.

She immediately reared back. "Omigod," she muttered, covering her face with her hands. "We have an *audience*." She glared up at William when he chuckled, then turned her glare on Trace when he snickered. "This is not funny! It's bad enough they're after me to ask out every single male who walks in the door—regardless of *age*; I didn't need them to see me kissing their new pet project."

When they both only laughed harder, Maddy gave them one final glare and stormed limping toward the door. She suddenly stopped with her hand on the knob and looked back. "Oh, okay, dammit! You're still invited to dinner tonight."

Trace nodded. "Thanks, Peeps. William and I will be there at six sharp."

Maddy's chin dropped nearly down to her chest.

"I hope your brother will be home this evening," William added, "as I am quite looking forward to meeting Rick."

Maddy snapped her mouth shut then opened it again, but she couldn't seem to so much as squeak. Her shoulders slumping in defeat, she turned around and quietly limped inside.

Chapter Five

William felt the evening was going quite well, considering the people crowded around Patricia Lane's dinner table ranged in ages from nine years old to twelve hundred. Little Sarah, though, appeared more interested in the various conversations going on than in eating; Trace and Maddy were too busy catching up with each other to realize they weren't the only people at the table; Rick was more interested in his food than in talking to anyone; and Maddy's mother, Patricia, seemed quite interested in William—particularly regarding his interest in her daughter.

William could have bowed down to Trace for tricking Maddy into inviting him to dinner, right after he hugged him for daring the lass to kiss her *boyfriend*.

Kenzie had informed William that Maddy's cousin was stopping by to visit her, so he'd had a good idea whose arms he'd found wrapped around her down by the river. But knowing the best way to size up a man was to threaten him, William had approached them rather aggressively. And not liking the idea of anyone's arms around Maddy but his own, cousin or nay, the threat had for the most part been real.

Which Trace Huntsman had immediately realized.

As for sizing up his reaction, William had immediately decided he liked Trace. He'd been impressed not only by the man countering his threat by offering one of his own, but Trace had in turn sized up William by reading *Maddy's* reaction.

William knew right then he was dealing with a fellow warrior, as well as with a man who was equally determined to find out who had slapped her.

"Mabel told me you were in the military with Kenzie," Patricia Lane said to William. "Were the two of you in the same unit or something, and that's what brought you to Midnight Bay? I've heard fighting together forms a strong bond between men."

"Yes, we're fellow warriors," William said, smiling at the older though more reserved version of Maddy. "We've even been known to occasionally fight on the same side."

That stopped Maddy and Trace's conversation, making Maddy frown and Trace look thoughtful.

"I'm not going to summer rec tomorrow," Sarah said, once again injecting a comment at a lull in the conversation that had absolutely nothing to do with anything.

"But you have to go to rec," Maddy told her. "Gram's going to Mrs. Bishop's house to bake pies tomorrow, and you can't stay home alone."

The young girl lifted her chin. "Rick sleeps until noon and then watches TV when he gets up, so I won't be alone. And I have to stay home because I'm going to be really sick tomorrow when I wake up."

Maddy felt Sarah's forehead as she eyed her daughter curiously. "You don't have a temperature or look sick. I predict you'll be just fine tomorrow morning," she declared with a tender smile.

Sarah leaned away to glare at her. "That's the problem with having a mother who's a nurse—you think you know everything!" the girl cried, sliding back her chair and running out of the room.

"Let her go, Mom," Maddy said over the sound of footsteps stomping up the stairs when she saw her mother push back her own chair. "I'll talk with her at bedtime. I have an idea what's bugging her," she finished with a sigh, dropping her head in her hands to stare down at her plate.

"What's summer rec?" William asked.

"It's a program the town puts on for the kids while school's out," Patricia explained. "They play sports, do arts and crafts, swim, and sometimes take field trips." She looked toward Maddy, who was still staring down at her plate. "Aren't they going to Oak Harbor tomorrow, to the state park? Sarah's been looking forward to that field trip all summer. Maddy, do you have any idea why she doesn't want to go all of a sudden?"

Madeline lifted her head, and after darting a quick glance across the table at William, she looked at her mother. "I imagine it's because Billy's fiancée lives in Oak Harbor."

"So?" Patricia said.

"So, all of Sarah's little buddies also know his fiancée lives there, and the snotty little girls will start pointing out the bus window at every woman they pass and say, 'Is that your new stepmom, Sarah? Cool, you can play dolls with her!' Or maybe the snotty little boys will say, 'Is that the hottie your daddy knocked up, Sarah? I heard my uncle say he must have balls of brass to be boinking something that young.'"

"Madeline Marie Lane, they're only children!" Patricia cried. "They don't know what a hottie is, much less what knocked up or . . . or boinking means. And I don't appreciate that kind of language at the table."

Maddy snorted. "I knew more about sex when I was ten than

I do *now*. And trust me, they know exactly what those words mean, and they won't be shy about explaining them to Sarah."

"And this is why she doesn't wish to go to summer rec?" William asked. "The other children are teasing her? But it's not unusual for a divorced man to remarry."

"The girl he's marrying is *eighteen*," Maddy growled. "She just graduated from high school *two months ago*."

Rick tossed his fork onto his plate, shoved his chair back, and stood up. "And word is she's *four* months pregnant," he sneered. "Sissy never hid the fact she wasn't interested in any of us high school boys, not when there were real men around, ripe for the taking. Look up *whore* in the dictionary, and you'll find a picture of Sissy Blake."

"Richard!" Patricia cried.

Rick glared at his sister. "Sarah's not the only one getting teased around here."

"Sarah is nine, Rick, not nineteen," Trace said evenly.

William saw the teenager's hands ball into fists. "Yeah, well, having my cousin broadcast a Mayday that he saw a mermaid in the Gulf isn't helping, either!" Rick kicked his chair out of the way so hard it banged to the floor. He stormed out to the porch, slamming the door hard enough to make the windows shudder.

Maddy jumped to her feet to go after him.

William also stood up, intending to head her off.

But Trace—who remained seated—captured her by the wrist. "Let him go," he said, gently pulling her back down into her seat. "I'll check on him in town tonight, and keep him out of trouble."

"I think they gather down at Pinkham's gravel pit," Maddy whispered, darting a worried glance at her mother before looking back down at her plate.

William silently picked up Rick's overturned chair and then sat down.

"I'm sorry, William," Patricia said, her face flushed with embarrassment. She gave a nervous laugh. "We're usually more civilized when we have company."

"Ye needn't apologize, Patricia. A family squabble at mealtime is music to my ears. My sister could throw a tantrum that rattled the rafters. My poor sainted mother spent half her time chastising Gabby, and the other half defending her to our father."

"You have a sister?" she asked with a hesitant smile. "Is Gabby a nickname because she likes to talk, or is it short for something?"

"It's short for Gabriella, though the lass did like to speak her mind." Seeing Maddy's head lift curiously, William shot Patricia a grin, hoping to lighten the mood. "Even with her hair hiked up in a bun, Gabby didn't reach a man's armpit, but she had the temperament of a magpie."

"Oh, she sounds wonderful. Will she be coming to visit you in your new home? And your parents, too? I would love to meet your *sainted* mother," Patricia said gaily. "I believe we might have a lot in common," she finished with a grimace toward Maddy.

"I'm sorry, but all of my family has . . . passed," William told her.

The older woman's cheeks darkened. "Oh, I'm sorry for your loss, William."

"Don't fret yourself, Patricia. They've been gone for quite some time now. Maddy," he said. "Has Sarah told you the children are saying those things to her?"

"No, she's too embarrassed," Maddy admitted—even as her chin lifted much like her daughter's had. "But I've been getting plenty of feedback from the *adults,* though they're careful not to actually say Billy replaced me with another tight-assed, perky-boobed, man-trapping cheerleader to my face. Only they forget kids hear everything they're saying *at home,* and that the little snots are far less shy about repeating it."

"Well, hell, Peeps, why don't you tell us how you really feel?" Trace drawled.

Patricia stood up. "I think I'll go check on Sarah."

"I told you, I will talk with her just as soon as she's over her little pout."

Patricia rolled her eyes. "If she's anything like her mother, that'll take days."

"I never pout."

The older woman smiled. "That's right; you don't get mad, you get even. Trace, William, thank you for coming to dinner. We'll have to do this again . . . soon." She headed toward the hallway. "Don't worry, Madeline. I won't spoil your mother-daughter talk. I'm just going to have a *grandmotherly* chat with Sarah about . . . boinking," she trailed off, disappearing up the stairs.

Trace arched a brow at Maddy. "So that's what has your panties in a twist? Your ex-husband is marrying a younger woman, and that makes you feel like a *baggy*-assed, *saggy*-boobed, mantrapping cheerleader?"

"Billy is damn near old enough to be that girl's *father.*"

Trace snorted. "Apparently Billy Kimble is the one who never learned his lesson. Whereas you, Peeps, learned yours *too* well."

"What in hell are you talking about?"

Trace leaned back in his chair and folded his arms over his chest. "You asked me today what happened to the fun-loving cousin you remembered, and now I'm asking you the same question."

"She grew up!" Maddy snapped. "She had a kid with a jerk who *never* grew up, she spent five years in night school getting her nursing degree, buried her father and took on the responsibility of her fifteen-year-old brother, and spent the last four years trying to hold this family together."

"And while you were doing all that," Trace said quietly, "instead of growing up, you grew old."

"Twenty-seven is *not* old."

"No? So instead of being a pediatric nurse like you intended, you didn't choose to work at a nursing home to be around people you have something in common with?" He leaned forward in his chair. "You may have spent the last four years holding your family together, but you also spent those years hiding behind them, trying to distance yourself from your own man-trapping-cheerleader past. When was the last time you went on a real date?"

Maddy stood up so forcefully her chair clattered to the floor behind her. "My love life is none of your damn business!" She turned her glare on William. "And if you ever kiss me in public or threaten to spank me again, I will sic my *real* boyfriend on you." Her glare turned sinisterly smug. "He's a big, bad-tempered, bear-eating *bogeyman,* and he'll do anything I ask him to do because he loves me."

Apparently satisfied he'd been duly threatened and sufficiently warned, Maddy kicked the fallen chair out of her way and marched to the door. "I'm going for a walk," she said through gritted teeth. "And neither of you had better be here when I get back."

"What time should I pick you up Saturday?" Trace asked softly.

Maddy halted with her hand on the doorknob, looking incredulous. But then her shoulders suddenly slumped. "I'll be at the dock at nine," she said, quietly walking out the door and closing it softly behind her.

William looked at all the empty chairs, and smiled across the table at Trace. "I'm assuming dinner is over?"

"Christ, it's good to be home," Trace said, returning his smile.

"Is there a reason ye just pushed her like that?"

Trace's smile vanished. "To make sure there's still enough

fight in her to push back." He folded his arms over his chest again. "You threatened to spank her?"

William shrugged. "I was just blustering. But since it was the first time she'd met me, she couldn't know that I'd cut off my right arm before I'd hurt a hair on her head."

"Have you met Maddy's bogeyman boyfriend?"

"I'm afraid *I'm* the bogeyman," William said with a chuckle. "It's a long story best saved for another time, preferably when we're on our fourth or fifth drink. What's happening Saturday morning?"

"I'm taking Maddy out on my boat to show her my mermaid."

"*Your* mermaid? So you started the rumor going around town?"

"Not intentionally." Trace uncrossed his arms, pulled something out of his pants pocket, and flipped it across the table to William. "Have you ever seen anything like that before, Kill-kenny?"

William studied the front of the coin then turned it to look at the other side. "It appears quite old," he said, looking over at Trace. "I'm not sure about the writing on the back, but I have seen the symbol on the front before."

In the first unguarded gesture William had seen the man make since meeting him, Trace's jaw went slack in surprise. "You recognize the symbol?" he whispered. He stood up, his stance somewhat aggressive. "Where is it from? What does it mean?"

William also stood up, and flipped the coin through the air to him. "It's the mark of a strong arm," he said, heading across the kitchen and out onto the porch.

"A strong arm?" Trace repeated, following him outside.

William walked down the stairs to the driveway and turned with a frown. "I don't know the modern word for it. A strong arm," he repeated, searching for a better term, "as in a protector or a champion." He suddenly had a thought. "Like one of those knights of that table. Sir Galahad, I think his name was. And King Arthur. My friend Mabel told me these iron-clad warriors would receive some sort of token from a woman, and vow to be her champion."

"Mabel Anderson, the teacher? Eve's mother? She told you the story of King Arthur and the Knights of the Round Table?"

"Eve is married to my friend Kenzie Gregor, and I'm staying with them while my house is being built. And Mabel has been . . . entertaining me with such stories."

Trace looked down at the coin in his hand. "And this is the symbol for a knight?"

"Nay, it dates back much further than King Arthur's reign."

Trace narrowed his eyes at him. "How come you know what this ancient symbol is, but you don't seem to know much about knights?"

William shrugged. "I'm better versed in what went on before the ninth century."

"You're a historian, then?"

William glanced toward the path leading into the woods that he assumed Maddy had taken in an attempt to walk off her anger. He looked back at Trace, pointing at the coin in his hand. "If ye wish to find out more about it, ye need to look at the black magic being practiced several thousand years ago." He shrugged. "If I had to guess, I would say the coin is a request for a strong arm, and the writing on the back is either the name of *who* is in need of a champion, or a warning as to where the threat is coming *from*. Where did ye say you got the coin?"

"There is no such thing as magic, black or otherwise."

"No?" William darted another glance toward the woods then smiled at Trace. "Then why are ye taking Maddy out to show her your *mermaid* on Saturday?"

Trace shoved the coin in his pocket, took a deep breath, and returned to the guarded warrior William had first met. "Maddy's a big girl," he said, gesturing toward the woods. "She can take care of herself."

"I noticed some strange markings on several of the trees back there," William said, "and I can't decide what sort of animal made them. So I'd rather the lass not have to take care of herself when I can do a better job of it."

"Good luck with that, my friend," Trace said with a chuckle. He headed toward his truck, opened the door, and looked back. "You go save your girlfriend, and I'll go find out what in hell possessed Rick to slap his sister."

Chapter Six

William untied the horse he'd left behind the old barn next to the Lane's house, and started leading his only source of transportation down the forest path dappled with lengthening shadows from the setting sun.

He'd purchased a four-door pickup truck last week, but he hadn't been able to use it to come here this evening. Modern society had so many blasted rules governing everything a person did, William wasn't sure he'd ever grow accustomed to living in this century. He couldn't drive his new truck on the roads without a license, and even with the learner's permit Mabel had helped him get, he still couldn't drive it unless there was somebody in the seat beside him. And after the little incident a few days ago . . . well, Mabel had suggested that maybe he should ask Eve or Kenzie to help him practice.

Eve had kindly volunteered, but they hadn't made it halfway into town when she'd asked him to stop the truck, gotten out, and walked the two miles back home. And Kenzie had said hell would freeze over before he'd ride in a vehicle with the power of three hundred horses that was being driven by a hardheaded Irishman.

Maybe tomorrow he'd ask Elbridge to go for a ride with him, William decided, or Samuel or Hiram. He'd learned he preferred a man in the seat beside him, as women had an annoying tendency to scream whenever they thought he came too close to something. He'd tried calmly explaining to Eve that he hadn't *really* hit the mailbox, because if it hadn't been leaning into the road like that, it wouldn't have pushed in the truck's large mirror on her side. That's when she'd gotten out, bent over and braced her hands on her knees for several minutes, and then silently started for home.

Maybe Trace would consider riding with him, since the man appeared in control of his nerves. And they seemed to get along quite well—although that would likely change when he found out William had withheld some important facts about the coin.

But *somebody* had to help him practice for his driver's license; he couldn't keep riding Kenzie's mares around town whenever he wanted to go someplace. Christ, he wished he could still fly. Considering all the vile unpleasantries he'd been forced to endure as a dragon, having the ability to soar through the air with the speed and skill of an eagle certainly had been a major advantage.

Not being able to make love to a woman for several long centuries, however, had been a major drawback.

William stopped walking to cant his head and listen, as he tried to decide where the sound of an occasional hollow thump was coming from. He started off again at a more urgent pace, pulling the horse into a trot when he decided it was coming from the general area where he'd seen the strange markings on the trees.

When he drew close enough that he could hear growled breathing as well as occasional sobs, he tied the mare to a branch, veered off the path, and snuck through the forest as quiet as a field mouse. He stopped at the edge of a small clearing just as he saw Maddy draw back and swing a large stick, striking a tree so violently that pieces of dead bark flew some twenty paces away.

But it wasn't until he noticed the tears streaming down her cheeks that he finally understood what was going on. Trace might have pushed Maddy to see if she still had some fight in her, but what the man couldn't have guessed was that the only target the woman dared push back at was some old dead tree.

It was then William realized that while holding her family together for the last four years, Maddy had quietly been coming apart inside. She was alone in a sea of people, having no broad shoulder to lean on when the journey got difficult, no one to discuss things with in the wee hours of the night when problems appeared far worse than they were, no partner to confide in who could hold her in his arms and whisper that everything would be all right, then make love to her until she couldn't remember what had been bothering her in the first place.

No, the only witness to her tears was an old dead tree.

With the growl of a wounded animal backed into a corner, Maddy took another mighty swing at the well-battered trunk, hitting it so forcefully this time that the stick flew from her hands, and she fell to the ground—her cry of surprise turning to heart-wrenching sobs as she lay there weeping in utter defeat.

Feeling as if he'd taken the blow to his chest, William dropped to his knees. Not since burying his family had he felt such despair, as he knew from personal experience that Maddy wasn't angry at the world near as much as she was angry at herself.

It was obvious to him from what she'd said at the table tonight, that she felt like a dowdy old spinster going through the motions while her ex-husband had retained his youthful vitality. She may have tried to defend her life to Trace, but in actuality, the people she cared for at the nursing home were emotionally younger than she was.

And she knew it, and it hurt.

William understood far too well the hopelessness of feeling that sort of isolation. Hadn't he himself repeatedly lashed out when he'd been a dragon, only instead of an old tree that couldn't fight back, he'd gone after a mangy old bear, or any other entity—animal or demon—he could find, in an attempt to ease the gnawing in his gut?

William silently watched Maddy cry herself out for several minutes, the pain squeezing his own chest nearly unbearable, until she finally straightened to a sitting position and wiped her eyes and face with the palms of her hands.

And that's when he decided that if he accomplished only one thing with this second chance at life he'd been given, he would see that Maddy never had to take out her frustrations on a tree again. If she had the urge to lash out at something, he would stand as her target; if she required a shoulder to lean on, he would give her his; and if she needed to whisper her fears in the wee dark hours of the night, he would be the one to hear her. Kneeling there in the bushes, William vowed on the souls of his dead mother and sister that whenever Maddy felt old and saggy and heavy of heart, he would do everything in his power to show her how young and alive and vital she was.

She finally stood up, finished drying her face on the hem of her blouse, and then ran her fingers through her hair in an attempt to tame it. With a deep breath that ended with a lingering sob, she squared her shoulders and started walking toward home.

William quietly got to his feet and silently ran back through the woods. He untied the mare and led her trotting several hundred paces back toward the house before he turned around and began casually strolling toward Maddy.

She stopped when she rounded a corner and spotted him, her eyes widening at the sight of the large horse before narrowing on him. "I told you to be gone when I got back," she said, her voice raspy from crying.

He kept walking until he reached her and pulled the mare up beside him to pat its cheek. "I remembered that ye had a sore knee, and Rose here suggested that we give ye a ride home before we head back to An Tèarmann."

"*Rose* suggested you give me a ride?" she asked, the barest hint of a sad smile twitching one corner of her mouth.

"Aye, she's quite thoughtful that way, despite being Scots," William said, running his hand over the mare's large nose. He suddenly stilled when he noticed Maddy staring at his arm. "Are ye upset that I let Janice use her money card to order my watch?" he asked, pulling his cuff back even more as he held his wrist out to show her the watch. "The others assured me it would be okay."

"Huh?" It took her a moment, but she finally lifted her gaze from his arm to his face. "Oh, no, it's okay," she said, her eyes straying to his wrist again.

"Then come." He stepped to the mare's side. "I'll help ye up."

"She's not wearing a saddle. I can walk. It's not that far."

"A saddle's more trouble than it's worth; don't worry, Rose is as gentle as a spring lamb. And the less ye use that knee, the quicker it will heal. Come on," he urged, pulling her in front of him so she was facing the horse.

She clutched his hands when he set them on her waist. "The both of us will be too heavy for her."

He chuckled. "Six of us wouldn't be too heavy for her, but I intend to walk." She tried to step away, but he didn't let her go. "You're not afraid of horses, are ye, Maddy?"

That did the trick. She grabbed Rose's mane, then raised her leg for a boost. "I'm not afraid of a silly old horse, even one that's bigger than the car I'm driving."

William lifted her by the waist then waited to make sure she was settled before stepping away. "Ready?" he asked, trying not to laugh when he saw her eyes had gone wide at being tossed up like a sack of feathers.

He started walking down the path and smiled to himself, remembering the night Eve and Maddy had gotten falling-down drunk to bolster their nerves as they walked along a dark road after Maddy's truck had ended up in the ditch. Since he'd been a dragon at the time—which they decided had to be a hairless moose—and was inadvertently the cause of their driving into the ditch, he'd gotten Kenzie to fetch them home. When Kenzie had found them and in turn carried each woman to his truck, Maddy had been drunkenly adamant that she was going to lose a few pounds before her own knight in shining armor finally showed up to sweep her off her feet.

The next day, William had asked his dear friend Mabel what a knight was, and that's when she'd told him the tale of King Arthur. And with twinkling eyes filled with speculation more than amusement, she'd also explained that even though Maddy might have been jesting, she was probably secretly hoping that a big, strong, handsome hero would come riding into town and rescue her and love her forever.

"It's true that Rose *is* the one who suggested we come give you a ride," William said into the peaceful silence. "But where she was being thoughtful, I admit I have a more selfish motive, as I have a favor to ask."

He heard Maddy sigh. "Sure, why not, seeing how you've probably figured out that I'm a pushover when it comes to people asking me for favors."

William kept facing forward so she wouldn't see his smile.

"Ye can say no if ye want; I won't be offended. But if ye do say no, then maybe could you give me some advice instead?"

"What's the favor?"

"I've purchased a truck, but I'm not allowed to drive it on the roads alone with only a permit. I was wondering if you'd consider riding with me while I practice for taking the test to get my license."

"You don't drive?"

He frowned at the path ahead, wondering how to answer without revealing the fact that he'd been in this century only a few months and a *man* only a few weeks. And he *could* drive, just not very well. "I'm getting used to all the rules about things like blinkers and horns and road signs and such, and I'm still trying to figure out what all the buttons scattered throughout my truck do." He glanced over his shoulder. "Did you know there's even a button to turn on a wire in the seat that warms a person's bum?"

That got him a full-blown smile. "You're going to find yourself using that button a lot come January. So that's the favor? You need someone to drive with you?" Her smile vanished and her eyes narrowed. "Why doesn't Kenzie or Eve take you driving? Or Mabel? The only requirement is that they have a valid driver's license, and Mabel still has hers."

William returned to watching the path in front of him. "They have gone with me, but I'm finding it difficult learning all your blasted rules, and I really don't wish to take up that much of their time."

"And if I say no, then what's the advice you want?"

"I wondered what you'd think of my asking Elbridge or Hiram or Samuel."

"Omigod, not Hiram," she said with an outright laugh. "He can't remember where his room is most of the time! The two of you would end up in Canada."

William felt her laughter easing the knot in his gut. "And Elbridge?"

"Elbridge would probably love to help you, and so would Samuel. Charlotte and Lois, too. They so need to feel needed." Maddy sighed again. "Um . . . it was really thoughtful of you to ask their advice about building your home. Your visits mean a lot to them."

He stopped walking and turned to face her. "I wasn't being thoughtful; I need their advice far more than they need my visits."

She gave him the strangest look—as if she didn't quite believe him—but then her gaze strayed to his hands as he absently wove the reins through his fingers, and her breath sort of hitched, as if she'd momentarily forgotten to breathe.

"So by suggesting that I ask Elbridge, are ye saying *you* don't wish to ride with me?"

"Huh? Oh, no . . . I could go with you once in a while." She patted Rose's neck, her eyes locked directly on his. "If you can get Kenzie or Eve to bring your truck to the nursing home and leave it, Elbridge or one of the others can go out with you in the morning, and I'll go with you on some of my lunch breaks. No," she said, suddenly shaking her head. "They wouldn't like you leaving your truck at the home overnight if you're not a resident, for liability reasons." She shrugged. "I'll have to think about how we can make this work."

"I have an idea," he said, turning to walk down the path again. "Why don't you drive my truck to work every morning, and then drive it home at night?"

"Because that would mean I'd have to go to Eve's house to get it every day."

"Or ye could give Eve her car back and drive my truck all the time."

"No!" she yelped so suddenly, William stopped and turned

to her. "I can't let people see me driving your truck. Everyone would get the wrong impression."

"And just what would that impression be?"

"That we're a couple."

He started walking again. "Forgive me; I was under the impression ye didn't care what people thought."

"I don't," she snapped.

"Then what's the problem?"

"Okay, then. Let's just say I don't want to feel indebted to you."

He stopped walking and turned to her again. "How does your helping me learn to drive make you indebted to me? I would be the one beholden to *you*."

"If your truck's so fancy it has heated seats, it cost more than I make in two years. I don't want that kind of responsibility. What if I scratched it, or worse, what if I drove it into a ditch when some big hairless moose flew out in front of me?"

William started walking again to hide his smile. "It's only a truck, lass. Scratches won't make it any less useful, and its feelings won't get hurt if ye drive it into a ditch. And the good part is you won't get hurt, either; it's a large, safe truck, unlike that old one of yours that's parked behind Kenzie's barn."

He heard her sigh again. "You don't understand," she whispered.

Deciding she'd had enough pushing for one night, William relented. "Never mind, lass," he said. "I will figure another way."

He led her back to her house in silence, reminding himself that handling prickly little hedgehogs required patience, until the wee beasties were comfortable enough with a person to relax their quills. William led Rose out of the woods into the dooryard, and saw Sarah sitting on the steps of the porch, her chin in her hands, looking quite glum.

That is until she spotted them—or more specifically Rose.

"Mom! You're riding a *horse*!" the girl cried, running down the stairs.

But she immediately scampered back onto the porch when they drew close, when she realized Rose was so large she could run under the mare's belly by only ducking her head.

William reached across the stairs, picked Sarah up, and settled her onto Rose's back in front of her mother. "And now *you're* riding a horse, too," he said with a chuckle at her surprised look. He started leading them around the yard. "And when ye go to summer rec tomorrow, you'll have something to tell all your friends."

"I'm going to be sick tomorrow."

"Ye know, you remind me of my little sister, Gabby; she used to get bouts of illness quite often, too, whenever our father would tell her to go outside and play."

"She did? Would she throw up and everything?"

"Quite often, actually. Papa would push her out the door, but she'd cling to his leg and throw up on his boots. So he would pick her up and carry her to our mother."

"I bet Gabby got to stay home when she was sick," Sarah said, turning to give Maddy a defiant glare.

"Nay, Mama would clean her up and take her outside for a walk. This went on almost the entire summer Gabby was ten, until one day, my sister overheard our father say that the village healer would have to cut off all her hair to cure her."

"He wanted to cut off all her hair?" Sarah asked, grabbing her own hair as she leaned back into Maddy. "D-did your mother let him?"

"She didn't have to, because Gabby finally told Mama *why* she kept getting sick."

"Why?" Sarah whispered, holding on to Rose's mane to lean toward William. "What was making her sick?"

He turned at the end of the driveway and started back toward the house. "Well now, it turned out the village children were teasing Gabby so badly that just the *thought* of playing with them made her sick."

"It did?" Sarah tapped William on the shoulder to make him look at her. "Wh-what were they teasing her about?" she whispered.

"Anything they could think of. And when they couldn't think of anything, they just made things up."

"But why? Didn't they like your sister? Was she mean and snotty to them?"

"Sarah," Maddy said, pulling the girl back against her. "Let Mr. Killkenny finish his story, and please don't insult his sister."

William started walking again. "I don't believe Gabby was at all mean and . . . snotty. She was quite shy around people, actually, as she preferred the company of animals. At least she was shy until she turned thirteen."

"What happened at thirteen? Did she discover boys were good for something other than throwing rocks at?"

It was Maddy who'd asked that question, and William realized the woman would have her hands full soon enough, as Sarah grew up in her spitting image.

"Nay, Gabby merely found her voice. And her backbone. And a vocabulary that would put yours to shame," he added with a chuckle.

"So why did your dad decide not to cut her hair off?" Sarah asked.

"Gabby told our mother about the children teasing her."

"And did your mother make them stop?" William glanced over his shoulder in time to see Sarah frown up at Maddy. "I-I don't want you to talk to them, because then they'll think I'm a sissy for tattling."

"Our mother didn't do anything," William said. "Gabby did it herself."

Sarah blinked at him. "She did? How?"

"Once Mama explained why the children were teasing her and suggest how she could make them stop, Gabby put a stop to it."

"What did your mama tell her?"

"That the other boys and girls were jealous."

"Jealous? Of what?"

"My sister was quite an accomplished young lass, and could ride a horse better than the boys could, and hit a target with her slingshot from over twenty paces away." He smiled at both of them. "And boys being boys, they didn't like knowing a lassie could outride them, so they tried to discourage her with their teasing."

"And the girls?" Sarah asked.

"My sister was quite pretty, with long dark hair and a smile that would make even a curmudgeon break into a grin." He nodded to her. "Just like you, Sarah. And girls being girls, they would start teasing Gabby about any little thing they could find, hoping to make her feel bad about herself so they'd feel good about themselves.

"You think I'm pretty, just like your sister?"

"Nay, lass, I think you're beautiful just like your mother. Ye have your mama's beautiful brown eyes, and when ye smile, it's like the sun just peeked from behind a cloud and the whole world lights up."

Sarah turned to look up at her mother. "He said we're beautiful," she whispered. "And that we have beautiful eyes."

Maddy hugged her daughter and kissed the top of her head. "Should we believe Mr. Killkenny, or do you think he's just shining us on?"

"You're beautiful," Sarah whispered. She nodded. "So I guess we can believe him." She looked at William. "What did Gabby do to make them stop teasing her?"

"She practiced the art of misdirection."

"What's misdirection? Is it something . . . I can learn?"

Since he'd run out of driveway, William started leading Rose on another turn around the yard. "Misdirection is really quite simple. When a person says something ye don't like, you ask them a question."

"I don't get it. How does that stop them from teasing?"

"If ye ask the person about something he or she might find fascinating, they will forget all about what *they* said to talk about what *you* said." He stopped and looked at her. "Take for instance that you're on the bus tomorrow, and one of the boys says something to you that ye don't like. You just ask him if he's ever ridden a warhorse. And when he says no, ye tell him that *you* have."

"But I haven't."

William gestured at Rose. "Aye, but ye have, lass. You've been riding a warhorse for the last twenty minutes."

"Rose isn't a warhorse; she's a big old plow horse."

"This mare has never pulled a plow or been put in a harness. She's descended from the great warhorses of highland warriors. In fact, she's won prizes at the Scottish summer games down on the Maine coast six years running, before her son, Kenzie's powerful stallion, Curaidh, stole the honor from her."

"But I'm not *really* riding her, so I'd be fibbing. I'm just sitting on Rose while you lead her around."

William tossed the reins over the mare's head, then reached up, captured Maddy by the waist, and slid her to the ground—leaving Sarah sitting on the horse all by herself. "Pick up the reins," he told the girl, taking hold of Maddy's wrist when she started to reach for her daughter. "Sarah's okay; she's a big, smart, brave lass who can command a warhorse to do her bidding."

"I-I can?" Sarah whispered, looking skeptical even as she picked up the reins.

Threading his fingers through Maddy's, William started walking down the driveway again. "Gently pull on the right rein, Sarah, to tell Rose ye wish to follow us."

"Don't kick her sides," Maddy added, craning her neck to watch. She glared at William as she tried to wiggle free. "Honest to God, Killkenny, if that horse so much as burps and she falls off, I am going to kill you," she hissed softly.

"Rose has been letting little girls boss her around all her life," he quietly assured her. "Sarah is safer on that horse than on one of those big yellow buses." He stopped walking to face Sarah. "That's good, lass. Now, turn her around and head back toward the house."

The girl pulled the left rein out as far as her arm would reach, and Rose obediently turned and ambled toward the house. "Look, Mom! I'm riding a *warhorse*! I can't wait to tell everyone tomorrow. They're going to be so jealous!"

Maddy blew out a heavy sigh, and William felt her fingers relax in his. "I'm a little jealous myself," she said, one side of her mouth lifting crookedly. "I only got to sit on Rose and be led around."

He squeezed her hand. "You and Sarah could come to Eve's tomorrow when ye get off work, and the three of us could take a ride after dinner. And you could have a warhorse all to yourself."

She looked down at her hand in his; her breath sort of hitched like it had before, and she looked up and studied his face for the longest time. "You know, I think I *would* like to go for a ride tomorrow evening."

He let go of her hand to lift Sarah off the mare and set her on the porch step. "The sun's set," he told her, "so that must mean it's your bedtime."

"I go to bed at nine."

"That gives ye seventeen minutes to climb the stairs, scrub your face clean, and put on your pajamas," he said, holding up his watch to show her the exact time.

"Oh, no, you don't," she countered, waggling her little finger at him. "You're not tricking me into thinking it's a race." She reached out and patted the mare's large nose. "Good night, Rose." The girl suddenly gasped. "Wait right here!" she instructed, spinning around and running into the house. "Gram! Bring your camera! I need you to take a picture of me on a *warhorse.*"

She ran back out onto the porch and held her arms out to William. "Can you lift me up on her again, please, Mr. Killkenny? I need a picture to show them on the bus tomorrow, because they'll never believe I really rode a warhorse if I don't have proof."

William looked at Maddy, and when she nodded, he picked the girl up and set her on Rose's back. Sarah immediately picked up the reins again. "How do I make her back up, so no one will be in the picture but me and Rose?"

"Just give a gentle tug on both reins, and make a soft clicking sound with your tongue. When ye want her to stop backing up, relax the reins."

"Oh, my God," Patricia said, stepping onto the porch just as Sarah started backing up the mare. She clutched her chest, turning horrified eyes on her daughter. "Maddy, she's just a baby."

"No, Mom, she's a big, smart, brave lass," Maddy said, holding her hand out for the camera. "And she's going to show everyone at summer rec *tomorrow* that she rode a warhorse."

Still looking more worried than impressed, Patricia handed the camera to her daughter. Maddy stepped away, held the little box up and peered at a tiny screen on it, then pushed a button several times. The camera gave several sudden flashes of light, and William flinched every time.

He had no idea what in hell a camera was, although he guessed that if Sarah was asking for a picture, it must capture her image somehow. He sighed to himself; he'd have to ask Mabel about it tomorrow, during their morning walk.

And then maybe he'd ask Janice to order one for him.

Maddy slid the camera into her pocket and helped her daughter off the mare. "Remember what Mr. Killkenny told you about the art of misdirection, Sarah. Timing is important. I'll print out the pictures for you tonight, but you don't show them to anyone until someone says something you don't like. Then you ask if they've ever ridden a warhorse, and *then* you whip out the photos." She gave Sarah a hug and nudged her toward the house with a laugh. "That will certainly misdirect the little snots."

"Gram, I'm going to the state park tomorrow, and we're going to study the mud flats," Sarah said as she led her grandmother back into the house. "We gotta find my rubber boots. And I need a plastic pail and old spoon, so I can dig up some clams," she continued, her voice trailing off as she dragged Patricia deeper into the house.

"Thank you," Maddy said, turning to smile at William.

"For?"

"For bolstering Sarah's confidence and giving her some ammunition against their teasing tomorrow. That was very sweet of you."

"There ye go again, thinking I'm sweet and thoughtful. Have ye not considered that I might have a more selfish motive?"

"Like what?"

"Like maybe if ye feel kindly toward me, you'd reconsider using my truck instead of Eve's car, so Elbridge can take me driving." He lifted his hand holding Rose's reins. "The mare's fine for getting around town, but it's hard to strap pieces of lumber to her back for the house I'm building. I need my driver's license."

Maddy stared at his hand holding the reins for several seconds, but then her shoulders suddenly slumped. "Okay, I'll use your truck."

"No, I've changed my mind," William snapped, grabbing Rose's mane and swinging himself onto her back. He turned the mare and started riding away. "I've decided I don't like feeling beholden any more than you do."

"Look, I told you I'd use the truck, and I will," Maddy snapped back, following him down the driveway.

He pulled Rose to a halt and looked down at her.

"I'm not doing it for you; I'm doing it for Elbridge," she continued, her glare as fierce as a battle-hardened warrior. "And Sarah and I will be at Eve's tomorrow after work, and I want my horse to be wearing a saddle," she finished, pivoting around and storming back to the house.

He started down the driveway again.

"And William?" she called out.

He turned to find her smiling at him—rather sinisterly—from the porch.

"You're not the only one who can have an ulterior motive," she said, spinning away and disappearing into the house.

Chapter Seven

William balanced the saddle over the stall door, but then stilled when the sun shining through the barn window flashed off the face of his watch. "Have ye ever thought of wearing a timepiece, Gregor?" he asked Kenzie, who was in Curaidh's stall, brushing the stallion.

"What for? I just have to look at the sun or stars to know what time it is."

"Aye," William agreed, turning his wrist to study the watch. "But I wonder if men in this century don't wear them for some reason other than telling time."

Kenzie stopped brushing. "Ye mean like jewelry?" He grinned. "Have you taken a fancy to adorning yourself like a woman, Killkenny?"

William opened Rose's stall door with a snort and began brushing the mare. "Did ye happen to notice how Maddy kept staring at my arm all through dinner? She told me she didn't mind that I let Janice at the nursing home order the watch for me, but I've caught her eyes straying to it quite often. And the ladies at the home seemed quite adamant that I needed it to go with my new look. I just wondered if watches have some sort of appeal to modern women."

"Eve wears a watch. And she bought Mabel one with a large dial that's easier to see." Kenzie looked across the aisle and shrugged. "They have no appeal to me."

William rolled the cuffs up on his sleeves another turn, deciding he'd ask Mabel what was so special about watches. "I'm afraid we have a bit of a problem with our spoiled little harbor seal friend," he said, leading Rose out of her stall. "Ye know the rumor going around that a mermaid was spotted out on the Gulf? Well, Maddy's cousin Trace Huntsman told me last night that he's the one who inadvertently started it."

Kenzie set his arms over Curaidh's stall door, his face darkened with concern. "But the magic should be shielding the pup's true nature, and all anyone should see is a common harbor seal. We can't even see past her mask, so how in hell could Maddy's cousin know she's really a woman?"

"That's the gist of our problem, I'm afraid. And apparently the pup has realized he can see her, because she gave him a coin."

Kenzie stiffened. "Did she also *speak* to him, or tell him her name or where she's from? Or what century?"

"I don't know what sort of exchange went on between them. I didn't ask too many questions or let on that I knew anything about her." William picked up the saddle, settled it on Rose's broad back, and tightened the cinch. "When Huntsman showed me the coin, I told him only enough to encourage him to confide in me in the future."

"Did you recognize the coin?"

"Only what was on the front, which was the mark of a strong arm." He scowled across Rose's back at Kenzie. "It was the same symbol I found on a large stone on my property that eventually led me through time to you."

Kenzie grinned. "Aye, ye told me how happy you were to learn that your salvation lay in the hands of a highlander." He just as suddenly sobered. "And the pup's, it appears, may lie in the hands of a modern warrior."

"A warrior who knows nothing about magic, and doesn't even believe it exists."

Kenzie went back to brushing Curaidh. "It looks as if he'll be learning about it soon enough. Was there anything else on the coin other than the symbol?"

"There was writing on the back," William said, going to the next stall and opening the door. "But I didn't recognize what language it was. Maybe I should suggest that Trace show you the coin. You could describe it to your brother, and maybe he can tell us what we'll be facing when whoever the hell is after that pup tries to take her back."

Kenzie stepped out of Curaidh's stall and untied Rose from where William had left her. "When the old witch was trying to prevent me from helping you, Matt explained that her energy was beyond his reach. Providence wouldn't allow either him or Winter to interfere."

"But he's Cùram de Gairn," William said in surprise, "one of the most powerful of all the drùidhs. Between the two of them, I thought there was nothing they couldn't do."

"They couldn't change you back into a man, could they?"

"Only because it was something I had to do for myself. It was my *thinking* that needed to be changed before my physical condition could be."

"Exactly," Kenzie said with a slow grin. "And so it is with our pesky little pup. She needs an attitude adjustment a hell of a lot more than she needs a strong arm. But for some reason, Trace sees her as she truly is, and she's mistaken that as a sign that he can help her."

William returned Kenzie's grin. "Then I guess we're about to become an army of three, are we not? We just have to explain the magic to Huntsman and teach him how to handle a sword."

"Not so fast," Kenzie warned. "Not until we get a better handle on what we're up against. The energy pursuing the pup is close; I can feel it. But it seems to be hovering just out of our reach, trying to decide how best to handle *us*."

"Then maybe while we're waiting, I'll ask Huntsman to teach me about modern weaponry."

"That might be wise, actually," Kenzie said, giving Rose's ear an affectionate scratch. "Maybe it's time we both embrace modern warfare and see how it holds up against the magic."

William finished brushing the horse Sarah was going to ride all by herself—much to her mother's horror, he figured. But the lass was nearly *ten*; she should have been riding a horse on her own for four or five years already. And Tulip was so gentle she didn't even kill the flies that plagued her, and would only swat them away.

He chuckled to himself as he tossed the saddle onto her back. Kenzie's mares had come from Greylen MacKeage, Winter's father, who apparently in a moment of weakness, had told his daughters that they could name all of his horses. And being girls, they of course had named every one of his noble beasts after a flower.

But that didn't seem to stop the mares from throwing amazing colts.

"I'm thinking I should start building my barn already," William said. "Do ye suppose Matt would sell me one of his young stallions?"

Kenzie gave him an incredulous look. "You expect the man to sell you a horse that you intend to pay for with money *he* gave you?" He snorted. "Christ's blood, Killkenny, that's ballsy even for you."

William ignored that, even as he thought that getting one up

on a highlander—especially a powerful drùidh—was little consolation against the sheep-stealing bastard's ancestors who had
constantly raided his homeland.

"Couldn't you feel me kicking you under the table?" Eve asked,
handing Maddy a soapy plate.

Maddy ran it through the rinse water and started drying it
off. "I thought you were playing footsie with your husband and
kept getting mixed up." She smiled at her friend. "Pregnancy
does addle one's brain."

"I was kicking *you* for spending the entire meal trying not
to openly stare at William. Every time I looked over, you were
watching his hand go from his plate to his mouth. I swear, if I
had heard you sigh one more time, I was going to throw my
milk at you."

Damn if Maddy didn't sigh again just picturing William eating.
"Hey, what can I say?" she said with a grin, taking another plate
from her. "I have a thing for masculine forearms and big broad
hands. Come on," she said, nudging Eve with her hip. "Don't you
think it's sexy when a guy rolls back his cuffs and exposes all that
hair-covered muscle? I personally like how a man's forearm tapers
into a tight wrist and then flares into a broad, powerful hand."
She fanned herself with the plate. "I swear, I could come just
watching those powerful hands roam all over me."

Eve stopped in the middle of handing her another plate and
gaped at Maddy. She shook her head. "My God, you need a date
worse than I thought. If you don't get those hormone levels
back in the safe zone, you're liable to hurt yourself."

"It's going to take more than a date to cure my case of horn-
ies; what I need is a down-and-dirty, full-blown affair."

Eve blinked. "Good Lord, you're serious. But you were staring at *William's* forearms. I thought big, strong, manly men like
Kenzie and William scared the bejeezus out of you."

"Men like that used to scare the bejeezus out of me. But I've been thinking that if Billy Kimble has the balls to bang some eighteen-year-old twit, I sure as hell ought to have the courage to do the same."

"You want to bang an eighteen-year-old twit?" Eve asked deadpan.

"No!" Maddy choked on a laugh. "Although I have heard that the younger you get them the more trainable they are."

"Madeline Kimble!"

Maddy darted a look toward the living room, where Sarah was telling Mabel and Patricia about her triumphant field trip today, as well as explaining the art of misdirection to them. "I've decided I'm going to jump Killkenny's bones," Maddy whispered, smiling at her friend's shock. She leaned closer. "But whatever you do, don't tell him, because I want it to be a surprise."

Eve opened her mouth but nothing came out, and Maddy plucked the plate out of her hand with a laugh. "But I need a plan; something other than just walking up to him and saying, 'Hey there, Willy. Would you mind letting me blow your socks off—or anything else you might have that needs . . . blowing?'" She reached over and lifted Eve's mouth closed. "What? You don't think I'd dare?"

"Maddy," Eve hissed, taking hold of her arm and dragging her out onto the porch. "William Killkenny isn't some eighteen-year-old twit; he's like Kenzie and Robbie MacBain and the MacKeage men who helped rebuild our house." She arched a brow. "Are you forgetting what happened to Susan? You so much as even bat your big brown eyes at William, and he's going to have you naked before you can even ask him if you can . . . if he's got . . . ." She sighed. "What happened to him being an uncouth, lecherous caveman you don't want anything to do with?"

"Have you *looked* at him lately?" Maddy asked, waving toward the barn where the men were saddling the horses for their ride. "The guy not only cleaned up well, he literally takes my breath away. And you should see him with our residents. He's sweet and thoughtful, and he sincerely likes them. So what's your problem all of a sudden? I thought you wanted me to take an interest in William." Feeling prickles of heat rise to her cheeks, Maddy smoothed the front of her blouse. "Or do you think William wouldn't be interested in *me*?" she asked softly.

"No! What would make you say something like that?"

Maddy tucked her escaping hair behind her ear, suddenly having second thoughts about her grand plan to seduce William Killkenny. She gave a self-conscious laugh. "We both know I'm not exactly a sex kitten. I mean, really; my girls never did perk back up again after I had Sarah, and I could lose twenty pounds and still not fit into my old cheerleader uniform. And the last time I had a tan and sun-streaks in my hair was in high school."

"You're beautiful," Eve growled.

"Yeah, I know. I have beautiful brown eyes and a smile that lights up the world, just like my nine-year-old daughter." She snorted. "And we both know how men love fondling a woman's eyes."

Eve shot her a scathing look. "My God, how did we go from your wanting to blow William to your blowing yourself up?"

Maddy sighed. "I think I'm in the early stages of menopause—one minute I'm horny as a toad, the next I'm feeling sorry for myself and can't stop crying, and then the next minute I just really, really want to hit something. And sometimes I'm all three at the same time! It has to be my hormones getting ready to croak."

"You are not going through menopause!" Eve hissed. "You're twenty-*seven*."

"Yeah, but some days I feel *seventy-seven*," Maddy shot back, although she couldn't help but smile at her friend's ferocious glare.

"Oh, it's your hormones, all right. Only they're not croaking, they're getting ready to explode all over the first man brave enough to get you naked."

"But you just said—"

"What I was *trying* to say," Eve snapped, cutting her off, "is that if you jump William's bones, you'd better be prepared for the consequences. I'm not trying to scare you off, Maddy. I'm trying to tell you that he's not like the men around here." She glanced at the barn before lowering her voice. "Remember how I kept complaining about how old-fashioned Kenzie was? Well, I have a feeling William's even more old-fashioned." Eve grabbed Maddy's shoulders and shot her a smile. "Nobody wants to see you and William together more than I do. But because I'm your very best friend, it's my duty to warn you that you'll be getting more than you bargained for if you pursue this. You remember how you told me you thought Kenzie was an all-nighter kind of guy?"

Maddy nodded, smiling smugly. "And I was right, wasn't I?"

"Well, I suspect William is an all-*weekend* kind of guy."

"All weekend?" Maddy rolled her eyes. "I wish. Billy was good for twenty minutes, half an hour tops, and that was before Sarah was born and we had all the time in the world. All weekend?" she repeated in a whisper.

Eve nodded. "You start an affair with William, I bet that from the minute you drop Sarah off at Billy's on Friday to when he brings her back Sunday afternoon, William won't let you see the light of day."

"Wow. All weekend," Maddy repeated, looking toward the barn. "I can't imagine spending two full days in bed with a man."

"And nights," Eve added with a snicker.

Maddy stepped away and lifted her boobs, then watched gravity drop them back into place. "Holy hell, I'm going to have to start working out."

"So does that gleam in your eye mean you're going for it?" Eve asked.

Maddy looked toward the barn again, and saw Kenzie and William leading three huge horses out of the barn—two with a saddle and one without.

And damn if William didn't have his cuffs rolled up even farther.

She looked back at Eve. "Hell yes, I'm going for it. I have six years of repressed hormones threatening to explode." She shot her a smile. "If for no other reason, I have to do it for my health."

"Are ye ready for a good ride, Maddy?" William asked, stopping at the bottom of the steps to grin up at her. "We'll take it slow and easy the first few times, so ye don't get too sore, and then we'll really get daring." His eyes sparkled in the low-hanging sun. "I promise, lass, once ye see how fun it can be, you'll be begging me to do it every chance we can."

Maddy grabbed Eve when she heard her friend gasp. "I'll get Sarah," she said with a strangled gasp of her own, pulling Eve into the house. She barely got the door closed before she bent over in full-blown laughter even as she pointed at Eve, who was laughing so hard she was sputtering. "Don't say it!" Maddy yelped, wiping her eyes with the back of her hand. "Omigod, I think I just peed my pants!"

Chapter Eight

✖

"I'm going to be sick," Maddy whispered, clutching her stomach.

Eve laughed, pushing her hands out of the way to finish buttoning her blouse. "You are not. That's just your hormones doing a happy dance."

"I can't believe I let Lois and Charlotte badger me into asking William on a date. I swear when he said yes I nearly threw up. And I couldn't do a damn thing right the rest of the day." She gave a nervous laugh. "I think I put Mem's dentures to soak in ginger ale, and I know I sent Hiram home on the Lynx bus without any socks."

"It's August. He probably wasn't even wearing socks."

"But Hiram's not a day camper; he lives there!" Maddy covered her face with her hands. "What have I gotten myself into? It's been so long since I've been on a real date that I've forgotten what to do!" She dropped her hands when she heard Eve laughing again. "You think this is *funny*?"

"I think this is payback," Eve said with a lingering chuckle.

"Or are you forgetting helping *me* dress for my date with Kenzie not that long ago? I have about as much sympathy as you had for me that night. Come on," she said, pulling Maddy over to her old vanity. "I need to dab concealer on that bruise—you know, the bruise you won't tell me how you got?"

"I fell off the porch."

"Who slapped you, Maddy?"

Maddy stared at herself in the mirror, eyeing the faded bruise near her hairline, and then walked over and plopped down onto her bed. "Okay, but I don't want this getting back to Mom. Promise me she won't find out."

"I promise," Eve said, sitting on the bed beside her.

Maddy wrapped her arm around Eve. "You are my very best friend in the whole world, you know that? And I'm sorry for not telling you, but I . . ." She took her arm away and shrugged. "But I was embarrassed that my snotty little brother got the best of me."

"*Rick* hit you?"

Maddy nodded. "It happened when he came home one night three sheets to the wind. I'd been sitting in the kitchen in the dark waiting for him, getting madder with each hour that went by. And when I heard him drive in and went outside in time to see him stumble out of his truck, I decided I'd had enough."

"And the two of you got into a fight?"

"I stood blocking the door and said he wasn't coming into the house in the condition he was in. I told him I was sick and tired of his staying out until three in the morning at least four nights a week, stumbling upstairs and falling into bed, and then sleeping all day. And yeah, I guess you could say it turned into a fight. He got all belligerent, said some nasty things, and tried to shove his way past me." She took a shuddering breath. "I said some nasty things back and grabbed his arm to stop him from going inside."

She lifted her hand to her cheek. "I don't think he intended to hit me; he just lashed out trying to make me let go of him. But his hand caught me on the side of my face, and it felt as if my head exploded. I staggered back, groping for the porch railing, but I missed and fell down the steps."

"Was he at least sorry he hit you?" Eve asked.

Maddy gaped at her. "He was drunk. And since I was no longer blocking the door, he stumbled into the house and went to bed."

Eve took hold of her hand. "Maddy, why didn't you tell us Rick was getting out of control? Kenzie could have talked to him for you."

Maddy stood up, walked to the mirror, and started dabbing concealer on what was left of her bruise. "Rick is my problem, not yours and Kenzie's. I'm dealing with it." She sighed. "He only started drinking in the last couple of months, really; before then it was just occasional high school parties. But once he graduated, he suddenly stopped working on old man Henderson's fishing boat and started staying out several nights a week and coming home drunk. It's been getting worse the closer he gets to leaving for college. I think he's sort of scared, you know? But he'll relax once he adjusts." She smiled sheepishly. "Then again, maybe I'm the one who should relax—I never should have confronted him like that."

"Don't you dare make this sound like it's your fault! Did he at least apologize?"

"No, because I think when he saw my face and that I was limping, he was too ashamed to say anything. He still goes out most nights, but he hasn't come home falling-down drunk since."

"He's the one who needs a good slap in the face," Eve hissed, coming to stand beside her. "He hit you, and then he pretends it never even happened."

"He's just a kid, Eve."

"He's almost *twenty*. If he's big enough to flatten his sister, he should be man enough to apologize. And he should be working instead of sleeping all day."

"He helps out on the docks once in a while for gas and spending money."

"He should be contributing to the household."

"I'm handling it," Maddy growled, tossing the makeup onto the vanity, only to be instantly contrite. "I'm sorry. I know you're just trying to help."

"Because I love you. And because it's killing me to see you running around with a huge smile on your face all the time, when you're barely holding it together inside. When was the last time you did something just for yourself?" Eve gestured at her head. "You have what's-her-name at the nursing home cut your hair because you won't even take the time to drive to Oak Harbor and go to a real salon."

"Elvira is a good stylist."

"And the only new outfit I've seen you buy in the six months since I moved back is a new set of scrubs for work."

"Oh, please," Maddy said, rolling her eyes. "You've been watching too many Oprah shows. I do not have martyr's syndrome; I just don't have time to do my nails and put cucumbers on my eyes and sip mint juleps."

She took a step back when Eve's expression suddenly turned . . . scary.

"But as of tonight," Eve said, dragging her toward the hall, "everything changes. You are going on a date with a handsome, hairy-armed man, and you're going to forget about everything except having fun."

Maddy tried resisting, but she might as well have tried pulling a freight train to a stop. "Slow down, dammit; I'm not ready to have fun with William. You said it yourself that he's too much man for me. He's going to eat me up!"

"God, I hope so." Eve sneered, dragging her down the stairs. She stopped at the bottom, gave her a quick inspection, and wagged her finger at her. "Honest to God, if you're wearing your panties when you get home tonight, I will never speak to you again," she whispered—throwing Maddy's own damning words from two months ago right back in her face. Eve undid the top button of Maddy's blouse. "The minute you get to the restaurant, you order a drink and chug it down," she continued. "But only *one* drink, just to relax. And then be very specific when you order your food," she added deadpan, "or you'll find yourself eating lobster until it's coming out your ears."

"Anything else?" Maddy drawled, fighting a smile.

Eve spread Maddy's collar to expose more of her hiked-up cleavage and then grabbed her hand to lead her toward the kitchen. "You do the driving tonight."

"I can't drive if I'm drinking."

"*One* drink. But trust me, if you drank an entire fifth, you'd still be safer than letting William drive. Here's your date," she said when William stood up from the table where he'd been talking to Sarah.

"Wow, Mom, you look pretty," Sarah said, sounding more surprised than complimentary. She suddenly frowned. "Isn't that your Thanksgiving skirt? How come you're wearing it tonight? It looks hot."

Maddy knew the girl was talking about the temperature and not her sex appeal. And hadn't she just had this discussion with Eve? She didn't care what Eve thought; William had threatened to spank her if he ever caught her in short shorts again, and she wasn't taking any chances by wearing a short skirt.

Apparently, Killkenny wasn't a leg man.

"The weather report said we might have showers tonight, and my other dresses would have been too cold." *And really too short,* she silently added.

Okay, time to make eye contact, she decided, and see if she could keep from throwing up. She looked at William, only of course her eyes went directly to his arms first, and yup, his cuffs were rolled almost up to his elbows.

"I picked these myself, for the prettiest lass around," he said, holding out a fistful of . . . good Lord, he'd picked *goldenrod* off the side of the road!

Maddy reached for them, but in a mirror image of Eve's first date with Kenzie, Eve plucked them out of her hand. "Okay, you two," she said, herding them toward the door. "Sarah and I are going to make popcorn and watch *Harry Potter* until Mom and Patricia get back from Bingo."

William stopped on the porch and turned to them. "When I was with Trace this afternoon, he told me that every Wednesday, there's something called ladies' night at the bars in Ellsworth," he said. "Would ye prefer to go there instead of the restaurant?"

"No!" both Maddy and Eve yelped at once.

"I mean, I'm really quite hungry," Maddy said more demurely. "And we can have a drink with our meal if you'd like. Unless . . . unless you want to go dancing?"

"No," William said quickly, though he didn't shout it like they had. "I mean, that is, unless you want to?"

"No," Maddy said. "I prefer Rhapsody in Oak Harbor."

William started to take her arm, but Eve took hold of *his* arm and stopped him, and Maddy saw her friend glare directly into his eyes. William sighed heavily, reached into his pants pocket, and took out his truck keys.

He handed them to Maddy. "I thought you might like to drive this evening," he said, smiling tightly. "So I can concentrate on learning the road signs. I've been told there's also a set of traffic lights in Oak Harbor."

The tight knot in Maddy's belly suddenly eased, and she all but skipped down the stairs to the shiny new, fire-engine-red pickup truck Eve had driven William and Mabel over in earlier. The plan, apparently, was that Maddy would drive William home and keep his truck to use, and Eve would take her car when Mabel got back from Bingo.

"Okay, Willy," Maddy said, climbing into the driver's seat. "But it's also your job to watch for flying moose."

Christ's blood, he hated feeling out of his element. And Kenzie reciting to him a list as long as his arm about the rules of dating had confused William more than helped. What was it with this century, that there were so many blasted rules?

In his homeland, when a man found a lass who was willing, they got straight to business. And if they both felt they'd had a good time, they continued on together until one or both of them found someone else they fancied more.

And permanent unions were always political, not for love.

Love was a woman's notion, anyway, invented to make her feel secure enough to have bairns. Whereas in this century, people got married and never had children, often staying together even if the woman was barren.

After finally winding down from explaining modern courtship in the barn late this afternoon, Kenzie had suddenly handed William a box of little packets. William had ripped open one of the packets, unrolled the little disk, and stared at the thin tube in confusion. That is until he realized *what* in hell it was, and exactly *how* he was supposed to use it. That's when he'd started cursing.

Kenzie had walked out of the barn laughing, tossing a final warning over his shoulder that Eve had promised to run William through with a sword if he knocked up her very best friend.

William frowned out through the windshield, trying to remember some of the things Mabel had suggested he talk to

Maddy about. "They've set the foundation for my house," he said, grabbing the door handle when she turned out of the driveway and brought the truck up to speed rather quickly.

"Already?" she asked. "So, did you set it in the sheltered cove like Samuel suggested or up on the bluff where Elbridge thought it should go?"

"I wished to place it far out on the point, where it would be surrounded by water on three sides. Charlotte and Lois liked that spot, because every room would have a good view, but the men persuaded me that the storms called nor'easters would likely sweep it away. And they said it would cost a small fortune to heat, and that I'd constantly be washing the salt spray off the windows."

"So, where are you building it?"

"High up on the bluff where Elbridge suggested. Everyone seemed happy with the decision by the time we left."

"What kind of house are you building? A New England Cape or something with a more modern design?"

"It's going to be more like an Irish keep."

"You mean, like a castle?"

"Nay, it won't be that big. It will have only eight bedrooms."

"Eight!" she said, glancing over at him. "That's a pretty big bachelor pad. It's going to take a year to build a house that size."

William slowly started to relax and finally let go of the door handle. Maddy appeared to be quite a good driver, as she sped through the winding road much as he liked to do, only she didn't let the tires stray onto the gravel. He needed more practice, he guessed, because it seemed if he moved the steering wheel only a wee bit, the damn truck would bolt for the ditch.

"Robbie MacBain found a good local carpenter for me," he told her, "and the gentleman agreed to hire more men so I can be moved in by next spring. Was that a Stop sign?" he asked, looking over his right shoulder as a signpost went rushing by.

"No, it said Yield. It was a triangle, not a hexagon."

He relaxed and faced front again. "I have a question to ask ye, Maddy."

"About driving?" she asked, slowing the truck down slightly.

"Nay, I like your driving. And soon you'll be riding a horse the same way. The question I have is about dating. Is it common practice for a woman to ask a man out on a date?" He looked over when she didn't answer and saw that her cheeks had turned a soft pink. "I only ask because Hiram made a comment about young women today are always chasing after anything in pants."

She still said nothing, though her cheeks did darken. She slowed the truck rather abruptly, bringing it to a full stop right beside a red sign that said Stop, then turned right and shot off again.

"Hiram then went on to say the affliction seems to be contagious, as even the older women like Lois and Charlotte have started being quite forward. So, is a lass asking out a man common practice or not?"

"Hiram is ninety-one years old," she finally said. "When he started dating, women had just won the right to vote."

"So is that a yes?"

He heard her sigh. "It's a sometimes, okay? Sometimes women ask men out, because if we have to wait for *them* to ask *us* out, it might never happen."

"I was going to ask you out," he said softly.

She slowed the truck again and blinked over at him. "You were?" She snapped her eyes back to the road, and the truck resumed its speed.

William suddenly decided that modern society could take all of its blasted rules and shove them. "I was thinking that after dinner, we might drive to Dragon Cove and I could show you my house."

Maddy glanced over at him, her gaze straying to his watch again before she looked back at the road. "I . . . I think I'd like that."

And that's when William knew that no matter what century it was, certain things between a man and a woman would never, ever change.

Chapter Nine

Thanks to Mabel insisting that he take her out to lunch three times a week to learn how things worked in this century, William had become very comfortable eating in restaurants. And tonight he found he quite liked the concept of dating as well, as he couldn't remember spending a more entertaining and enlightening meal with a lovelier woman. And a rather talkative one, too; the more Maddy drank the more she talked, and the more she talked the more enchanted William became. She'd even admitted that Eve had said she could only have one drink to calm her nerves—a little tidbit she'd thrown out after finishing her fourth glass of what she'd called a Long Island Iced Tea.

William had taken a sip at her insistence, and decided it wasn't like any tea he'd ever tasted; the fumes alone could have brought down a bear. When he'd asked why she felt the need to calm her nerves, Maddy had explained how dating was like riding a horse, and that when a person repeatedly fell off, they sometimes needed a little liquid courage to climb back on again. Then she'd gone on to say she was limiting herself to only four drinks tonight, as five seemed to be her tipping point for outright stupidity.

William had followed the waiter to the bar when she'd obviously lost count and ordered her *fifth* drink, and he'd instructed the man to cut the liquor down to a quarter and replace it with more of the tea. He was pleased Maddy was comfortable enough to let her guard down with him, but he preferred his women *consciously* willing.

He'd limited himself to two drinks of warm straight whiskey, unwilling to let his own guard down as long as Maddy was in his care.

All in all, he felt the evening was a success thus far. In fact, he even got to drive. Maddy had handed him the keys as they'd stood up to leave—after gulping down her sixth drink—saying she certainly wasn't drunk but maybe it would be better if he drove. And seeing how she appeared relaxed and rather agreeable, he figured she wouldn't start screaming if the truck decided to stray off the pavement of its own accord.

It was his first experience driving at night, and he found that once he left the town of Oak Harbor and was traveling a dark road, the headlights were more of a hindrance than a help. He tried to turn them off, but no matter which button he pushed he couldn't make them go out. Total darkness would have allowed his eyes to adjust, whereas the headlamps only shone a few hundred paces in front of the truck, so he had to go very slow for fear something would suddenly appear in front of him.

Maddy complimented him several times on the drive back to Midnight Bay, and said he should be able to get his license very soon.

William decided the more time he spent with the lass, the more he liked her.

He slowly made his way down the dirt road going into his

land, stopped at the edge of the cove, and shut off the engine. And *still* the lights didn't go out.

"Are the blasted lights going to stay on all night?" he muttered.

Maddy giggled. "They're on a timer; they'll go out in a minute or two. They stay on so you can walk to the house without tripping over anything." She giggled again, only to end with a hiccup—which made her giggle *again*. "I haven't been down this road since high school," she said. "We used to come here to drink and go parking."

"How does one *go* parking? If you're parked, you aren't going anywhere."

The dash lights let him see her surprise. "You've never been *parking*?"

"I believe we're parking right now, are we not?"

Her expression went from surprised to intense.

The headlights suddenly went out, plunging them into darkness, and Maddy hiccupped again—which was followed by another giggle. She blindly reached over and grabbed his arm. "We're certainly not going to be able to park in this truck. The console is keeping you way over there." There was enough moonlight that William could see her smiling somewhat expectantly as her fingers feathered over his forearm. "But I guess that's why they make backseats," she said huskily.

He glanced over his shoulder and would have laughed if he hadn't known she was serious. Full-grown men and women made love in backseats? Christ, he'd get a leg cramp just trying to undress her.

Maddy hiccupped again, but no giggle followed as she pulled her hand away.

"Come on," he said, opening his door—which brought on the *interior* lights this time, allowing him to see her cheeks had turned a lovely pink as she stared down at her hands in her lap.

"Let's head up to the bluff so I can show you my building site. Wait, stay there; I'll walk around and get you, so ye don't trip and fall."

He held on to the truck to guide himself around to her side, as he couldn't see the ground because apparently the interior lights were also on a timer. He took hold of her hand as she slid out, and immediately closed her door.

"Just stand here a minute until the lights go out and your eyes can adjust to the moonlight," he suggested, lacing his fingers through hers. "Are ye cold, lass?" he asked when she hugged herself with her free arm. "Your long skirt might be warm, but your blouse is sleeveless. Here, I'll give ye my shirt," he said, letting her go to unbutton it.

"No! I mean, you should probably leave it on," she said, her voice sounding even huskier as she stopped him by grabbing both of his wrists.

The interior lights suddenly shut off. William felt her fingers flex on his wrists, heard her breath hitch, and suddenly her hands were gone and she hiccupped again.

But no giggle.

His eyes having adjusted to the moonlight enough to see that she'd gone back to hugging herself, William unbuttoned his shirt, pulled the tails out of his pants and shrugged it off, and then wrapped it over her shoulders.

"Omigod," he heard her whisper on an indrawn breath, which was quickly followed by a strangled hiccup.

"Slide your arms into the sleeves," he told her. As soon as she did, he took her hand and started leading her up the new road the crew had carved through the trees. "I believe you're going to have your stockings blown off, lass, once we reach the bluff."

"Omigod," he heard again, only this time it came out more as a squeak.

"Can ye see well enough?" he asked. He wrapped an arm

around Maddy's waist and tucked her against his side when they reached the uneven ground of the building site.

She hiccupped so violently that she stumbled anyway, and William stopped and turned to face her. "I believe I have a cure for what ails ye," he said, threading his fingers through her hair to cup her face in his palms. He tilted her head and covered her mouth with his own just as her soft sweet lips parted in surprise.

Her hands gripped his wrists, her breath hitched, and she leaned into him. Aye, he knew exactly how to cure what ailed the lass.

And she seemed to like his medicine. In fact, she parted her lips even more, and her sweet, delicate tongue found his. She trailed her fingers down his forearms, then back up, then down again before moving them in a feathery path up his naked torso. She splayed her hands over his back and pulled herself into him, the entire length of her body melting against his.

She started making soft little sounds, her hands kneading his muscles. William tucked her head in the crook of his arm and deepened his kiss even as he reached down and cupped her bottom, her mewls turning to moans when he pulled her against his groin. She started trembling again, but William knew she wasn't cold. Without breaking their kiss, he turned them both as he searched for a place to lay her down.

The moonlight shone off a thick cloth covering some building material, and he reluctantly tore his mouth from hers, smiling openly at her protest. "It's just temporary, lass," he said, leading her to the cloth. He tugged it free and dragged it—towing Maddy with him—to a patch of grass, and tossed it down, pulled her back into his arms, and settled his mouth back over hers.

The moment she melted into him again, he eased them both down onto the makeshift bed he'd made, settling beside her to wrap her in his arms.

Only the lass seemed to have another idea; she hiked up her billowy skirt to slide a leg over his hips, and swung up to straddle him. "I'm afraid it's *your* stockings that are going to get blown off, Mr. Killkenny," she said with a throaty giggle, her hands splaying across his naked chest as she pressed her womanhood against him. But when he tried to reach for her, she captured his wrists, leaned forward, and pinned his hands beside his head.

"Not so fast, big man. I've been waiting a rather long time for this. You just lie back and relax," she whispered, her big dark eyes locked on his. "And enjoy the show."

She thought *she'd* been waiting a long time? Hell, he'd been several centuries yearning to get his hands on a woman again!

She hesitated to see if he would obey, then straightened—which served to press her rather provocatively onto the growing bulge in his pants. Having absolutely no intention of just *watching*, William slowly slid his hands under her skirt—relishing every inch of her silky thighs—and grasped her hips.

She stilled in the act of unbuttoning her blouse. "I thought you weren't a leg man," she said as he worked his fingers beneath her underpants to palm her soft, wonderfully feminine bottom.

"Not a—what could have given ye that impression?" he asked, even as he used his grip to slide her along the length of his shaft.

"N-never mind," she said with a breathless moan, squirming intimately against him. She hurriedly finished unbuttoning her blouse and shrugged it off along with his shirt, only to reveal a small lacy garment that looked to be strangling her bosom and causing an intriguing amount of flesh to spill over the top.

"Christ's blood, can ye breathe in that thing?" he asked, every last bit of his blood shooting to his groin. He bolted upright with every intention of helping her out of the garment, eager to taste her sweet flesh.

But she reared away with a gasp of surprise. William lifted his hands to catch her from falling backward—which in turn lifted her billowy skirt up, exposing her bottom to the ocean air.

She immediately lurched forward and reached back to pull it down, driving her bosom into his face. He fell back with a muffled grunt of surprise when something hard and pointy nearly poked out his eye.

With a yelp of horror, she tried scrambling off him, driving the air from his lungs when she shoved herself off his chest, her knee damn near emasculating him. William bolted upright to protect himself and caught her flailing arms. He rolled them both over to pin her to the cloth as she continued to try to push her skirt—which was tangled up in his legs—back into place.

"Maddy, darling," he whispered, working to keep the edge from his voice, "what say we just lie here for a while and enjoy the moonlight?"

She suddenly hiccupped, and William tucked her against his side with a sigh of defeat, guessing that if drink number five was her tipping point for stupidity, number four must be her point of calamity.

Either that or they were *both* out of practice.

Maddy couldn't remember ever being so embarrassed.

But then, she'd never tried to make love while keeping most of her clothes on before, either. That's why she'd worn this skirt; because it was full enough that she could just pull it up, slip off her panties, and straddle William. And the thin lace on the top half of her bra was supple enough that she could tuck it under to expose her nipples while still keeping her boobs jacked up. It was all part of her perfect plan of seduction; she could blow William's mind with sexy underwear and a little mystery and show off her good assets while keeping her flaws hidden.

"Can I ask ye a question?" he said over the sound of the gentle surf washing against the rocks below.

"No." She'd had to mutter her answer into his naked chest, because he was holding her plastered against him, apparently afraid she would attack him again. She took as deep a breath as his embrace would allow and let out a sigh. "Okay, what?"

"That tiny garment you're wearing around your bosom; is there metal in it?" he asked, rubbing his eye with his free hand. But then she saw him hold it up in the moonlight and rub his fingers together as if they were wet.

Maddy popped up as far as his grip would allow. "Are you *bleeding*?" she asked, touching his cheek just below his eye. When she felt her own fingers come away wet, she shoved her hand down the front of her blouse to her bra. "Omigod, my underwire worked free and poked you in the eye!" she cried in dismay. Utterly humiliated now, she tried to get up so she could go jump in the ocean and drown herself.

He pulled her head back down to his chest with a chuckle. "It's not a mortal wound, lass. So what's an underwire?".

Maddy went still. He hadn't really just asked that, had he? "It's a wire, or rather a set of wires, sewn into a bra to shape a woman's breasts and . . . jack them up."

"Why?"

"So we don't trip over them," she snapped, trying to wiggle free again.

Only he still wouldn't let her go. "I see. No, actually, I don't," he said. "Why would a woman feel the need to shape her breasts in an unnatural way, and . . . jack them up? It looks very uncomfortable."

Was this guy for real? She decided she didn't want to jump in the ocean; she wanted to throw *him* in. "To maintain our youthful figure," she growled, "after we have a baby and all our parts head south." Since he wouldn't let her pop her head up to glare at him, she unthinkingly poked him in his side. "Did you just fly in from another planet or something? Don't they have Wonderbras in Ireland?"

"Hush, lass," he said, capturing her hand so she couldn't poke him again. "Just lie back and listen to the surf. Isn't it a beautiful evening?"

She couldn't hear anything but his strongly beating heart because one ear was plastered against his *naked* chest and the other one was covered by his big, strong, wonderfully masculine hand.

"I believe I'll like living here," he continued. "This coast reminds me of home."

Not wanting to be hushed again, and enjoying the lilt of his soothing voice and the heat of his pleasant-smelling chest, Maddy let out a yawn, only she wasn't able to cover her mouth because he was still holding her hand.

Obviously a very polite man, he decided to cover it for her.

He lifted her chin as he resettled their positions, and brought his lips down over hers, kissing her gently. But then he threaded his fingers through her hair to tilt her head back, apparently so his tongue would have an easier time making deep, delicious love to her mouth.

Every hormone in her body started doing a happy dance again, and Maddy moved restlessly against him. God, she hoped he wasn't one of those slow and gentle and really considerate lovers. That might be fine halfway through a weekend, but tonight she wanted it fast and hard and   dammit, she didn't need him to be considerate, she needed him *now*.

Maddy reached into her eye-poking Wonderbra—that she was sending back to the company first thing tomorrow with a nasty letter—and pulled out the condom she'd tucked inside it when Eve hadn't been looking, for just in case she found herself in the backseat of a shiny new pickup with a caveman turned sexy hunk.

But hey, she was flexible, and a moonlit bluff overlooking the ocean worked equally well—though the old canvas tarp left something to be desired.

Maybe she could lie on her skirt.

Better yet, maybe she'd get William to lie on her skirt, and she would lie on him.

She pulled her mouth from his and held the condom up to his face. "Here, you open this, while I open your pants," she said raggedly, reeling from his kisses as she fought to keep her hormones from exploding—at least until he was inside her.

Oh, God, just the thought of him sliding inside her made her shudder.

She wiggled down his beautiful, barrel-chested torso, unable to keep from running her lips over him as she did—gratified to feel him shudder in response.

God, he tasted as good as he looked.

"Maddy, darling," she heard him say in a strangled growl, his hands grabbing her shoulders when she started unbuckling his belt.

Not about to let him turn this into another wrestling match, she got right back up in his face. "Here's the deal, Killkenny," she ground out. "I haven't been laid in forever, okay? I don't want sweet kisses in the moonlight—even though you certainly can kiss—and I sure as hell don't need an hour of foreplay or any other romantic crap. We're both consenting adults, we both knew where this evening was headed the moment I asked you out, and I don't know about you, but I'm about one second away from exploding."

She grabbed his hand holding the condom and held it in front of his face again. "So just open the damn thing. You want to play touchy-feely; you can touch and feel all you want—*after.*"

She went back to unbuckling his belt, the task made difficult because she was shaking uncontrollably now, either from hormone overload or abject fear he was going to stop her. She unzipped his pants and tried to work them down his hips, only now she was having difficulty because he was really, really aroused—thank you, God.

He finally sprang free and Maddy stopped breathing.

Oh man, she was *so* ready for this.

She wrapped her hands around him with a hum of pleasure, and he said her name in a strangled groan, every muscle in his body tightening in response.

Maddy's insides clenched with anticipation.

Only she couldn't decide if she wanted to taste him first, or feel him inside her.

No, dammit, she really couldn't wait any longer.

And hey, nothing said she couldn't blow his socks off *after*.

Intending to sensually slide the condom down over him herself—though he certainly didn't seem to need any more stimulation—she looked over to find him still holding the unopened packet. "Oh, give it to me and I'll do it," she said, grabbing it and tearing it open with her teeth. Her happy-dancing hormones turned into a mob of impatient rioters the more she handled him, and her hands shook uncontrollably as she finally got him safely sheathed. She scrambled up to straddle him—fully prepared to push him back down if he sat up again—desperately needing to feel him inside her.

Only he wouldn't fit!

No matter how she wiggled or moved, she couldn't make it happen! Whimpering in frustration, she started to grab his hand to make him help her, but suddenly stopped in mid-reach. Prickles of blazing fire scorched her cheeks as she stared into his moonlit eyes filled not with lust but with concern, and the full scope of what she was doing suddenly brought her crashing back to reality.

She pushed off him with a cry of horror to *really* go jump in the ocean.

But he snagged her skirt and pulled her back into his arms, rolling her onto her back with dizzying swiftness. "Shhh, easy, lass," he whispered, brushing her hair off her face. "There is nothing you can say or *do* or even think, that should ever make you feel the need to run from me, Madeline." He trailed his lips over her cheeks. "And I swear there is nowhere you will ever be safer than in my arms." She felt his hand slide up under her skirt, his fingers slipping under the elastic of her panties. He slowly pulled them down her legs, the heat of his broad palm making her shiver. "So let's see if I can't help ye finish what ye started, lass," he whispered.

His empty hand returned, tracing a slow, fiery path back up her leg, and Maddy suddenly realized he hadn't fit because she'd still been wearing her panties!

"Ye have the softest, silkiest skin," he murmured, his lips brushing her ear as her skirt somehow went the way of her panties. But even as she wondered how he'd managed to un-button its waistband—considering it had taken her forever to get the damn thing buttoned at home—an involuntary moan erupted from her throat when his hand returned to find the seam of her opening.

He softly toyed with her slickness, and all her rioting hormones snapped to attention, collectively focusing on his finger gently sliding inside her. His thumb brushed across her sensitive bud—ever so lightly and then with increasing pressure—and Maddy almost wept at how wonderful it felt. She bucked upward with a soft cry of delight as she clenched around his salaciously talented finger.

"Come for me, Madeline," he whispered against her lips, sliding a second finger inside her. "Give me your pleasure, lass."

His unbelievably talented thumb set a rhythm that sent her

flying over the edge before she even knew what was happening, and she came hard and fast and so violently that it tore another scream from her—which William immediately captured by lowering his mouth over hers.

His fingers continued to move inside her; pulling lingering spasms that rocked her gently as his thumb caressed her soothingly. He slowly backed away from their kiss, and she felt him shift beside her—getting to his knees, she thought, her mind still reeling with the force of her orgasm.

He started fumbling with the band of her bra. She wanted to tell him it clasped in the front, but it suddenly loosened all on its own, and Maddy instinctively grabbed to catch it as the cool night air washed over her nipples. Not fast enough, she immediately grabbed her breasts instead, to keep them from falling off her chest. She blinked up at him looming above her kneeling between her open thighs, his broad shoulders blocking the moonlight and making it impossible to see his face.

"Do not hide yourself from me, Madeline," he said roughly, gently pulling her hands away. "Let the moon bathe your beauty," he whispered, replacing them with his own large, masculine hands.

And his oh-so-talented fingers gently kneaded her breasts, his thumbs brushing both her nipples at once before he softly pinched them, making her moan in pleasure.

"Now that's a sound as sweet as any I've heard in a while." He lowered his weight down in order to replace one hand with his mouth, and ran his tongue in a slow circle around her areola before closing his lips over her eager nipple and suckling.

Maddy arched into him with a cry of encouragement. He lavished attention on each nipple in turn, the alternating heat of his mouth and the cool ocean air raising havoc with her senses. She touched him everywhere she could reach, kneading the muscles on his arms and shoulders, as he worked her into such a frenzy that she braced her feet on the ground to lift her hips, and came again just by rubbing intimately against his shaft.

And being the polite and obviously considerate man that he was, he rode the entire explosion outside her; then just as she started to ebb, he eased inside her with one long, smooth stroke that pulled even more clenching spasms from her as she stretched to accommodate him.

He made a guttural sound, lifting up onto his hands and throwing his head back to seat himself even deeper. "Again, Madeline," he said through his teeth. "Let me feel your pleasure tighten around me."

Sucking air into her lungs with enough force to crack a rib, she gaped up at him.

That is until he moved. He drew nearly out and drove into her again, and Maddy forgot all about the need to breathe as her mighty hormones snapped back to attention, apparently far more ready than she was for yet another spin around the universe.

He set a rhythm that sent her senses spiraling inward again, tightening into a knot of building tension. But when she dug her fingers into his chest because she really needed something solid to hold on to, and incoherently pleaded that he not flat-out kill her with another orgasm, he pressed his thumb intimately against her.

"Once more, Madeline," he urged tightly, using his other hand to lift her onto his thighs and thrusting even deeper.

It was simply too much; Maddy exploded, rocketing into the universe and back with such dizzying speed that her cry of fulfillment came out as a hoarse, keening whimper. He went utterly still above her, both hands on her hips holding him sheathed deeply inside her as her spasms continued pulsing for what seemed like forever.

Oh God, if he moved right now he really would kill her.

But not only did he move, he suddenly pulled out of her and pressed his hand over her mouth just as she was trying to suck much-needed air into her lungs!

Chapter Ten

"Hush, lass. Don't make another sound," he whispered against her ear, his weight suffocating as she squirmed to get free. "And do exactly as I say."

Maddy went very still, alarmed by the tone of his voice.

"We're going to get up and quietly walk to my truck. Understand?"

She nodded, willing to do anything he wanted if it would get her breathing again.

He hesitated briefly, his hand on her mouth easing, and then suddenly lifted off her. Maddy sat up, panting as quietly as she could, and groped for her clothes while he fastened his pants, even as she looked around for what had caused the sudden change in him. But he pulled her to her feet and started leading her away stark naked!

"My clothes," she hissed, turning to find them.

"Hush!" he growled, swiping his shirt off the ground without breaking stride as he dragged her down the path through the trees.

Maddy didn't protest, glad she at least was still wearing her sandals. And since he seemed to be able to see where he was walking, she spent her time trying to pierce the darkness of the woods, hoping to figure out what had spooked him.

She scrambled closer to William, bumping into him as she picked up her pace. Oh God, what if it was that bear-eating, hairless moose she'd almost hit on her and Eve's ride back from Oak Harbor a couple of months ago?

"You're safe, Maddy," he said softly. "Just keep walking."

Since he was talking, she decided she could, too. "Wh-what's out there?"

"Hush," he said, squeezing her hand.

Fine. She didn't want to talk to him anyway. She grabbed her boobs to keep them from repeatedly bumping his arm, and concentrated on walking instead of watching the woods when she realized that every rock and stump looked sinister.

The truck came into view, and William stopped next to a large pine tree and handed her his shirt. Maddy immediately put it on, and then gave him a nudge with her shoulder to get him moving again as she fumbled with the buttons. He didn't budge; instead pulling her against his side as he scanned the woods, his head tilted in a way that said he was listening more than seeing.

It was then she noticed the knife in his hand, as well as the way he was holding it; with the blade running back along his wrist, just like she'd seen Trace hold his knife once when he'd been home on leave. Like all fighting men did, he'd explained to her, when they meant business.

She took a shuddering breath.

William's arm tightened around her. "We're going to walk to the truck, and you're going to get in the driver's seat," he said, bending to whisper in her ear as he continued scanning the trees. "Reach in my pocket and get the key, and when you get in, put it in the keyhole but don't start the truck. Under-stand?"

She nodded, and then slipped her hand in the pocket he turned toward her and took out his key, making sure she didn't press any of the buttons on the fob.

She tugged on his arm to get him to lean over. "Hey," she quietly said in his ear. "I could hit the panic button on your key fob, and all the lights would come on and the horn would blast, and that would scare away whatever the hell's out there."

"No noise. Is there a way to stop the interior lights from coming on?"

"I'm pretty sure there's a button that will shut them off."

"Just as soon as you open the door, push it."

"The lights are still going to come on when I open it."

"Just get them off as soon as ye can. Then get in and lock *your* door but not the others." He gave her another squeeze. "You're doing fine, lass."

Fine? She was too friggin' scared to panic!

He took hold of her hand again and slowly approached the truck. Maddy heard a noise to their right and tried to *run* the rest of the way.

But William held her back. "Just keep walking," he said, keeping his attention on the direction of the noise. He let go of her when they reached the truck and turned his back to her. "Get in, shut off the lights, and lock only your door," he repeated.

A low, menacing growl came from the shadows off to their right, and every hair on Maddy's body rose in terror. She stopped breathing completely when she heard another growl just off to their left.

"Now," William growled with equal menace.

She yanked open the door, blinking against the sudden light as she fumbled with the buttons on the dash until they went out. She scrambled up into the seat and shoved the key in the ignition, but didn't close her door. "William, get in!" she cried, trying to scoot over the console.

He closed the door for her, but before she could protest, he opened the back door and climbed inside. "Lock all the doors!"

Maddy groped at the buttons, and finally heard all four locks click.

William moved around behind her, bumping her seat, and she turned to see him reaching behind the back of the rear seat. Her eyes widened when his hand emerged holding a . . . sword?

"Can ye start the truck without the lights coming on?"

"I don't know how!" she cried, gripping the steering wheel.

He squeezed her shoulder. "It's okay, Maddy," he said calmly. "There appears to be enough room for ye to turn around without having to back up." He continued scanning the woods surrounding them on three sides. "If there are any small trees in the way, just drive over them."

"Wh-what's out there?"

"I'm not sure, lass," he said, giving her shoulder another reassuring squeeze. "I only caught the shadowed outline of what looked like a wolf."

Maddy took her first full breath in twenty minutes. "You must have seen a coyote, then; we don't have wolves in Maine." She reached down to the key but didn't start the truck. "But if it didn't run from us, the poor thing could be rabid. Just as soon as we get to Eve's, we'll call the sheriff and report it."

His hand on her shoulder disappeared. "Start the truck, and drive out the road."

Taking another deep breath that went a long way to settling her nerves, Maddy started the truck, put it in gear, and drove in as tight a circle as she could, barely missing a tree she never would have been able to drive over. Not that there was any need to anymore. Coyotes, even rabid ones, couldn't get them now.

"Um . . . William?" she said, driving up the narrow dirt road. "Is there any particular reason you keep a sword behind your backseat?"

"Because I don't own a gun yet," he said, leaning his arms on the two front seatbacks as he alternated between watching out the windshield and glancing behind them. "I hope to purchase a rifle, but even so, Trace told me that it can't be loaded in a vehicle." He snorted. "Which makes no sense; what good is an unloaded gun? And he said I can't carry a handgun without a permit, either."

"And you feel the need to be armed because . . . ?" She glanced over at him briefly and then laughed softly, more from relief than amusement. "What? Are you afraid of the big bad bogeyman, Killkenny?"

"Are ye saying you're not?"

"Hey, I told you; the bogeyman is in love with me. Maybe that was *his* shadow you saw, and he was growling at *you*. Maybe he's jealous."

But she suddenly slammed on the brakes when a large animal leaped off the road and into the woods in front of them.

"Don't stop!" William snapped. "Step on the gas."

Maddy did as he said, gripping the steering wheel fiercely. "That was one hell of a big coyote," she whispered, slowing the truck to a less reckless speed when she hit a bump that lifted her off her seat.

"Speed back up," he instructed. "And no matter what ye see, don't stop."

"Omigod, there's two of them! Behind us!" she cried when she glanced in her rearview mirror and saw two monstrous coyotes chasing them. "No, three!"

She slammed on the brakes again when the headlights fell on

another one standing in the middle of the road in front of them, its eyes reflecting like glowing coals. Its lips were curled back, exposing the biggest fangs she'd ever seen on *any* animal.

"Drive, Maddy!" William ordered, nudging her shoulder. "Run over it if ye have to. Just don't stop."

She pushed down on the accelerator and the truck lurched forward. Only instead of getting out of the way, the animal leaped directly at them, snarling so fiercely that she heard it over the revving engine. Maddy screamed, giving the wheel a jerk to avoid it, but just as quickly jerked it back when branches scraped her outside mirror. The animal slammed into the top of the passenger side of the cab and tumbled into the woods, the impact sending spider veins through the glass. She screamed again when not ten seconds later, the truck suddenly rocked violently, as if something had jumped into the back bed.

"Drive as if the hounds of hell are after ye, Madeline!"

She pushed the gas pedal all the way to the floor and didn't let up until she reached the main highway. She stomped on the brake to slow down only enough to make the turn—and screamed again when whatever was in the bed suddenly slammed into the rear window with enough force to shatter it into a thousand spider veins.

"Dammit, William, what are they!" she cried, tromping down on the gas again as they careened onto the highway. The tires squealed, and the truck fishtailed toward the ditch just as she heard a bloodcurdling scream—which hadn't come from her!

She glanced in her passenger-side mirror to see whatever had been in the bed get flung out as she straightened from the fishtail, the taillights showing a large ball of fur rolling down the pavement and into the ditch.

"William! What *are* they?" she cried again, her eyes glued on the road ahead as she pushed the truck to a dangerous speed.

"You're doing fine, Madeline," he said evenly, patting her

shoulder. "Just keep going as fast as ye can, and drive directly to Kenzie's house."

"No! We're only a few miles from my home, and I need to make sure Sarah is safe from . . . whatever those things are! I have a couple of my dad's rifles and a shotgun at the house. I need to get home."

"Ye can't, Maddy. You'll be putting Sarah and Patricia in danger if ye do. The beasts have your scent now, and you'd be leading them right to your family. Drive to Kenzie and Eve's."

"M-my *scent*?" she whispered. Oh, God, what in hell was going on? "But for all we know, there could be more of them out there, and I need to get my daughter— Omigod!" she cried when she glanced in the rearview mirror. "They're still following us!" She looked down at the speedometer. "I'm doing seventy!"

"I need ye to go to Maddy's house," William said, only it took her a moment to realize that he wasn't talking to her. "And bring Patricia and Sarah to An Tèarmann."

Realizing he was talking on his cell phone, Maddy sensed him turn away as he lowered his voice. "We have company, Gregor. Close the storm shutters. It's best ye leave before we get there, so ye won't be followed. I will be on watch until ye get back."

There was a moment's silence but for the sound of the laboring engine, before she heard William continue, only in a language she didn't recognize. She glanced in the rearview mirror again, growing truly terrified when she didn't see anything behind them.

She flinched when William's hand came to rest on her shoulder again. "Kenzie will bring Sarah and Patricia to his house," he told her. "When ye reach the road to An Tèarmann, don't slow down any more than ye have to." His fingers lightly dug into her. "You're doing really well, lass."

"No, I'm not!" she cried, taking a hand off the wheel just

long enough to swipe the tears welling up in her eyes. "I won't be doing *well* until I know my baby is safe. Give me the phone so I can call Mom. I can't have Kenzie just suddenly show up at the house; she'll think something terrible has happened to me."

"You drive; I'll dial the number and then hold the phone for ye."

She gave him the number, and while he dialed, Maddy wracked her brain as to what she could say that wouldn't give her mom a heart attack. "Hey, Mom," she said calmly when Patricia picked up the phone. "No, everything's just fine, except William and I just heard on the radio that the sheriff and state police are chasing some criminals in the woods around Midnight Bay. And, well, William said he'd feel better if you and Sarah weren't in the house all alone. So he just called Kenzie and asked him to drive over and get you, and bring you and Sarah back to Eve's house. What? No, it'll be quicker if Kenzie comes and gets you; we . . . we're heading back from Ellsworth right now, and we'll meet you at Eve's. Rick? Oh, don't worry about him, Mom. He's with his buddies, and . . . and I think they were all going to Oak Harbor tonight. He's safe, but I just want to make sure you and Sarah are safe, too."

She glanced in her rearview mirror and then back at the road. "Get Sarah dressed and be waiting downstairs for Kenzie. But stay inside and keep the doors locked, and don't open them until Kenzie actually gets out of his truck and comes up onto the porch to get you, okay? Yes, I love you, too. I'll see you soon."

She pulled her ear away from the phone to let William know she was done. "Wh-what about Rick?" she asked when she heard him close the phone. "There's a good chance they're all down at the gravel pit."

William's hand returned to her shoulder. "I spent the afternoon with Trace, and he told me he'd be shadowing Rick this evening. And your cousin impressed me as a man who can handle any situation that might arise. I doubt our . . . visitors will head that far inland, anyway." He gave her a squeeze. "Ye have my word, Maddy; Kenzie will keep Patricia and Sarah safe."

"I don't know what those things are, William, or why they're chasing us," she whispered, swiping her eyes with the back of her shaking hand. "I-I don't know what's happening."

His grip tightened on her shoulder. "Ye don't have to know right now," he said softly. "Ye only have to deal with it. This will all be over soon, and when the sun's shining tomorrow, it will seem to be nothing more than a bad dream."

She instinctively slowed down when they reached town, and even put on her blinker! "Oh, God, I'm losing my mind!"

William actually chuckled. "Ye need to wait a little longer before ye do. When we get to An Tèarmann, turn in a wide arc so your side of the truck is right by the steps. Then shut off the engine, but don't get out until I tell ye to. Understand?"

If he asked her if she *understood* one more time, she was going to scream.

No, wait; she'd already screamed so much her throat hurt.

She took a fortifying breath. "I understand."

And then she put her blinker on again to turn into Eve's farm! Squinting against the array of floodlights lighting up the dooryard like high noon, Maddy swung the truck in a wide circle, stopped it right beside the porch steps, and shut off the engine. "Okay, let's get the hell inside."

"Nay. You'll be going in, but I'm going to keep watch outside."

She snapped her head around. "You can keep watch *inside,* where it's safe!"

He cupped her cheek in his palm, his deep blue eyes glistening in the floodlights. "You're quite a woman, Madeline. I've known battle-hardened warriors who couldn't have done what you did tonight."

"Please come inside with me," she whispered.

"I can't find out what's going on from inside the house." He pulled her closer as he leaned in and kissed her, then disappeared.

Maddy heard his door unlock, and twisted to see him get out—taking his sword with him. She spun around and opened her door, and he helped her out of the truck.

"You'll be holding your daughter in your arms soon," he said, leading her up the stairs. "How long ago did Kenzie leave?" he asked Eve when she opened the front door.

"He called to say he just got to Maddy's house, and everything is quiet there," Eve said, grabbing Maddy's other arm and pulling her away from William.

"And the pup?"

"She's in the back room. Kenzie brought her in before he left."

William nodded. "Lock up behind me," he said, disappearing back outside.

Maddy pulled away from Eve and ran to the door—since that was her only view outside because all the windows had heavy metal storm shutters covering them. "I want him to stay inside!" she cried, watching him slip into the shadows beyond the barn.

"William can take care of himself," Eve said, reaching around Maddy to lock the door. She took hold of Maddy's arm again. "Come on, I bet you could use a drink."

"How can you be so calm about this?" she hissed, pulling away. "Eve, there are *wolves* out there, huge, vicious, snarling monsters! They attacked the truck, and they chased us halfway here!" She hugged herself. "I've never even seen dogs that big; they were the size of ponies. And they had glowing red eyes and fangs larger than my fingers. And I was doing seventy miles an hour, and they were keeping up with us!" She pointed at the door. "And William is out there with only some stupid sword that looks old enough to be an antique, and you're calmly telling me I need a drink? I need a *shrink*!" She suddenly stiffened. "No, I know what this is. Somebody slipped something into my drink at Rhapsody, and I'm hallucinating. This is all some weird dream. It has to be!"

"Shhh, don't wake up Mom and Daar. It's going to be okay," Eve said, wrapping her arm around her. She led her to a chair at the table and made her sit down. "You're safe now, and that's all that matters. And Sarah and Patricia will be here soon."

Eve went to the cupboards, took down a bottle of scotch, poured about two shots' worth into a tumbler, and came back and handed it to her. "Sip this; it'll calm your nerves. You can't let Sarah and your mom see you like this, Maddy, or you're going to scare them. I have no idea what excuse Kenzie came up with to get them over here."

"I called them on William's cell phone," Maddy explained after taking a large swig. She wiped her chin with her sleeve, having spilled some because she was shaking so badly. "And I told them the sheriff and state police were searching the woods for criminals."

Eve pulled a chair over and sat down facing her. "That was quick thinking." She gently pushed the glass toward Maddy's mouth. "Drink it all up, and you'll be feeling like your old self before it even hits your belly."

Maddy downed the rest of the glass, wiped her mouth again, and hiccupped. "Oh, shit," she muttered, handing the glass to Eve. "I forgot I already had enough Long Island Iced Teas tonight to float a lobster boat."

Eve reared back in horror. "But you were only supposed to have one! And you just let me give you two more shots?"

Maddy smiled at her and hiccupped again.

And then she giggled, already quite punch-drunk at being

inside a brightly lit, storm-shuttered house that even Godzilla couldn't break into. She hiccupped again. "Where in hell is William when I need him?" she muttered. "He has the perfect cure for hiccups." She leaned toward her friend and lowered her voice. "You won't believe this, but he can actually *kiss* hiccups away." She flopped back in her chair with a sigh. "Man-oh-man, can that man kiss."

"Um . . . where are your clothes?" Eve asked.

"Up on the bluff next to William's new house," she said, waving in that general direction. She suddenly sat up. "Omigod! His building crew is going to find them tomorrow morning when they come to work."

"Don't worry," Eve assured her. "They can't know who the clothes belong to—unless you left your purse up there, too?"

"No, that's in William's truck."

Eve arched a brow as she leaned back in her chair. "So, he kisses good, he can cure hiccups, and he obviously knows how to get a woman to part with her clothes. Anything else I should know about concerning your manly man?"

"Yeah. The manly *man* tried to kill me with sex."

Eve's eyes widened. "Madeline Kimble, he did not."

"He did. Why do you think they call it *the little death*? Well, guess what, my very best friend, I died three times in less than ten minutes! Or maybe it was four," she murmured, trying to think back.

"Exactly how many Long Island Iced Teas did you have?"

"I can't remember—four or five. Or maybe it was six. No," she said, shaking her head. "I distinctly remember telling William that five drinks make me stupid, so it had to be only three or four."

"We agreed on *one,* just to calm your nerves."

Maddy snorted. "An entire fifth wouldn't have calmed my nerves. And *you* agreed to only one; I didn't agree to anything.

Hey," she said with a frown, "is that a pen sticking out of your cleavage?" she asked, squinting at Eve's chest.

Eve looked down, then back at Maddy. "I was balancing the store's bankbook when William called Kenzie, and I guess I just stuck it in there." She laughed. "Being pregnant, it's the first time I've ever had anything even close to cleavage. So let's get back to William's almost killing you. Was that before or after you parted company with your clothes?" she asked, arching a brow.

"Both. We had a couple of wrestling matches trying to determine who was blowing whose socks off, but because he's bigger and stronger and . . . and hairier than I am, he won. I got embarrassed, and then I got so humiliated I wanted to throw myself in the ocean. Only William wouldn't let me, and he told me there's nothing I can say or do or think when I'm with him that should ever make me feel embarrassed," she said, just now remembering that part. And how good it had made her feel at the time, and how . . . safe. "And then he tried to kill me with sex."

"And of course you weren't at all trying to kill *him*, were you?"

Maddy glared at her, just to let her friend know how serious she was, but then her mouth turned up in a smile all on its own. "Well, the first time *was* quite nice, thank you very much; and the second time was . . . well, quite surprising, actually. But then he *insisted* that I come a third time, and since I was still trying to catch my breath from the first two times, I kept trying to tell him no. But my stupid hormones wouldn't listen to me, either. I think *they* were drunk, and didn't want to stop partying."

She leaned forward and lowered her voice again. "Honest to God, I swear I saw stars. And I really couldn't breathe, and then William suddenly covered my mouth with his hand, and told me we were walking down to the truck. But I was *naked*. And he wouldn't let me gather up my clothes; he just started dragging me through the dark, scary woods, and my boobs were flying all over the place!"

She grabbed her breasts through his shirt. "I think he cut my bra off with a *knife*," she whispered. "I know he has one; I saw it in his hand. But not until later, when we were headed to the truck. And he looked like he really knows how to use it. Oh, and he keeps a sword behind the seat in his truck. Isn't that weird?"

Eve shrugged, but then she frowned. "Why would William cut off your bra? All you had to do was unclasp it."

"I think he was getting impatient because I wasn't taking it off myself." She made a face. "But more likely, he was mad at the damn thing for poking him in the eye."

"You poked him in the eye?"

"I didn't—my bra did. One of the underwires must have worn through, and when I shoved my boobs in his face because he'd lifted my skirt up over my shoulders during one of our little wrestling matches, the wire poked him just below the eye." She nodded at her friend's incredulous look. "It drew blood and everything. Didn't you see the small cut just below his eye just now?"

Eve had both her hands covering her mouth, trying to hold in her laughter.

Maddy glared at her again. "You think his trying to kill me is funny?"

"No," Eve said, now holding her protruding belly. "Honestly, no. But really, Mads, I can just see the two of you fighting over who was going to seduce whom." She shook her head. "I don't think I've ever met two better-matched people than you and William, especially when it comes to . . . oh, let's call it your *enthusiasm* for the opposite sex, shall we?"

Maddy gasped so hard she nearly fell off her chair. "Are you calling me a slut?"

"No!" Eve said, still laughing. "Are you forgetting how determined you were that I jump Kenzie's bones the first time you laid eyes on him? And I'm pretty sure William loves women just as much as you love men, especially women brave enough to wrestle him to the ground trying to blow his socks off."

"*Stockings,*" Maddy corrected. "He calls them stockings. And I was half drunk at the time." She smiled crookedly. "If I'd been just a little more sober, I would have remembered to take my panties off first."

Eve was back to covering her mouth with her hands.

A horn tooted out in the dooryard.

Eve stood up, and Maddy panicked. "Omigod! What am I going to tell Mom about my clothes?" she cried, looking down at herself. "And Sarah! I can't let my daughter see me wearing only a man's shirt!"

"Calm down," Eve said, going to the door to unlock it. "Tell them you fell off the pier in Oak Harbor or something and that William gave you his shirt to wear."

"No, I told Mom we went to Ellsworth," Maddy said, chasing after her. She switched directions, grabbed the bottle of scotch off the counter, and shoved it into the cupboard. "I know—I'll tell her that as we were walking out of the restaurant, the sprinklers came on and soaked me."

Patricia walked in, Kenzie right behind her, carrying Sarah.

"She fell asleep halfway here," Kenzie said, continuing through the kitchen. "Which bed do ye want me to put her in?"

"Lay her down in the blue room," Eve instructed quietly. She turned to Maddy and Patricia. "Maddy, you can sleep with Sarah, and Patricia, you can have the room right next to Mom's."

"Madeline, where are your clothes?" her mom asked.

"I fell off the pier, and William gave me his shirt."

"What were you doing at the Ellsworth pier? There's no restaurant down there."

Damn, she'd gotten her stories confused. "Oh, William took a wrong turn, and when we ended up at the Union River boat ramp, I suggested we go for a moonlight stroll down on the docks. Yeah, that's when I fell in; when I tried to feed a seagull some leftovers out of my doggy bag, and the ungrateful thing attacked me."

"Where is William?" her mom asked, looking around.

Maddy tucked her hands behind her back and crossed her fingers, silently praying for forgiveness. "He's in the barn. I think one of the animals isn't feeling well." She yawned. "Wow, I'm beat. And you must be, too." She took her mother's arm and started leading her toward the stairs in the living room. "I know it's no fun having the phone wake you up and then being told you have to leave in the middle of the night, but I really thought it was better to be safe than sorry."

Patricia stopped at the foot of the stairs and leaned away from Maddy. "Good Lord, Madeline, you smell like a distillery. And your eyes are bloodshot." She grinned—one of those smug "I'm your mother, and you can't fool me" grins. "So you had a couple of drinks at the restaurant, suggested to William that a walk down by the water was just the thing after dinner, and you fell into the river because you were more tipsy than you realized."

Maddy dropped her head to hide her smile. "Jeesh, I can't ever get anything past you, can I?" she muttered, walking up the stairs behind her laughing mother. "I sure hope you give me some pointers when I finally let Sarah start dating in another . . . oh, fifteen or twenty years from now."

Chapter Eleven

"Christ, Gregor, it was one hell of a scary thing last night. I had *Madeline* with me," William growled, staring out at the gently swelling ocean. "There was no warning, no sense of danger—nothing. One minute I'm making love to the lass, and the next minute they're just . . . *there*. The goddamned beasts scared the hell out of my woman."

"*Your* woman, Killkenny?" Kenzie repeated, glancing over and lifting a brow.

William glared at him. "She willingly gave herself to me, and I accepted. I don't care what century it is, that makes her *mine*. At least, for as long as we both agree," he muttered, looking back at the ocean. But then he grinned to himself. "And I'm thinking it's going to take quite some time for me to tire of the lass." He looked at Kenzie again. "Ye should have seen her last night, Gregor. Madeline has the heart of a warrior; she kept her head about her, doing exactly as I told her when I told her, and she drove my truck like I ride a horse. Aye," he said, leaning back to recline on his elbow. "I have a fear I might never tire of her."

Kenzie chuckled. "If ye fear anything, it should be that *she* will tire of *you*."

William scoffed that away. "Nay, I've learned enough about Madeline in the last few days to know how to keep her interested." He lay back and laced his fingers behind his head to smile up at the fading stars. "But being a highlander, I can understand why ye think women aren't easy to keep, seeing how ye had to get your pixie with child to catch her."

"Your skills as a warrior are exceeded only by your arrogance, Killkenny. After last night, you'll be lucky if Maddy even speaks to you again."

William grinned again, pleased that he at least knew which of *Kenzie's* buttons to push. "Were they a scouting party, do ye suppose? Trying to find our weakness?"

"Most likely. And now they know yours. You'll be sleeping on Maddy's knoll, I'm afraid, until this is over."

William sighed. "If not for her daughter, I could be sleeping in Maddy's bed."

"Christ, I wish I knew where Fiona has gone off to," Kenzie growled, shaking his head. "For as protective as she is of that pup, I don't understand why she's disappeared all of a sudden. She would have been a great help last night; she might have seen them coming and been able to warn you."

William snorted. "Your little sister would likely have helped them kill me." He glanced over at Kenzie. "Could she have gone back in time, do ye think? Maybe the pup gave her a clue to where she was from, and Fiona is looking for answers."

"Aye, that's what I've been thinking, too," Kenzie said.

"Don't worry, Gregor; the little termagant can take care of herself." He chuckled. "In fact, if it truly is a man chasing our pup, I pity him. If Fiona discovers his identity, he best be sucking his sack up in his belly, or he's liable to find his voice several notes higher."

"She has good reason to hate men, Killkenny."

"Aye," William agreed. "I just wish she'd learn that not all of us are bastards."

"With luck, she will someday. Were ye able to get a sense of what the wolves truly were or where they're from?"

"They felt . . . old to me, far older than I am, even." He sat up. "Maybe even as old as the coin Trace got from our pup. Ye didn't say anything when he showed it to you yesterday afternoon, but did ye recognize the writing on the back? He said he believed it was Sanskrit, but I've never heard of that language before."

"Nor have I, but there was something familiar about it. I made a drawing of the coin and sent it over the phone line to Matt. Maybe he can tell us something, as he has access to the collected knowledge of the ancient worlds."

William lay back down just as the first hint of dawn faded the stars. "Something—or *someone*—other than me chased the demon beasts off as they were approaching An Tèarmann. Could Daar have had anything to do with it?"

"Nay, he has almost no power left."

"Did Eve use the fancy pen ye gave her for protection?"

"I made sure she had it on her, but she said the pen never sensed any danger near the house."

William sat back up. "Do you suppose it was some other entity, then? Could there be more than one person after our spoiled little seal?"

Kenzie stood up and smiled tightly. "If there is, then our job just got more complicated. It's beginning to look like we *will* have to get Huntsman involved. When we meet him at the gravel pit this afternoon for another gun lesson, we'll have to see if we can't begin persuading him that the magic is real."

William also stood up, groaning with fatigue. "And then

maybe we can introduce him to the pup?" he asked, walking beside Kenzie as they headed back to the house. "I'm curious to see them meet face to . . . whisker," he said with a chuckle.

"Nay, not yet. We need to make sure where we stand with Huntsman before we reveal all our secrets."

"And Maddy?" William asked, reaching out to stop him. "Just how much am I supposed to reveal to her?"

"Nothing."

"I was afraid you'd say that. Then how in hell am I supposed to explain what happened last night?"

"Ye don't. When Eve got her first taste of the magic the night she rescued me on the cliff, I realized the next morning that it was something she had to ease into on her own. If I'd hit her over the head with a bunch of explanations, she would have decided I was crazy. And from that point on, she wouldn't have believed anything I told her, and that really would have put her in danger. You said yourself you're worried they have Maddy's scent now. You alienate her trying to explain the magic, she very well might turn her back on you. And you can't protect what ye can't get near."

"And you don't think last night did that already?"

"It matters not how she feels about you now; she's involved whether ye wish her to be or not." Kenzie started walking again. "So it looks as if you'll have to use that arrogant Irish charm of yours, my friend, if ye wish to remain close enough to *your woman* to keep her safe."

Maddy sat on a stool in Eve's store, trying not to drop crumbs on the floor as she slathered the miniature loaf of banana bread she'd stolen off the table with butter. "So you honestly don't think all the stuff that's been happening around here lately isn't it bit strange?" she asked Eve. "I mean, really, you had to rebuild your home into a virtual fortress because of all the weird storms that keep hitting the bay. And that was no moose we saw that night; that was the same creature that ate that bear and those kayakers said they saw in Dragon Cove. And now there's a rumor about a mermaid going around. Oh, and let's not forget the pack of coyotes that chased us last night," she said, giving an involuntary shiver.

"So they're no longer wolves the size of ponies?" Eve asked.

Maddy gave her a sheepish grin. "I've decided I had a lot more to drink last night than I realized. So to block out my . . . um . . . lovemaking debacle, I instead built the coyote thing up to mythic proportions." She shrugged. "It's the best explanation I can come up with, considering I broke the front and back windows out of William's brand-new truck by hitting two of the poor animals."

"Did you tell anyone about last night?" Eve asked, perusing the baskets for something to snatch for herself.

"Are you kidding?" Maddy snorted. "My cousin mistook a harbor seal or porpoise for a woman, and now the entire town is saying Trace Huntsman saw a mermaid." She widened her eyes in mock horror. "Dragons and mermaids in Midnight Bay, oh, my!" she whispered, breaking into laughter.

Eve snatched a cinnamon roll out of one of the baskets, unwrapping it as she walked over and sat down behind the counter. "Personally, I think it's mass hysteria," Eve said. "You know, like when we were walking down that dark road and heard a noise, and suddenly every tree looked like the bogeyman. Well, somebody saw what they decided was a dragon, and suddenly we have all sorts of mythological creatures running around. Add a couple of freak storms into that mix, and Midnight Bay has become the new Twilight Zone." She broke off a piece of the gooey roll but stopped with it halfway to her mouth and smiled at Maddy. "And that, my friend, is how legends are born, which conveniently ups the tourist trade, which in turn ups our incomes. I'm sorry Trace got stuck being the brunt of the latest rumor, but tell him if it's any consolation, every store owner in town thinks he's a hero," she finished, popping the piece of roll in her mouth then immediately licking her fingers.

"Yeah, well, I know it's all a bunch of malarkey, but I didn't imagine those coyotes stalking us last night, and that's why I'm not taking any chances. At least not until the game warden hunts them down and shoots them."

"What do you mean, not taking any chances?" Eve asked around another bite of roll. She stopped chewing. "Exactly what is that gleam in your eye all about?"

Maddy nudged her purse on the floor with her foot. "I dug out my forty-caliber Glock, and I intend to carry it everywhere from now on."

Eve swallowed, her eyes having gone huge. "You have a gun in your purse? An honest-to-God *handgun*?"

"Well, my dad's 30–30 rifle sure as hell won't fit in there."

"But Maddy, you can't run around with a gun in your purse!"

"I have a permit that says I can."

"You do? You actually got a permit to carry a concealed weapon? When? You just saw the . . . coyotes last night."

"Oh, I've had a permit since I was twenty-one." She shrugged. "And for some silly reason, I've kept renewing it ever since I got it."

"But why did you get it in the first place?" Eve gasped. "You divorced Billy when you were twenty-one! But I thought the two of you parted on good terms. Did he threaten you or something?" she ended in a whisper.

"Billy? Of course not! He's the one who bought me the gun." Maddy smiled at her friend's confusion and decided she might as well add to it. "It was a *divorce* gift from Billy. He bought me the gun, went to the firearms safety class with me, and then helped me get my permit."

"But why?" Eve repeated.

Maddy shrugged again. "I didn't move back home until my dad died. I rented a house halfway between here and Oak Harbor when we got divorced, and Billy said he didn't like the idea of my living alone with a three-year-old kid, so the least he could do was make sure I could protect myself."

"But what about Sarah? Maddy, you can't run around with a loaded gun in your purse. You have a child who could get hold of it."

"Have you ever tried to work the action on a forty-caliber Glock?"

"I don't even know what a Glock is!"

"It's what they call a Tupperware gun, because half of it is made from ballistic plastic so it won't be so heavy—though when it's full of bullets it's not exactly light. But I have all I can do to jack a shell in the chamber myself, so Sarah certainly couldn't. And it's really only sort-of loaded. In fact, that's why Billy didn't want me to have a revolver; because you just have to pull the trigger on most of those."

Eve's gaze dropped to Maddy's purse before slowly rising back to her. "You honest to God are walking around with a gun?"

"Drunk or not, *something* attacked us last night, and I don't intend to ever find myself in that kind of helpless situation again. Instead of falling asleep last night, every time I closed my eyes, all I could see were huge, pointy fangs and glowing red eyes, and all I could think of were vampires and werewolves." Maddy suddenly had a thought and jumped up off the stool, brushing the crumbs from her hands. "I should use the rest of my lunch break to go to the library and see if silver bullets kill werewolves like they do vampires." She straightened from picking up her purse and canted her head. "I wonder if gun stores even sell silver bullets."

"Madeline Kimble! Will you get *serious*," Eve hissed, walking around the counter and snatching her purse from her. Her arm dropped, nearly dropping the purse on the floor. "My God, it weighs a ton!" She spread the flaps to peek inside. "Where is it? I don't see any gun."

Maddy took the purse from her, held it by the strap, and pulled down a hidden zipper between the two compartments. "Billy also bought me the purse when he bought the gun; see, it's a holster purse. It has a secret padded compartment in the middle, and you access it from the outside."

Eve was gaping at her again but then suddenly pulled Maddy's hand away and reached inside the compartment herself. She stilled, and looked at Maddy. "You're sure it's not loaded?"

"There are bullets in the magazine but not in the chamber. What, you think I want to shoot myself in the hip if I bump into anything? Not that it would go off; it also has a safety." She looked toward the front door and then nodded at Eve. "Go ahead, pull it out. I know you're not afraid of firearms; you hunted with your dad all the time."

"I carried the binoculars, and he carried the rifle," she said, even as her hand emerged holding the pistol. "Holy shit, Maddy, this is a small cannon."

"Billy said just showing it to anyone bothering me would probably be enough to make them run like hell, because most guys won't stick around very long when they see a woman with a gun in her hand. But if that doesn't work, I just have to fire at the ground, and they'll skedaddle."

"When was the last time you shot it? Don't you have to practice regularly?"

"After we went home this morning, I dug it out of our gun

safe, dropped Sarah off at rec, then drove to Pinkham's gravel pit before work." She grinned broadly. "And I blew three beer cans to smithereens from fifty feet away."

Eve slid the gun back into the compartment with a grin. "You know what? I say good for you. I like the idea of knowing you can take care of yourself."

"And my daughter and Mom and even my residents. What if those coyotes really are rabid, and they show up on the River Run grounds when people in wheelchairs and using walkers are outside? We'd never get everyone inside in time."

"Are you going to tell your boss about the gun?"

"Heck, no—Doris would have a coronary. I'm legal, and as far as I'm concerned, only you and I have to know I'm carrying it. I especially don't want Mom finding out."

"What about William? Are you at least going to tell him?"

"What for?"

Eve arched a brow. "You don't think it's only fair to warn a man that the woman he's dating is armed?"

"*If* we were dating, then . . . maybe I'd tell him."

"You and William are no longer dating? After he blew your socks—I mean your stockings off three times last night? Um, does *he* know you're not dating?"

Maddy slung the strap onto her shoulder, only to wince when the heavy purse slammed her hip. "If he can't figure out that last night wasn't exactly a woman's idea of a fun time, then maybe he really did fly in from another planet."

Maddy looked her friend directly in her eyes. "What's going on, Eve? How come William seemed to know that the shadow he saw wasn't just some dog? And how come Kenzie didn't even question him when William told him to go get Mom and Sarah? And they spoke in some language I've never heard before. Who are these two mystery men who just showed up in

Midnight Bay, one soon after the other? You know I love Kenzie and that I'm really happy for you, but honestly, Eve, your husband is more than a little bit old-fashioned. I know we tease each other about him being your knight in shining leather, but Kenzie is . . . he's . . . there's something . . ." She sighed. "All this strange stuff started happening right around the time he moved to town. And last night, I think *William* scared me more than the coyotes did; he was so controlled and . . . focused. And as I stared at your storm shutters trying to fall asleep, the only thing I kept thinking about was how much he reminded me of Trace." Maddy touched Eve's shoulder. "Will you please tell me who Kenzie and William really are and what's going on? I know you know, because you wouldn't be acting so calm about last night if you didn't."

Eve got such a pained look in her eyes that Maddy's chest started to hurt.

"I-I can't tell you," Eve whispered, giving her a wrenchingly sad smile as she reached out and took Maddy's hand, and held it between hers. "I love you like a sister, but please don't ask me to break my word to my husband. I can tell you this much, though: William and Kenzie are noble, caring, capable men, and I would trust either of them with my life—and with the life of my child. And so can you, Maddy. No matter what happens in the coming days, please, please, trust William."

Maddy pulled her hand away to hug herself. "Okay, now you're freaking me out. What's going to happen in the coming days?"

Maddy jumped when the bell over the door suddenly tinkled, and Eve pulled her toward the counter when a customer walked in. "That's something you'll have to ask William," she said softly. "But until *he* tells you what's going on, you're just going to have to trust him. And you can trust Kenzie, too. And me," she finished, plastering a smile on her face when the customer approached them.

"I-I'll see you later," Maddy said, more than a little confused as she turned away. Feeling as if her very best friend in the whole world had just punched her in the stomach, she quietly walked out the door.

Chapter Twelve

"Is there a reason you two ladies are moping around my station?" Maddy asked Lois and Charlotte when Charlotte sighed for the fourth time in as many minutes. "If your faces get any longer, you're going to trip over them."

"Elbridge told William that he knew a good place to have his truck windows replaced over in Oak Harbor, and they left over three *hours* ago," Lois said.

"And they took Hiram with them," Charlotte added. "And it's a four-door pickup, so there wasn't any reason we couldn't have gone, too."

"You just know Hiram's going to suggest they stop at the Dairy Queen for a hot fudge sundae," Lois muttered. "It's been ages since I've had soft-serve ice cream."

"And the sprinkles they serve here are nothing but colored wax," Charlotte added. "The Dairy Queen has good sprinkles."

Maddy felt her own face grow long. "William was here?" she asked.

Not that she wanted to see him or anything. She was just

surprised that he hadn't even bothered to come say hello. He should have at least checked to see how she was doing today; the last time she'd seen him, he'd been running into the shadows carrying a sword. "Wait, how did William get here?" she asked.

"He drove his truck," Lois said, her tone implying that was a silly question. "The windshield was smashed, but you could still see out it."

"He drove himself here? Alone?"

"Of course, alone," Lois said, again implying Maddy was crazy for even asking. "The man might have money, but he's not so uppity that he'd have a chauffeur drive him around."

"He said the windows got smashed when he hit an animal last night on your way back from Oak Harbor," Charlotte said, frowning at her. "His being new to the area, you should have warned him that deer are a major road hazard at night."

Lois scrunched up her face, adding a few more wrinkles. "How come you didn't tell us about hitting the deer, so we'd know at least *something* interesting happened on your date?" She made a *tsk*ing sound. "I still can't believe you didn't have the good sense to grab the boy by the cheeks and kiss him good night."

"You expected *me* to kiss *him*?"

"Well, of course," Lois said, this time her tone implying Maddy was an idiot. "You asked him out; it was up to you to take the initiative. You young women can't have it both ways, you know. If you want equality, that means you have to be equally willing to chance getting your feelings hurt."

"Excuse me?" Maddy asked, intrigued by Lois's thinking even if she couldn't quite follow it.

"Don't you know that men have been taking chances of being rebuffed by women ever since we lived in caves?" Lois asked, her tone back to implying Maddy should have known that. "Haven't you ever felt a young man's damp palms on your face the first time he kissed you? That's because he was sweating bullets, afraid you were going to rebuff him."

"Or knee him in the groin," Charlotte added with a snicker.

Maddy blinked from one woman to the other. Either she was punch-drunk again from sheer fatigue, or she *was* an idiot for feeling hurt that William had been here and hadn't come to see her.

Not that she wanted to see him or anything.

At least not until she could decide how she felt about last night.

"We're really disappointed in you, Maddy," Lois said, her face growing long again. "We thought you had the courage to put the moves on a sexy, handsome man who eagerly accepted your invitation to go out."

Oh, what the hell, Maddy decided. It looked as if all three of them needed a little pick-me-up. Giving them a sly grin, she leaned over the counter. "Okay, then, ladies—what if I told you the truck windows got smashed because I was practically sitting on William's lap and had my tongue halfway down his throat when that deer suddenly jumped out in front of us?"

Both women gasped so hard they nearly fell over, and Charlotte grabbed the counter when her knees obviously went weak.

"No!" Lois cried, her eyes growing huge. "Madeline Kimble, you didn't!" She slapped the counter, making Charlotte flinch. "You did! You attacked the devil in the front seat of his own damn truck!"

"Shhh," Maddy said, looking up and down the hall and then toward the sitting room. "This is just between the three of us, understand? I especially don't want the men to hear about it. Hiram already thinks I'm a loose woman for asking William out." She brushed down the front of her scrubs and shot the ladies a conspirator's smile. "A girl has to protect her reputation, you know."

"We promise, we won't say a word," Charlotte whispered, also looking up and down the hall before leaning closer. "So? How was it?"

"Yeah," Lois echoed. "I bet that big boy can kiss the socks right off a girl."

Maddy felt her cheeks prickle and wondered what in hell had possessed her to make up such an outrageous lie. She stifled a snort. A Long Island Iced Tea hangover is what, coupled with too little sleep. "I can't really say how good a kisser William is," she told them. "We were just getting started when we hit that . . . animal. And for the record, I wasn't wearing socks, I was wearing sandals."

"And your pretty red lace pushup bra?" Charlotte asked. "You know, the one you had Janice order from Victoria's Secret last year, along with a matching pair of panties?" She leaned closer again. "And your scandalously short denim skirt; did you wear it, too, and that pretty yellow peasant blouse you can slip off your shoulder?"

Good Lord, did *everyone* think she was a slut?

Maddy sighed, realizing that she did have a tendency to dress like one sometimes.

"Earth to Maddy," Lois said, waving her hand in front of Maddy's face. "If you weren't going to stop by last night, you were at least supposed to bring in a picture this morning, to show us how you looked."

"You should always take a picture the night of your first date," Charlotte told her, "so you'll have it to look back on after forty years of marriage."

Maddy laughed. "That would mean I'd have enough pictures to fill an entire album, I've been on so many first dates." She shook her head. "I just haven't been on a whole lot of second dates."

"That's because you're too picky," Lois chided. "You keep waiting for Prince Charming to come sweep you off your feet and carry you away to his castle to live happily ever after."

"I am not picky, I'm discerning. And when was the last time you saw Prince Charming walking down Main Street in Midnight Bay?"

"I think William looks like a prince," Charlotte said, her eyes turning dreamy. "He has really broad shoulders, and that goatee makes him look quite regal." She leaned into the counter again, her smile somewhat . . . scheming. "And he's building a castle down on Dragon Cove. It's even going to have a tower. I bet that's where he puts the master bedroom."

"Can't you just picture William carrying his princess up all those steps to his tower bedroom?" Lois said, taking over Charlotte's fantasy. She slapped her hand over her bosom. "And not letting her leave until she agrees to marry him?"

Maddy started laughing. "Okay, that does it. I am calling the grange women and telling them no more historical romance novels allowed in the books they bring here. It's time for a reality check, ladies. A mean old witch turned Prince Charming into a frog, and I draw the line at kissing frogs."

"Even if they come bearing gifts?" a deep, lilting voice asked.

Only the owner of the voice had to drop his package on the floor to catch Charlotte when she gasped so hard that she really did fall.

"Whoa there, Charlotte, my sweet," he said, clutching her to his chest just in the nick of time—which, of course, made her knees give out.

So William swept her into his arms, looked around, and set her in the wheelchair just down the hall. His eyes contrite, he leaned over and smiled down at her as he started wheeling her back toward the nurses' station. "Forgive me, Charlotte. I didn't mean to make ye swoon."

Charlotte giggled like a schoolgirl, reaching up to pat his face. "You're so good for this old woman's heart, William. I swear if I was thirty years younger, I'd have asked you out before Maddy had worked up the courage to yesterday."

Realizing that she was smiling like a schoolgirl herself, Maddy instantly sobered when William's eyes locked on hers. "Hello, Madeline," he said softly. "How are ye feeling today? Were ye able to get any sleep last night?"

"Now, William," Lois said, touching his arm. "Maddy's not some shrinking violet, and it probably isn't the first time she's crashed into a deer." Her eyes took on a twinkling smile. "And the accident certainly wasn't *your* fault," she drawled. "It's a known fact that men aren't good at . . . multitasking."

Maddy hung her head with a groan. Yup, her outrageous lie was going to come back and bite her on her baggy ass.

"What in hell is this thing?" Hiram asked, straightening from picking something off the floor—which for Hiram was no easy task—then holding it up for everyone to see.

Lois grabbed it from him with a shriek of dismay, stuffing it under her shirt as she spun around to stare wide-eyed at Maddy.

Knowing that her face was two shades short of purple, Maddy could only stare down at the lump under Lois's shirt being made by her red lace Wonderbra.

Silence settled with a sickening thud.

Charlotte leaned over the side of her wheelchair and picked up the bag William had dropped in order to catch her, the crinkling of paper sounding like firecrackers going off. Everyone turned toward Charlotte, just in time to see a pair of matching red panties slip out of the bag and drop back to the floor.

William cleared his throat. "Yes, well," he said gruffly, picking them up, the skimpy material disappearing in his large hand. He took the bag from Charlotte, stuffed the panties into it, but then his hand reemerged holding a small white box. He tucked the paper bag under his arm and thrust the box toward Maddy, two flags of red coloring his cheeks. "This is for you," he said. "It's a little something I had Janice include in the order she made on her computer last week."

Honest to God, she couldn't move to save her soul, she was so mortified.

He set the box on the counter in front of her then pulled the paper bag from under his arm. Rolling the end of it tightly closed, he set it on the counter next to the box. "I, er . . . I retrieved your clothes this morning," he whispered, the red on his cheeks intensifying.

Silence descended once again.

"Maddy," Lois quietly hissed out the side of her mouth, the older woman's eyes boring into hers. "Open William's gift."

"Come on, Maddy," Charlotte said quite loudly. "Show us what he got you."

She stared at the box as if it held tiny venomous snakes.

"Oh, good Lord," Lois snapped, reaching out with one hand, the other hand still holding the bra under her shirt. She picked up the box and thrust it at Maddy. "Where are your manners?"

They're in the paper bag with my clothes, along with my dignity.

She didn't know how she managed it, but Maddy took the box from Lois, and with shaking hands that made the task nearly impossible, she lifted off the cover and stared down at a tiny . . . dragon?

"Well, what is it?" Charlotte asked, pushing out of her wheelchair and walking up to the counter. "Oh my, it's beautiful! Take it out, Maddy, and pin it on your blouse." The older woman spun to look at William. "No matter how much we tried, Janice wouldn't tell us what else she ordered for you. She only said that you have excellent taste when it comes to jewelry."

She spun back around to Maddy, leaned into the counter, and lowered her voice to a whisper. "Janice also said it was painted enamel over solid gold and that she knew you were going to love it." She pushed Maddy's hand holding the tiny dragon—which was green and brown with bright yellow eyes and a red tongue—toward Maddy's chest. "Will you pin it on?" she gritted, using her eyes to gesture behind her at William. "You're going to hurt his feelings."

Maddy nearly stabbed herself pinning it to her scrubs, industriously watching her fingers work so she wouldn't have to look at William. God, she couldn't believe he'd brought her clothes here. Just as soon as he left, the questions would start, and now she was going to have to think of *another* lie.

"Maddy," Lois hissed in a whisper again, leaning as far as she could over the counter. "Thank him."

For what? For showing everyone her underwear?

After only three tries, she finally lifted her gaze to his. "Thank you. It's beautiful."

His marine-blue eyes glinting with humor, he nodded ever so slightly. "You're welcome, Madeline."

"Oh, I get it!" Hiram suddenly injected. "He got her a dragon because he's gonna be living on *Dragon Cove*." He nudged Elbridge standing beside him. "See, Elby, I remembered." He suddenly frowned, looking at Lois. "I still don't know what that thing is I picked up off the floor. It fell out of the bag William dropped to catch Charlotte."

"It was a bra, Hiram," Elbridge said quietly.

Hiram swung toward William. "What you doing with a bra, boy?" Both of his bushy brows rose. "You ain't one of them young fellows who like sneaking into girls' rooms to steal their undies, are you? What were they called, Elby, back when you were in college?" he asked, nudging Elbridge again.

"Panty raids," Elbridge said with a chuckle.

Hiram scowled, pointing a crooked finger at William. "I don't care how nice a fellow you are, you're too old to be raiding women's panties, Killkenny. That's college punk stuff, and we don't cotton to you embarrassing our Maddy like that. Friend or no friend, you raid her panty drawer again, you'll find yourself dealing with us."

Her heart melting into a glob of sentimental mush, Maddy raced from behind the counter and wrapped her arm around Hiram. "Calm down, Mr. Man," she said as she led him away. "William didn't steal my underwear; he was returning it to me. I left some of my clothes at my friend's house. You remember Eve Anderson, don't you?"

"Mabel Anderson's daughter?" Hiram asked as she guided him toward his room. "That curly-haired little blond thing who looks like a miniature Shirley Temple?"

"Eve's all grown up now, Hiram. She's married to Kenzie Gregor, the man who took you on the picnic down to Dragon Cove the other day."

She stopped at the door to Hiram's room and looked back toward the nurses' station to see everyone staring after her. "You're going to hurt Katy's feelings if you don't all go in and work on your picture albums with her," Maddy told them, gesturing toward the sitting room. "She drove all the way to Ellsworth Sunday, using her own gas, to buy more scrapbooking supplies for you."

"Well, I guess I should finish up the album I started for my granddaughter," Elbridge said, heading toward the sitting room. He stopped and turned back to nod at William. "We'll go out driving again tomorrow morning," he told him.

William started pushing Charlotte's wheelchair. "Thank you, Elbridge. I appreciate the pointers ye gave me today," he said, his voice trailing off as he followed Elbridge into the sitting room.

Instead of following the others, Lois reached under her blouse and pulled out Maddy's bra. She started to slip it in the paper bag on the counter but suddenly held the bra up with a frown and spread it open. She immediately headed toward Maddy.

Maddy finished leading Hiram inside his room. "You look like you could use a nap, Mr. Man," she said, settling him on his bed. She reached down and slipped off his shoes. "And when you wake up, it will be time for supper. I believe they're having your favorite, three-bean salad and chicken noodle soup."

"I like three-bean salad," he said with a tired sigh, lying back on his pillow. "But it don't like me. It gives me gas. I ain't hungry, anyway," he murmured as she took off his glasses and set them on his nightstand. "William bought me a double fudge sundae at the Dairy Queen." He grabbed Maddy's hand when she finished tossing a light blanket over him and frowned up at her. "I spilt some of it in the back of his truck when he suddenly stopped quick, because Elby told him he had to let the man crossing the street go ahead of him. I ain't riding with them tomorrow, I don't think." He tugged on her hand to get her to lean closer. "Don't say I told you so, but William can't drive worth a hill of beans."

She patted his arm. "I promise, I won't say a word to him, Hiram. You just have a good nap now."

Only he still didn't release her. "I can see why he hit that deer last night. He drives like he owns the road. If you ever find yourself riding with him, don't ever scream, okay? Even when you see a mailbox go whizzing by your window at sixty miles an hour, just try to ignore it. I think screaming unnerves the man."

"I promise, I won't scream," she said. She leaned over and kissed his wrinkled cheek. "And thank you, Hiram, for defending my honor just now. I love you for that."

He gave her hand a squeeze, then let her go with a har-rumph. "Ain't none of us here gonna let some young punk mess with our favorite girl," he muttered, rolling onto his side and closing his eyes. "We might be old, but we ain't dead yet."

She patted his arm with a laugh. "Sweet dreams, Mr. Man," she said, walking out of the room—only to nearly run over Lois standing just outside the door.

Lois glanced up and down the hall and then held up Maddy's bra by its straps. "Did you know your pretty bra is ruined?" she asked, turning it to show her the band. "Look, it appears to have been cut with something sharp. See, not even the elastic is frayed. And here," she said, her fingers pushing up one of the cups. "The underwire has poked through. Didn't you just get this last year?"

Maddy took it from her and held it up to study the strap. And yup, it sure as hell looked like it had been cut with a knife.

"I noticed a small scratch under William's eye," Lois said. She canted her head and tapped her chin. "Hmm . . . now, if I were practically sitting in a gentleman's lap while he was driving down the road, and I happened to have my tongue halfway down his throat when a deer suddenly jumped into the windshield of the truck, I would probably rear up in sur-prise, and my chest would probably clam the gentleman right in his face."

"Lois," Maddy hissed.

"And," the woman continued, "I suppose one of the under-wires in my bra might pop out and poke him in the eye . . ." She frowned, still tapping her chin. "I don't know how the band could have gotten sliced clean through, though." Her eyes sud-denly took on an impish twinkle. "Unless the gentleman gal-lantly took out a knife and cut my bra off before it could scratch my lovely breast. Hmm . . . but that would mean my blouse would have been unbuttoned for the underwire to have poked him in the eye."

"Lois Manning," Maddy said with a laugh. "You are outrageous!"

Lois shot her a wink. "That's the best thing about getting old, Maddy girl. We can be as outrageous as we want, and just who's going to stop us?" she said, pivoting on her heel and heading toward the sitting room.

Lois approached William in the hall, who, having spotted Maddy, was heading toward her. The older woman tapped her own cheek as she passed him. "That's what they make backseats for, William. The P on your shifting column stands for Park," she said, her laughter trailing down the hall as she disappeared into the sitting room.

William stopped in front of Maddy and looked down at the bra in her hand, a faint hint of color padding his cheeks as he lifted his gaze. "I am honestly sorry for embarrassing you in front of your residents. That's why I hunted around for something to put your clothes in and found a paper bag."

Maddy felt her own cheeks growing warm. "Y-you cut my bra off me," she whispered, mostly because she couldn't believe it herself. She held up the two ends of the band to him. "With your knife. D-did you cut off my skirt, too?"

"Nay, just the button."

"William, you cut off my bra," she repeated, shaking it at him.

He took the bra from her and shoved it into his rear pocket as he stepped forward, crowding her against the wall. "And I'll cut it off again, if I ever see such an offensive garment binding your bosom that way."

"Wh-what?" she said, pressing into the handrail that ran the length of the hallway when he leaned even closer.

He palmed her flaming cheeks in his hands and captured her gasp in his mouth.

Maddy grabbed his wrists with every intention of stopping him. But then his lips started sipping hers with devouring softness. He tasted like hot fudge and salt air, and . . . desire. She felt her hormones rallying, some of them heading straight to the pit of her stomach and some racing to her head, making her dizzy enough that she had to use her grip on his wrists for support instead.

"I've been waiting all day for another taste of you," he whispered, trailing his lips across her cheek toward her ear. "Wanting to slide deep inside you again and feel your sheathing heat tightening around me."

Maddy's knees buckled.

He released her face to prop her up in his arm, his mouth returning to hers as he pressed into her, his tongue tracing the fullness of her lips, teasing her to respond. His gentle assault sent her mind reeling with images of broad shoulders blocking out the moonlight, of her clutching his masculine arms, of him buried deep, deep inside her.

His mouth blazed a scorching trail to her ear again. "And ye can leave your underpants at home from now on, too," he whispered, his teeth gently raking her lobe. "And I'll keep a box of those little packets in the truck."

A box?

A whole *box*?

Maddy shivered, either from anticipation or . . . regret; she didn't know which.

Because she'd already decided she simply didn't have the courage to go out with him again. She had a speech ready and everything; only at the moment she couldn't seem to remember any of the words.

His mouth returned to hers when she somehow managed to bring her hands up to his shoulders, but for some reason she couldn't seem to push him away. His kiss sang through her veins, his probing tongue demanding and wickedly salacious.

"Does the bogeyman know you're messing with his girlfriend, Killkenny?"

William tore his mouth free and leaned his forehead on hers. "Go away, Huntsman. Can ye not see I'm busy?"

Maddy tried to push him away but soon realized she'd have better luck pushing through the wall behind her. William straightened, and when she tried sidestepping away, he planted his hands on the wall on either side of her shoulders, even as he turned his head to look at Trace.

"We were supposed to meet at the gravel pit."

Trace's grin broadened. "I'm headed over there right after I visit with my favorite cousin." He nodded in the direction of William's hip. "I hope that's not your idea of a slingshot, because those underwires will definitely throw off your aim."

"Well, shit," Maddy growled, ducking under his arm and slapping William's rear pocket until she could snag the bra dangling out of it. She stepped away from him and turned to glare at both men. "Why don't we just run the damn thing up the flagpole out front so *everyone* can see it!"

"Now, Peeps," Trace said with a chuckle. "Don't get your panties in a twist . . . or are those in his other pocket?"

She pointed the hand holding the bra at him, realized what she was doing, and stuffed it into the front pocket of her scrubs. Suddenly remembering the bulk of her prepared speech, she smiled—somewhat tightly—at William. But then she hesitated.

She couldn't flat-out dump him in front of another guy; that was just plain cruel.

She looked at Trace. "Why are you two meeting at the gravel pit?"

"We're going to do some target shooting."

"But I wanted you—" She glanced at William, smiled tightly again, and turned and walked away. "Don't let me keep you, then."

"Wait, what were you going to say?" Trace asked, following her.

"Nothing. I've changed my mind," she said, going behind her station. She saw the paper bag, quickly snatched it off the counter, and tossed it onto the floor beside her chair. Glancing down the hall to see William walking into Samuel's room, guessing he was going to cheer up his friend, who wasn't feeling well today, she arched a brow at Trace. "So, are we still on for Saturday?"

"Actually, that's why I stopped in. I've decided I don't want you puking all over my boat."

"But what about your mermaid? I thought you wanted me to see her."

"William offered to go with me, so that lets you off the hook."

Maddy leaned away. "You're taking William instead of me?"

"Hey, I thought you'd be pleased that I'm getting along with your boyfriend." He snorted. "Considering how I couldn't stand to be in the same room with Billy Boy."

"Look, we both know William is not my boyfriend, so quit calling him that."

Trace arched a brow. "Does that mean you'll let any old guy walk in here and stick his tongue down your throat?"

"We went on one date, and one was quite enough, thank you very much. I was going to break the news to him just now, but I didn't want to do it in front of you. I'm discerning but not cruel."

Trace looked down the empty hallway, then back at her. "I don't think Killkenny is going to be that easy to dump, Peeps. He strikes me as a man who goes after what he wants and doesn't stop until he gets it. And I'd bet my boat that he wants you."

"Look, if you want to be his new best buddy, that's fine with me. But I feel I should warn you, the guy is weird."

"Weird how?" he asked, tensing. "As in perverted weird or your typical I-can't-boss-him-around weird?"

"As in guarded, focused, and . . . lethal weird. And the guy is way too controlled. In fact, last night, he reminded me of you."

Trace relaxed, folding his arms over his chest. "Thanks. I think."

"Oh, you know what I mean. Which, come to think of it, is probably why you do like him." She waved him off. "Go on, get out of here. Go shoot beer cans with your new best buddy," she said, sitting down and grabbing Samuel's chart.

"Maddy."

She looked up at him. "What?"

"You will stop mothering Rick. And don't bother waiting up for him at night anymore; he's on my watch now, and if he so much as even raises his voice to you, he'll be answering to me."

Maddy's hand flew to the side of her face. "He *told* you?"

"After a little . . . prodding." His eyes hardened. "And I told him that if I ever hear of him striking a woman—any woman— ever again, he won't be able to . . . well, let's just say he's decided to see things my way."

Maddy shot out of her chair. "Did you threaten him? Dammit, he's just a kid!"

"Not anymore, he's not. And you," he growled, leaning over the counter to get right in her face, "will stop coddling him. And if I ever catch wind of you giving him so much as a dime, it'll be years before you can put your hair in a ponytail. Got that?"

"He's my baby brother," she growled right back at him. "Which makes him my responsibility, not yours."

Trace was around the counter and had her backed up against the medicine cabinet before she could even gasp. "I own him for the next two weeks," he said ever so softly. "He'll be sleeping on my boat at night and working his ass off every day, earning the money for his college supplies. You so much as buy him a pillowcase, and one inch of hair comes off." He reached up and pulled the band off her ponytail, taking a lock of her cascading hair and holding it in front of her face. "Buy him a pencil, and another inch comes off."

"He lost his father when he was fifteen, Trace."

"And he just lost his big sister last week, when he punched her and left her lying in the dirt."

"Is there anything I can help ye with, Huntsman?" William asked.

Trace dropped Maddy's hair but stood his ground, keeping his dark gray eyes locked on hers. "Thanks, Killkenny, but I was just asking your girl here if she'd like me to give her a haircut. I'm hoping she decides to keep it long, though." He kissed her forehead. "Rick needs this more than you do, Peeps. Let him go so he can grow up." He turned and walked away. "I'll see you at the gravel pit, Killkenny."

"I also hope ye decide to keep your hair long, Madeline. And though he might never have come right out and told you, I believe Rick prefers it long, too."

Maddy ran shaky fingers through her mess of hair, and with a shuddering breath, she walked back to her chair, sat down, and opened Samuel's chart.

It took her a moment, staring down at the blurred writing, to realize that she was alone. And it took her the rest of the afternoon to grudgingly admit that *maybe* Trace was right and that she *might* have been babying Rick a little too much.

And when she finally walked out of the River Run Nursing Home later that afternoon, just wanting to go home and fall into bed and sleep for a week, Maddy realized that Trace might also be right about William not taking no for an answer. Because parked next to where she'd left Eve's car this morning was a fire-engine-red pickup truck with glistening new windows.

And Eve's car was nowhere to be found.

Chapter Thirteen

*A*pparently in an attempt to further ingrain himself into her life, Maddy also found a brand-new, fire-engine-red, state-of-the-art cell phone propped up on the steering wheel when she finally got in the truck. He'd left a short note—written in painstakingly neat lettering—saying it was already programmed with all the important numbers she would need, and he hoped she liked the color.

William Killkenny might be having a hard time knowing which buttons to push on his truck, but he seemed to know exactly which ones to push on *her*.

"Dammit to hell," she whispered, dropping her head onto the steering wheel.

The man kept kissing her senseless.

But he also scared her spitless.

So how in hell was she supposed to deal with the guy, when on the one hand she was desperately attracted to him, and on the other hand he frightened her?

She'd been able to handle Billy, because deep down her ex-husband was just a big kid at heart, who didn't have a secretive or calculating cell in his body. Whereas William seemed as old as time itself when he got all guarded and focused and controlled, and she'd bet her red panties that he had more secrets than King Tut's tomb.

Life had been harried but basically uncomplicated with Billy, despite their having Sarah and being married so young. Their grab-the-world-by-the-ass passion had quickly waned when reality hit; Billy had been forced to give up his dream of college to work two jobs to support them, and she'd alternated between taking odd jobs, going to night school, and changing diapers.

She thought of him as Billy the Bastard, not because he'd broken her heart but because he'd shattered her dream of happily-ever-after, making her wonder if true love even existed. And he sure as hell hadn't ever been a soft place to land whenever she'd felt herself falling into an abyss of desperation.

William, however, might be too complicated for her; that is, if she ever got brave enough to dig her dreams out of mothballs and open her heart again. She'd thought she'd found the courage to do just that a few weeks ago, when she'd watched Eve pick up the pieces of her own shattered dreams and dare to fall in love with Kenzie. Heck, she'd even put on her short shorts and pushup bra and actually flirted with the men who had helped rebuild Eve and Kenzie's home after one of the freak storms had left it in ruins.

But then William had walked right up to her in the town square, stark naked and looking like a caveman, and kissed her. And ever since then, she'd been vacillating between wanting to jump his bones and wanting to take Sarah and move to Alaska.

"God, Susan, I wish I had your balls," she muttered, pressing the palms of her hands to her stinging eyes. "Hamish MacKeage carried you off to a mountain hideaway, and I'm sitting here in

Prince Charming's truck, afraid that instead of a tragic little frog, he's the big, bad bogeyman."

Maddy pulled on the front of her scrubs and twisted the material to look down at the pin William had given her, having to wipe her eyes again to dry her welling tears. She truly did like it; the colorful dragon was reared up on powerful hind legs, its front claws curled to strike and its wings stretched in flight, looking lethal and formidable and yet . . . enchanting.

Not unlike the man who had given it to her.

She supposed she'd have to wear it to work every day from now on, or she'd never hear the end of it from her residents.

Trying to remember the last time anyone had given her jewelry, Maddy gave her eyes one last swipe, finally turned the key William had foolishly left in the ignition, and started the truck. She pulled out of the parking lot and stopped at the street, looking both ways in indecision.

Left would take her home, and right would take her to Eve's.

She turned right in defeat, suddenly deciding that she was naming her pin Willy Dragonheart—the manifestation of her dreams and nightmares.

"What do you mean, your car was totaled?" Maddy whispered, her skin tightening as she stared up in horror at Eve standing on her porch. "How badly was William hurt? Did they take him to the hospital in Ellsworth?" she asked, all the blood pooling in her feet as she started inching to his truck.

Was he dead and Eve just didn't know how to tell her?

Her friend snorted. "William doesn't have a scratch on him, according to Kenzie. Apparently the man drove my car right off a gravel bank at the beginning of Pinkham's pit, got out and walked to Kenzie and Trace, and started target practicing as if nothing had happened."

Maddy's horror rushed out in a relieved sigh, only to be replaced by suspicion. "He drove off a bank high enough to total your car, and he didn't even get a scratch?"

Eve shrugged. "It's possible if he was wearing a seat belt and the airbags went off. Come on. Let's go inside and have some iced tea."

"No," Maddy said, hiking her purse up over her shoulder and turning to walk out the driveway. "I'm going to start for home."

Eve ran down the steps. "Maddy, you can't walk home! It's eight miles!"

"Well, I'm not driving William's truck home," she said, turning to walk backward as Eve followed. "I refuse to be seen driving that damn thing around town."

"But why? He can't use it, so you might as well."

She arched a brow. "You really think driving off that gravel bank was an accident?"

Eve stopped. "You think it wasn't?"

Maddy also stopped. "I think that William is just devious enough to believe that taking away my only transportation will make me dependent on him." She reached into her pocket and pulled out the cell phone. "Look what else he gave me this afternoon," she hissed, holding it up as she started walking again. "One more link in the chain he's trying to wrap around my neck."

Following again, Eve's expression turned pained. "That wasn't calculating, Maddy. William knows you don't have a working cell phone, and he was just being thoughtful."

"He told me he's not thoughtful; that everything he does is for selfish reasons."

"Then after what happened last night, maybe he *selfishly* doesn't want to be constantly worrying about your not being able to call for help."

"Oh, I'm keeping the phone, and making lots of new friends in China and Australia and Brazil. But he can keep his truck." She stopped walking again. "I'm not a charity case, Eve," she whispered, fighting back tears. "Don't you remember how *you* felt when everyone in town was telling you to go after Kenzie because he could solve all your problems? W-well, I don't need a knight in shining armor to rescue me, either." She swiped at her eyes. "And I sure as hell don't need some man bullying his way into my life, acting as if he's my Prince Charming."

"But what if he is?" Eve asked softly. "Please don't make the mistake I almost made. My own stubbornness nearly cost me the man of my dreams."

"I stopped dreaming about happily-ever-after the day I moved into a dumpy old house with a three-year-old child, and I didn't even have two nickels to rub together. If it hadn't been for Billy's parents not wanting their granddaughter to starve, I couldn't even have bought cereal."

"William Killkenny isn't Billy, Maddy."

Maddy gave a brittle laugh. "No, he's not. He's worse. If I found the courage to believe in happily-ever-after again and then fell in love with William, I wouldn't survive it not working out this time, Eve. And I can't take that chance, because I have a little girl who needs a mother that's sane."

"Please come back to the house, Maddy. Kenzie will be back soon, and he'll give you a ride home."

"I'm not up to battling William right now."

"Then call your mom to come get you."

"She took Sarah to Ellsworth after rec today to shop for school clothes."

"What about Rick?"

"I don't think I'm allowed to speak to Rick anymore."

"Then Trace," Eve snapped when Maddy started walking again. "Call your cousin to come get you."

Maddy didn't even bother to turn around even when she realized Eve wasn't following her anymore. "Trace is the reason I can't even talk to my brother. And he's at the pit with Kenzie and William, so who do you think will show up here if I call him?"

"Maddy!"

She stopped and turned to her friend. "That's quite a club you're a member of, Eve; you know, the exclusive club you can't tell me anything about? Only it seems my cousin has been invited to join."

"Maddy, *please.*"

She gave her friend a weak wave, and turned at the end of the driveway and started walking up the road. It was three miles to town, and she had another five miles to her house after that, so she picked up her pace. Knowing Eve was right now on the phone to Kenzie, she hoped at least to make it to town where she could hitch a ride before William came looking for her.

"What's the matter, Killkenny?" Kenzie asked. "Are ye having a wee bit of trouble with *your woman?*"

William glared out the windshield. "What in hell is wrong with the women of this century?" he muttered. "Christ, you'd think I'm the pox-marked village beggar for the merry chase Madeline is giving me." He finally turned his glare on Kenzie. "I was doing quite well with the lass until those damned wolves showed up. And now I find out that I frightened her last night more than they did. When we told Trace what happened, he said Maddy's warning to him finally made sense. Apparently the woman not only believes I'm . . . weird, but guarded, controlled, and lethal."

"You are."

William went back to watching the road, even though he knew Maddy couldn't have gotten this far yet. "That should give her a sense of security, not drive her off."

"Do you remember how reluctant Eve was to let me help her at first?" Kenzie asked, slowing down as they approached town. "It appears that women today don't wish to be taken care of, and they no longer need their men to be warriors, because they have sheriffs to keep them safe."

William snorted. "I didn't see any sheriffs last night."

"And they don't want us to fix their problems for them," Kenzie continued, putting on the blinker and then turning down the road to An Tèarmann. "I believe women today just wish for us to listen while they discuss their problems out loud with themselves."

William looked over at him in surprise. "Are ye saying we not only can't fix their problems, but that we can't even *suggest* how to fix them?"

Kenzie chuckled. "This may come as a surprise to you, Killkenny, but women are just as capable as men when it comes to dealing with most problems, only they prefer to approach them with understanding instead of a sword."

"But sometimes a good smack with the flat of a sword can keep a wee problem from becoming a big one. There, she just bolted into the woods."

"I saw her."

"Drive right by," William said, unfastening his seat belt. "And let me out around the next curve."

Kenzie pulled to a stop down the road, then grabbed William's arm to keep him from getting out. "It's not the flat of your sword she fears, my friend, but more likely the blow you could deliver to her heart. Eve told me Maddy realizes there's more to us than meets the eye, but she thinks that's only part of the reason Maddy's acting skittish."

"Did the pixie explain the magic to her, then?" he asked hopefully.

"Nay. I know it's hurting both women, but Eve will keep

her word to me. Have ye decided yet what your intentions are toward Maddy?"

William got out and turned to look across the seat at him. "Right now my only intention is to see what color undergarments she's wearing today."

"Ye can't seduce her into liking you, Killkenny."

William gave him a sad smile. "Is that why you highlanders carry such long swords, Gregor, to make up for the length of your cocks?"

"One of these days, I really will make you sorry for finding the stone that led you here." Kenzie's mouth twisted wryly. "Unless *your woman* beats me to it."

William shut the door with a laugh, but instantly sobered once he started walking up the road toward little miss maddening Maddy. Why in hell couldn't the lass just relax, and let them enjoy the pleasure of each other's company? There was no need for her to be afraid of him, only he didn't know how to make her believe that.

Well, except he had discovered that when he was loving her mouth—and her luscious body—she did seem to forget that she feared him.

But Christ, he couldn't keep her perpetually naked.

Or could he?

William rounded the corner just in time to see Maddy peeking out of the bushes.

But when she spotted him, she quickly disappeared again.

Oh, she was a smart little hedgehog, having the sense to make sure they hadn't seen her. Aye, she was already coming to know him quite well.

He continued walking a short way past her, then pulled out his cell phone and hit the speed dial for *her* phone. He then stopped and faced the woods on the opposite side of the road, peering into them as if searching for her.

He heard the loud musical tone of her cell phone go off—followed almost immediately by an unladylike curse—and then he heard her bolt deeper into the woods. He took off after her, jumping the ditch and pushing through the bushes, breaking into the old-growth forest without slowing down.

Chapter Fourteen

William was surprised to see Maddy run not in the direction of town or An Tèarmann but deeper into the woods. He was also surprised by how fast she was, considering her large purse kept sliding off her shoulder and bumping against her hip, more than once snagging on a branch and almost yanking her to a halt.

He'd have to have a talk with her, he decided, about shedding cumbersome gear if she ever found herself being pursued by anyone other than him. The lass needed to realize that her belongings were not as important as her life. William leaped over a fallen tree that had forced her to veer slightly, and finally moved to intercept her.

Only his gut suddenly knotted at the stark fear he saw in her eyes when she glanced over her shoulder and realized he'd closed the gap between them; and he nearly gave up the chase when he heard her cry of panic as she grabbed a tree and swung herself to suddenly change direction.

But he was well past the point of letting her go, and had been for days now.

He caught hold of her shoulder and spun her toward him, wrapping his arms around her and twisting to take the brunt of their fall. And then he simply held her against him as she struggled like a cornered animal, her ragged, panting whimpers far more wounding than her pummeling fists.

He got one arm around both of hers, using his other hand to cup her head to his. "Hush, Madeline," he whispered into her hair, wrapping his legs around her when her knee jerked close to his groin. "Just lie here with me and catch your breath," he crooned, clutching her to him with the same desperation he felt in her struggles.

She went utterly still, holding herself arched tensely away from him. "Please, I just want to go h-home," she whispered, finally admitting defeat and going limp.

He loosened his arm around her, and brushed a tear off her cheek with his thumb. "I'll take ye home, Madeline. Just as soon as we catch our breaths, we'll walk back to An Tèarmann and I'll drive ye home."

She hesitantly tested his grip.

But finding himself still unable to let her go, he released her only enough to let her sit up, then turned so she was tucked against him as he leaned against the tree he'd slammed into bringing her down. Apparently realizing that he wasn't giving her the option of moving away, she buried her face in his shirt with a shuddered sob.

He slowly ran his fingers through her tangled hair, carefully working small twigs free. "I told ye there would never be a reason for you to run from me, Madeline," he said thickly. "If you are frightened, run *toward* me, not away. If you're angry, give *me* your wrath. And when you are confused or heavy of heart or simply tired, my strong arm is yours for the asking." He kissed the top of her head. "Everyone needs a safe shelter to run to, Madeline; let me be yours."

"I-I can't," she whispered, her voice quavering. "I might not survive."

He tucked his finger under her chin and tilted her head back to look at him. "I won't ever let anything happen to you."

She leaned away, continuing to stare directly into his eyes. "Maybe it's not about you at all," she said, her voice raw as she tried to catch her breath. "Maybe it's about me," she continued in a raspy growl, lifting her hand to tap her bosom. "I only have one heart to give, and I'm not risking it on a man who expects me to trust him but who refuses to trust me in return."

William took his first relieved breath when her cheeks colored with budding anger. He pulled her head back to his chest—ignoring her protest—so she wouldn't see his scowl. Dammit to hell, she had him by the short hairs! He'd decided he agreed with Kenzie: explaining the magic would likely send her running forever.

But not explaining who he really was to her was making her run anyway.

"I would ask a favor of ye, Madeline."

"No, dammit. No more favors."

"I promise not to be offended if ye say no." He took a shuddering breath of his own. "And if ye do say no, I will never bother you again."

She went completely still for several heartbeats. "You'll just w-walk away?"

"Aye . . . if you say no."

She started to tilt her head back to look at him but then suddenly settled against his chest again. "What's the favor?" she whispered.

"Take me as your lover."

Her head popped up so fast that she nearly clipped his chin. "What?"

He fought to stifle his grin as he watched a blush spread

across her cheeks. "Take me *only* as your lover," he repeated softly. "Keep your heart tucked safely in a box under your bed, but give me your body."

Her lashes dropped to hood her eyes from him, and her blush intensified. "A-and if I say no, y-you'll just walk away?" She looked directly at him again. "Just like that, you'll stop giving me gifts and coming to the nursing home? And you'll s-stop kissing me?"

"No more gifts or kisses, but I would like ye to keep the pin and cell phone." He took another painful breath. "And if ye insist, I will stop visiting Elbridge and the others."

"And if I say yes?" she asked in a tremulous whisper.

"Then we are both free to indulge our senses." He squeezed her gently. "I have but one stipulation: I admit to being somewhat possessive, so as long as we are enjoying each other's company, I must be the only man in your life."

She dropped her gaze to his hand resting on her thigh, letting the silence of the forest settle around them.

"Do I have to give you an answer right now?" she asked, not looking at him.

He gently brushed his thumb on the inside of her thigh and felt a small quiver run through her. "How about if you give me your answer tomorrow morning, when I get back from my ride with Elbridge?"

Silence settled between them again.

"Do ye need longer?" he asked. "Because I have to tell ye, lass, I'd prefer to know where I stand with you sooner rather than later." He smiled crookedly when she looked up. "Because if ye do say yes, I would like to clear up last night's unfinished business between us as soon as possible."

"We have unfinished business?"

"You're not one of those women who likes to leave a man . . . hanging, are ye?"

"Hanging?" she repeated, her brows drawing together in a frown. But then her eyes suddenly widened and her cheeks turned a lovely pink again. "You mean . . . you didn't . . . omigod, you didn't!"

Unable to stop himself, William threaded his fingers around the back of her neck and pulled her mouth toward his. "Just one more taste of ye, Madeline, just in case ye say . . . no," he murmured against her lips.

But when he hesitated, she leaned forward and softly touched her lips to his.

Using all the restraint he possessed—and some he borrowed from the devil himself—William held back from claiming her mouth.

His patience was rewarded when her arms came around his neck just as she gave a small hum of frustration, and her tongue sought his—only to pull out and begin tracing the contour of his lips.

His restraint shattering with her boldness, he canted her head to capture her teasing tongue, and got serious about loving her mouth. He devoured her softness, sipped her sweetness, and almost shouted with joy when she melted against him.

But he quickly realized that if he didn't stop, there was a very real danger that he really would find out what color underclothes she was wearing. And as delightful as that might be in the short term, it certainly wouldn't help him reach his ultimate goal. He broke their kiss and pulled her head back down to his chest again, smiling at her initial protest and then her sigh of contentment.

His beautiful, maddening Maddy, he thought, stifling his own sigh, so full of passion and yet so frightened by it. It wasn't so much him she was afraid of, he was coming to realize, but herself.

He would like very much to meet her bastard ex-husband

who had stolen her courage to open her heart to another man. When he'd asked, Trace had told William that Billy Kimble hadn't made it past puberty, and that if Maddy hadn't divorced the bastard six years ago, she probably would have killed him by now out of sheer frustration.

Apparently his cousin, Trace had said, had started taking on the role of caregiver when she'd found herself raising a husband right along with her daughter. Then, when her father had died, she'd moved home to finish raising Rick and had even begun mothering her mother. It was easier, Trace had said, for Maddy to focus on everyone else than it was to deal with her own insecurities.

William knew he was pushing her to do exactly that by asking her to give him only her body; and that if she did, she would more often than not push back with the fierceness of a bear if she felt anything other than lust start to blossom between them.

A large buck suddenly snorted not a hundred paces behind them and went crashing away in alarm at discovering that he no longer owned the woods.

Maddy scrambled off William's lap with a yelp of surprise, and he grunted at the sharp pain that suddenly shot through him when her knee drove into his groin, the blow completely unmanning him.

"William! Come on," she hissed in a whisper as she crawled away and started fumbling with her purse. "It's those wolves. We have to get out of here!"

Rolling into a tight ball of agony, William fought for breath even as he wondered how his not wringing her neck would help her decide to give herself to him.

"Come on!" she cried, tugging his sleeve. "The woods are getting dark. William, I don't know which way the road is!"

"N-not wolves," he gasped. "It was a—" He snapped his

mouth shut when he saw the huge gun clutched in her hands, her arms stiffened to hold it pointed into the woods as she knelt over him. "Christ's teeth!" he shouted, clamping his hand over hers as he sat up. "What in hell are ye doing with a gun!"

She started wrestling him for control of the weapon, and when her knee came too damned close to his groin again, William spun her around and slammed her back against his chest. Not knowing exactly where her finger was but hoping it wasn't on the trigger, he repositioned his grip over the barrel and twisted the gun free, immediately tossing it out of her reach.

"William!" she cried, struggling to go after it. "The wolves!"

He wrapped both arms around her in a bear of a hug, and squeezed her until she squeaked. "Maddy, darling," he rasped, fighting to keep the edge out of his voice. He spread his legs so that she was sitting on the ground instead of his throbbing groin, but he didn't dare loosen his arms. "That was a buck snorting."

She went very still, tension humming through her. He brushed her hair back with his jaw, so his lips could touch her cheek. "What are ye doing with a gun, lass?"

"Protecting myself!"

"Where did ye get it? Was it your father's?"

He felt her take a deep breath. "Billy bought it for me when we got divorced."

William knew he couldn't have heard right. "Why would he have done that?"

"So I could protect myself," she repeated, her tone exasperated. "I was moving to a house in the middle of the woods with a toddler, and he wanted me to have it for security."

Oh, aye, he really wanted to meet Billy Kimble, preferably on a dark night with no one around. "Are ye saying the bastard handed you a gun and just walked away, leaving ye alone in a house in the middle of nowhere with a child? *His* child?"

"You mean, as opposed to leaving me in the middle of no-where without any way to protect myself?" She twisted just enough to glare at him. "He took me to firearms classes and helped me get a permit. I don't call that just walking away."

All of the little pieces suddenly fell into place, and William realized that the mask Maddy had built around herself was as complex and as powerful as the one he had worn for several centuries; only where he'd become a dragon everyone feared, she'd become a giving person everyone couldn't help but love.

He repositioned her to face away from him again, so she couldn't see the anger in his eyes, and made sure it wasn't in his voice. "Eve told me it's common knowledge that you divorced Kimble, but right now I would have the truth from ye, Madeline. Who asked for the divorce?"

She started struggling to get away, but he merely tightened his arms around her.

"Ye tried for three years to make your marriage work, didn't you?" he whispered against her face, feeling her cheek grow cold with paleness. "But Billy Kimble wasn't interested in being a husband and father, was he?"

"He loves Sarah," she rasped.

"But he never loved you. Did you love him?"

She said nothing.

"Or were ye only a young lass clinging to the hope that you could make it work?"

Her head dropped forward, and William felt burning tears fall onto his hands. "I wanted to love him," she said softly.

"Shhh," he whispered, turning her in his arms so she could bury her face in his shirt. He smoothed down her hair. "I'm sorry to say so, but I'm glad ye didn't succeed."

"W-will you do me a favor?" she stammered.

"Yes."

He heard her breath hitch in surprise at his quick

declaration, and then he felt her shudder. "Will you please not tell anyone that Billy's the one who wanted the divorce?"

"Ye have my word." He ducked his head so she could see his smile. "And could ye do me a favor?" he asked, brushing her damp cheek with his thumb. "Could ye not tell anyone ye had me rolling on the ground in agony with only a flick of your knee?"

He watched her frown, and then her eyes suddenly widened. Seeing that she was about to unman him again as she tried to leap up, this time he all but *threw* her off his lap and then immediately rolled to the side and sprang to his feet.

"Omigod, I'm sorry!" she cried.

He smiled, though she was too busy staring at his crotch to see it. "How sorry?"

She lifted her gaze to his face, her own face blistering red. "Really, really sorry," she said, dropping her gaze to his crotch again.

"Because I'm thinking ye look more worried than sorry."

She looked up. "Worried about what?"

"That ye might have indefinitely postponed clearing up our unfinished business."

She gaped at him, but then a faint smile worked its way into her eyes. "Is there anything I can do to . . . speed up your recovery?" she asked, deadpan.

William felt most of his blood rush to his wounded groin, and turned away with a bark of laughter before she could see the effect she had on him. "My God, woman, you need a keeper," he said, going over and picking up her purse and then her gun. He turned to her in surprise. "Christ, this thing weighs more than your whole purse."

"It's the nine bullets that make it so heavy," she said, holding out her hand.

He gave her the purse but continued studying the weapon. "Have ye actually shot it?" he asked, looking at her.

He saw her chin lift. "I shot it this morning before work."

"So those were your shell casings we found at the gravel pit?" She held her hand out for the gun again.

"Maddy, I know ye said no more gifts, but would ye let me buy ye a new weapon? One a little less heavy, and that would fit your hand better?" he asked, carefully turning the handle toward her as Trace had shown him—only to flinch when she merely grabbed it and stuffed it into the side of her purse.

She stilled when she saw him step to the side. "Hey, don't worry; I don't keep a bullet in the chamber. That way, if Sarah got hold of it, she couldn't accidentally shoot herself." She smiled at him. "And thanks, but I like this gun," she said, slipping the strap over her shoulder and patting her purse. "It's big enough to scare the bejeezus out of people, and Billy said that if I ever have to actually shoot someone, they won't be able to get up and start chasing me, whereas anything smaller might just piss them off."

William laced his fingers through hers and started walking toward the road, only just noticing how dark the woods were getting. She might be right about the gun's stopping power, but he didn't care that she was carrying her ex-husband's parting gift.

But if he'd learned anything about maddening Madeline, it was that pushing her was like trying to herd chickens. He led her to the road in silence, and when they reached the bushes, he had to let go of her hand so she could jump the ditch. But he found himself smiling again when she slipped her hand back in his as they started walking toward An Tèarmann.

"If I give ye a ride home and just drop ye off, how will ye get to work tomorrow morning?" he asked.

"I suppose I could have Mom drop me off, but then she'd have to take Sarah to rec and come pick us both up tomorrow night." She sighed. "I guess I'm going to have to try to get a car loan now instead of saving up for one." She frowned at him. "You didn't drive Eve's car off that gravel bank, did you? You got out and then rolled it over the edge."

He grinned. "I suppose I did."

"But why?" she asked, looking back at the road they were walking on. "I realize you might be a bit . . . obsessed about getting your way, but I can't believe you'd wreck a perfectly good car just so I would have to use your truck."

"I was doing Kenzie a favor by destroying that demonic machine."

She stopped walking. "What are you talking about?"

He started them walking again, seeing that if he didn't get her home soon, she was going to fall asleep on her feet, as he'd noticed her steps faltering with fatigue. "If that car were to get in an accident with something even as small as a mailbox, the mailbox would win. I don't like the idea of you and Sarah riding in anything smaller than my truck, any more than Kenzie would want to see Eve driving that car again. Would ye promise me that when you buy yourself a new vehicle, you'll choose a large truck?"

She laughed. "Trust me, if I ever win the lottery, I will buy myself the biggest, baddest SUV they make."

He noticed the air starting to chill as they drew near An Tèarmann, a soft sea breeze pushing fog in off the ocean. "Are ye chilled, Maddy? Would ye like my shirt?"

She laughed again, anxiously this time. "Keep your shirt on, Killkenny," she said, her voice husky as she glanced down at their clasped hands. "But if you're chilly, maybe you should *roll down your sleeves*," she finished in a near growl, suddenly picking up her pace.

She stopped when they reached the driveway. "Eve can take me home."

"I said I would drive you, and I will."

"But then you'll be driving back here without anyone accompanying you, and that's illegal. And it was illegal today, when you came to the home all alone."

"I've decided I don't like that rule."

She smiled at that. "And if you don't like something, you what . . . either ignore it or bash it over the head with your *sword*?"

He frowned at that. "Ye dare tease me, when you're walking around with a gun in your purse that weighs as much as a car?"

Still holding his hand, she started walking in the driveway. "I tell you what—while I'm deciding whether or not to . . . grant your favor," she said thickly, "I will *borrow* your truck this one time and drive myself home. And that way, it will be at the nursing home for you and Elbridge to use tomorrow."

"Deal."

They stopped by the driver's door of the truck; and William opened it but stopped her from getting in. "Is there anything I can say to help you make your decision?"

There was still enough light from the setting sun for him to see color rise to her cheeks. "If I say yes, you would hold yourself to the same stipulation about not seeing anyone else?"

He grinned. "That's the thing with possessive men—like dogs, we're too busy guarding our territory to be sniffing out new ones."

That brought her color up a notch. "And the gifts would stop?"

His grin vanished. "Aw, lass, I am having such fun shopping on the Internet with Janice." She tossed her purse across the console with a snort, and William couldn't help but wince. "Are ye sure there isn't a bullet in the chamber?"

She climbed into the truck and looked down at him. "I'm *pretty* sure," she said with a cheeky grin. But she suddenly sobered. "One more question."

"What would that be?"

"Will you tell me who you really are?"

"Yes." He saw her jaw go slack and smiled. "But not today. Or tomorrow."

"Then when?" she snapped.

"When you're ready."

"That's not an answer."

"You have my word, Madeline. When you are ready, I will tell you everything."

She sat there fuming at him for several heartbeats, and then her shoulders slumped. She turned away and reached for the key.

"Another thing ye might wish to think about as you decide tonight," he said, causing her not to start the truck—though she also didn't look at him. "And that's if you are prepared to let your bogeyman boyfriend go."

She looked at him. "He's not real, William."

"Oh, I'm thinking he's quite real to you, and quite safe, because ye feel he can't steal your heart—at least not as long as ye have it tucked away in a box under your bed." He canted his head at her. "I tell ye what; how about that if you do agree to my favor, I give you something I hold equally dear, and you can keep it safe for me?"

"What is it?"

He shook his head. "I'm no more ready to open my box than you are to open yours." He smiled. "Maybe someday we'll each work up the courage to finally open them together." Her shoulders slumped again, and he could see her fatigue. "Go home, Madeline, before ye fall asleep," he said, moving to close her door.

"William," she said, although she was looking at the steering wheel and not him. "I-I want to say yes," she said, her voice whisper-soft.

"I know ye do, lass. And I want very much for you to say yes."

"But I'm scared."

"I know that, too. But remember, ye have my word that you'll not find a safer place than in my arms." That said, he softly closed the door and stepped back.

She stared out at him, and William gave her a tender smile, then turned away and started walking toward the barn. He heard the truck start behind him and stopped at the door just as Kenzie walked out, obviously also having heard the truck.

"I'm seeing, but I'm having a hard time believing," Kenzie said. "How did ye get her to change her mind?"

William stared at the taillights disappearing up the road, wondering why the devil himself expected a man to settle for possessing only a woman's body, when even a fool knew her true value lay in her heart. "It's simple, really. I just opened the gates of hell and walked in."

Chapter Fifteen

"*I* believe I know why they kicked ye out of your war, Huntsman," William said as Trace walked up behind him. "I've guided legions that made less noise than ye do."

"Would you have preferred I didn't announce my arrival?" Trace asked with a chuckle, sitting down beside him. "No offense, Killkenny, but I'd rather not have to explain to Maddy why I slit her boyfriend's throat defending myself."

William snorted and handed Trace a bottle of the ale he'd bought at a store Elbridge had suggested he stop at. It wasn't mead, but at least he could stomach it.

Trace took the bottle, held the label up to the moonlight, and also snorted. "You drink this rotgut warm?"

"Half the taste is lost when it's chilled."

Trace twisted off the cap and took a sip, made a sound of disgust, and then took a longer swig. "You intend to camp out here every night?"

"I can't very well camp out in her bed, now can I? Not with her mother and young daughter in the house."

"I see she's using your truck."

"Only until I work up the nerve to give her the new SUV hidden in Kenzie's barn."

Trace spit out a mouthful of ale. "Good luck with that. I'm shocked you got her to use your truck even temporarily. You try to give her that SUV, and she's going to get behind the wheel only long enough to run you over."

William chuckled, deciding he'd have to ask Mabel what a lottery was, and how he went about having Maddy win one. "So, Huntsman, what did ye think of our . . . target practice this afternoon?"

Trace said nothing at first, staring down at Maddy's house for quite some time before he spoke. "I've spent most of the last ten years in just about every country in this world. You don't think that's the first time I've seen a hocus-pocus dog-and-pony show, do you? There are witch doctors in the Pacific who not only can light a fire with the tip of their finger, but can also walk across the glowing coals without burning their feet." He took another swig, gave a small shudder, and glared at William. "As for what Kenzie did next . . . well, he should never do that in front of a man holding a gun."

William chuckled, and took a sip from his own bottle. "Aye, I was quite surprised the first time he did it in front of me, too. But not nearly as surprised as I was that he showed you some of what he's just recently mastered." He sighed. "But it seems modern man has spent the last few centuries trying to distance himself from his true nature, so I suppose it's not your fault for being skeptical of the magic."

"That's wasn't magic; there has to be sound science behind those tricks." He looked down at the bottle in his hand. "I could probably figure out how he started the fire, but that panther thing was . . ." He looked over at William. "It takes a lot to rattle me, but I'm still trying to come to terms with what I saw."

"I have a good friend who's a scientist," William said, twisting the cap off another bottle of ale, wondering why anyone would bother buying such wee bottles. "And Camry told me that the line between science and magic is growing thinner with each new discovery and that one day, when it completely disappears, man will realize he's wasted centuries proving nothing. We are what we are, Huntsman, and it matters not if we like it, only that we accept it."

"Then what's the point of even being born?"

"*The point* is different for everyone, and is rooted in whatever lessons we need to learn—or that we can teach one another." He grinned over at him. "And I just recently learned that we are our own worst enemies, far more than what's out there," he said, sweeping his bottle in an arc to encompass everything around them.

"So you're saying the wolves that attacked you and Maddy last night aren't really the enemy, so we really don't have to worry about them?"

"Hell yes, we need to worry, just as we must deal with the energy that sent them. And that's the very core of the problem. Our individuality gives us free will, but there are always those who wish to impose *their* will on the rest of us. Whoever sent those wolves here is after your mermaid, and you, Kenzie, and I are all that are standing between her and untold horror."

Trace drained the last of his ale, gave another shudder, and shook his head. "I'm having a hard time wrapping my mind around what you're saying."

William chuckled again. "Welcome to the magic." He handed him another bottle, then leaned back on his elbow. "The woman who gave ye the coin came seeking Kenzie, but apparently when she realized you could see her true nature, she decided to ask for your help as well. So while you're fighting whatever demons got ye kicked out of your war, ye need to decide if you're also willing to fight hers."

Trace stared down at the unopened bottle in his hand. "How does one fight something he can't see and doesn't know anything about?" he asked softly.

"Ye use whatever weapon ye have at your disposal; sometimes it's a sword or a gun, and sometimes it's your smarts," William said, looking down at the light shining from Maddy's kitchen window. "And sometimes ye simply fight with all your soul."

Trace followed William's line of sight. "Are you in love with my cousin?"

William took another sip and then wiped his mouth with the back of his hand. "Nay, I'm not certain I'm capable of loving anyone."

"Then why are you messing with her?"

William glanced over when he heard the edge in Huntsman's voice. "Because if there's even a glimmer of hope that I *can* love, then I would wish to love Madeline. And if I find that I can't, then I'll settle for taking such good care of her that she will feel loved."

Trace snorted. "Trust me, women know the difference. So what happens if Maddy won't settle for anything less than love?"

"Then I will let her go . . . before I break her heart."

Both men turned at the sound of a screen door slamming, and William sat up when Maddy came running out of the house, hiking her purse over her shoulder as she ran down the stairs.

"Sarah! Sarah, where are you?" she shouted, her voice verging on panic as she stopped in the middle of the driveway. "Sarah, answer me! Sarah!"

William sprang to his feet, but before he could take even a

step, Trace tackled him to the ground and then quickly ducked to avoid William's fist. "Sarah crawled out her bedroom window and is chasing fireflies," he said in a rush.

"And ye did nothing?" William growled, shoving him away.

Trace's grin slashed in the moonlight. "She actually started calling them like pets, in whispers so her mother wouldn't hear."

"Dammit, Sarah, where are you?" Maddy shouted, now in a full-blown panic.

William attempted to jump to his feet, but Trace tackled him again. "Goddammit, Huntsman," William hissed, this time catching the bastard square on the jaw. Trace rolled away and lunged to his feet, the moonlight glinting off the knife in his hand.

"Sarah!" Patricia also shouted as the screen door slammed again.

"Oh, Sarah!" William heard Maddy cry in relief. "Didn't you hear me calling you? What are you doing out here? You're supposed to be in bed!"

While keeping half his attention on Huntsman, William turned to see Maddy drop to her knees and hug her daughter.

"The kid's almost ten," Trace said, straightening from his defensive stance. "Maddy used to sneak all the way over to my house at that age to spy on me after her parents had gone to bed. Why do you think I call her Peeps?"

"She didn't sneak through woods filled with wolves."

Trace ran his hand along his jaw and then slid his knife into the back of his belt.

William also straightened, suddenly realizing there was a reason the man hadn't been worried about Sarah. "Who's with her?" he asked.

"Rick started whining about missing his niece, so I brought him over. It was his idea to climb up to her bedroom and bring her out to catch fireflies."

William sat back down and picked up his overturned bottle of ale. "You ever interfere in my business with Maddy again, Huntsman, and I will be the one explaining why I killed her cousin."

"What the . . . why in hell did she bother to bring her *purse*?" Trace asked, looking down the knoll.

William glanced down to see Maddy sliding the strap of her heavy purse over her shoulder again as she led her daughter back into the house. "Because she has a gun in there big enough to blow a hole the size of my fist in a man."

Trace gaped at him. "She's carrying a handgun in her purse?"

"It was a parting gift from her bastard ex-husband, so she could protect herself and Sarah. She claims she has a permit to carry it and that she doesn't keep a bullet in the chamber."

"Those were her shell casings we found at the pit. Holy shit, Billy gave her a forty-caliber cannon." Trace grinned. "She has good aim; she blistered those beer cans."

"Can ye talk her into carrying something smaller?" William asked, spitting out a piece of dirt he nearly swallowed when he'd swigged down what was left of his ale.

"Why don't *you* talk her into a smaller one, since you like buying her things?"

"It appears my gifts unnerve the woman, but she might accept one from you."

Trace folded his arms over his chest. "Do you want her to have a different gun because you think she needs a different one or because you don't like that this one is from Kimble?"

"What in hell sort of man gives a woman a gun as a divorce gift?"

Trace grinned. "A stupid man, apparently. He's lucky she didn't turn it on him."

"He knew she wouldn't. Madeline is too damned softhearted for her own good."

"Most women are," Trace said. "It's in their DNA."

William snorted. "Then ye haven't met Kenzie's sister. That's one woman I'd hate to see holding a gun in her hand." He chuckled. "Or, rather, her wing."

"Excuse me?"

William eyed Trace speculatively. "Fiona Gregor is a red-tailed hawk—as well as a flaming shrew. She's not all that fond of men, though I suppose she may have good reason. I just don't like how she's decided that other than her two brothers, all the rest of us are bastards."

"What do you mean, she's a red-tailed hawk?"

"Just that. She died giving birth to her son in the eleventh century, but she showed up here as a hawk soon after Kenzie moved to Midnight Bay. Only she's been missing almost a week now, and we're starting to worry about her. Before she disappeared, Fiona wouldn't let your mermaid out of her sight, and Kenzie fears she's gone off on her own to deal with whoever is after the pup."

"The pup?"

"You see a woman swimming in the bay, Huntsman, where everyone else sees only a harbor seal pup."

Trace was back to gaping again. He suddenly bent over, grabbed another bottle of ale out of the box, twisted off the cap, and downed half of it.

William chuckled. "Getting drunk won't make it any less confusing, my friend."

"I never get drunk."

"Aye, a warrior can't afford to let down his guard long enough to enjoy some of the simpler pleasures." William looked toward the house and saw that the downstairs lights had gone off; the only one left on was in Maddy's bedroom. He wondered if she was right now tucking her heart into a box and sliding it under her bed.

God, he hoped so.

"Wait, you said something about Fiona's two brothers. Kenzie has a brother?" Trace snorted. "What is he, an elephant?"

William looked back at him and grinned. "Nay, Matt's a wizard."

Trace downed the last half of his ale in one swallow.

William took two more bottles out of the box and handed one to him. "Sit down, Huntsman. I believe I promised to tell ye the story of Maddy's bogeyman boyfriend, and I guess now's as good a time as any."

"Are you sure you've got everything you need for the weekend?" Maddy asked, stuffing the mail she'd just gotten out of the mailbox into her purse. She glanced over to make sure her daughter's seat belt was fastened and the airbag was off and finally pulled out of the driveway, already ten minutes late.

Sarah made an impatient noise as she twisted in her seat to look around the truck, apparently tired of getting asked the same question every Friday morning. "I'm only going to be twelve miles away, Mom. And if I forgot anything, Sissy usually has it."

That's because Sissy Blake's only nine years older than you, Maddy wanted to shout. *And the spoiled-rotten snot gets whatever she wants, and for some inexplicable reason, she wants your daddy.* "I'm sorry I got a little carried away scolding you last night, Sarah, but you scared the dickens out of me when I went to check on you and found your bed empty."

"Rick put a ladder up to my window and asked me if I wanted to catch fireflies." Sarah began pushing all the buttons on her door, making her window go up and down and the doors lock and unlock. Then she started adjusting all the vents she could reach, so the air-conditioning blew on her hair. "This is a really nice truck. Is it ours?"

Maddy smiled to herself, deciding to wait and see how long it took the little imp to realize that her seat was getting hot. "No, it's Mr. Killkenny's. We're just borrowing it for this morning, because Eve's car was . . . in an accident. I'm going to buy us a new car, but it might take a couple of days, so Gram will have to drive us around next week."

Sarah started running the windows up and down again. "I like the leather seats, only they're a lot warmer-feeling than Dad's cloth ones," she said, giving a squirm. "And I like that this truck's so smart it automatically turns off the airbag, so I get to sit in the front. Instead of a car, can we get a new truck like this one? Maybe red, too?"

"Sorry, kiddo, not on the salary I earn—unless you don't mind eating macaroni and cheese every day for the next six years."

"Why don't you just marry Mr. Killkenny, and then he can move in with us and Gram, and that way we can use his truck all the time? Now that Sissy's moved in with Dad, he gets to drive the new car her parents gave her for graduation."

"I don't think getting a vehicle is a very good reason to marry someone, do you?"

"Well, you could have Mr. Killkenny's baby," Sarah suggested, looking at Maddy with absolutely serious eyes. "That's why Dad's marrying Sissy." She suddenly smiled. "And that way, I'd get *two* new brothers or sisters. And I like Mr. Killkenny, because he doesn't treat me like I'm five." She suddenly wrinkled her nose. "When I spend the weekend at Dad's, Sissy's always trying to *mother* me."

Maddy grinned out the windshield. "She's going to be your stepmother, Sarah, and she's just trying to make sure you like her. Now, let's get back to your climbing out your window last night, young lady. Is there a reason Rick didn't walk into the house and take you out the *door* to go firefly hunting?"

Sarah gave a little snort, and Maddy glanced over at her in surprise. Good Lord, had *she* snorted when she was nine? "Out with it, Sarah Jane, what did Uncle Rick say about why he didn't come inside and get you?"

Sarah glanced over, her big brown eyes looking far too old for her age. "He said Trace decided you and Uncle Rick needed a vacation from each other, and that's why he's sleeping on Trace's boat. But he missed me, so he snuck up to my window after you put me to bed." She smiled, looking like a little girl again. "It was fun, Mom. I've never crawled out my bedroom window before."

"And if I ever catch you doing it again, the television gets turned off for an entire month," Maddy told her, figuring that in a few years, the girl was going to lose her television rights for forever.

God, she was growing up fast.

"So, will you get pregnant so Mr. Killkenny will have to marry you?"

Maddy put the brakes on at the intersection a little harder than she intended and blinked over at her daughter's expectant expression. "Um . . . you do know that getting pregnant *first* and married *after* isn't the way it's supposed to work, don't you?"

"You got pregnant before you married Dad. And so did Sissy."

"Who told you I did?"

"Sissy. She said Dad has a thing for cheerleaders."

Dammit to hell; she was going to have to sit that little cheerleading snot down and explain to her that Sarah was *nine,* not nineteen. "That's because we were both . . . we didn't . . . both Sissy and I were too young to know any better," Maddy said with a sigh. She reached over and gave a soft tug on one of Sarah's long braids. "But you will have the benefit of my experience, young lady, and will do things in the proper order. First comes love, then comes marriage, and *then* comes the baby carriage. Got that?"

Maddy glanced up into her rearview mirror when she heard the rev of a powerful engine behind them and saw a dark-visored, red-helmeted head looking at her over the tailgate. Realizing that she was just sitting at the Stop sign holding up traffic, she looked both ways and pulled out onto the main highway.

Checking her mirror again, she saw the motorcycle come up behind her and then suddenly pass. Only instead of zooming by, the idiot slowed down when he got beside her door, gave a wave with his left hand, and then zoomed ahead, slipping back into the lane in front of her just in time to miss an oncoming car.

"Oh, man, I'd give anything to ride on a motorcycle," Sarah said, watching the bike lean into the upcoming curve and disappear.

"Not as long as I'm your mother," Maddy said with a laugh.

"I bet Mr. Killkenny could talk you into letting me ride one."

"What makes you say that?" she asked, looking over in surprise.

Sarah snorted again. "Yeah, like you would have let me ride a warhorse all by myself if he hadn't pointed out that I'm not a kid."

"That's different. Mr. Killkenny knows horses, and I trusted his judgment."

"What if he had a motorcycle? Would you let me go for a ride with him?"

Maddy gave a quick bark of laughter. "Mr. Killkenny has all he can do to drive this truck, Sarah. I sure as hell wouldn't let you on the back of a motorcycle with him."

Sarah held out her hand. "A quarter, please."

"Damn," Maddy muttered, reaching into the change pocket of her purse.

Sarah giggled, motioning with her open palm. "Make that two quarters. But I think I'm upping it to a dollar for each cuss word. That way I'll be rich enough to buy my own car by the time I'm sixteen."

Chapter Sixteen

"What are you guys doing hanging around out here in the sun?" Maddy asked as she walked up to the group of residents gathered at the front entrance—some of them in wheelchairs, some using walkers, and all looking more excited than a bunch of kids on Christmas morning.

"We're waiting our turn," Charlotte said. "I'm next."

"Your turn for what?"

"A motorcycle ride."

"Excuse me?" Maddy said with a gasp, looking around for a motorcycle. She looked back at Charlotte. "Who's giving rides?"

"William."

"*Killkenny?*" she squeaked.

Elbridge chuckled. "It seems the boy went out and bought himself a bike a few days ago. And it seems the women," he said, waving toward Charlotte, "have all decided they want to be biker babes when they grow up."

"Oh, Maddy, you just wait until you see it," Charlotte said. "It's candy-apple red, it looks like it just beamed down from outer space, and the air literally rumbles when he revs the engine."

"The leather jacket he got at the dealership is thicker than the one we ordered for him, and he also got two matching helmets," Janice said from her wheelchair, pulling the brim of her bonnet down as she squinted against the sun. "But I told him we could have gotten them cheaper on the Internet, and to check with me first before he buys any other accessories."

Maddy felt her panic growing and scanned the parking lot again, then looked toward the road. "Who's on the bike with him right now?"

"Lois," Charlotte told her. "She said it's been over thirty years since she'd ridden on a motorcycle, but that she figures it's like riding a bike."

Maddy turned wide eyes on Elbridge. "But William can't keep his truck on the pavement," she whispered. "You told me yourself that he keeps oversteering."

Elbridge started to say something but stopped when the sound of a downshifting engine rumbled the air. Maddy spun around just in time to see the idiot who had passed her earlier pull into the parking lot—a tiny woman on back wearing a candy-apple red helmet and a leather jacket that looked ten sizes too big for her, clinging to William as if her life depended on it.

He made a loop around the parking lot and came to a stop in front of everyone, took the bike out of gear and revved the engine a few times before he shut it off, dropped the kickstand, and pulled off his helmet.

Maddy immediately ran over and took hold of Lois. "Let me help you," she said, wrapping an arm around her waist as the older woman set one foot on the ground and wrestled her other leg over the bike. But then Maddy had to continue holding her when she realized Lois was unsteady on her feet as she fumbled to take off her helmet with trembling hands.

"Here, let me get that for you, Lois, my sweet," William said, reaching under her chin and unsnapping the strap.

Maddy was expecting to see terror-filled eyes, but when the helmet came off, Lois Manning was beaming from ear to ear. "Holy hell, William, you certainly know how to show a girl a good time."

"It's my turn now," Charlotte said, taking the helmet and shoving it down over her head. "Hurry up, give me the jacket, too."

"Wait!" Maddy cried, having to lift the visor to look at her. "Charlotte, I don't think . . . I wish you . . ." She looked into the older woman's excited eyes and blew out a sigh. "Does Doris know you guys are out here taking turns on a motorcycle?"

"She had the first ride," Elbridge said. He shook his head. "Didn't seem to care that she was wearing a skirt and heels. Apparently the woman has a wild streak."

Seeing that Lois was steady on her feet now, Maddy grabbed hold of William's shirtsleeve and pulled him a good distance away from everyone. "What are you doing?" she hissed, turning her back to the residents. "William, they can't be riding a motorcycle at their age, especially not with . . . look, it's not that I don't think . . ." She took a calming breath. "How long have you been riding motorcycles?"

"Three days, if ye count since sunrise this morning."

"Three days?"

"Don't worry. I'll give you a turn right after Charlotte."

"Three *days*? William, you can't even keep your truck on the pavement!"

Apparently not realizing she'd just insulted him, his grin widened. "When I saw the ad on the television, I realized a motorcycle was what I should have. It's exactly like riding a horse, Maddy; I get to use the weight of my body to guide it, and there are fewer buttons to deal with."

Maddy could only gape at him, utterly speechless.

He suddenly clasped her face in his hands and leaned down and kissed her rather robustly, obviously on a motorcycle adrenaline high. And instead of stopping when the claps and whistles and catcalls started behind them, he wrapped her in his arms, tucked her head into the crook of his elbow, and kissed her senseless.

She finally had to poke him in the ribs so he'd at least let her breathe, but her reprieve lasted all of two seconds before he started kissing her again.

The whistles and clapping increased, although the whistles were hoarsely blown wind and the catcalls had turned downright bawdy.

Well, bawdy for eighty-year-olds.

Maddy gave up and dropped her purse on the ground with a dull thud—ignoring William's flinch—and wrapped her arms around his waist and kissed him back.

Well hell, if she'd known that was all she had to do to make him stop, she would have done it sooner. Because the moment her tongue started dueling with his, he lifted his head and smiled down at her.

She frowned up at him. "I don't believe I've said *yes* yet."

"I don't believe you've said *no* yet, either."

"William, a motorcycle is the most dangerous vehicle on the road."

"Nay, Madeline, not for me. The moment I sat on one at the dealership, it was like slipping into a second skin." He kissed the tip of her nose then smiled down at her again. "I won't let anything happen to your residents, lass. I didn't let the speedometer go over seventy, and I made Lois lift her visor at every Stop sign so I could see how she was doing."

"William, you're going to have to help me up!" Charlotte called out. "Come on, you've got the rest of your life to kiss

Maddy. Dr. Petty's coming this morning, and I want my turn before he gets here. If he sees me riding a motorcycle, he'll have a coronary, and then I'll have to break in a whole new doctor."

"Oh, go on," Maddy said, giving his chest a pat as he finally let her go. "Your biker babe is getting impatient." She reached down and picked up her purse, and started walking with him back to the bike.

It really was a beautiful motorcycle, although it looked more like a rocket with two wheels attached. It was obviously designed for speed more than riding double, and Maddy believed William *would* feel more in control if it was like riding a horse.

He swept a positively giddy Charlotte into his arms and carefully set her on the tiny piece of leather that passed as a backseat. He immediately slipped his leg over the bike and plucked his helmet off the handlebar. "The rule book said I have to wear one of these blasted things until I've had my license for a year, but the damn thing is more of a hindrance than a help and keeps rubbing my whiskers," he muttered, slipping it down over his head.

Maddy lifted the visor and then tapped the dial where she assumed the speedometer was. "Forty, William," she said, figuring if she lowballed his speed, he wouldn't do more than fifty. "You keep it under forty miles per hour."

"Yes, ma'am," he solemnly agreed, although his eyes were smiling. "Are ye ready, Charlotte, my sweet?" he asked, turning to grin back at his passenger.

Charlotte wrapped her arms around his waist tightly enough to choke a horse, her squeal of delight drowned out by the rumble of the starting engine. He put it in gear, kicked up the kickstand, gave Maddy a nod, and slowly—and very smoothly—drove off.

It was as she watched them pull onto the road that she had a thought. "Omigod, he's not allowed to carry a passenger on a provisional license, is he?"

"No," Elbridge said with a chuckle from beside her. "But then, William told me he's decided simply to ignore any rule he doesn't like."

"He does seem to have acquired that habit," Maddy said with a laugh, taking hold of the back of Janice's wheelchair. "Come on, everyone. Let's get out of this sun before Dr. Petty finds half his patients looking like cooked lobsters."

Having spent a good portion of the morning following Dr. Petty on his rounds, Maddy finally sat down at her station to go over everyone's chart and reread her notes. Then she wrote several memos to Paula, the weekend day nurse, highlighting any changes in meds or treatments. After placing the last chart in the file stand, she leaned back in her chair with a sigh, glancing up at the clock to find that she had twenty minutes before her appointment with Elvira.

Eve might think she was neglecting herself by not going to a salon in Oak Harbor or Ellsworth, but Elvira was one of the great perks of this job. Doris also had Elvira do her hair and even brought her husband in for haircuts. Heck, the whole staff had their hair done at the River Run Nursing Home, creating a win-win arrangement for everyone, especially Elvira. The woman really was good, and Maddy suspected that feeling needed was more rewarding for Elvira than the generous tips everyone gave her.

Maddy noticed the mail crammed in her purse down by her feet, and pulled it out and started thumbing through it. She tossed the bills into one pile, tore up the credit-card offers and other junk mail and tossed them into the recycle bin, and put the catalogs in another pile to let the residents browse through.

She stopped when she reached an envelope from the University of Maine addressed to Richard Lane. God, she hoped it was a letter saying his bill was paid in full; with grants, scholarships, and a small student loan, he shouldn't owe them another dime. Maddy used a letter opener to slice along the top, pulled out the single sheet of paper, and frowned as she read it.

And then she reread it several more times.

It took her three tries to stuff the letter back into the envelope because she was shaking so badly. She shoved the envelope into her purse and then picked up the phone and called Midnight Bay's harbormaster, making up some lame excuse for why she needed to know the minute Trace Huntsman's boat docked. As soon as she hung up, she went over and locked her purse in the medicine cabinet, and then headed down the hall to her appointment with Elvira.

But she slowed as she approached Hiram's room and stopped outside his door. Taking a calming breath and plastering a smile on her face, she walked in. "How are you feeling, Mr. Man?"

It took him a few moments, but Hiram finally stopped staring out the window and looked over at her, his eyes still somewhat distant. "I'm feeling a wee bit more tired than usual." He gave a weak snort. "Dr. Petty said I'm entitled, considering I wore out my body working in the woods for sixty years. But that man don't know squat. All those years logging the forest are what's kept me moving this long."

Maddy smiled, realizing that more than one of the residents had begun using the term *wee* ever since William had started visiting. "He also said that if you're not back up to snuff by tomorrow, maybe you should consider going to the hospital in Ellsworth for a few days," Maddy reminded him.

He shook his head and patted the bed beside him. "Ain't nothing they can do to treat old age in a hospital."

Maddy sat down with a sigh, feeling as old and tired as Hiram.

He took hold of her hand. "You know how I said I've been hanging around so long because I'm afraid to die, Maddy girl?"

"I remember," she said, a lump rising in her throat. She reversed their grip. "And at the rate you're going, you're going to outlive me."

He shook his head again. "I don't think I got any fight left in me." His fingers tightened around hers. "I know you didn't like it this morning when I made sure that *do not resuscitate* order is still on my chart, but will you . . . if the end turns out . . ." He looked down at their clasped hands. "I'm scared, Maddy. I've told you my father got kicked in the head by a horse, and that I watched him linger in pain for nearly a week before he died." He looked at her. "I was seven, and I remember sitting on the front-porch steps that whole last night, covering my ears to block out his screaming."

Maddy forced a smile, rubbing her thumb along the back of his large but withered hand. "That was over eighty years ago, Hiram. You have my word; you won't feel any pain when . . . your time comes. We have medicine we can give you now that they didn't have back then."

"I don't want to scream, Maddy," he whispered. "I don't want all my friends to hear me carrying on and scare them like I was." His frail fingers tightened again. "I don't want you crying, either, you hear? And you don't let everyone get all depressed like they did when Amos died. This place was like a funeral parlor for weeks."

"How about instead of a wake, we have a party?" she suggested, determined to lighten his mood. "We'll have the kitchen bake an apple spice cake with cream cheese frosting in your honor and put balloons and streamers up all over the place."

He gave a weak snort. "You want to throw me a party *after* I'm dead?"

"Okay, then; I'll rally the troops and we'll start planning, and Monday afternoon you'll wake up from your nap to a surprise party."

"It ain't a surprise if you just told me."

Maddy rolled her eyes with a laugh and stood up. "I had to tell you; surprise parties are the leading cause of heart attacks after the age of ninety."

He made a harrumphing sound and settled back on his pillow. "I love you, Maddy girl," he whispered, closing his eyes with a sigh.

"I love you, too, Mr. Man," she whispered back, covering him with a light blanket and then going to the window and drawing the shades.

"I told William I was afraid," Hiram said just as she started to leave.

She stopped in surprise. "You did? But I thought that was our little secret?"

"I didn't mention the screaming part; I just told him I was scared of dying because I don't know what comes next. And you know what he told me? William said there ain't nothing to be afraid of, because it ain't any different than being born. He said there's people on the other side who'll take care of me until I get adjusted to being dead, just like there's people here to help babies grow up to be adults. He said being born and dying are the exact same thing, only we're going in the opposite direction."

"And so you're not afraid anymore?"

"Not about dying, I ain't—just about screaming."

"I promise, I won't let you scream."

"But what if I start in dying at night or on a Saturday or Sunday?"

Maddy pulled her cell phone out of her pocket. "I can be reached anytime and anywhere, and everyone has instructions to call me even before they call Dr. Petty. I will be here in two shakes of a lamb's tail, Mr. Man."

He closed his eyes again and snuggled into his pillow. "Okay then; I guess that makes me all set to die."

Maddy stared at him for several painful heartbeats, then quietly walked out the door and headed to the shampoo room down the hall—though she held on to the handrail because everything was quite blurry.

Seeing that Charlotte, Lois, Janice, and Elvira were inside waiting for her, Maddy took a minute to compose herself and wiped her eyes with her hands. She finally walked in, sat down in the shampoo chair, and then actually flinched when Elvira settled the cape over her shoulders.

"Mem said you better go show her the minute you walk out of here," Lois said. "Hey, have you been *crying*?"

"Land sakes, girl," Charlotte said. "I've never seen anyone more scared of change than you are."

Maddy gave them all a hesitant smile in the mirror. "I know. But thankfully I have you to give me a good kick in the butt when I need one."

"You're absolutely sure you want to do this?" Elvira asked as she pulled Maddy's ponytail free and ran her fingers through her hair.

"Of course she is," Janice answered for her. "Just make sure she doesn't end up looking tacky, like some of those overprocessed brassy blondes who do their own hair."

"Yes, not too heavy on the highlights," Lois added. "She needs to look like her hair's only been kissed by the sun."

Charlotte giggled. "Not like William just kissed her, or she'll be *solid* blond!"

Elvira quickly ran a brush through Maddy's hair and then wove it into a long braid down the back of the cape. Maddy stared at herself in the mirror and flinched again when Elvira picked up her scissors.

Lois patted her shoulder. "You close your eyes, sweetie, and when you open them again, you'll see a whole new woman looking back at you in the mirror."

Maddy closed her eyes and felt her other shoulder get a pat. "And no peeking," Charlotte said. "Or we'll tape your eyelids closed. It's taken months of badgering, but you'll soon see how right we are."

Maddy heard Janice's wheelchair move closer, and then felt her arm being patted. "You're going to look just like a movie star, Maddy," Janice said.

"No," Lois said, "she's going to look like a princess. And Prince Charming is going to gallop in here, sweep her up in his arms, and ride off into the sunset."

"No," Charlotte contradicted. "He's going to put her on the back of his motorcycle and zoom her off to his castle and then carry her up to his tower bedroom."

Still keeping her eyes closed because she was afraid they really would try to tape them shut, Maddy snickered. "Or maybe Prince Charming is going to take one look at me and hop on his bike and speed off into the sunset all by himself."

All three women patted her at once, only not quite so gently this time.

Maddy felt a tug on her thick braid and took a shuddering breath when the cold steel of Elvira's scissors touched the back of her neck. "I-I hope this doesn't take too long," she said, trying to distract herself from the feel of the blades sawing through her hair. "I have an errand I need to run just . . . as soon . . . as Prince Charming gets back from his driving lesson with Elbridge," she stammered, her voice trailing off as a bead of sweat slipped down her cleavage.

And suddenly, she felt rather dizzy and weightless at the sound of the scissor blades clinking shut when they ran out of hair.

"You going to that new shop I heard about in Oak Harbor?" Janice asked. "To buy some pretty new underwear because your red bra got ruined?"

Pouncing on this new distraction, Maddy opened her eyes to glare at Lois in the mirror. "You told them my bra was cut?"

"No," Lois said, her own eyes gleaming. "*You* just did. I only told them the underwire wore through."

"No peeking!" Charlotte yelped, stepping over to the counter. "Elvira, where's that tape you use to make those curls on Mem's cheeks?"

"They're closed!" Maddy cried, snapping her eyes shut again—but not before she'd watched Elvira set fifteen year's worth of her hair on the counter.

"I found the tape," Charlotte said. "And if I see you peeking again, I'm using the whole roll." She patted Maddy's arm. "Trust us, dear. This is for your own good."

Maddy forcibly relaxed her muscles, figuring it was too late to turn back now. Both Katy and Doris came in occasionally to check on her progress over the next hour, and even Samuel came shuffling in, the old man giving a chuckle as he declared she looked like a television antenna with all the foil on her head.

But Maddy kept her eyes closed the entire time, wondering what had possessed her to finally give in to the women. She reached under the cape to touch Willy Dragonheart on her chest, deciding it *might* have had something to do with William.

Or she might be trying to shove little miss knocked-up Sissy Blake off her high horse, as well as make Billy the Bastard do a double-take.

Then again, maybe she was doing this just for herself; after all, there was nothing like a new hairdo to make a girl feel twenty-seven instead of seventy-seven.

"Maddy," Katy said, from what sounded like the doorway. "The harbormaster just called to say your cousin's boat is heading into port."

"Did he say how many boats are ahead of him at the co-op?"

"Three. He figures they'll be tied up at the dock for almost two hours."

"Katy!" Maddy called out, not knowing if the girl had left or not, as she still refused to open her eyes.

"Yeah?"

"Are William and Elbridge back yet?"

"Nope. But Elbridge told me his granddaughter is stopping by this afternoon, so they should be back soon."

"What time is it now?"

"It's a quarter past one. I have to go; I need to change Mem's bed before she falls asleep in her chair. Don't forget to come show us your new do."

"It's after *one*?" Maddy yelped, opening her eyes. "You guys all missed lunch!"

Charlotte jumped up with the tape in her hands, and Maddy snapped her eyes shut. "They're closed!"

Not that it mattered, because Elvira had turned her chair away from the mirror as she began working her fingers through Maddy's hair to blow it dry, apparently not trusting her not to peek.

"We didn't miss lunch; we've been taking turns going to the dining room," Lois said loudly over the dryer. "Elvira took her turn while the bleach set up."

"What, you felt you had to leave someone on guard at all times?" Maddy loudly drawled. But then she stuck out her lower lip. "Nobody brought me back anything."

"It would have tasted like bleach," Janice said with a laugh.

"Okay, ladies," Elvira said, shutting off the dryer. She pulled off Maddy's cape and turned her chair a hundred and eighty degrees. "Presenting Miss Madeline Kimble, River Run's sexy new head nurse!"

Maddy opened her eyes and blinked at the woman staring back at her in the mirror. She reached up and touched the loose, highlighted curls cascading around her face. "Did you give me a perm, too?" she whispered, blinking again.

"No, sweetie. I told you there were curls under the weight of all that hair."

"Oh, Maddy," Charlotte said, also touching her hair. "They're beautiful. *You're* beautiful. Just look how those soft curls make your big brown eyes sparkle."

"You look just like your daughter," Lois said in an almost reverent whisper as she walked up beside Maddy to stare in the mirror. She shook her head. "You'll never get into a bar now, no matter what card you show. You don't look a day over sixteen."

Maddy couldn't stop staring at herself. "I-I didn't look this good in high school," she whispered, shaking her head and watching the loose curls flutter back into place.

"So are you going to take our advice more often now?" Lois asked.

Maddy eyed her curiously. "Advice about what?"

"Everything" Charlotte said, waving her hand. "Remember what William said—we have several centuries' worth of collective wisdom."

"To begin with," Lois continued, glaring at Maddy in the mirror, "you're going to start letting us pick out your clothes."

Maddy stood up to look at Lois directly. "What's wrong with my clothes?"

"You might look like a sixteen-year-old, but you have to stop dressing like one." Lois swept her arm in the general direction of Maddy's body. "You don't need to jack up your boobs so high that you look like you're choking, and a little less leg showing leaves something for a man's imagination."

"And makes them eager to undress you," Charlotte added.

Maddy narrowed her eyes at the women. "Did William put you up to this?"

"Put us up to what?" Lois asked innocently. "To suggesting

that you start dressing like a sophisticated young woman instead of a teenage tramp?" She snorted. "Of course not. William's a man, isn't he? He'd just as soon you wear pants low enough in the back to give you a second cleavage."

"Or that you wear nothing at all," Charlotte added. She grabbed Maddy's arm. "Come on, let's go show you off."

After one last glance at herself in the mirror as they led her away, Maddy quickly found herself at the center of a parade that made its way to every room in the nursing home—including the kitchen—where she would then have to twirl like a ballerina, shake her head to make her curls move, and let everyone touch her new hairdo. It was when she was on display in the sitting room, performing for the day campers, that she spotted William and Elbridge pulling into the parking lot.

"I have to go," she told everyone, bowing repeatedly as she backed out of the room. "I have an important errand to run."

She ran down the hall, got her purse out of the medicine cabinet, raced to the shampoo room, and grabbed her braid off the counter. She stuffed it into her front pocket and ran outside just as Elbridge and William were getting out of William's truck.

She waved at Elbridge heading inside as she rushed up to William. "I know I'm contradicting myself, but can I borrow your truck? I have an errand I need to run."

William stood stone-still, staring at her in stunned silence.

Maddy nervously touched her hair, just now remembering her new look and realizing she'd shocked him.

"Ye cut your hair," he whispered, also reaching up and touching one of her curls. "And it's blond in places."

"I . . . um . . . I've been planning to cut it for months," she whispered back, uncertain whether or not he liked it.

He let go of the curl and gently feathered his fingers through her hair, letting them slowly glide all the way through before doing it again. And every time his fingers came to the end of the curls that stopped at her neckline, he would linger to rub them between his fingers.

Unable to tell what he was thinking, she wet her lips and his gaze dropped to her mouth—even as his fingers continued moving through her hair, sending salacious shivers down her spine.

"The truck?" she asked hoarsely. "Can I borrow it?"

"Hmmm."

"Can I borrow your truck to run my errand? I'll have it back in an hour."

Wow, she'd impressed herself, getting out two whole complete sentences.

Which seemed to be more than William could do; he just grunted.

His gaze lifted from her mouth, stopped briefly at her eyes, then continued up to her hair again, where he watched his fingers slide through her curls.

Maddy felt herself starting to melt—and it wasn't from the blazing sun. "C-can I have the keys, please?"

His fingers stopped and wrapped around the back of her neck, and he pulled her forward as he leaned in—only instead of kissing her, he brushed his lips over her hair.

"I-I'll only be gone about an hour," she managed to croak, her insides clenching and her legs turning to rubber.

He grunted again.

Or maybe it was more of a guttural moan.

"And before you take off on your motorcycle, could you go visit with Hiram, if he's awake?"

Wow, another whole sentence.

"Maddy! The harbormaster just called back to say Trace's boat is off-loading," Katy shouted from the entrance.

Maddy tried to remember why she cared.

William straightened away with a sigh.

She placed her hand on his chest when she felt herself sway toward him, and looked up to find him running his *eyes* through her hair now.

"Well, Maddy?" Charlotte shouted from the entrance. "Does he like it?"

She was pretty sure she nodded.

Since he wasn't handing her the keys, she slowly backed away, bumped into the mirror, and then worked her way to the door handle. "Um . . . are the keys in it?" she asked, even though she couldn't remember why she needed them.

Please stop staring at me so I can breathe, she wanted to shout.

Maybe . . . maybe she should stop staring at him.

She groped for the door handle, pulled on it, and the interior buzzer went off the moment the door opened.

Which meant the keys were in the truck.

So Maddy got in, too.

But her purse nearly made her fall back out when she sat on it.

It would probably help if she watched what she was doing instead of watching William watch her. She pulled her purse free and tossed it onto the passenger seat, then pulled the seat belt around and clicked it shut—all without taking her eyes off him, the loud ding of the key buzzer keeping pace with her thumping heart.

You can do this! she silently screamed, groping for the key and pulling it out just enough to stop the infernal beeping. *Stop looking at him! Just close the door and start the truck, and go . . . somewhere.*

Somewhere important, she thought.

She was also pretty sure that she had a time constraint.

But there was something else nagging at the back of her mind; something she was supposed to do first.

"Maddy!" Charlotte shouted from the entrance. "If you're

going to the docks, bring me back some rock seaweed so I can make us some more face cream."

Fairly sure she nodded again, Maddy finally managed to close the door and turn the ignition at the same time, starting the truck as she continued to stare at William staring at her—his marine-blue eyes gleaming in the hot August sun.

She groped at the window buttons when she suddenly remembered the something else she needed to do. She rolled down the rear window, realized her mistake, and rolled down her window.

"Um, are you still interested in that favor you asked for yesterday?"

His eyes grew guardedly intense, and he nodded ever so slightly.

Maddy took a deep breath. "Then . . . yes."

She'd intended to say more; something cheeky that she'd thought of last night as she'd lain in bed staring up at her ceiling. But when his eyes went from intense to downright dangerous—though he remained utterly still except to nod again—Maddy reversed the button and rolled her window back up.

She adjusted one of the vents to blow directly on her flaming face, pushed down on the brake, pulled the gearshift into drive, and slowly pulled away—not daring to glance out the window at him again.

She did look in her rearview mirror when she reached the road and saw William still standing there in the middle of the parking lot staring after her—his cuffs rolled up his sexy arms and his large, masculine hands balled into fists at his sides.

Chapter Seventeen

"*I*sn't she beautiful?" Charlotte asked, coming to stand beside him.

"She steals my breath," William managed to get out, still staring at the road even though Maddy had long since disappeared.

"She did it for you, you know, though I'm not sure *she* knows it," Charlotte said. "I believe our Maddy girl has taken a real shine to you."

Finally able to pull his gaze away from the road, William looked down at the aging sprite smiling up at him. "I believe I've taken a shine to her, as well."

Charlotte's worn face took on a few more wrinkles as she frowned. "Only she's terribly gun-shy, so you're going to have to be patient with her." She shook her head. "Lord knows we've all spent the last four years trying to crack that armor she's wrapped around herself, but Maddy's got a defense system the Pentagon would envy." She smiled again. "But then, that's a large part of her appeal. You let anyone try to mess with any of us here, and she'll break every rule on the books making sure the doctors and our families don't bully us into doing anything we don't want. And if you really want to piss her off, just try messing with her family. Sarah is Maddy's whole world, and so are her mother and her brother, Rick."

She chuckled gaily. "Why, I remember last fall when Rick got into some trouble at school; you'd have thought a three-day suspension was a death sentence for the boy. But Maddy was afraid Rick might lose his chance at a college scholarship." She shook her head. "I don't know what dirt she had on Principal Adams, but she ambushed him outside the supermarket one day, and the suspension mysteriously disappeared."

William suddenly stiffened, his gut twisting in a knot as he remembered seeing Maddy's braid of hair in her pocket as well as Trace's threat to cut it off if she attempted to mother Rick anymore.

Holy hell, she wasn't running an errand; she was going to war with her cousin!

He turned to Charlotte and took hold of her shoulders. "Did Katy just tell Maddy that Trace's boat is at the dock?"

"Yes, she did," Charlotte said, her eyes widening at his tone. "Maddy apparently called the harbormaster and asked him to let her know when her cousin was coming in to off-load his catch. I believe that's where she's going on her errand. That's why I asked her to bring me back some seaweed."

William gave her a quick kiss on her forehead. "Thank ye, sweet Charlotte, but I have to run now. We'll continue our conversation later, okay?"

"Okay," she said in surprise when he released her and ran to his motorcycle.

He slipped into his leather jacket but tossed the helmet on the grass instead of putting the damn thing on. He started the engine and shot out of the parking lot, only briefly glancing for traffic before speeding off toward the harbor.

Dammit to hell, something had gotten Madeline's under-pants in a twist all of a sudden, and he would bet his new mo-torcycle it concerned Rick.

But she had to go through Trace to get to the boy.

William wasn't worried Trace would harm her; it was Hunts-man he was concerned about!

He downshifted and turned onto the narrow lane leading down to the docks, just missing a truck loaded with shellfish as he skidded to a stop when he saw Maddy walking—no, *marching* down the ramp to the fishing boats off-loading their catches.

He flipped down the kickstand and started running. He reached the top of the ramp and came to a stop just in time to see Trace leap off his boat to intercept Maddy. William slowly walked down the ramp but stopped at the bottom, deciding to see how this played out before he chose sides.

"What are you doing here?" Trace asked, folding his arms over his chest.

"I need to talk to my brother."

Trace shook his head. "That's not going to happen, Peeps." He started to say more, but his eyes suddenly widened and he dropped his arms in surprise, taking a step back. "What in hell did you do to your hair!"

Maddy reached in her pocket and pulled out her braid. "I cut it before you could!" she snarled, slapping it against his chest, putting her whole body behind the blow and shoving him off the dock.

Huntsman grabbed the braid as he fell back with a grunt of surprise that turned to a shout of outrage when he hit the water. Maddy immediately scrambled onto the boat and grabbed Rick's arm as he ran toward the stern in disbelief.

"You dropped out of college!" Maddy cried as she spun him around to face her. She waved an envelope in his face. *"Per our phone conversation on August 19,* the letter says, *you are no longer enrolled in this semester's classes.* You dropped out of school!" she shouted, waving the letter at him again. "Why?"

"Because I don't want to go!" Rick shouted back. "I never wanted to go!"

"But without an education, you'll be stuck here the rest of your life." She grabbed his shirtsleeve and started dragging him toward the dock. "You are calling the university right now and telling them you've changed your mind."

He jerked out of her grasp. "No. This is *my* life we're talking about, not yours. I'm old enough to make my own decisions, and I've decided I'm not going. I don't want to work a nine-to-five job in some stupid office. I want to fish, just like Dad did," he said a little more softly, though still roughly.

Trace heaved himself out of the water and climbed over the stern, still clutching Maddy's braid in his hand. "Get off my boat, Maddy," he ground out. "Now!"

She swung toward him and started waving the envelope at Trace. "You put him up to this! Goddammit, Trace, he needs to go to college!"

"You walking off this boat or swimming?" he asked, advancing on her.

She actually took a step back, and William started forward. But he just as suddenly stopped when Rick shot around Maddy and placed himself between his sister and his cousin.

"Don't touch her," the boy said through clenched teeth, his hands balling into fists as he took up a defensive stance. "Or I swear I'll knock you flat on your ass."

Trace moved to go around him.

Rick took a wild, poorly aimed swing, the blow catching Trace on the side of the head and causing him to stagger backward.

Maddy screamed and grabbed Rick, trying to pull him away. "Are you nuts? Come on, let's get out of here!"

Rick shrugged her off and lifted his fists when Trace straightened.

Maddy tried to move around Rick to get between them, but the boy swept her back with his arm. "Stay back," he ground out, his attention on Trace. "Jesus, Maddy, why'd you piss him off like that?"

"Oh, I'm pissed, all right," Trace growled, shaking the braid at her. "You think this bought you the right to shove me in the water and then board my boat? I am shaving you *bald*."

Two other fishermen started toward Trace's boat, but William stepped into their path. "I believe this is a family matter, gentlemen," he said softly, making sure his tone spoke for him. "What say we let them work this out between themselves?"

While Trace was busy glaring at Maddy, Rick took another swing at him, this time catching the man square in the jaw. "Run, Maddy!" Rick screamed, reaching down and shoving a large coil of rope toward Trace's feet as he staggered backward again.

"Rick, come on!"

"I'm right behind you, sis!" he cried, grabbing another coil of rope and throwing it at Trace as he tried to catch his balance.

Maddy scrambled onto the dock and started running toward the ramp, but spotted William and ran to him instead. "Omigod! Do something!" she cried when she looked back and saw Trace had her brother cornered against the wheelhouse. She tugged on William's sleeve, pulling and then pushing him toward the boat. "You have to save Rick!"

William spun her around so her back was to him and wrapped his arms around her to stop her from going to save her brother herself.

"William!" she cried, stamping a foot. "You promised to be my strong arm!"

"I only promised to save you, not your brother," he said.

He gave her a squeeze when she started struggling, and leaned down to whisper in her ear. "Take a moment to see what's happening, Madeline. Ye already have a strong arm coming to your rescue. Did ye not notice how your brother put himself between you and Trace? Let him be your hero, Maddy, instead of you always being his."

She stopped struggling. "But Trace could really hurt him," she whispered, watching the two men face off against each other.

"Do ye honestly believe your brother's punch could have connected if your cousin hadn't allowed it?"

She sucked in a surprised breath. "He *let* Rick hit him?"

"And do ye not think that with his training, Huntsman didn't see your intention to push him in the water before you even decided to do it?"

"But why?" she asked, turning to look up at him.

"Because he loves you and your brother, lass. You're looking at the problem between you and Rick from *your* perspective, Maddy, where Trace sees both sides. Rick isn't a little boy anymore, and your cousin is trying to point that out to you."

She went limp in his arms, and William saw her shoulders slump.

"Decide, Madeline," he whispered against her hair, "if ye want to be Rick's mother or a sister he can look to for support."

She took a shuddering breath, and William opened his arms when he felt her spine stiffen. He watched her walk back down the dock to the boat.

"Leave him alone, Trace."

Huntsman turned to her and folded his arms over his chest. "Give me one good reason why I should let him get away with punching me."

"Because if you beat him up, you'll be fishing all by yourself."

Trace shrugged. "I'm going to be fishing alone in another week, anyway, when he heads off to college."

William watched Maddy glance toward Rick, then hold out the envelope to Trace. "He changed his mind and isn't going, because he wants to fish like our dad did."

Trace took the envelope from her and spread open the top, but instead of pulling the letter out, he glared up at her. "Isn't it against the law to open other people's mail?"

Maddy clasped her hands behind her back. "I guess I forgot. But I'm pretty sure I'll remember to never open his mail again."

Trace rubbed his jaw, squinting up at her. "I don't know. He did sucker-punch me—twice. And if I let him get away with it, my reputation will be shot."

She snorted at that. And then she sighed and looked over at Rick. "I'm sorry for not listening to you and for pushing you to go to college. It was my dream, not yours." She looked back at Trace. "You're allowed *one* free punch if you feel you need to save face, but you can't punch Rick."

Trace's eyes widened, and he took a step back. "You expect me to punch *you*?"

"William, will you let Trace punch me?" she called back over her shoulder, not even bothering to look at him.

"No, Madeline."

Still looking at Trace, she shrugged. "William keeps insisting on protecting me, so I guess you'll have to punch him instead."

William choked back a bark of laughter, wanting both to kiss Madeline and to throw her into the harbor. But he sobered right fast when Trace leaped onto the dock and headed toward him.

Huntsman stopped in front of him, his eyes shining with amusement, and held out his hand. "Here, I believe every strong arm needs a token from his lady," he said, handing him Maddy's braid of hair. Trace turned to his cousin. "If you don't mind, Peeps, I'm going to take a rain check on the free punch and save it for when you *really* piss me off. Come on, Killkenny," he said, heading up the ramp. "I need to get some dry clothes out of my truck. And rumor has it there's a madman racing through the streets of Midnight Bay on a motorcycle all hours of the day and night, and I don't know if you're aware of it, but I have a thing for fast bikes myself."

William looked back to see that Maddy was already standing in the boat, wrapped up in Rick's arms, softly weeping. He smiled at the realization she would be seeing her brother quite differently from now on, and followed Trace up the ramp.

"When did ye learn the boy didn't want to go to college?" he asked, moving up beside Trace.

"That night we had dinner at Maddy's, when I hunted him down and we had a little talk. He told me he'd saved up enough money working for an old fisherman all through high school to put a down payment on his own boat. His dad, actually, is the one who started the savings account with him about a year before he died."

Trace opened the door to his pickup and started stripping right there in the parking lot, using the door to block anyone's view. "Neither of them told Maddy or Patricia, because both women were determined the boy would go to college. And then, after their father died, Rick said he never told Maddy about the money because he was afraid she'd make him use it for tuition."

"Rick truly prefers fishing?" William asked.

"He's a completely different person when he's on the water. Hell, you'd think he'd hatched out of a lobster trap. He's sharp and confident and so damned focused it's scary. And he knows the industry better than most thirty-year veterans. I've actually been making a profit since he came onboard."

William glanced back toward the dock and saw Maddy and Rick sitting on the stern, simply talking.

"I've been waiting for Peeps to explode for days now," Trace continued, pulling a dry shirt down over his chest. "But her cutting her hair and effectively neutralizing my threat," he said with a chuckle, "well, I sure as hell didn't see that coming." He shot William a grin. "Any more than I anticipated she'd let you take the fall for her."

William returned his grin. "That one blindsided me as well." He looked down at her wet braid in his hand. "Though not nearly as much as her cutting her hair."

Trace sat inside the open door to pull off his boots. "I'm guessing the new hairdo had more to do with you than with me. So, what are you two lovebirds up to this weekend?" he asked, tossing his wet boots into the back bed of the truck. "Sarah's with Billy, so that leaves Maddy free for the next two days."

William gazed toward the dock again. "I'm not sure, actually. After what happened the other night, I have a feeling even suggesting we *go parking* in my truck is out of the question, much less up on the bluff at my house site."

Trace straightened from slipping into a dry pair of jeans and started threading his wet belt through the loops. "Well Christ, Killkenny, that's why they invented *motels*."

Chapter Eighteen

"You reserved us a cabin at Seashore Hideaway?" Maddy whispered, sinking down in her seat as she glanced around.

William frowned over at her. "Is there a problem?" he asked, looking at the office and then at the cabins scattered in a grove of tall oaks down by the ocean. "Trace said this was a clean, well-run establishment."

"You asked Trace to recommend a *motel*?" she squeaked, her face turning bright pink as she looked at him in horror.

"Nay, he's the one who suggested I bring ye to a motel, seeing how going parking no longer appears to be an option for us. What in hell's the matter, Madeline? I thought you'd be pleased to have a nice bed instead of an old cloth on the ground."

"But . . . but . . ." She waved toward the office even as she sank farther in her seat. "Samuel's daughter owns Seashore Hideaway. If she sees me here with you, she'll tell Samuel, and then everyone at the nursing home will know we . . . that you and I are . . . wait, you *told* Trace we're having an affair?"

William dropped his head onto the steering wheel with a

groan. "Christ's teeth, I don't think I've ever had so much trouble getting a lass out of her underpants," he muttered. Keeping his head on the wheel, he turned just enough to glare at her. "Maddy, darling," he said softly, not even caring if she heard the edge in his voice, "what do ye suggest we do, then? Because I'm still *hanging*."

Her eyes widened, her lips forming a perfect O.

William straightened with a heavy sigh and reached to start the truck.

Maddy covered his hand. "We'll stay here," she said huskily.

"I don't want to embarrass you to your residents." He smiled tightly. "I believe I've done quite enough of that already."

"You can go in and register while I wait in the truck," she said, still holding her hand over his. "Just make up a fictitious name for me and tell them I'm . . . your wife," she finished, her blush kicking up another notch.

"Are ye sure?"

"Yes, William, I'm sure." She gave him a slow smile. "And you don't have to worry about getting me out of my panties, because I'm not wearing any."

He sucked in a breath as his gaze snapped to her lap. "I'm glad ye didn't tell me that earlier," he growled thickly, "or there wouldn't have been a mailbox left standing between here and Midnight Bay."

She laughed at that, though a bit nervously, and pushed on his shoulder. "Go register. I'll just stay here and hide," she said, sinking back down in her seat.

Not giving her time to change her mind—or find another problem—William bolted from the truck and practically ran to the office. But he hesitated at the door. He'd been counting on Madeline to help him register, as he wasn't quite sure what was expected, not having dared to ask Mabel how one went about renting a place to spend a weekend of debauchery with a good friend of her daughter's.

He looked back at the truck and saw just the top of Maddy's head peeking at him, and waved at her and then walked inside. "I called this afternoon and reserved one of your cabins," he said to the woman behind the counter—who did look a bit like Samuel.

"Your name, please?" she asked, giving him a smile and then tapping a few keys on her computer.

"William Killkenny."

She glanced at him in surprise. "William Killkenny? Would you happen to be the gentleman my father's been telling me about? Samuel Keating? He lives at the River Run Nursing Home over in Midnight Bay."

William inwardly groaned even as he smiled at the woman. "I'm sorry; I don't know anyone named Keating. It must be another William Killkenny you're referring to."

She shrugged and hit a few more keys on the computer, and then held out her hand. "If you'll just give me your credit card, I'll run it through and give you your key. The reservation says you asked for two nights. Is that correct?"

"I don't have a credit card. I intend to pay with cash."

She blinked at him and dropped her hand. "Oh. Okay. Then I'll have to see your driver's license, Mr. Killkenny. The law requires I photocopy it, and keep it on file."

William reached in his back pocket, took out his wallet, and handed her the piece of paper they'd given him when he'd taken his written test.

She took it with a frown. "This is a learner's permit."

"I've only just recently moved here from Ireland."

Still frowning, she walked over to a machine on the side counter, slapped the paper onto a piece of glass, and pushed a button that made a bright light come on.

"This says you live in Midnight Bay," she said, reading his permit as she walked back with it and the piece of paper the machine had spit out. She looked at him again. "That's quite a co-incidence, there being two William Killkennys in Midnight Bay."

He merely shrugged, saying nothing.

She handed him back his permit and shot him what appeared to be a secretive smile. "We don't have many locals who stay here, at least not for two . . . whole nights."

William felt beads of sweat break out on his forehead. Why in hell did everything have to be so bloody difficult in this century? For chrissakes, all he wanted to do was bury himself in Madeline's softness. "The friends I've been staying with have company, and I offered to give up my bed," he said tightly.

She glanced out the window. "Are you alone, Mr. Killkenny?" She suddenly laughed. "Of course not, you need a licensed driver if all you have is a permit."

"My wife is with me."

She tapped a few more keys on her computer. "Her name?"

"Gwendolyn," he said, figuring he was well on his way to hell already, so he might as well speed up the journey by using his poor sainted mother's name.

While the woman typed "Gwendolyn" into her computer, William stuffed his permit back in his wallet. Another machine spit out two more pieces of paper, and she slid one toward him, along with a pen.

"Sign right here, Mr. Killkenny. That will be three hundred sixty-eight dollars and seventy-two cents." She smiled apologetically. "That's our summer rates, but they'll lower to off-season at the end of September . . . if you happened to find yourself needing a . . . bed again."

William took out four hundred dollars and handed it to her. "Keep the change," he said, snatching up the second sheet of paper, assuming it was his receipt like at the restaurants. He started for the door, just wanting to get the hell out of there. "Give the extra to the woman who cleans, if ye wish."

"Mr. Killkenny!" she called out. "Your key."

Dammit to hell. He spun around and strode back to the counter. "Thank ye."

"It's cabin seven, the last one on the right by the beach. There's coffee in the room, and breakfast is complimentary at our diner. Just show them your room receipt," she called after him.

He waved the receipt over his shoulder as he went out the door. "Thank ye."

He got in the truck and started the engine before he even finished settling into the seat. "Open the glovebox and put those boxes in your purse," he told Maddy, who was practically sitting on the floor now.

William forced himself to drive slowly down the narrow path toward the cabin.

"Ten?" Maddy suddenly squeaked, her gaze snapping to him. "You bought *ten* boxes of condoms?"

He pulled up beside cabin seven, shut off the engine, and looked at her. "That was all they had at the supermarket."

Her expression turned horrified again. "You walked into the Shop 'n Save in *town,* and bought *ten boxes of condoms*?" she said in a near shout.

William took all of the boxes out of the glovebox and stuffed one into his shirt pocket, and then shoved the others into her purse on her lap. "Get out of the truck, Madeline," he commanded softly, opening his door and getting out.

Seeing her staring at him through the windshield, wide-eyed and utterly still, he started around the front of the truck with every intention of carrying her inside. But she suddenly scrambled out, and slinging her heavy purse over her shoulder, scooted past him and ran up onto the porch.

William got the key out of his pocket, crammed it into the lock, and opened the door. He pulled her inside and pushed her back against the closing door. He covered her mouth with his own—not even flinching when her purse hit the floor.

She didn't balk or complain or get all shy on him all of a sudden; nay, she met his demand with a hunger that rivaled his own. Only instead of wrapping her arms around his neck, she pulled his shirttails out of his pants and started unbuckling his belt.

He gathered up fistfuls of material in his hands, wondering why in hell the woman kept wearing such long skirts. And what did he find when he finally got the hem high enough to slide his hands beneath it? As promised, he didn't find anything but soft, sweet flesh, and he splayed his hands over her bottom and pulled her to his groin.

Or at least he tried to; but not surprisingly, Madeline was in his way, busy shoving her own hands down the front of his pants. He actually shouted into her mouth when one hand cupped him, the other wrapping around his rock-solid shaft.

He stepped back, not releasing her luscious bottom, so that she came with him, and broke their kiss only long enough to find the bed. Prepared to ward off a wrestling match if she got it in her head to start fondling him again, William forced himself to give up the prize in his palms and took hold of her shoulders. He eased her back onto the bed and planted his palms on either side of her, using his knees to spread her thighs.

"Condom," she panted, reaching into the shirt pocket.

"Ye have three seconds to get it on," he ground out.

It took her five seconds just to get the damn packet open because her hands were shaking so badly, and William suffered through a good half-minute of sweet torture as she worked it down over him.

Not even sure if she had succeeded, but having reached the limit of his patience, he shoved her hands away so he could touch her intimately; and finding her sleek and wet and ready, he pushed into her. Her breath quickened, and she gave a long, keening moan. He pushed deeper at her sound of pleasure, his entire body humming with tension at the feel of her heat quivering around him.

"Are ye okay, Madeline?" he said through gritted teeth.

"Oh God, y-yes," she got out raggedly.

William bent at his elbows to bring his mouth close to hers. "Then hold on, lass," he whispered, his smile turning feral when her eyes suddenly widened in alarm.

But being a wise woman, Madeline clutched his arms, digging her fingers into his muscles as she braced herself. William pushed all the way into her, then withdrew, then thrust even deeper; slowly at first then with increasing speed. When he was certain she could handle him, he finally closed his own eyes to concentrate on the feel of her penetrating heat surrounding him.

He took her hard and fast, her cries of encouragement pushing him right up to but not quite over the edge of no return. He rose up to clasp her hips, pulling her into his thrusts. "Come for me, Madeline," he urged, spanning her hip bones and using his thumbs to spread her folds, exposing her to his ministrations.

"Now Madeline."

"Omigod, William!" she cried, her hands clutching his arms as she tossed her head, her soft curls sticking to her dampened face.

"Come, Madeline," he demanded, his own sweat dripping onto her clothes—which he hadn't even bothered to take off her.

As the first tremors of her climax shuddered around him, William felt his control slip another notch, and when she cried out and bucked upward, she finished pulling him into her maelstrom of ecstasy.

He could have wept, she felt so damn good clenching around

him. William held himself deeply inside her, letting her power-ful spasms rock him to his very core, and several centuries of torturous despair ended with his own raw shout of fulfillment.

He very carefully lowered himself onto his elbows, keeping enough weight off her so she could breathe, and threaded his fingers through her damp curls. He began kissing her cheeks and closed eyelids, savoring her lingering quivers as they con-tinued pulling at him deep inside her, and he started gently thrusting again.

"Again, Madeline," he whispered, nipping her earlobe as her hot breath fanned over his neck and shoulder, her ragged pant-ing pushing her still-confined breasts into his chest. "Again," he urged, increasing the speed and depth of his thrusts until he felt her begin to tighten around him with rebuilding tension.

He reared up—ignoring her protests, which soon turned to sounds of approval when he shed his shirt—and reached down and unbuttoned her blouse. He lifted her up and pulled it off her, only to find another one of those damned eye-poking undergarments. He smiled at the realization she was testing his threat, and while she was busy driving him crazy by running her tongue over his chest, he reached down to his boot and pulled out his knife. Three quick cuts at the band and straps, and he immediately laid her back and settled over her again, loving her kiss-swollen lips as he resumed gently rocking her with his thrusts.

"Come for me, Madeline," he whispered tightly, trailing his tongue down her neck, briefly stopping to sip at her racing pulse when she threw her head back. William continued his mouth's downward journey, pulling the offending garment off and tossing it away as he gently closed his teeth over one of her nipples.

She gave a husky moan, her legs jerking as she arched her back into him again, her fingers sharply kneading his ribs. He moved to her other breast, his thrusts forcing him to suckle her swaying flesh before finding her other nipple and pulling it into his mouth. She planted her feet, bucking her hips up to meet him, and her sheath tightened violently around his shaft as she cried out her pleasure. William went perfectly still, embedded deep inside her, and let her spasms finish draining him.

He very carefully pulled out and collapsed beside her with a groan of contentment, smiling when he looked over to see her peaked nipples rising and falling as she panted uncontrollably. He rubbed his own chest, turning to smile up at the ceiling as he pictured the claw marks she'd likely left on him.

"Y-you cut off my bra again," she raggedly whispered as she pulled her blouse over to cover herself.

Rolling to face her, William snatched it away and tossed it on the floor behind him. "I warned ye, lass. You keep putting them on and I'll keep cutting them off."

Her big, beautiful eyes widened, and except for her heaving chest—which she had covered with her hands now—she went perfectly still. "You're serious," she whispered.

"Aye," he said, pulling her hands away. "Do not hide your beauty from me, Madeline. Clothed or naked, a man desires to see his lover's curves." He used a finger to trace the shape of one plump, heavy breast. "It's the movement of your sweet curves that tempts a man, lass, and makes him hard with the thought of your soft flesh yielding to his. Do not hide from me the very thing that makes you a woman."

Her blush traveled down from her face to her neck and then spread across the very curves under discussion, and she tore her gaze from his to stare up at the ceiling, her ragged panting only now beginning to ease.

"Um . . . please don't take this the wrong way," she whispered, not looking at him. "But while we're on the topic of the do's and don'ts of our . . . our affair, I was wondering if you . . .

could please stop demanding that I come again before I'm even halfway recovered." She finally looked over, giving him a tentative smile. "I mean, really, it's very sweet and immensely generous of you to make sure that I'm having a good time and everything, but you're *killing* me."

"Sweet?" he said, propping his head on his hand to smile at her. "There ye go again, lass, thinking I'm sweet and thoughtful and generous, when I assure you, I am anything but." He arched a brow. "Have ye not considered that maybe your pleasure only serves to heighten mine, when you shudder around me with the force of storm waves crashing to shore?"

She blinked at him, apparently trying to decide if he was serious.

He ran his finger down the side of her face, down her damp neck, and down over the swell of her breast until he reached her nipple, which he then gently pinched, giving a chuckle when her breath quickened and she arched into his touch with a soft moan. "I'll settle for nothing less than *all* ye have to give me, Madeline," he continued thickly, palming the weight of her breast. He leaned down as he lifted it to his mouth, suckling the nipple before releasing it with a gentle pluck, causing her to moan and start panting all over again.

He rose over her, forcing her down onto the pillow, and brought his mouth to hover just slightly above her swollen lips as his eyes bore into hers. "And when ye think ye have nothing left to give, I'm going to demand even more, because that's my nature," he whispered. "Which should answer some of what ye asked me the other day; part of who I am is a demanding lover, and I require a woman who not only is strong enough to meet my demands, but also brave enough to accept that part of me."

He finally kissed her sweet lips, and then rolled onto his side again and propped his head on his hand to arch a brow at her again. "Any other questions or complaints?"

She rolled toward him, her expression unreadable as she stared at him for several heartbeats and then finally shook her head.

William planted a light but loud slap on her luscious bottom, giving a satisfied grunt at her gasp of surprise, and rolled off the bed. "Ye have exactly five minutes to *recover*," he said over his shoulder as he walked to the bathroom. "And while you're at it, ye might as well get the other boxes out of your purse and set them on the table beside the bed."

Chapter Nineteen

"*M*adeline," William said, giving her rump a shake. "I need ye to wake up, lass."

Maddy flailed out trying to swat him away, wondering if murder by sex was a prosecutable crime. Honest to God, she very well *could* die if they made love one more time. "Ten more minutes," she muttered into her pillow, too tired even to open her eyes.

"Up, Madeline," he said more insistently. "Now."

She felt the blanket being pulled off her, and groped to catch it. "Did you take Viagra or something?" she growled, rearing up to chase after the blanket. "There isn't a man alive who should be able to—" She snapped her mouth shut when she saw he was fully dressed, his hair wet from the shower. "What's going on?" she asked in alarm, looking at the bedside clock to see it was two in the morning.

"I need ye to get up and get dressed. There's a storm coming, and I'm taking you to An Tèarmann."

Maddy dropped her head in her hands with a groan. "These

cabins have been standing here for fifty years, William; I think they'll survive another storm."

He lifted her up by the shoulders, stood her on her feet, and turned her facing the bathroom before she could yelp in surprise. "Ye have five minutes to shower and get dressed," he said, grabbing onto her shoulders again when he realized her legs wouldn't work, and then guiding her through the door.

She finally woke up enough to walk out of his hands. "I am getting damn tired of you bossing me around," she grumbled, closing the door none too gently.

"Get used to it, lass," he said, his muffled reply accompanied by a chuckle.

Maddy blinked at herself in the mirror, and raised her hand to touch her swollen lips. Holy hell, she looked like she'd been loved to death. She trailed her fingers down her neck, stopping at the pale mark right over her pulse, and then let her gaze stray down to her breasts. She suddenly smiled, trying to remember the last time her body had carried the evidence of being so . . . *ravished* was the only word that came to mind; she looked as if she'd been thoroughly and expertly ravished.

"I'm not hearing the water running," he said through the door.

"Hold your horses, I'm still waking up," she muttered, turning on the shower. *And trying to move without wincing*, she refrained from adding.

Good Lord, she really was going to have to start working out if she wanted to keep up with him. Not that she hadn't done a bit of ravishing herself, she thought with a satisfied smile, stepping under the spray with a moan of pleasure. She'd been quite prepared for William when he had returned from the bathroom beautifully naked and obviously ready for round two.

Maddy lathered her short curls with the motel shampoo, pleasantly surprised by how easy it was to wash her hair now.

If William had thought his little speech—or had it been a threat?—about being a demanding lover was going to intimidate her, he'd soon learned differently. She'd pounced on him the moment he'd crawled into bed, and if he'd been wearing stockings . . . well, they would have been blown all the way to Ireland.

The condoms were definitely a pain in the ass though, and first thing Monday morning she was calling her doctor and either going on the pill or having an IUD put in.

"Three minutes, Madeline."

Jeesh, what was his problem? Did her big hulking *strong arm* have a phobia about storms? She frowned, ducking her head under the spray to rinse off. She didn't remember the weather man mentioning anything about rain. She shut off the water and stepped out, quickly drying off and wrapping the towel around her, frowning again when she realized that she had a blouse and skirt to put on, and that was all.

"You are such a slut," she muttered, even as she grinned at herself in the mirror. She liked feeling slutty, she decided, as well as desired by a man who obviously knew his way around a woman's body.

She flipped on the blow dryer. William certainly had learned more about *her* body in the past six hours than her ex-husband had learned in four years. Poor Sissy. She snorted; then again, maybe Billy was the one she should pity.

The bathroom door opened. "Ye don't have time to dry your hair," he said, taking the dryer and shutting it off. He held out her blouse and skirt. "Get dressed."

Instead of taking the clothes, Maddy clasped his face and pulled him down. "Don't worry; you won't melt in the rain," she whispered, just before she kissed him.

He apparently wasn't in such a hurry that he couldn't kiss her back. He wrapped his arms around her and deepened the kiss, and Maddy felt every last one of her overworked hormones rally to attention with a groan. But he suddenly stepped away and headed back into the room—taking her towel with him!

"One minute, Madeline, and you're getting in the truck, dressed or not."

She didn't even bother to close the bathroom door; she just snapped out her skirt and bent over to slide her feet into the waistband, facing the room and making sure her dangling anatomy was visible to him—pretending not to notice him watching her.

It was as she was picking up her blouse that she noticed that the trash can in the bathroom was full. She slipped into her blouse and started buttoning it, frowning down at the can. "Why are all the unused boxes of condoms in the trash?"

"Because I threw them in there," he said, coming to stand in the doorway.

"But why?"

"Because the damn things are more bother than they're worth. They're such thin little pieces of nothing that over half of the ones we did use tore apart."

"They tore when you were taking them off, you mean?" she whispered, still staring down at the trash can.

"Nay, while we were *using* them."

Maddy felt all the blood drain from her face, and had to grab the sink when her knees buckled.

"I was willing to wear them because ye felt they would keep you from getting with child, but I see no reason to continue using them if they're not going to work."

They'd torn *during* sex?

"Come on," he said, taking her hand, carrying her purse and sandals. "I want you to drive." He led her outside barefoot, stopping only long enough to close the door behind them before dragging her down the steps and to his truck.

She pulled away when he opened the driver's door, having to grab her skirt when a powerful gust of wind suddenly lifted it. "I think you better drive," she said, backing away. "I'm not . . . I can't . . ."

They'd torn *during* sex?

"Madeline," he said, pulling her into his embrace. "There's nothing to be afraid of, lass," he whispered, his arms tightening when she started to tremble. "We can still get to An Tèarmann before it hits."

She bunched his shirt in her fists with a sob. "They tore *during* sex!"

"What in hell are ye talking about?" He set her away, but only so he could toss her in the driver's seat. "Come on, you can talk about what's bothering ye while you drive," he said, closing her door and running to get in the passenger side.

Maddy stared through the windshield at the black, churning ocean.

"Madeline!" he snapped. "Drive."

She flinched, then started the truck, put it in reverse, and cut the wheel and shot backward. She just as quickly slammed on the brakes, but not quickly enough to avoid hitting a large tree, which made the truck bounce with the impact.

"Maddy, darling," he said, reaching out and taking hold of the back of her neck, his thumb covering her racing pulse. "I really need ye to focus on what you're doing right now, lass," he said gently. "I'll fix whatever is bothering you tomorrow, I promise. Take a deep breath, put it in gear, and slowly drive up to the main highway."

She obediently took a deep breath, pulled the shift lever down to drive, and turned the wheel and drove up the narrow winding path.

"Good girl," he said calmly, his thumb giving her still-racing pulse a caress before he took his hand away.

She pulled out onto the main highway, and then had to turn on the wipers when they drove into a deluge of rain that pelted the truck in wind-blown sheets. He wasn't going to be able to fix anything tomorrow, because the damage was already done. Maddy tried to remember the date of her last period but instead found her mind trapped in her kitchen ten years ago, when she'd told her parents she was pregnant with Billy Kimble's baby—and the look of utter disappointment that had crossed her father's face before he'd gotten up from the table to go watch the news.

"Could ye speed up a bit, lass?" William asked, his voice still gentle but edged with urgency. "It's okay, Maddy. Whatever's wrong can be fixed."

"The condoms broke, William." She took a shuddering breath. "And I could be getting pregnant this very minute," she whispered, briefly glancing over at him. "How are you going to fix that?"

"If you are with child, then we'll get married."

Maddy swiped at a tear running down her cheek. "Yes, let's do that, seeing how it worked out so well for me the last time."

"I am not your ex-husband, Madeline."

"No, you're worse." She swiped at her eyes and shook her head. "I-I can't go through that again," she whispered, more to herself than to him.

His hand returned to her neck, his fingers splaying through her hair. "There's also a very good chance that we didn't make a child tonight, lass. But if we did, we will deal with it together."

"Look out!" she suddenly cried, slamming on the brakes when an animal shot across the path of the truck, another one right behind it. "Omigod! It's those wolves!" She stomped down on the accelerator. "William, they're back!"

He opened the console between them and pulled out a handgun that made hers look like a peashooter. "Just keep driving," he told her, working the action to load it.

"Y-you don't happen to have silver bullets in there, do you?" she asked with a semihysterical laugh as she glanced in her rearview mirror.

"What are ye talking about?"

She was traveling way too fast for her headlights, especially considering that she couldn't see more than a hundred yards because it was raining so hard, but she figured she'd just as soon run over one of those wolves, anyway. And since this conversation was a tad better than their previous one, though no less frightening, she decided to go with it. "The only way to kill a vampire is either to drive a stake through its heart or shoot it with a silver bullet; so I'm guessing they'd both work on werewolves."

"Werewolves?"

Lightning was flashing almost continuously now; brightly enough that she could see the trees bending in the wind, but the deafening rain was too loud to hear any thunder. Gusts strong enough to rock the truck were starting to hit with increasing frequency, sometimes nearly pushing them off the pavement. "Werewolves are really men who turn into demon wolves at night, and come out searching for human prey."

"Works for me," he muttered, glancing over his shoulder to look out the rear window. He turned back to face forward. "We're nearing town. There's no one on the road tonight, so don't even slow down."

She gave another hysterical laugh, her knuckles starting to ache from clutching the wheel as she worked to avoid the branches littering the road. "Gee, I should be getting really good at this by now. Oh shit, look out!" she screamed, cutting the wheel and hitting the brakes when the headlights illuminated a huge oak tree lying across the road in the town square.

"Go around! Drive right through the top branches."

Only as she stomped down on the accelerator to push

through the tangle of branches, another large tree crashed down onto the hood of the truck, bringing them to such an abrupt stop that both airbags exploded.

"Christ almighty, what in hell was that!" William shouted, slapping at the bag in front of him. "Maddy, are you all right?" he asked loudly over the rain pelting the roof, his hand groping her shoulder. "Madeline!"

"I-I'm okay," she said in a daze, feeling her face. Finding her nose was bleeding but at least still where it belonged, she reached out to William and gave him a pat. "Are you okay?"

"What just exploded in our faces?" he asked, tugging on the deflated material and eventually ripping it away.

"Those are airbags; they pop out when you crash, so your face hits them instead of the dash or steering wheel." She pushed her own airbag out of her way and felt around for the button to turn on the interior lights. But she hesitated; though the engine had died in the crash—likely because a massive branch had folded the hood nearly in half—one headlight was still shining, allowing her to see they were almost completely surrounded by the thick limbs of a large oak tree. The windshield was severely cracked on William's side, but it hadn't shattered all the way through.

"Um . . . do you want me to turn on the interior lights?"

"Nay, not yet. Are ye sure you're okay? Are ye bleeding anywhere?"

"My nose is bleeding, but not badly," she said, using the airbag to wipe it and then shoving the material through the steering wheel out of her way. "Do you want me to turn on the cargo light, so we can see behind us? Maybe I can back us out . . . if I can get the truck started again."

But before he could answer her, a loud, keening howl sounded to their right—really, really close—and Maddy sucked in a whimpering breath.

The one remaining headlight blinked out, plunging them into total darkness except for the red glow of the rear taillights reflecting off the rain-soaked leaves behind them.

Maddy screamed when the truck suddenly rocked, and she could just make out four large canine paws standing on the hood right in front of them, a vicious snarl raising the hairs on her neck.

"Don't move," William whispered, having leaned closer so she could hear him over the sound of the rain. He slowly groped for her hand and shoved her purse in it. "Get out your gun and put a shell in the chamber. Can ye do that, Madeline?"

"Y-yes."

"But don't shoot unless they actually make it inside. I don't want the bullet to finish shattering the glass."

"T-they?"

"There's another one on my side and one more working its way through the branches in front of us. When I tell ye, turn on the cargo light in the back, and we'll see what they think of that."

"We'll see—but what if it pisses them off?" she asked, dropping her purse on the floor in order to work the action on her gun.

He patted her knee. "You're doing excellent, Madeline. Okay, turn on the light."

But just as she was reaching for the button, a snapping mouth and two huge paws leaped out of the leaves and slammed into her window. Maddy screamed and tried to bring her gun up, but William covered it with his hand. "Don't shoot!"

She started quietly sobbing, her entire body wracked with tremors. "Wh-what are they? Why are they after us?"

"Steady, Madeline. You're safe inside the truck."

The snarls were suddenly overridden by a bone-chilling roar, just as something heavy landed on the roof of the cab, rocking the truck again.

"T-that wasn't a wolf," Maddy stammered—only to scream when whatever was on the roof landed on the wolf on the hood.

And as the truck shook and shuddered, it looked to Maddy like the mother of all cat and dog fights was taking place not three feet in front of her.

"Yes, take that, ye bastards!" William shouted. "Let's see how ye like dealing with a soul warrior!" He squeezed Maddy's arm when she screamed again, when the two fighting animals slammed into the windshield as the wolf tried scrambling up over the cab to get away. "You're going to be okay now, lass. Help has arrived."

"H-help?" she hoarsely sobbed. "William, that . . . it's . . . that's a *panther*!"

More yelps sounded over the pounding rain, and the leaves shook and the truck shuddered violently. Something slammed into the back fender, and what sounded like an angry feline hiss was followed by several more yelps moving away.

It stopped raining so suddenly it was like someone had shut off a faucet, and the air outside the truck started to glow an eerie green. Maddy whimpered again when the truck rocked, and she turned in her seat to see . . . to see . . .

"W-William, is t-that a tiger?" she whispered in the stark silence, staring at what looked like the mother of all Bengal tigers sitting in the back bed of the truck, staring at them through the rear window. Its head was nearly as wide as the whole back window, its sharp green eyes the size of tea saucers; and when it opened its mouth to run its tongue lazily over its snout, Maddy saw fangs longer than her fingers.

"William," she whimpered, slinking down in her seat.

"Easy," he said just as softly. "He's not here to harm us."

"Y-you *know* him?"

He studied her face. "He's an old friend, Madeline, and he's on our side."

She blinked at him. "We have a side?"

William actually grinned at her and reached out and squeezed her hand—the one that still happened to be holding her gun. "Aye, lass—the good side."

The truck suddenly started rocking back and forth, and Maddy looked over her seat to see the tiger make a circle and then suddenly lie down with a yawn.

And then she heard the passenger door open.

"William!" she hissed, grabbing his arm. "What are you doing?"

He got out, practically dragging Maddy with him because she refused to let go of his shirtsleeve, even as she stole a frantic glance at the bed of the truck. William turned as soon as his feet hit the ground, and very gently pried her hand off.

"It's okay, Madeline. He'll protect you while I'm gone."

"Gone? But you can't *leave* me here!"

"I have to go after Ke—the panther. You'll be perfectly safe, I promise. Just stay in the truck until I come back for you."

"William, no!" she cried, reversing their grip and trying to pull him back inside. She looked back and saw the tiger watching them intently, although it was still lying down. "Please don't go out there. Those wolves could come back."

He shoved his pistol in his belt and took hold of her wrist, and gently pried himself loose. He then opened the back door, reached behind the seat, and pulled out his antique sword— only now it was in a leather sheath with long straps. He closed the rear door and stepped back to look in at her as he slid the straps over his shoulder, settling the sword diagonally across his back. He smiled. "I wouldn't leave ye if I wasn't certain you are safe here, Madeline. But I really need to go help the panther."

"Why can't *he* go help the panther?" she asked, nodding toward the tiger.

"Because he's not allowed to, lass." He started to close the door but hesitated. "You stay put until I get back, ye understand? Lock the doors and don't open them for . . . anything. And Madeline?"

"What," she snapped, glaring at him.

He smiled. "Whatever ye do, don't shoot the tiger."

Chapter Twenty

$\mathscr{M}$addy held her breath as she watched William force his way through the branches, stopping only to look the tiger in the eye and give it a nod—to which the tiger nodded back!—before he disappeared into the oak leaves glistening in the eerie green light. Maddy collapsed over the console and buried her face in her hands with a shuddering sob, unable to believe he had left her.

Alone.

With a *tiger*.

This had to be some stupid, bizarre dream.

Yeah, that's what this was. It was really last night, not to-night, and she was in her bed at home, having fallen asleep while trying to decide if she wanted to have an affair with William. And she was so afraid she might fall in love with him that she'd dreamed up this bizarre scenario. First he would try to kill her with amazing sex—because only in her dreams could a guy have that kind of stamina—and then he'd leave her alone in a truck with a man-eating tiger that was supposedly going to protect her from man-eating wolves.

Oh, and why not throw in a large black panther—which William simply *had* to go help—just to make things really interesting.

She cried harder, her loud sobs echoing in the stark silence of the truck.

Until she heard what sounded like slurping. Maddy slowly sat up, turned in her seat, and saw the tiger's large tongue *licking* the rear window.

He stopped to stare at her.

Only she couldn't stifle an involuntary sob, and the tiger licked the window again.

She sucked in her breath and held it, and he stopped.

And then she screamed when music suddenly started blaring, and pulled her legs up with a whimper when something moved against her bare feet on the floor.

Finally realizing it was her cell phone ringing and vibrating, Maddy snatched up her purse, dug around inside it, and found the phone. Glancing over to see the tiger's intense eyes focused on her, she opened the phone, praying to God it was William.

"Hello," she whispered tightly. "Maureen?" she squeaked, keeping a wary eye on the tiger. "What? He thinks he's starting to die *now*?"

The tiger perked up, and Maddy lowered her voice. "He can't, Maureen. You tell Hiram he has to wait until morning to start dying."

Maureen, the weekend night nurse at River Run, went silent, and Maddy realized just how absurd that had sounded. "Look," she said, closing her eyes and hanging her head. "I really, really can't get there for . . . until after sunrise," she told her, assuming that when the sun came up, everything—including her affair with William *and* the torn condoms—would evaporate into the ether where they belonged.

"Is he really dying, or could he have just had a bad dream?"

she asked, figuring there might be an epidemic of nightmares going around. "Have you called Dr. Petty? No, I realize he has the DNR order, but we need an order for pain medication if . . . if he needs it. Petty needs to come in."

She sighed again. "Okay, look; you tell Hiram that I will be there just as soon as I can. And Maureen? If he starts having pain, could you . . . oh, never mind. I'll try to find a way to get there," she finished, closing the phone.

She simply couldn't bring herself to ask Maureen to dispense that kind of medication without a written order. Maddy dropped her head into her hands and quietly started sobbing again. What in hell was she supposed to do now?

She'd given her word to be there for Hiram, but she was stuck in this stupid truck with a stupid tiger, abandoned by a man who'd promised to be there for *her*.

Oh God, she didn't want Hiram to die!

She wanted all of her residents to live forever, so they could keep badgering her into being a better person. Every day she went to work was an adventure; somebody would do or say something outrageous that would make her keel over in laughter, all of them worse than Sarah when it came to making her stay one step ahead of them.

They kept her sharp and grounded; and like William, she valued their wisdom.

And, by God, she'd promised Mr. Man, and no stupid wolves or stupid tiger were going to stop her from keeping her word. And if William Killkenny thought she was going to just sit here in his stupid smashed truck while he ran off to battle evil forces . . . well, he was about to discover there was a *wee* bit more to the woman he wanted to have an affair with than just a bunch of horny hormones.

Maddy started looking around for her sandals, and thanks to the eerie green light she found them on the backseat. She slipped them on, crawled over the console into the passenger seat, and opened the door a crack—all the time watching the tiger.

It immediately sat up.

She just as immediately pulled the door shut.

The truck rocked when the big cat jumped out of the bed on the passenger side, and Maddy hit the button to *lock* the door.

Standing on the ground now, its head level with the window, the tiger stared at her; its ears perked forward, its breath fogging the window, and the tip of its pink tongue lolling out between its monstrous fangs.

Well, shit. How come it let William walk right by without paying him any mind, but when she tried to get out, the damn cat decided to get out of the truck, too?

"Go away. Shoo," she said, waving it away, her voice sounding unusually loud in the eerie silence. "Go haunt someone else's nightmare."

It started licking the glass.

Maddy hung her head to stare down at the gun in her hand. *Don't shoot the tiger,* William had said.

But the tiger was stopping her from getting to Hiram.

Well, it and a bunch of demon wolves.

The passenger door suddenly opened—even though she honest to God had *locked* it—and Maddy scrambled back across the console with a frantic yelp, hitting her hip on the steering wheel and banging her head into the driver's window. She brought her gun up even before she'd finished righting herself, but the tiger was gone.

And now she didn't know if she was relieved or even more terrified.

The leaves rustled just outside the door, and she could see its fat tail sticking out between the branches, and just barely make out its sharp green eyes staring back over its shoulder at her. It made a soft snuffling sound and moved slightly deeper into the tree—taking the eerie green light with it.

"No, come back! I promise I won't shoot you. Just don't abandon me, too!"

It made that gentle sound again—half purr, half woof, and sort of . . . encouraging.

Maddy climbed back over the console and slid her feet to the ground. Keeping her gun raised, she looked around the dark foliage and tangle of tree branches and took a shuddering breath just as she heard a few drops of rain hit the roof of the truck.

The nursing home was less than a quarter-mile away, across the library lawn and just up the side road. "Wait!" she called to the cat, turning to get her purse. "I have to leave William a note, or I'll never hear the end of it," she muttered, deciding that talking to a tiger had to be less insane than talking to herself. "But please don't start talking back to me," she whispered as she dug in her purse for something to write on.

She glanced over her shoulder. "Don't leave," she pleaded, actually holding up the pen and a paycheck stub. "I'll just be a second, I promise."

Seeing that the cat was still standing there, its eerie green glow illuminating her side of the truck—the driver's side being pelted with wind-blown rain now—Maddy quickly scribbled her note: "Gone to nursing home."

She leaned in and set it on the console, slung her purse over her shoulder, and turned to the tiger. After checking to make sure the safety on her gun was on, she took a deep breath and started fighting her way through the branches toward the library.

As soon as she broke free of the tree and stepped onto the soggy lawn, she immediately thought of the very first time she'd met William. It had been raining then, too, and he'd walked out of the library with Eve's mother in his arms, right after a blinding flash of white light had lit up every window in the three-story building.

The same building everyone had been pointing rifles at because they claimed a dragon had been seen carrying Mabel inside.

A dragon no one had seen since.

Rain started pelting Maddy's back, and the wind lifted her skirt. "Dammit, wait up," she called out, running to catch up to the tiger ambling across the library lawn as if it *knew* where she was going. She peered into the darkness surrounding them, able to see the wind was still blowing and that it was still raining buckets—except inside the bubble of green light.

"N-nice cat," she whispered, following it. "You're a really big fellow, aren't you?"

The damn cat had to weigh as much as a moose, and she guessed that if it decided to eat her, she'd be gone in one gulp. "M-my little girl, Sarah, would love to meet you," she said, needing to fill the silence so she wouldn't hear her mind screaming that she was crazy. "We've been reading *The Chronicles of Narnia,* and you sort of remind me of one of the main characters, Aslan. Only he's a lion, not a tiger."

Maybe that was why she had panthers and tigers and wolves in her nightmare; she'd been reading a book about talking animals. "But Aslan could talk," she added.

The tiger suddenly stopped. Maddy actually bumped into its tail and immediately scurried back with a squeak. It turned its massive head, and honest to God, it looked as if it was scowling at her.

She backed all the way to the edge of the light, until she felt raindrops hitting her shoulders. "Hey, I didn't write the book, C. S. Lewis did. I'm just telling you what Lewis did in his . . . story. I really don't mind that you can't talk in my dream. In fact, I'd probably freak out if you did." She smiled. "You have really

beautiful eyes, you know that?" she said, figuring a little flat-
tery wouldn't hurt. "And the prettiest stripes I've ever seen on a
tiger."

Not that she'd ever seen a real live tiger before.

"Um . . . do you think we could get going? Hiram's *dying*,"
she said, taking a hesitant step forward.

The cat made that snuffling sound again and started walking
toward the street. Maddy ran to catch up but suddenly stopped
when the tiger leaped over the ditch separating the lawn from
the road. Water was gushing from the torrential rain, and seeing
that it had to be at least two feet deep and four feet across, she
decided there was no way she'd be able to jump it.

"Wait!" she shouted when the cat started walking up the street.

It stopped and looked back at her.

"I can't make it."

Honest to God, she'd swear the tiger sighed. It finally walked
back to her, turned around, and stuck its tail across the ditch.

"You expect me to *grab a tiger by the tail*?" she said somewhat
hysterically, even as she slowly reached out and touched it.

The end of the thick tail suddenly curled around her wrist
and gave her a gentle tug toward the ditch.

"Wait!" she cried again, groping to shove her gun in her
purse. She took hold of the tail with both hands. "Okay. On the
count of three, I'm going to jump and—"

She hadn't even finished giving her instructions when she
suddenly went sailing across the ditch, landing halfway into
the street on the other side. "Holy shit!" she yelped, untangling
the tail from around her wrist. "Th-thank you."

The tiger started trotting up the street, and Maddy ran to
keep up, weaving her way around large fallen branches, being
careful not to slip on the wet leaves littering the pavement. "Just
as soon as I wake up, I'm going to write all this down," she told
him. "I'm sure this would make a best-selling book!"

They reached the nursing home, jogged side by side across the parking lot and stopped at the entrance. "Okay, as much as I would love to bring you inside," she said, pulling her gun out of her purse, "I don't think that's such a good idea." She dropped the magazine of bullets out of the handle and tucked it in her purse. "I know, maybe you could go help William and that panther, seeing how I'll be all safe inside." She worked the action, popping the bullet out of the chamber, but it fell onto the ground and rolled right between the tiger's massive front paws.

Without even thinking about what she was doing, Maddy bent down, and using her shoulder to nudge the big cat out of her way, she scoffed up the bullet—only to jump back in surprise when she felt a rough, warm tongue lick the side of her face.

"Omigod! Was that a kiss or a *taste*?"

The cat made that feline woofing sound again, and turned around and sat down facing the parking lot.

"Okay," she said, inconspicuously wiping the side of her face. "You just sit right here until William comes looking for me, if you want." She shoved her gun into her purse. "I have to go now. Thank you for bringing me here . . . Mr. Tiger." She put her hand on the door but hesitated. "If you ever find yourself on Back Ridge Road, you stop by my house and I'll give you some . . . meat or something. Good-bye, now," she said when he didn't even bother to turn around.

She went inside and ran down the softly lit hall, stopping at Hiram's open door and taking a steadying breath before she stepped inside.

Maureen turned in her chair and immediately stood up when she saw Maddy. "He's napping right now," she said, walking to the door and leading Maddy back into the hall. "His pulse is weak, and his breathing is shallow, but he doesn't seem to be in any pain."

Maddy took a relieved breath and wiped her hand over her face. "Okay; I'm going to change into my spare set of scrubs, and then I'll sit with him. Does . . . is everyone else still asleep?" she whispered.

"Yes. And I called Doris to let her know, though I ended up having to call her cell phone like I did you, because it appears this section of town is the only part with power. But she called back and said she couldn't come in because the storm's knocked trees down all over, and the electricity's out in most of town."

"What about Dr. Petty? Were you able to get hold of him?"

Maureen shook her head. "No. The main line to Ellsworth must be down. I couldn't even get his answering service. I tried the hospital but couldn't get through to them, either." Her eyes worried, Maureen hugged herself. "It's like Midnight Bay is cut off from the rest of the world."

Maddy patted her arm. "At least you're not alone anymore. You go in and sit with Hiram in case he wakes up, and I'll relieve you as soon as I change."

"But how did *you* get through the storm?"

"I . . . um, I made it as far as the library and ran the rest of the way."

"Then why aren't you soaked? It's raining cats and dogs out."

Maddy blinked at her, then merely shrugged and headed down the hall. *More like wolves and tigers and panthers,* she was tempted to say. "I'll be right back. If he wakes up, tell him I'm here," she called softly over her shoulder.

She went into the room behind the nurses' station and opened a cabinet where she kept an entire change of clothes, including sneakers. She pulled her panties up under her skirt, then her scrub pants, and then stepped out of the skirt. Turning her back to the door, she slipped out of her blouse and put on her bra, then pulled her top down over her head as she turned back to the cabinet—giving a quiet shriek when she saw a man standing at her nurses' station, smiling at her.

He looked to be in his early forties; tall, broad-shouldered, and casually dressed in a rich golden polo shirt. His hair was deep auburn and quite short, and his sharp green eyes were crinkled at the corners of his tanned, chiseled face.

"Can I help you?" Maddy asked, wondering how long he'd been watching her.

"My car is in the ditch down the street," he said with a slight accent she couldn't place, "and this was the only building with lights on." He looked up and down the hall, then at her. "Is this a home for the elderly?"

"Yes." She stuffed her purse in the cabinet, then grabbed her socks and sneakers and walked out to the station. "It's the River Run Nursing Home."

He nodded. "Would you mind if I hung out here with you folks until the storm eases, or at least until morning when I can get a tow truck?"

Maddy sat down and started dressing her feet. "Sure, we don't mind. We can even scare you up a cup of coffee if you'd like." She nodded across the hall. "We have a sitting room and a television, so just make yourself at home."

He thrust his hand across the counter when she stood up. "Dr. Lewis."

Instead of shaking his hand, Maddy grabbed it like a lifeline. "As in a medical doctor who's able to write prescriptions?"

He looked at her curiously. "As in a doctor who would need a good reason to write one."

"I have every hope you won't have to, but we have a dying patient, and . . . well, I promised Hiram we could give him something if he starts feeling any pain."

"Have you called an ambulance?"

She finally let go of his hand when she realized she was still clutching him and shook her head. "He has a DNR order; he's ninety-one, and he seems to just be shutting down. Maureen tried calling our regular doctor but she couldn't get through to anyone."

"Would you mind if I see his chart? I would need to see the DNR, and I'd like to read up on him before I prescribe anything."

Maddy looked in the stand, didn't see Hiram's chart, but then she found it open on the lower counter right in front of her. "His name is Hiram Fields, and other than occasional bouts of forgetfulness, he's in amazingly good health," she said, handing him the chart. "Or he had been until yesterday, when he complained of feeling unusually tired."

Maddy started to ask Dr. Lewis to see his credentials but then suddenly changed her mind. She didn't want to know if he was a certified doctor or not right now; that way she could always say she forgot in the heat of the moment later, if anyone asked. Just as long as he wrote the order on Hiram's chart and was well on his way to wherever he was going before anyone checked, they would all be covered. And she was willing to do anything, even jeopardize her own license, to keep Hiram comfortable.

"Would you like to see my credentials?" he asked, setting the chart down and reaching toward his back pocket.

Dammit, had the guy read her mind? Maddy shook her head and walked around the counter into the hall. "There will be plenty of time for that later," she said, heading toward Hiram's room. "And hopefully, we won't need an order from you."

He fell into step beside her. "If you don't mind, I'd like to meet Mr. Fields."

"Oh, of course." She stopped in the doorway and motioned to Maureen.

"Maureen, this is Dr. Lewis," she said when the older woman approached, her expression curious. "His bad luck just happens to be our good luck. Dr. Lewis's car is in the ditch, and he came here when he noticed we still had power. He's a medical doctor, and he'd like to take a look at Hiram."

Dr. Lewis gave Maureen a slight nod and then walked into the room.

Maureen stopped Maddy from following. "A stranded motorist walks in here, and he just happens to be a doctor?" she whispered. "Did you check his credentials?"

"Not yet, but I will if Hiram needs anything."

"How come he isn't soaked from the rain, either?" she asked, looking upward, where they could both hear the rain pounding the roof.

Maddy went perfectly still. *More important, how did he get past the tiger?*

"Wait right here," she said, running down the hall to the entrance. She grabbed the corner to swing around it and came to a sliding stop at the door.

The tiger was gone.

Maddy opened the door and was blasted by gale-force winds and driving rain that blew under the wooden canopy. She immediately stepped back inside.

Where in hell had the tiger gone?

She walked down the hall, hoping it had gone to help William do . . . whatever William was doing.

"What were you looking for?" Maureen asked.

Maddy shrugged. "I thought I heard someone knocking on the door. Why don't you go in the kitchen and see if you can't find us a snack? Is there any coffee on?"

"No, but I'll make a new pot while I'm at it." Maureen hesitated and touched Maddy's arm. "I know how much Hiram means to you, Maddy," she said softly, her eyes sad. "Every weekend, all he does is talk about his Maddy girl, and tonight, as I tucked him into bed, he told me how your new hairdo made your eyes look as big as dinner plates. I . . . I'm sorry."

Maddy patted Maureen's hand. "We knew when we signed on for this job that we were going to fall in love with them, and then have to watch them leave us."

"I'll go make the coffee. How do you take yours?" Maureen asked, giving her a final pat and dropping her hand.

"Just wave some cream at the cup." Taking a deep breath, Maddy walked into Hiram's room. "Hey, Mr. Man," she said, giving him a big frown. "What's the idea of calling me out in the middle of a nor'easter at three in the morning?"

"Maddy." He patted the bed beside him with a big smile. "Have you met Dr. Lewis?" he asked, waving at the man sitting in a chair on the other side of the bed.

"Yes, as a matter of fact, I have."

Hiram grabbed her hand and pulled her down next to him. "He just asked me if I really had my heart set on dying today," he told her.

"And what did you tell him?" she asked softly.

"I told him I got to go soon, because everyone's waiting for me." Hiram slowly gazed around the dimly lit room, then back at her. "They started coming around midnight, and now the room's so crowded I don't think another one will fit in."

"T-they?" Maddy whispered, also looking around.

He squeezed her hand. "My family, girl. And a good number of my old friends, including Rufus, my best buddy, who drowned when he was twelve." He pulled her closer so he could whisper to her. "My papa said he's mighty sorry for hollering and scaring me like that, but he explained he didn't even know he was doing it." He tugged on her hand when she tried to look around again. "You can't see them because they're dead."

"But you can?"

He grinned. "That's because I've already started in dying."

He pulled her closer again. "It's just like William said; I ain't got nothing to be afraid of, because everyone's gonna take good care of me once I'm all the way dead."

Maddy took a shuddering breath, and since she was already so close, she gave his weathered cheek a kiss. "I'm glad for you," she whispered, just before she straightened and turned away so she could wipe her eyes.

"But I ain't going until William gets here," Hiram said. "He gave me a message to give to his sister, only I can't remember all what I'm supposed to tell her. I think it was about a warhorse and a ribbon or something, but I got so excited about knowing I was going to meet his family, too, that I forgot to listen close. And I don't want to mess it up, because I think William really misses them—especially his sister."

"I don't know when he'll get here," she said, glancing briefly at Dr. Lewis before looking back at Hiram. "It might not be for a day or two."

"That's okay; I can wait. And you know what?" he said. "I ain't got even a wee bit of pain. In fact, I feel the best I have in years. Even my bunions don't hurt." He squeezed her hand. "But you'll stay with me anyway, won't you? I mean, just in case."

"I'm not going anywhere."

He snuggled back into the pillow with a sigh. "I love you, Maddy girl," he said, closing his eyes.

"I love you, too, Mr. Man," she whispered, holding his frail hand as she unsuccessfully fought back her tears, watching him drift off to sleep.

Chapter Twenty-one

It was one of the longest nights of Maddy's life, and by eight o'clock that morning, it still wasn't ended. The storm continued to rage with hurricane-force winds and torrential rain, and even though it was well past sunrise, it could have been midnight for how dark it was outside. The nursing home still had power, but they couldn't get any television or radio stations, and even their cell phones had stopped getting out. Maddy was beginning to agree with Maureen; it felt as though they were completely cut off from the rest of the world.

And there still wasn't any sign of William.

Or the tiger.

Nobody had come into work at seven, and the residents weren't waking up!

It was as if time had simply stopped.

Hiram continued drifting in and out of sleep; he'd wake up, discover he was still alive, and close his eyes and start softly snoring again. When he did stay awake for more than two minutes, he was quite lucid—considering he was telling Maddy stories about all the people in the room that only he could see. But then he asked if there was anything she wanted him to tell her daddy, just in case he happened to run into Charlie Lane in the hereafter.

Maddy had nearly lost it right then and there, but had somehow managed to give him a thankful smile, and told him to tell her daddy that she loved him and that everyone was doing okay. But then she'd remembered to have Hiram also tell him that Rick was following in his footsteps, and becoming a fisherman just like he'd hoped.

And then she'd said she needed to use the bathroom, and that was why she was standing out in the hall right now, bawling like a baby.

"D-did he pass?" Maureen whispered, rushing up to her.

Unable to speak, Maddy just shook her head.

A pair of large hands turned her into a broad chest, and two well-muscled arms wrapped around her. "Easy there, Miss Kimble," Dr. Lewis said, patting her back. "I can see how difficult this is for you, but Mr. Fields seems to be waiting for that gentleman to show up, and I don't think he's going to let go until he does."

Utterly mortified to be crying all over a doctor—not to mention a complete stranger—Maddy forced her emotions under control and tried to step away.

Only his arms tightened and his patting turned to gentle rubbing. "If it's any consolation, I believe Hiram is actually enjoying himself," he said, his warm breath fanning over her hair.

Maddy stiffened, suddenly uncomfortable. It might be unprofessional to cry on a doctor, but it was really inappropriate for him to be soothing her like . . . like . . .

"Maddy, I think we should start waking up the residents," Maureen said. "I'm starting to really worry about them."

God bless the perceptive woman! Forcibly pushing on the

hand holding her head down, and with Maureen actually helping by pulling at her, Maddy finally managed to step free. "Excuse me, Doctor," she said, smiling apologetically, "but we really need to see to the others. I'm sorry; that was very *unprofessional* of me."

He smiled, his green eyes glinting in the dim hall lights. "Everyone needs a shoulder to cry on sometimes, Miss Kimble, so please don't apologize. As for the residents, why not let them sleep in this morning? It will be a lot less stressful for them than waking up to this terrible storm and then learning that Mr. Fields is dying."

"But it's unnatural," Maddy said tightly, restraining herself from visibly shuddering because she could still feel his arms around her—probably because he was still embracing her with his eyes. "Especially that they're all asleep at eight in the morning. If you will excuse us, Dr. Lewis, we have work to do," she said, pivoting on her heel and heading toward the nurses' station.

"Madeline," he said ever so softly as she walked away, making her stop to look at him. "I believe we can drop the formalities now. Please, call me Aslan."

Maddy went perfectly still, not even daring to breathe.

Aslan.

The Chronicles of Narnia.

C. S. Lewis.

One missing green-eyed, face-licking tiger.

And a way-too-forward stranger claiming to be a doctor, who very conveniently showed up when they needed one, with not a drop of rain on him.

"Aslan is a very uncommon name," she said, staring down the hall directly into his bright green eyes.

"It's from C. S. Lewis's book *The Chronicles of Narnia*," he said. "Maybe you're familiar with it? My mother was fascinated by all the talking creatures and named me Aslan after the lion. When I was . . . oh, almost *ten,* I think, she and I read it together."

Maddy's heart started pounding.

"Hey, isn't that the book you and Sarah are reading together?" Maureen asked.

"No, we read it when she was *eight,*" she blatantly lied.

Aslan Lewis nodded, the glint in his eyes intensifying. "I believe I'll sit with Hiram while you tend to your other residents, then," he said, shooting her a wink and then walking into Hiram's room.

"He's the one acting unprofessional," Maureen said, looping her arm through Maddy's and leading her toward the nurses' station. "Doctors do not hug nurses, and they sure as hell don't wink at them," she added, stopping to face her. "What in hell is going on here, Maddy? I feel like we're standing in the middle of the Twilight Zone!"

"I honest to God don't know, Maureen."

Maureen glanced down the hall and visibly shivered. "Yeah, well, that guy gives me the creeps. Do you think it's okay to leave him alone with Hiram?"

Maddy shrugged. "He's been alone with him several times this morning while we were checking on everyone. And Hiram seems comfortable enough with him." She straightened her shoulders on a deep breath. "Come on, let's get everyone up, and maybe this place will start feeling normal again. We can let Charlotte and Lois and Elvira loose in the kitchen, and they can conjure up some scrambled eggs and toast for everyone," she said, inwardly wincing at even uttering the word *conjure.*

"Okay," Maureen said, also stiffening her spine. "You get Charlotte and Lois, and I'll head in the other direction and wake up Elbridge." She smiled. "He might be eighty, but it'll feel good to have another man around." But then she frowned. "I just wish I could get through to my husband on his cell phone. I can't believe he hasn't shown up here looking for me by now."

"But you told me Doris said all the roads are blocked by trees and downed wires."

Maureen went back to smiling. "Sean would walk the whole six miles if he had to, figuring I was stuck someplace between here and home. I swear, if I'm so much as ten minutes overdue, he's in the truck coming after me." She laughed. "That's what forty years of marriage does to a couple; if he doesn't call from the woods every three hours, I usually go looking for *him*," she finished, heading toward Elbridge's room.

"Maybe someday I'll be lucky enough to have that problem," Maddy said with a chuckle, heading in the opposite direction toward the room Charlotte and Lois shared.

It took more effort than usual to get everyone up and dressed and ready to face the day, and their one bed-ridden resident, Mem, was quite put out that she couldn't watch the morning news to get the latest on the storm. Charlotte and Lois and Elvira, acting as though she'd just given them the keys to the kingdom, had practically run to the kitchen to cook breakfast for everyone.

Charlotte had been wearing enough flour to make a loaf of bread when the women had rolled out a cart almost an hour later, loaded with enough divine-smelling food to feed a small nation, and Maddy figured it was going to take the kitchen crew a week to clean up the mess the women had made. Janice and Samuel and Elbridge had immediately gone to Hiram's room, and Hiram was sitting up in bed, holding court, telling them about his ethereal visitors. Feeling bummed at not being part of the party, Mem talked Maddy and Maureen into putting her in a wheeled recliner, and they'd pushed the frail woman into Hiram's room with everyone else.

Now they were all sitting around in wheelchairs or on the

spare bed, eating perfectly cooked eggs and homemade biscuits, a small island of people weathering both the storm outside and the one in their hearts as they all tried to comfort a dying friend.

Only Hiram seemed oblivious to both storms. "Maddy girl," he said, scowling at her as he set his fork on his empty plate. "This is a right nice get-together, but it ain't exactly the party you promised me." He waved at the room. "You didn't put up any of them streamers, and you forgot the balloons." But then he smiled at her. "I'll let it go, though, if'n I can have a piece of my apple spice cake. You got candles for it, I hope."

Maddy didn't know what to say; forget the candles, she didn't have a cake!

"It's not your birthday, Hiram," Mem scoffed before Maddy could say anything. "You only put candles on *birthday* cakes."

Hiram went back to scowling, only at Mem instead of at Maddy. "I've had ninety-one birthdays, woman, but I only intend to have one dying day. And I think I should get to blow out some candles." He looked at Maddy and smiled again. "Only I just need one, okay? I don't think I got enough wind in me to blow out any more than that." He rubbed his belly. "But I got plenty of room for lots of cream cheese icing."

Silence descended, and it was all Maddy could do not to burst into tears. She didn't have an apple spice cake with cream cheese frosting, because this party wasn't supposed to happen until Monday afternoon.

"Would you like me to help you carry Hiram's cake from the kitchen, Madeline?" Dr. Lewis asked, standing up. He smiled at Hiram. "Because if your cake is the one I saw in the cooler, Mr. Fields, it's going to take two people to carry it."

Hiram's face lit up. "Is the icing thick, and it's all decorated up fancy?" He suddenly scowled. "Not with flowers, I hope. I don't want one of them girly cakes."

"The icing was at least an inch thick," their mysterious guest said. "And the cake I saw was decorated with a forest of trees. I do believe there was even an axe and crosscut saw on it. Is that appropriate for a man who spent sixty years in the woods?"

Honest to God, she was going to kill him. They didn't have a cake, and this . . . this bastard was building Hiram up for a huge disappointment.

Maddy stood up. "Yes, Dr. Lewis, I believe I *would* like your help," she said tightly, spinning around and heading for the door.

"There's some streamers left over from the Fourth of July," Lois said, following.

"And there's still helium in the tank," Charlotte added, also following.

Maddy smiled at the two women as they rushed toward the sitting room.

But then Lois suddenly stopped and turned to her. "I never saw a cake when we were cooking breakfast, and I must have been in that cooler twenty times this morning."

"That's because there is no cake," Maddy said.

"Then why did Dr. Lewis say there was?"

"That's what I intend to find out." Maddy forced herself to take a deep breath and let it out slowly, hoping to calm some of her anger. "Maybe I can whip up some frosting and spread it over bread or something. Meanwhile, we can at least put up streamers and balloons," she finished, gesturing for Lois to continue her mission. "That will ease some of his disappointment."

Lois gave her a concerned look and then headed after Charlotte, disappearing into the sitting room. Maddy stood with her arms crossed and waited for Dr. Lewis.

"What in hell do you think you're doing?" she hissed the moment he stepped into the hallway. She grabbed him by the sleeve and pulled him away from the door. "Why did you tell

Hiram you saw a cake in the cooler? Now he's going to be heart-broken when I have to tell him there isn't one."

"Is that cake for someone else, then?" he asked. He suddenly reached up and touched one of her curls. "You have got the sexiest eyes I've ever seen on a woman, Madeline, and when you're angry they positively snap with fire."

She jerked away so quickly that she bumped up against the hall railing. "I don't know who the hell you are, but you are *out* of here," she growled, pointing toward the entrance. "Now!"

He arched a brow. "And just what are you going to do if I don't leave? *Shoot* me?" He shook his head, and his eyes crinkled with laughter. "Apparently you're no more afraid of me than you are of your boyfriend."

"What in hell are you talking about?"

He crowded her back against the handrail, the heat of his body sending shivers down her spine. "Isn't Killkenny expecting you to be waiting in his truck for him when he gets back?" He rubbed her curls between his fingers. "Where I come from, women do as they're told or suffer the consequences."

"W-where exactly are you from?"

"Not Narnia, that's for hell sure." He leaned closer, bringing his mouth within inches of hers. "You're not really all that enamored with Killkenny, are you?" he asked softly. "Because I happen to know he'll never be able to give you what you need. Come with me, Madeline. Walk away with me right now, and I will give you the world."

Maddy wasn't sure where she got the nerve, but she smiled ever so sweetly. "Thank you, but I believe I'll stick with a man who has the balls to go fight a pack of demon wolves instead of hide in a nursing home with a bunch of old people."

He straightened away, his scowl fierce enough to turn her to toast.

Maddy kicked her smile up another notch. "William

Killkenny has already given me more than I even realized I wanted. And I'd run off with . . . oh, let's say a *dragon* before I would with someone lower than pond scum who tries to poach another man's girlfriend the moment his back is turned." She stepped out from between him and the wall in the direction of the kitchen, but turned back. "I'm going to put a candle in a loaf of bread, and if you're still here when I get back, I do believe I *will* shoot you."

Apparently Maddy had been standing in front of the open cooler so long that Maureen had decided she'd better come save her from Dr. Lewis again. But as soon as the woman turned to look in the cooler herself, she gasped.

"Where did that come from?" she whispered, reaching out and touching the cake. She blinked at Maddy. "I . . . it . . . I swear that wasn't there two hours ago," she said, waving at the cooler. "It's so big it takes up an entire shelf!"

There was even one big fat candle shaped like a pine tree sitting smack in the middle of the damn thing. Maddy decided she really was going to have to write all this down the moment she woke up, because it was simply fantastical. Only she probably wouldn't include Pond Scum's lecherous proposition, since this was going to be a children's book.

Maureen plopped down on the stool beside the center island and dropped her head in her hands with a tired sigh. "I'm getting too old to be working the night shift," she muttered. "I swear I'm losing my mind."

Maddy wrapped her arm around her, also giving a deep sigh, only hers was more resigned than tired. "One of Hiram's invisible visitors must have put it in the cooler."

Maureen looked up between her fingers. "That is not funny." She suddenly dropped her hands and grinned drunkenly. "Because it's probably true."

"Maddy! Maureen! Come quick!" Elvira shouted, running into the kitchen. "William's here, and he's hurt."

"William!" Maddy cried, chasing after Elvira, who was already running back down the hall. "Where is he?" she asked, catching up with her, Maureen also following at a run. "How badly is he hurt?"

"They laid him on the bed in Hiram's room. He's covered in blood!"

Maddy used the door casing to pivot around and came to a sliding stop. "Let me through," she said, carefully pushing past the sea of people crowded around the bed. "Oh, William!" she cried, reaching out for him.

Kenzie caught her hand. "It's not all his blood," he said quietly enough that only she could hear as he turned her to face him. He gave her a shake to make her look at him. "But Trace thinks he might have a cracked collarbone, and there's a deep slash on his arm that needs to be sewn shut. They said there's a doctor here."

"He's not a real doctor, and I'm not letting him anywhere near William," she hissed, pulling away. Then she had to shove Trace out of her way. She gently brushed her fingers through William's wet hair as she studied his pupils, and she smiled when she caught him studying her back. "Don't look so worried, big guy," she whispered. "I'm a much better nurse than I am a driver."

"It looks like the ligaments haven't been damaged," Maureen said, having unwrapped the bloody rag covering the lower half of William's right arm. "But it's going to need several layers of stitching." She looked at Maddy. "We have to get an ambulance here; we're not set up for the kind of care he needs."

"That's not going to happen," Trace said. "None of the roads are passable, and the storm isn't showing any signs of letting up."

"Maureen, you worked as a trauma nurse for several years," Maddy said.

"Fifteen years ago." Maureen straightened and threw back her shoulders. "But I guess it should be like riding a bicycle. I'll go see what I can scare up out of the supply cabinet. Come on, people," she said, looking around. "We all need to pitch in and get organized. You two men," she said, looking at Kenzie and Trace. "I need you to wheel Mem back to her room—no, take her to the sitting room. Janice and Elvira, you go with them and take Samuel with you. Elbridge, you find a cart and put several pans of hot water on it and wheel it back in here; then you can sit with Hiram. Charlotte, get us more sheets and lots of towels. Lois, you come with me." She looked at Maddy. "You get him undressed, and I'll send Lois back with supplies to clean him up." She looked around as if checking to see if she had everyone. "Have you seen Dr. Lewis?"

Maddy shook her head. "I found out he's not really a doctor."

Maureen looked at Trace and Kenzie. "There's been a man here since around three this morning, but he seems to have suddenly vanished. Could you two search the building for him after you drop off Mem?"

"We will," Kenzie said, taking hold of the back of Mem's recliner.

"I'm going to stay and help Maddy," Trace said. He grinned at Maureen. "With your permission, ma'am."

"You can help her undress him, but then clean yourself up," she said, glancing at his wet and muddy clothes. "How much of that blood is yours?" she asked, touching the gash on his arm.

He shrugged. "Not enough of it to worry about right now."

"Mr. Gregor?" Maureen asked.

He stopped in the doorway and looked back at her. "I'll survive until after you tend to William," he said before wheeling Mem out into the hallway.

Everyone else had already headed off on their assignments,

and Maddy turned her attention back to William when she felt him pat her bottom.

"I seem to remember telling ye to stay in the truck until I got back."

She started unbuckling his belt. "I left you a note."

"Ye also left the door open. The whole interior was soaked, and your note is probably halfway to Ireland by now."

"Trace, get his boots off," she said, unbuttoning William's shirt, only to suck in her breath when she saw the ugly bruise just above his left pectoral muscle.

"William," Hiram hollered. "Are you going to be okay?"

"Yes, Hiram, I am. I have a good nurse."

"Ain't she, though?" Hiram said. "She came all the way here through this storm when Maureen called and told her I had started in dying."

"You're dying?" William said, trying to lift his head to look over at the other bed.

Maddy held him down. "He can wait a bit longer."

"My whole family's here, William," Hiram continued. "Just like you said they'd be. Only I think they're getting impatient."

"You tell them they've waited all these years," Maddy said, working William's wet pants down with Trace's help. "They can wait another day or two. And if you want a piece of your beautiful cake, you're going to have to wait until William is all patched up, so he can have a piece with you."

When Maddy saw the knife Trace had taken from William's boot and set on the nightstand, she scoffed it up and stuck the blade in William's shirtsleeve, stopping to smile at him. "Let's see how you like having *your* clothes cut off."

He actually smiled and relaxed back into the pillow. "Have at it, lass."

Trace covered him with a blanket, and Maddy grabbed her cousin's sleeve just as he turned to leave, pulling him to lean over the bed. "That guy Maureen mentioned," she whispered so Hiram wouldn't hear. "I think he's the . . . tiger William left me with," she said, glancing at William and then nodding at his frown.

She took a deep breath. "Maureen called my cell phone when I was in the truck, and told me Hiram was dying. And the tiger heard our conversation, and he somehow opened the door and started walking to the nursing home . . . taking his bubble of light with him." She glanced at Trace to see his reaction, only to find his expression unreadable. "I came inside and the tiger sat down by the front door, but while I was changing into my scrubs, this guy suddenly showed up at the nurses' station, claiming he was Dr. Lewis and that his car was stuck in a ditch down the road. Only he wasn't wet from the storm, and when I went to look, the tiger was gone."

"Did he say anything in particular," William asked, "that would make ye think Dr. Lewis was really the tiger?"

Maddy felt her cheeks grow hot. "I-I just have a feeling. He mentioned something I'd said to the tiger on our walk here."

"What aren't you telling me, Madeline?" William asked. "What did he do?"

She went back to cutting off his shirt.

Trace stopped her. "Okay, I need to know why you aren't totally freaked out by what's going on here."

She gave a humorless laugh and went back to cutting off William's shirt. "I'm saving up for a total mental breakdown later." But then she grabbed Trace's sleeve when he started to leave. "Um . . . just don't shoot the tiger, okay?" She smiled tightly. "He might be a jerk, but I do believe he's on our side."

"*Our* side?" Trace softly repeated, his storm-gray eyes searching hers.

She took another deep breath. "I became a member of your exclusive little club by default last night, don't you think?" she said, glancing down to find William staring at her just as intensely.

He nodded ever so slightly.

Trace pulled her across the bed to kiss her on the forehead. "Welcome to the magic, Peeps," he whispered, straightening away and walking out the door.

Maddy set down William's knife and gently pulled his shirt out from under him.

"When are ye going to tell me what the tiger did to you?"

She straightened with a laugh and threw his shirt on the floor. "When you're too old to even *lift* your sword." She suddenly sobered, staring directly into his eyes. "You are going to grow old, aren't you?" she whispered.

He shot her a wincing smile as he reached out and patted her backside again, and then cupped it with his large hand. "Aye, Madeline, we will grow old together."

"And you'll show me what's in the box you gave me last night when you picked me up, that you had me run up and slide under my bed?"

He arched a brow. "Is your box under there with it?"

Her throat closing with emotion, she merely nodded.

"And are ye ready to show me what's inside yours?"

His hand on her backside rubbed her soothingly when she started to tremble, and Maddy slowly nodded again.

"Then we will open them together." He scowled. "And then you will tell me *everything* that happened after I left the truck."

Elbridge walked in rolling a cart loaded with tubs of steaming water sloshing over the sides, followed almost immediately by Charlotte, her arms stacked so full of towels and sheets it was a wonder she could see where she was going.

Maureen came in looking ready to do battle, shooed everyone but Elbridge and Maddy out, and then went to work on William. It took them an hour and more than sixty stitches to close no fewer than five wounds on his body—most of the stitches in William's handsome, muscular right forearm.

All the time she worked, Maureen kept trying to decide what had caused the gashes, unable to believe William's explanation that it was merely flying debris from where he'd been caught in the storm. Personally, Maddy thought some of them were claw marks, and she'd swear the deep gash on his arm was from a sword.

She was a little disconcerted that William remained so calm through the entire procedure, considering they didn't have anything stronger than a topical anesthesia to take the sting out of the needle being pushed through his flesh, and only a couple of pain pills that didn't seem to make him even a little bit drowsy. But more often than not, it was William patting her bottom to reassure *her* that he wasn't in any pain—although he did give her a good squeeze every now and then while Maureen was working deep in his arm.

A half hour after they tied off the last stitch, they had him bandaged and lying on clean bed linens, and Maureen was off with her supplies to tend to Kenzie and Trace.

"How are you doing over there, William?" Hiram asked, having just woken up from another nap.

"I'm right as rain, Hiram," William said. "And you? How are you doing?"

"I'd be doing better if I could have a piece of my cake." He looked at Maddy expectantly. "Can we get back to the party now that William's all patched up? I feel myself fading, but I don't want to go before I get my cake."

She looked down to find William smiling at her. "Every man deserves to die with his belly full of sugar," he said. "And come to think of it, I'm having a hankering for something sweet myself." He arched his eyebrows. "So unless you're willing to crawl in this bed with me, I suppose I'll have to settle for some of Hiram's cake."

Hiram chortled like a teenager. "You be careful about flirting with our Maddy girl, William. When Doc Lewis stopped in to say good-bye, he told me to make sure I stay on Maddy's good side, or she just might help me along before I'm ready." He laughed again. "The Doc said she's got a tongue sharp enough to cut a man clean in half, and I reckon you don't need any more stitches right now."

William snapped his gaze to Maddy.

But it was Elbridge who spoke first, as he stood up from his chair beside Hiram's bed. "Did Dr. Lewis bother you, Maddy?" he asked. "You should have come and gotten me, and I would have escorted him out, storm or no storm." He suddenly frowned and looked at Hiram. "When did he come say good-bye to you? Almost everyone's been in here with you all morning."

Maddy saw Hiram frown in confusion. "I don't remember," he said, glancing from Elbridge to Maddy. He gave a confounded snort. "Maybe I just dreamt he came in."

"I'll go get your cake, Hiram, and tell the others to come in and watch you blow out your candle," Maddy said.

She started to turn, but William caught the hem of her shirt and pulled her to a stop. She reached out and placed her hand on his forehead. "That's quite a frown you have going there, Mr. Killkenny. Are you in very much pain? Maybe instead of those pills, I should give you a big fat needle full of painkiller."

"I will find out, ye know."

"And then what?" she whispered, leaning down so Elbridge and Hiram couldn't hear. "Believe it or not, William, I am quite capable of defending my own honor—*if* I happen to be feeling honorable, that is." She leaned in so that her lips were just brushing his ear. "But if I'm feeling dishonorable toward a man, I have been known to blow his stockings all the way to Ireland." She straightened, gently pulled his hand off her scrubs, and laid it over his stomach. "Any more questions or complaints?" she asked, throwing his words from the cabin back at him.

"Can I have ice cream with my cake?"

"And sprinkles," Hiram piped up. "And whipped cream."

"Hiram, you're going to overdose on sugar!"

He chortled again. "That's my plan, Maddy girl."

Maddy rolled her eyes to cover her horror that they were discussing his dying so casually, and turned and headed out of the room. "Come on, Elbridge. I'll get the cake while you get the others. I'm sure these two . . . gentlemen can babysit each other."

Chapter Twenty-two

Hiram's party had wound down sometime near noon, everyone having eaten so much ice cream and cake they couldn't stop yawning, and one by one, after giving Hiram a kiss on his cheek, the residents had left to go have naps. Maureen had said she was going to catch a few winks in the spare bed in Mem's room, and Kenzie and Trace were resting on guard at each end of the building.

It had taken William a good ten minutes to talk Maddy into curling up in bed with him, but the lass had been so tired she'd fallen asleep before he'd finished wrapping his good arm around her. He had then spent the next two hours quietly talking with Hiram, before the old man had given in to the lure of his ethereal visitors and fallen asleep for good this time.

Now William was just staring up at the ceiling, listening to the rain gently patter on the window as the storm moved away, remembering his horror at finding his truck empty when he'd insisted Trace and Kenzie help him get back to Madeline.

The last time he recalled ever being that scared was when

he'd galloped through the splintered gates of his keep and found his family, his people, and every damn animal he owned slaughtered and left to rot in the sun. That was the day he'd started his vengeful march toward hell, and last night, as he'd stared into the empty cab of his truck, he'd felt as though he had finally reached it.

He kissed Maddy's hair and then rested his lips on her soft curls with a sigh.

It wasn't that he'd thought Mac had failed to protect her; but rather, he'd been terrified the bastard had stolen her. Because if Maximilian Oceanus had decided he wanted Madeline for himself, there was a very good chance William had lost her forever. Protecting his woman from the evil was one thing, whereas protecting her from a powerful drùidh known to walk both sides of the magic just might prove impossible.

What in hell was Mac doing here, anyway?

William had recognized the magic maker immediately, although it had been the first time he'd shown up as a tiger. The bastard had plagued William for centuries, dangling the prospect of vengeance for his family under his nose. Mac usually claiming it wasn't within his power to grant, but then hinting it might be possible for the right price.

So was Mac here to continue their centuries-old sport or for another reason?

When William had told Kenzie about the drùidh's sudden appearance last night, the highlander had grown deeply concerned. Maximilian Oceanus was legendary in every century—revered by most, hated by many, and feared by all.

Except maybe not feared by Kenzie's brother, Cùram de Gairn, whose own legendary temper was equally well known. And anyone foolish enough to cross either drùidh . . . well, those who did live to tell of their misfortune usually wished they hadn't.

But Mac had taken an unusual liking to William for some reason, when the two of them had met on a battlefield in the thirteenth-century in middle Asia, when William had tediously been working his way through time toward Kenzie.

William suddenly stiffened, his arm tightening enough to make Maddy stir. He immediately loosened his grip and let out a sigh of relief when she remained asleep.

Dammit to hell, he knew why Mac was here! It was for the same reason he'd been in Asia back then: he was still chasing after his spoiled brat of a sister, trying to hold on to the slippery girl long enough to talk her into going home to face their father.

That damn harbor seal pup was Carolina Oceanus!

And she'd come here seeking sanctuary, hoping that Kenzie could protect her not only from her father, but also from being wed to a man she despised.

Which meant that the jilted bridegroom was probably the evil entity chasing her.

But Mac had told William that his father had retracted the proposal once he'd found out that his daughter had good reason to fear her betrothed. Only Carolina wouldn't stop long enough to hear the news from her brother.

Christ, Midnight Bay had become the battlefield of warring entities engaged in a domestic dispute over a headstrong girl with more power than she knew how to control yet, who was determined to choose her own fate.

And in her youthful impetuousness, she had chosen Trace Huntsman.

Maddy stirred again, but this time when William forced himself to relax, she didn't fall back into sleep. She blinked up at him, and then blushed profusely when she realized exactly what part of him she'd been holding on to under the blankets.

She pulled her hand away with a gasp and sat up, being

careful not to push against his chest, and then rubbed the sleep from her eyes as she looked over toward Hiram—only to go perfectly still.

William held her in place when she tried to get off the bed. "He's not there, Madeline," he told her gently. "He left us about an hour ago."

"You should have woken me up," she whispered, still staring at her friend.

"Why?"

She finally looked at him. "Because . . . so I could . . ." She buried her face in her hands. "He's g-gone," she said on a sob.

William pulled her to him, rubbing his thumb over her damp cheek. "He told me to tell ye good-bye and that he loved ye like a daughter. And he thanks ye for the wonderful party, and for the chance it gave him to leave everyone on a happy note."

"I-I wanted to be holding his hand."

"Nay, Madeline. Hiram said it was better if he left while you were sleeping, because he couldn't have handled the sadness he knew he'd see in your eyes. He was afraid that if you started crying he would, too, and said it just wouldn't be proper for a man of the woods to leave this earth bawling like a baby."

"I didn't want him to go, William."

"We're not meant to live forever, lass. Do ye not think ninety-one years was long enough for your friend?"

"No."

He chuckled and kissed the top of her head. "I believe Hiram thought it was. Be glad he was able to leave peacefully, lass. Not everyone does."

She tried to get up, but William held her against him; and obviously not wanting to wrestle with him in his condition, she relaxed with a sigh. "I-I have to get up," she said, although she made no move to do so. "I can't just leave him lying there."

"He's not there, Madeline; he's everywhere now. Did Mac try to take you with him when he left?"

She went perfectly still again. "Mac?"

"The tiger—Maximilian Oceanus. Did he ask you to run off with him or try to bully ye into going with him?"

He felt her suddenly relax, and his thumb brushed across what he realized was her smile. "I told Mr. Oceanus in no uncertain terms that I think men who try poaching other men's girlfriends are pond scum." She softly snorted. "I believe he left here with his tiger tail between his legs, knowing exactly what I thought of him."

William closed his eyes against the knot forming in his gut. "Maddy, darling, ye didn't send Mac away; ye merely presented him with a challenge. Men, like tigers, will chase anything that runs from them, and they won't stop until they catch it."

Apparently oblivious to his mood, she tilted her head back to smile at him. "Is that what you did, Mr. Killkenny? As soon as you realized I wanted nothing to do with you, the chase was on?" Her smile turned downright smug. "Have you ever stopped to consider that maybe that was my plan all along?"

Oh, she was definitely feeling quite proud of herself, and William pulled her head down so she wouldn't see his scowl. But she patted his chest and sat up, and then quickly scrambled off the bed before he could catch her. She glanced over at Hiram's body, and her eyes turned sad again.

"I need to go get Maureen so we can take care of him." She looked at the window and saw it was getting light, and that the rain had stopped. "William, are the wolves gone for good this time?"

"I'm afraid not. But knowing that Mac is here, I have an idea how we can stop them from returning. Before ye get Maureen, could you tell Kenzie and Trace that I need to talk to them?" he said, trying to sit up.

She ran back to the bed. "Oh, no, you don't. You are staying put until an ambulance can take you to the hospital in Ellsworth. That collarbone might be broken, and if you move around too much, it could pierce your jugular vein."

He arched a brow at her, trying not to laugh at her threatening glare. "Did ye happen to notice any old scars on my body while you were checking for new ones?"

She folded her arms under her breasts and arched *her* brow at him. "As a matter of fact, your body looks like you might want to trade in your sword for a weapon that doesn't require you to get within ten feet of . . . whatever you're fighting." Her scowl returned. "Because you obviously haven't learned how to avoid the *pointed* end of one."

That got rid of his desire to laugh. "Maybe I should *help* Mac steal you."

She snorted. "Trust me; he'd return me in less than a week." She leaned down right in his face. "And when I got back here, I would screw your Irish stockings on so tight they'd never blow off your feet again. Stay in bed."

That said, she spun around and disappeared before William could break into a full-blown grin. He was going to have to do something about the woman's belief that she could take care of herself, he decided, as he sat up and swung his feet off the bed, before she got into real trouble.

What he'd been trying to point out by pointing out his old scars, is that he had enough experience to know if his bones were broken or not. Only as soon as he stood up, William realized he had another problem, as he was as naked as the day he'd been born and saw no sign of his clothes.

A fact to which poor Charlotte's scream attested when she came barreling in through the door, which was followed by Lois's shriek as she came in behind her.

The three of them stood there staring at one another, until

William finally snapped the blanket off the bed and covered himself—though not quickly enough to stop both women from bursting into laughter as they ran down the hall to tattle to Maddy.

And for the second time that day William found himself terrified, only this time *of* Madeline instead of *for* her. He quickly crawled back into bed, covered himself up with the blanket, and looked over at Hiram. "I may soon be joining you, old man."

But instead of Maddy coming in to scold him, Doris walked in, looking like a drowned rat. She stopped with a startled gasp, and William looked down to make sure he was decently covered and then smiled at her.

"Mr. Killkenny! What are you doing here?"

He held up his bandaged arm. "Your staff was kind enough to tend my injuries when Kenzie and Trace and I got stranded here in the storm."

She suddenly noticed all the streamers and balloons and half-eaten cake, and then her gaze landed on Hiram and her eyes immediately turned troubled. "Oh, dear," she said, walking over to him. She touched his weathered cheek. "I am so going to miss him," she whispered. She sighed. "Well, he's in a better place."

"Oh, I believe Hiram thought this place was quite nice," William softly assured her. "In fact, he told me the only part he didn't like about dying was his having to leave all of you. Ye gave Hiram many happy years here, Doris, and he asked me to tell you that he appreciated your efforts. Especially your battle to stop them from cutting down that old pine tree next to the river that he loved to sit under, so he could smell the pine pitch on the hot summer days."

She looked over at him. "I didn't know Hiram was even aware that I was the one who stopped the owners from cutting it down. I believed everyone thought his handwritten petitions made them change their minds."

"Hiram knew it was you they eventually listened to, not him."

She looked back at her deceased resident and sighed again. "Let me have someone make up a bed for you in another room, Mr. Killkenny," she said, looking at him again. "So you don't have to be in here with him."

"I don't mind, Doris. And ye needn't bother, anyway; if the roads are passable, then it's time Kenzie and Trace and I got going. Um . . . if somebody could find me something to wear, that is," he said with a chuckle. "For I fear I've already scandalized poor Charlotte and Lois."

Speaking of the little devils, Charlotte and Lois popped their heads in the doorway, and Maddy walked in and tossed some folded material at him. "The open side of the thin robe goes in the back, and the thick one goes over it, with the opening in the front. Doris," she said, suddenly noticing her boss. "The roads are open?"

"The main road is," Doris said. She shook her head. "It looks like a category three hurricane came through Midnight Bay. There are crews working with chainsaws all over the place, and line trucks are clearing away the wires. I swear, it's going to take a month of Sundays to clean up this town. Only it's the strangest thing—the storm didn't seem to hit Ellsworth or even Oak Harbor." She walked over and hugged Maddy. "I'm sorry, Ms. Kimble," she said. "I know how much Hiram meant to you." She stepped back and waved at the decorations, smiling crookedly. "I see you all got together and sent him off in high style, though. I'm sorry I missed the party."

Kenzie and Trace walked in. "Eve's on her way to pick us up," Kenzie said. "Maddy, we'll give ye a ride home."

"I need to stay here and take care of William and . . . Hiram."

"The funeral home has already been called," Doris said, "and they're on their way. And the rest of the staff is trickling in, so we're all set here. Why don't you take the next few days off? At least until after Hiram's funeral, which will probably be on Wednesday. He already made the arrangements." She smiled. "From what hymns he wanted right down to the beautiful pine box he showed me a picture of."

"But—"

"You can take care of William at your house, Peeps," Trace said, cutting off Maddy's protest before she could make it. "That should keep you busy enough."

"But—"

"And I can sit on your porch and supervise as ye clean up your yard," William said, cutting off her protest again.

"But you can't—"

"Don't make me get out the hair clippers," Trace said quietly.

William saw Maddy's shoulders slump in defeat.

But he figured they'd soon straighten back up once she saw the new SUV he would now have to take out of Kenzie's barn.

Chapter Twenty-three

Maddy gave William a sweet little wave as she pulled out of her driveway, making sure not to let him see her smile. She looked into her rearview mirror when she reached the road, and chuckled out loud at the sight of him standing on her porch, scowling hard enough to hurt his face. She didn't know which was confounding him more, that she was leaving without him or that she hadn't even bothered to ask if she could borrow his truck.

She'd had some reservations about letting William stay at her house while he recuperated, but he'd been a surprisingly cooperative patient, and Maddy suspected he quite liked being fussed over by three women. While soaking up their attention like a thirsty sponge, William had in turn entertained everyone with stories of his own family, and spent hours sitting on the porch listening to Sarah read *The Chronicles of Narnia* aloud.

Rick had moved back home, only now instead of stumbling into bed at three in the morning, he was leaving at four to go fishing with Trace as both men plotted to add a second boat to their fleet. Patricia had been horrified to learn that her son had dropped out of college, but Maddy had stood beside Rick when he'd broken the news to their mother that he had inherited his dad's passion for fishing.

Yes, the Lane house was near to bursting with people, and despite dealing with demon wolves, lecherous tigers, and freak storms, Maddy couldn't remember ever feeling so happy.

And she wasn't nearly as scared as she thought she'd be.

She turned on the radio to her favorite country and western station, cranking up the volume until all eight speakers were thumping. When Trace had delivered the spanking-new, fire-engine-red SUV on Sunday, Maddy had seen William actually brace himself, as if he'd been expecting her to explode—or at least spit and sputter and tell him she was not driving this truck around town, either, for everyone to see. But she'd given a squeal of delight instead, and climbed in the driver's seat and started playing with all the buttons.

She might get stubborn sometimes but she wasn't stupid; it was a really badass truck. It had ten times the buttons William's pickup had, including a navigation system a rocket scientist would have trouble figuring out, and she really, really loved it. And she'd finally decided that what was the point of having a rich boyfriend, anyway, if she couldn't enjoy some of the perks?

Maddy chuckled again as she remembered William's expression this morning, when, on their way to Hiram's funeral, he'd finally realized that she had already made the truck her own. She'd folded a pretty throw blanket over the backseat, programmed the radio—which was satellite, thank you very much—to her favorite channels, filled the console with all her paraphernalia, and even slapped a bumper sticker on the back that said, "Nurses Do It with Intensive Care."

And just to see if she couldn't get *him* to explode, on their ride back she'd told him the truck would look really cool with a vanity plate that said "DRGNHRT"—after the pretty pin he'd given her that she'd named Willy Dragonheart.

He hadn't exploded, but he certainly had spit and sputtered.

The poor man; Maddy wished she could tell him to just quit trying so hard. He might not have had her at hello, but she'd definitely started melting when she saw him with her residents. And when he'd given her that small wooden box to tuck under her bed when he'd picked her up on Friday, and she'd realized he hadn't even *sealed* it . . . well, someone needed to look after the romantic sap before some perky-boobed, tight-assed hussy stuck her gold-digging claws into him.

She had planned to make this trip to Ellsworth on Monday, to talk to her doctor about that new Plan B morning-after pill she'd recently read about and to get a more reliable contraceptive, but since she'd started her period late Saturday night, it had taken away a good deal of the urgency.

So she'd made her appointment for Wednesday afternoon instead, and she intended to come home with several surprises for William: an IUD—because she didn't think he'd wait around for the pill to take effect—and a couple of cases of fine Irish ale that Trace had told her William liked. As for her third surprise, Mr. Killkenny was about to find out that he wasn't the only one who liked to give gifts. She was taking the nice little bequeathal Mr. Man had left her in his heart-wrenchingly sweet card—which had started her crying all over again when Doris had quietly handed it to her at the funeral—and buying William a token of her affection.

She'd found the perfect piece last night, when she'd gone online to browse local stores in Ellsworth, although at the time she hadn't known exactly what she'd been looking for. Figuring William wouldn't wear anything that even hinted at being jewelry, she had started looking for something he could carry in his pocket. But remembering the St. Christopher medal her mom had given her dad, which he'd worn on a long chain around his neck to keep him safe while fishing, she had eventually gravitated to the small medallions that were definitely made for manly men.

Even if she'd designed something herself, she couldn't have come up with a more perfect piece than the one she had found.

Maddy pulled into the liquor store just outside Ellsworth and bought three cases of ale and two slip-on bottle sleeves; one exclaiming *Your village just called to say they're missing their idiot*, and one that said *I'm so damn near perfect, I even scare myself sometimes.*

She then went to the jewelry store, bought the medal, and spent the twenty minutes it took them to engrave it picking out the perfect chain. She wanted one strong enough to survive William and long enough that he could slip it over his head and it would hang low enough on his beautiful broad chest that it wouldn't show even if he kept the top two buttons undone.

And then she made them gift-wrap it in very manly paper.

It was almost two hours later that Maddy walked out of her doctor's office, feeling a bit crampy but quite satisfied that she wouldn't have to worry about another unplanned pregnancy. She climbed into the SUV—which she'd parked at the end of the lot because she didn't want anyone dinging its beautiful doors— and opened the console. She rummaged through her bag of necessities, got out two aspirins, and popped them in her mouth.

But when she tilted her head back to take a swig of water, Maddy inadvertently glanced into the rearview mirror and saw Maximilian Oceanus sitting directly behind her—holding an open bottle of Irish ale in one hand and the medal she'd bought William in the other.

William sat in the backseat of Kenzie's truck, staring down at the three cell phones in his hand; one was Kenzie's, one was his own, and the third belonged to Trace. All three men had gotten text messages half an hour ago; all originating from Maddy's cell phone, all requesting they come to Dragon Cove.

The messages were signed "Mr. P.S."

William closed his eyes against the knot strangling his gut. Maddy had written the texts, and signing them "Mr. P.S." was her way of saying the man she'd called pond scum—to his face—had made her send them.

"Is there a reason you let Maddy go off by herself this afternoon?" Trace growled from the front seat.

"It doesn't matter," Kenzie said before William could answer. "Mac would have gotten hold of her eventually. Oceanus is well known for his patience."

"He's also known for wiping out entire civilizations when that patience has been pushed too far," William added, the knot in his gut starting to burn at the thought of Maddy doing the pushing. "So Mac's the one who's been holding Fiona," he said, rereading Kenzie's text message. He reread Trace's. "And Carolina must have stolen the coin from her betrothed, and Mac wants it as well as his sister."

"Then why get Maddy involved?" Trace asked. "Doesn't he think Fiona is enough of a trade for his sister and the coin?"

"Taking Maddy was personal," William said, snapping shut all three phones.

"Did you piss him off, Killkenny?" Kenzie asked.

"No, I believe Madeline did," he said with a sigh.

Kenzie drove right up to the bluff where William was building his home and shut off the engine. All three men sat silently, looking around the construction site, which was empty because the crew was still helping clean up Midnight Bay after the storm.

"Holy hell," Trace whispered, looking toward an outcropping of ledge.

William snorted. "Mac does love drama," he said, opening his door.

Kenzie also got out, and William could feel the tension humming through the highlander. "Don't worry. Mac has no intention of harming Fiona much less keeping her. In fact, he'll probably offer to *pay* you to take the little termagant off his hands."

"We don't show him Carolina until we see both Fiona and Maddy," Kenzie said.

Trace joined them—although Huntsman had needed to hold on to the truck as he walked around it, as he couldn't seem to take his eyes off the spectacle up on the ledge.

But then, it wasn't every day a modern saw a drùidh in full regalia.

"Are we supposed to be impressed?" Trace asked.

"No, I believe Maddy's the one he's trying to impress," William said. He started walking toward Mac, the other two men falling into step beside him.

"I would have expected you to build out on the point, Killkenny," Mac said. "And your new home isn't nearly as big as your old keep. What, are you not planning to have much of a family?"

William stopped ten paces from the drùidh, the others stopping beside him. "Since when have ye stooped to using helpless women as pawns, Oceanus?"

"Cùram de Gairn's magic made An Tèarmann impenetrable, which forced me to use the women," Mac said, apparently brushing off the slight. He nodded to Kenzie. "Tell your brother I said hello when you see him, Gregor." He winced. "I had hoped he would thank me for the gift I'm giving him, but now I'm beginning to worry he may take offense. And I thought my sister had problems," he added with a shudder.

William saw Kenzie stiffen. "What have ye done to her, Oceanus?"

Mac pulled back the edge of his large, billowing robe to reveal a woman tucked up against his left side, wearing the clothes of an eleventh-century Scottish lass and a horrified look on her face.

It was the first time William had ever seen Kenzie caught off guard; the highlander suddenly grabbed William's shoulder, his knees obviously going weak at the sight of the trembling, reddish-blond-haired, golden-eyed woman blinking out at him. "Fiona," he said on an indrawn breath.

William reached out to hold Kenzie back when he stumbled toward her, just as Mac stopped Fiona from trying to scurry behind him—in shame, it appeared.

"What in hell have ye done!" Kenzie shouted, his eyes moving to the drùidh.

Mac smiled, though it appeared forced. "She's my gift to you for taking *my* sister in and protecting her."

"Matt is going to kill you," Kenzie growled, his eyes filled with pain as he stared at Fiona. "Do you not think that if she wished to be human again, my brother would have done it himself? She was *at peace* as a hawk."

Mac actually winced. "So I've since learned." He sighed. "But it's done, Gregor. Give me Carolina and the coin, and you can have your sister."

"Go get her, Trace," Kenzie said softly, not taking his eyes off Fiona.

"I would see Madeline now," William said as Trace walked back to the truck. "And we want both women for Carolina."

Mac shook his head. "Madeline is not part of this deal, Killkenny. Did you come here prepared to give me what I want?"

William smiled tightly. "You may wish to rethink your request," he said. "Or you might find Carolina will like your . . . gift to her about as well as de Gairn will like his."

Trace walked up to them, his hand manacling the wrist of a spitting-mad young woman—who looked twenty-three or twenty-four years old—wearing only his shirt. "It would have been nice if someone had thought to bring her some clothes," he drawled, rubbing several scratches on his naked chest.

· William snorted. "We put a *harbor seal* in the truck. Give it up, lass," he told Carolina when he saw her try to bite Trace's hand. But Huntsman quickly subdued her by spinning her into him and wrapping both of his arms around her.

Carolina twisted to glare up at him. "You're supposed to be my strong arm," she hissed. "It's your duty to protect me, not hand me over." She turned her glare on her brother. "And you!" she spat. "I can't believe you're taking Father's side!"

Mac sighed again. "I'm on your side, brat. Everyone is, including your obviously reluctant strong arm *and* our father. If you would only stay put long enough, you'd know that he broke your marriage contract to Tamon the day you ran off."

She stamped her foot. "I'm still not going home! He's only going to find some other bastard to marry me off to." She lifted her chin. "I'm choosing my own husband, so you can go home and tell Father that I've chosen this man."

Trace's jaw went slack with surprise, as did his grip on Carolina. But instead of bolting, the woman spun around and wrapped her arms around his waist, smiling up at him even as she continued talking to her brother. "We're going to build a grand home on Midnight Bay in *this* century, and have lots and lots of babies and live happily ever after for a thousand years."

"Excuse me," Trace said in a strangled whisper, trying to peel the girl off him.

Kenzie Gregor stepped over and grabbed Carolina around the waist, lifted her off her feet to carry her up to the ledge, and stood her in front of Mac. "Here's your sister, now give me mine," he demanded, holding out his free hand.

Mac let go of Fiona and quickly manacled Carolina's wrist to his fist.

Kenzie pulled Fiona into his arms. The lass buried her face in his neck, and he carried her to a boulder a few feet from William and Trace. Sitting down and settling her on his lap, he clutched his sister, kissing her hair as he softly whispered to her.

"Huntsman," Mac said, drawing William's and Trace's attention again, "could I perhaps interest you in coming home with us to meet our parents?"

Carolina suddenly stopped struggling against her brother and turned to look at Trace expectantly.

"You could do a lot worse than having Titus Oceanus as a father-in-law," Mac added, his own look encouraging.

Trace grabbed on to William to keep from dropping to his knees.

William heard Mac sigh again. "I didn't think so," Mac muttered. "Just give me the coin then, and my sister will no longer be your problem."

Seeing how Huntsman seemed unable to move, William held out his hand. "Give it to me, and I will take it to him."

Trace reached in his pocket and slapped the coin into William's hand.

William walked up to Mac, but stopped just out of his reach, the coin clenched in his fist. "I will see Madeline now."

Mac folded back the other side of his robe.

It was William's turn to sigh, when he saw her hands were bound and she had a gag tied around her mouth. He looked at Mac. "Was there no other way ye could have subdued her?"

Mac grinned. "Like this, you mean?" he asked, flicking his arm holding Carolina.

A flash of smoke filled the air, and Carolina's shriek of protest faded to nothing more than a squeak when she shrank to the size of a kitten in Mac's hand. He very carefully slid her into an inside pocket of his robe, giving her a pat when her muffled protests turned to threatening curses.

Mac held his hand out to William. "The coin?" He arched a brow. "Or are you planning to keep it after all?"

"I haven't decided," William said, shoving the coin in his pocket. "Do ye despise your sister so much that you'd have her marry a man who can never love her?"

"My sister means as much to me as Gabriella meant to you," Mac growled. "And you don't have to love Carolina to be a good husband to her." He shook his head. "Why do you think I've been haunting you all these centuries, Killkenny? Carolina needs a strong arm, but she also needs a firm hand." He grinned. "Not only will my father give you his blessing, but he'll probably give you a kingdom."

William stepped up and untied the knot behind Maddy's head when she suddenly started choking.

"That wasn't wise," Mac said as the gag slipped free.

Maddy held her arms out for him to undo the thick rope binding her wrists, but William stepped away, returning his attention to Mac so he wouldn't see her glare.

He was pleasantly surprised, however, when she remained silent.

"Do ye really want a woman who doesn't want you, Oceanus?" William asked. "Because if you do take Maddy, she promised me you'll return her within a week."

"She *told* you I asked her to leave with me?"

"We have an agreement between us, and Madeline is an honorable woman."

"She's also bossy as hell," Mac said, although he was smiling as he said it.

"She has a daughter."

"I like children. In fact, I hope to have many of my own."

William eyed him speculatively. "Ye don't think family gatherings might be a bit awkward, sitting down to dinner with a man who bedded your woman before you did?"

Mac shrugged. "I can live with it, knowing I will be the *last* man in Madeline's bed. So let's get down to business, Killkenny. How much do you want for her?"

William couldn't believe that Maddy was remaining silent, considering they were bartering for her as if she were a horse. "She's not for sale."

"All women are for sale. Would you hand her over for . . . say, one thousand two hundred and sixteen years—plus one day? It's that simple, you know; I can send you back to one day before, and you can save your family."

William shook his head. "They're long dead and buried and resting in peace. I no longer have a taste for revenge."

Mac stilled in surprise. "You love her that much?" he whispered.

William felt the flames in his belly start to lick the outer edges of the empty hole where his heart should have been. "You and I both know that love is beyond my reach."

Maddy snorted.

"What?" Mac said, looking down. "Did you wish to say something, Madeline?"

"No, I just had a tickle in my throat."

He looked back at William. "How about if I give you Gabriella, then? I'll bring her to this century, and she can have an even more wonderful life than the one that was stolen from her."

"I know," Maddy suddenly piped up, smiling ever so sweetly up at Mac. "How about you find your own girlfriend instead of trying to buy someone else's? Even I can see William's going to say no to anything you have to offer. So either kill him and be done with it, or just take your sister and go home."

"Men do not kill each other over women," Mac said with a chuckle. "Where I come from, women are either liabilities or assets, but they are not worth dying over."

"Madeline," William growled when he realized she looked ready to punch Mac.

She turned her glare on him. "As flattering as it is to have two men haggling over me, I have to pick Sarah up from summer rec in half an hour." She looked up at Mac. "You know, I started out thinking you were lower than pond scum, but now I realize you're just a lonely, clueless geek. Have you ever tried *asking* a girl out on a date?"

"Do not bait him, Madeline," William softly warned.

"Hey, it's a legitimate question, considering I'm being bartered over like a piece of furniture at a yard sale." Her gaze traveled up the length of Mac's robe and settled on his face. "If my dweeb of an ex-husband can manage to nail *two* homecoming queens, why can't a guy with all your . . . resources get your own girlfriend? I'll tell you why," she said before he could answer. "Where William worked really hard to get me, you aren't even *trying*. Maybe instead of blackmailing him into marrying Carolina, you should ask him for pointers on getting your own woman. Really, even your little sister had the courage to go find her own boyfriend."

"Madeline!" William snapped.

But she continued to ignore him, as oblivious to his anger as she was to Mac's incredulousness. She suddenly lifted the edge of Mac's robe with her bound hands and peered down inside the pocket. "Trust me, Carolina, if you're at all attached to your beautiful hair, you'll forget about Trace." Maddy shook her head, making her short curls bounce. "See what Trace made me do just so I could talk to my brother? Last week my hair was nearly as long as yours."

William heard a small, horrified gasp come from inside the pocket.

Maddy straightened and smiled sadly at Mac. "It's too bad you didn't show up here sooner. I have a friend I could have introduced you to, and you wouldn't even have had to break a sweat to get her. In fact, all you would have had to do was show her your fancy robe," she said, wiggling the material before she let it go with a shrug. "Only Susan ran off with some gorgeous Scottish hunk a couple of weeks ago."

"Madeline," William growled.

"Hey, I know," she said. "The guy she ran off with had two other cousins who are single; maybe you could persuade one of them to marry your sister." She pulled Mac's robe out and peered into the pocket again. "Did you hear what I just said, Carolina? They're both really big and strong and gorgeous, and I bet they wouldn't even care that you have a brother who's a . . . wizard."

Opening the robe even more, she looked at William. "William, drop that coin in the pocket with Carolina, so she can give it to one of the MacKeage men."

Mac suddenly stiffened. "Did you say MacKeage?" He looked over at Kenzie. "Isn't your brother married to a MacKeage?"

Kenzie was still sitting on the rock, still cradling Fiona as Trace sat beside him—both men as amazed as William by how the negotiations had somehow turned to matchmaking. But then William suddenly stifled a smile; apparently little Sarah wasn't the only lass who had learned the art of misdirection.

"Matt married Greylen MacKeage's youngest daughter, Winter," Kenzie said quietly. "Who also happens to be Pendaär's heir."

"And the MacKeage men Madeline just mentioned?" Mac asked.

"Winter's cousins."

The drùidh studied Maddy in silence, and looked at William. "Are you *sure* you don't want Carolina? She comes with one hell of a dowry."

William pulled the coin from his pocket and handed it to him.

Mac sighed and looked at Trace. "What about you, Huntsman? Are you *sure* you don't want my sis—"

The drùidh suddenly grunted when Maddy drove her elbow into his ribs. "Trust me, that is not a good idea," she said, deadpan. But then she smiled. "I do believe there are several single MacKeage *females* living up in the mountains. Maybe while you're husband-shopping with Carolina, you could ask one of them for a date." She shrugged. "Who knows, maybe both you and Carolina will get lucky."

It was all William could do not to reach out and kiss her when he saw Mac's entire demeanor go from suspicious to downright interested.

He looked at William. "Are you *sure*, Killkenny?"

"He's sure," Maddy answered for him, a distinct growl in her voice. She walked over to William and leaned against him with a sigh. "I have a headache and really bad belly cramps," she whispered, "and if I don't lie down soon, I'm going to faint."

William wrapped one arm around her and looked at Mac.

Mac's shoulders actually slumped, and he nodded.

William turned away and started leading Maddy down from the ledge.

But she suddenly spun around, ran up to the drùidh, and held out her hands, palms up. "I want my medal back."

"You already have it; it's around your neck, under your blouse."

She looked down with a gasp and tried to pull her blouse away from her bosom, but her bound hands made it impossible. She thrust them out to Mac. "Will you please take this damn rope off me?"

Without Mac even touching her, the thick rope suddenly fell to the ground.

Maddy squeaked in surprise, but then quickly reached into her blouse and pulled out the medal hanging around her neck. She turned it over to look at the other side. "This isn't the medal I bought!" she said, glaring at Mac. "The inscription's the same, but the one I bought had a knight riding a warhorse on the front, not a . . . not . . ." Her words trailed off as she stared down at the medal.

"That is the appropriate symbol, Madeline," Mac said softly. He reached out and touched one of her curls, rubbing it between his fingers before dropping his hand. "Because where I come from, that is a woman's only power, and the one thing every man wants but cannot buy. Consider it my gift to you."

"Where exactly *are* you from?"

William watched Mac break into a slow grin. "Atlantis."

"The lost continent of Atlantis? But I thought that was only a myth!"

He winked at her. "Then I guess that means I am but a myth, too," he said, giving William a quick nod just as the air suddenly filled with smoke.

And when the sea breeze carried the smoke away, Maximilian Oceanus and his troublesome brat of a sister were gone.

Chapter Twenty-four

William sat beside Maddy on the floor in her bedroom, leaning against her mattress; the silence of the Lane household settled around them like a comfortable blanket, Sarah and Patricia and Rick long since gone to bed. Maddy was holding his small wooden box on her lap, and he was sitting cross-legged, a cedarwood chest the size of a small coffin in front of him.

She'd led him up the stairs ten minutes ago, but William had balked when she'd tried to bring him into her room. She'd giggled softly and pulled him inside; the house rule being that if she had a boy in her bedroom, the door must remain open, she'd told him even as she'd closed it. And then she'd said she was putting bars on Sarah's window in another couple of years and that no boy was ever making it past the kitchen. To which William had wholeheartedly agreed.

Maddy had then proceeded to drag what she'd called her hope chest to the middle of the room and pulled out the box he'd given her from under the bed just before she'd sat down and patted the floor beside her.

But when he'd sat down beside her, she'd suddenly gone silent.

"I hope Mac didn't frighten you too much this afternoon," he finally said.

She looked at him in surprise. "He never frightened me, not even when he was a tiger." She smiled. "I think he just pretends to be mean and scary so no one will realize he's really a cupcake."

"You *like* him?"

She nudged him with a soft laugh. "I like you more," she said huskily, looking down at her lap. "William, why didn't you seal your box?"

"Because I trust you with my secrets." He gently nudged her back. "Are ye ready to trust me with yours, Madeline?"

She took a shuddering breath. "In a minute," she whispered. She reached up behind her on the bed and took down her purse. "I've decided to stop carrying my gun," she said, fumbling with the zipper on the side.

"But I thought you felt safer carrying it."

She looked over at him and smiled. "I don't need it anymore; I have you."

William dropped his gaze, not wanting her to see how deeply she affected him.

She reached inside the compartment but then softly gasped, her hand emerging covered in short golden hair. She shook it off her fingers, and then drove her hand into the opening again, moving it around as if searching for something.

But all she pulled out was another fistful of hair. "What is this stuff?"

William picked some of it up and softly chuckled. "It's tiger fur."

She snapped her gaze to his. "Your friend turned my gun into fur?"

William nudged her shoulder again. "I believe he's your friend now, too, whether you want him for one or not." He chuckled. "Unless all those MacKeage women ye sent him after decide he's pond scum."

She made a harrumphing sound and shook the fur off her hand. And then she brushed it off herself, even spitting some out of her mouth as it floated through the air like milkweed. She finally set her purse on the floor, picked up his small wooden box, and went silent again.

William took a painful breath. "Go ahead, Madeline; open it."

He saw her hands were trembling as she slowly worked the lid free, and then she went perfectly still as she stared down into the open box.

"Do ye have any idea what that is, lass?" he asked, his heart pounding so hard it hurt to breathe.

"It's . . . I believe it's a dragon's claw," she whispered. She reached in and picked up the three-inch-long, razor-sharp claw. "It's . . . this is what you used to be."

"Nay, Madeline, it's who I *am*."

Her snort sounded like gunshot, and William actually leaned away from her thunderous glare, and then flinched when she suddenly thrust the claw in front of his face. "This is what you think you *are*?" she asked through gritted teeth, shaking it at him. "Some ugly, badass, *heartless* monster that sends everyone scurrying under their beds in fear?"

His mouth so dry he couldn't even swallow, William merely nodded.

She threw the claw across the room. It ricocheted off the wall, and before it had even clattered to the floor, she rolled onto her knees and slapped her hands on his cheeks; getting right in his face, her glare so fierce that he flinched again.

"What you are, William Killkenny, is an idiot. You also

happen to be the badass, *big-hearted* sap I am in love with. And if I ever catch you calling yourself a monster again, I will shave off every damn last hair on your body." She suddenly smiled. "Except on your arms—that hair makes me hotter than Lucifer's bride on her wedding night."

It took him several heartbeats to realize that somewhere in that little tirade, she'd mentioned something about loving him, and judging by her sudden look of horror, she also just realized what she'd said.

Where she'd been red with anger, she suddenly paled. William hauled her into his arms when she tried to bolt, and buried his face in her hair. "I won't let you take it back," he growled. "You are *my* woman now." She was trembling so violently she started making him tremble, too. "Say it again," he demanded thickly. He clasped her face in his hands, locking her gaze to his. "Again, Madeline. *Say it.*"

"I love you."

Christ, he thought his chest was going to explode. He used his thumbs to brush the tears on her cheeks, but when he tried to speak and couldn't, he pulled her forward and claimed her mouth.

He kissed her like a man deeply in love, hoping she wouldn't realize the difference even as he wondered how long he could deceive her. And Madeline kissed him back like a woman deeply in love; her trembling hands running through his hair, her body melting into his, her sweet lips tasting like heaven.

But when she moved to straddle his lap, William broke away and tucked her face against his neck, muffling her cry of protest. "We will stop now, before we scandalize your daughter and mother."

"You can't just leave me *hanging,*" she cried. "I want to feel you inside me."

He chuckled—though it held no humor—and held her looking at him again. "Get used to it, lass, as you will probably be hanging for months."

She went utterly still. "M-months?" she whispered. "You're *leaving*?"

"No, Madeline, I'm not going anywhere. But if ye wish to walk down the aisle at your grand church wedding, wearing your mama's gown and not be heavy with child, then you'll not feel me inside you again until our wedding night."

She tried to rear away, her face paling in horror. "You peeked! You looked in my hope chest!" she cried, struggling to get away.

William held her facing him, this time his chuckle was sincere. "Ye left me here all alone this morning with nothing to do but wander through your house. And when I came to your bedroom, your secrets called out to me."

"But that's not fair! I didn't peek in your box."

He sighed. "Madeline, a man stands no chance against a woman if he plays fair. It's our nature to use whatever we can beg, borrow, or steal to capture your hearts." He smiled. "Did Mac not tell you that it's something we all want but cannot buy?"

"It was still a rotten thing to do," she muttered, the color returning to her cheeks.

"Have I not repeatedly warned you that I'm a selfish bastard?" He pulled her forward and kissed the tip of her nose, then held her facing him again. "So knowing that I will never play fair, do you still wish to love me?" he asked softly.

She dropped her gaze to his chest, her eyelids hooding her expression from him as she took a shuddering breath. She reached under his hands and pulled a chain from her blouse, making him let go of her so she could take it off. She slid the chain down over his head and then patted the medal against his chest with a sigh.

"I tried as hard as I could not to fall in love with you, but it happened anyway. And no matter how hard you try to discourage me when *you* get scared, I'm never going to stop loving you." One corner of her mouth turned up. "Did I hear you say I'd be hanging until our wedding night? Was that a marriage proposal, Mr. Killkenny?"

"No, it wasn't," he snapped. He gestured toward her hope chest. "I believe a modern proposal involves candlelight and flowers, music and dancing, and an engagement ring. And then *months* to plan a wedding with flowers and music and *two* rings, and enough people to fill a cathedral." He cupped her face again. "And after your grand day, you would move into a house with enough bedrooms for four children, surrounded by a white picket fence. And I believe there was also a puppy on your list, a couple of cats, and a pony for each of the children."

"I-I was thirteen when I started that list," she whispered, two big fat tears running down her cheeks. "When I still believed dreams really could come true."

Instead of using his thumbs to brush them away, he sipped each tear off her cheek. "Ah, but they can, Madeline, when fate gives us a second chance."

She reached down and lifted the medal hanging around his neck and studied it for several silent heartbeats before she lifted her gaze to his. "I bought this because I wanted you to know exactly how I see you. It had a knight in shining armor riding to my rescue. I don't need candles and flowers and an engagement ring, or a big wedding, or a picket fence and ponies. Those are the dreams of a naïve young girl, and have nothing to do with love, really. But that little girl grew up, and the woman she became wants . . . just you," she ended on a whisper.

"Nevertheless, you are getting those things," he told her

just as softly. "Only the ponies will be warhorses, and the house will be a keep with *eight* bedrooms. And instead of a knight in shining armor, you'll be getting a devious, possessive strong arm who will demand more than you think you can give."

"Oh William, for a ninth-century warrior, you are such a romantic sap," she said, melting into him.

He stiffened. "How do you know what time I'm from?"

"Mac told me," she murmured against his chest, her own chest expanding on a sigh. "But I already guessed you weren't from this century."

"Ye did? How?"

She sat up to frown at him. "You're over thirty years old, and you can't even *drive*." She snorted. "And you own a *sword*. And you've asked me to explain everything from Wonderbras to airbags to *going parking*. Then I remembered a dragon had walked into the library carrying Mabel, but *you* walked out carrying her. And with Eve warning me that you were even more old-fashioned than Kenzie—who acts like he just stepped out of the Middle Ages—it didn't take long to figure out what was going on. Mac just filled in some of the missing pieces." She snorted again. "For someone who's supposed to be a powerful wizard, he sure is insecure. He spent the whole ride from Ellsworth telling me everything you've done, trying to dissuade me from loving you."

William reared away. "He told you *everything*?"

"Not everything. I stopped him when he started listing off all the women you'd been with, and where you'd been with them, and what you'd been doing with—"

He covered her mouth with his hand. "Exactly how did you stop him?"

She smiled behind his hand, and he quickly pulled it away when her tongue darted out to lick him. "I swerved off the pavement toward a bunch of mailboxes." She frowned. "Only I didn't notice the sheriff's car following me. When he stopped me for driving erratically, and then asked to see my driver's license and registration . . . well, imagine my surprise when I found out the truck was registered to *me*." Her smile returned, and her chin lifted. "I've decided I'm keeping it."

"Oh, ye have, have you?"

"Yup," she said, her chin lifting higher as her smile disappeared. "Even if you suddenly end our affair, I'm not giving it back just so you can give it to some perky-boobed, gold-digging hussy who only wants to take advantage of you."

William arched a brow. "So we've gone from having a wedding night back to being only lovers?"

"You told me that wasn't a marriage proposal."

He pulled her down to his chest so she wouldn't see his smile. "I did say that, didn't I? What else did Mac tell you about me?"

He felt her toying with the medal she'd given him. "He tried to explain why you'll never be able to love me."

William's blood suddenly went cold. "And?" he whispered.

She nearly clipped his chin when she popped her head up. "And I shut him up again. After checking my rearview mirror, I slammed on the brakes and made him spill ale all over himself." She scowled. "He must have stolen the three cases I bought you; they weren't in the truck when I went out to get them this evening."

She suddenly scrambled off his lap—making him grunt when she nearly unmanned him—and gestured toward the door. "You might as well go to bed, William. I'm feeling crampy again, which just reminded me that we can't make love even if we wanted to. The doctor said I shouldn't have intercourse for a couple of days."

William leaped to his feet. "Ye went to see a doctor today? Are ye sick, Madeline? Did we . . . did I hurt you the other night at the cabin?"

"No! I had an IUD put in so we don't have to mess with condoms anymore."

"What's an IUD?" he asked, grasping her shoulders. "And what do ye mean, ye had it . . . put in?"

She looked momentarily startled and then laughed. "It's a tiny little plastic device that the doctor placed inside my ute—my womb, so your little boys can't get to my little girls and make a baby."

William stepped away in horror and looked down at her stomach. "Ye let them put something *inside* you? Isn't it going to hurt when we . . . whenever you and I . . ."

"In another day I won't even know it's there." She stepped into his arms and grinned up at him. "And neither will you." She patted his chest. "So the only thing that's going to be *hanging* is your stockings, Mr. Killkenny, when they get stuck on a nearby tree."

Not even daring to kiss her again for fear he would scandalize *himself,* he turned away and walked to the door.

"William."

He stopped but didn't turn around.

"I love you."

He nodded without looking back, and quietly opened the door and walked down the stairs. He went outside and climbed the knoll, then sat down and stared at Maddy's bedroom window, watching her silhouette as she undressed for bed. When her room finally went dark, he lifted the medal she'd given him up to the moonlight and read the inscription engraved on one side.

Mine; until the end of time.

He turned it over, but instead of a knight on a warhorse, he saw a large heart bulging out from the flat medal, the ancient symbol of a strong arm carved into it.

And that was when William decided he had made it to hell after all, which turned out to be the unwavering love of a beautiful, lusty, courageous woman he was incapable of loving in return.

Chapter Twenty-five

$\diamondsuit$

$\mathcal{M}$addy stole a loaf of olive bread from the display table, grabbed a container of goat cheese and two oatmeal cookies, and sat on the stool across the counter from Eve. "Men," she scoffed. "And they call us women complicated. They even have their own secret language. I've seen them have entire conversations where they just nod and grunt at each other. And really, what's up with their idea that the less we women know, the better off we are?"

Eve opened the cheese and drove her knife into it rather forcefully. "They think they're being protective. I practically talked myself hoarse trying to persuade Kenzie that you weren't going to run through town screaming, 'Hide the children, the monsters are coming!'" She smiled sheepishly. "Are you sure you forgive me for not telling you about the magic?"

"For the tenth time, there is nothing to forgive. I would have done the same thing if William had asked me to keep a secret—even from my very best friend."

Eve broke off a chunk of bread and slathered it with cheese.

"I wish I could have met Maximilian Oceanus. Did he really show up dressed like a wizard?"

"Right out of a fairy tale, only he didn't have a pointy hat."

"Is he cute?" Eve asked just before she took a bite of bread.

"I can't really say; I never saw his sleeves rolled up."

Eve started choking and actually spat the bread back into her hand. "You are so bad." She arched a brow. "Did you honestly call him pond scum to his face?"

Maddy nodded. "I took it back, though. Mac really is a nice guy. Did I tell you he gave Hiram a beautiful cake before he died?"

"I'm sorry about Hiram, Maddy. I know he was special to you."

"Thank you. But since meeting William and Mac and realizing there's all this . . . stuff going on behind the scenes, I don't feel so sad. Hiram actually seemed to be looking forward to dying, once he saw everyone waiting for him." She leaned forward on the counter. "The old sap left me two hundred dollars in a sentimental card and said I should buy myself something pretty." She laughed. "But not one of those skimpy bras like he picked up off the floor that William had dropped. He actually wrote that in the card!"

"So what pretty thing are you going to buy yourself?" Eve asked. She bobbed her eyebrows. "Some really short shorts?"

"I used the money to buy William a medal." Maddy felt her cheeks heat up. "I had the jeweler engrave *Mine; until the end of time* on the back of it. And on the front it used to have a knight in shining armor, but Mac changed it to a heart with some sort of symbol carved into it." She hesitated. "And last night, I told William I loved him."

"And?" Eve whispered. "Did he say he loved you back?"

"No. But only because he doesn't know he loves me."

"Excuse me?"

Maddy set down her piece of bread. "William believes he's still an ugly monster who's incapable of loving anyone. I think it has something to do with what happened to his family back in the ninth century. Apparently William's home was raided and everyone was killed, and he went a little . . . crazy. At least that's what Mac told me. That's why William drove that old witch off his land—because he thought she could have done something to stop the massacre or at least warned him. And after she turned him into a dragon, he spent the next four years lashing out at everyone. But then he found some symbol Kenzie had left on a rock and spent the next two years fighting his way through time to get here."

Her jaw slack, Eve continued to stare at Maddy in disbelief.

Maddy nodded. "So, because he believes he lost his soul seeking revenge for his family, and because he spent six years acting and feeling like a monster, William assumes that he doesn't have a heart left to give me."

"But you believe he *does* love you?" Eve asked. "You're not worried that he might only be in lust with you?"

"Oh, it's love, all right," Maddy said, rolling her eyes. "The man's got it so bad he doesn't know if he's coming or going most of the time. One minute he's chasing me down with the desperation of a starving lion, and the next minute he's doing any devious thing he can think of to push me away." She leaned forward again. "Do you know he stole the diary I kept all through my teens? He snooped through my hope chest, found out my most intimate desires, and now he's planning to use them against me."

"Use them against you how?"

"By giving me every last one of them."

Eve was back to staring at her in disbelief—or maybe confusion.

Maddy sighed. "William is having a small cottage delivered

for him to live in while they're building his house, and I will bet you a manicure, a pedicure, *and* a facial that a white picket fence goes up around it in less than a week." She grinned. "And the stone on the engagement ring he's going to give me will be so huge I probably won't be able to lift my hand."

"He asked you to marry him?" Eve squeaked.

"Not yet. But every time I walked into a room at work this morning, everyone suddenly stopped talking. I think William has already enlisted my residents to help him plan a romantic evening to propose to me."

"So what are you going to do about his stealing your diary?"

"Absolutely nothing. If it makes him feel all smart and devious to grant my every desire, who am I to spoil his fun? Can you imagine having every one of your childhood dreams come true, including having a man get down on his knees and ask you to marry him?" She straightened with a laugh. "My God, if I remember correctly, I actually wrote down exactly what my dream guy would say. Talk about making it easy for him; William won't even have to come up with the right words."

"And when he finally asks, will you say yes?"

"Are you kidding? I've already started looking at bridal magazines!"

"But Maddy, you can't marry a man who can never love you."

"Haven't you been listening to me? He *does* love me; he just doesn't know it."

"And he'll never be able to say it," Eve snapped.

"Hell, Billy said he loved me all the time when we were first married, and he didn't have a clue what love was. William says he loves me a hundred times a day in a hundred different ways without uttering a word."

Eve jumped up from her stool and ran around the counter, nearly knocking Maddy over when she threw her arms around her. "I knew there was a reason I love you," Eve said, hugging her fiercely. "You are such a wise woman."

Maddy hugged her back even as she sighed. "If I'm so wise, then why can't I come up with a plan to make William *realize* he loves me?" She leaned away. "I can't just *tell* him he does; he'll never believe me. So help me figure out how to get him to figure it out for himself."

Eve walked back to her stool with a thoughtful look. "Why not try using *his* tactics?"

"How?"

"You said William is sneaky and devious, so why don't you get sneaky and devious, too? You just have to find out *his* secret desires and give them to him."

"But *how*? He doesn't exactly have a hope chest I can snoop through. And I've already given him everything I have, including my heart."

"You haven't given William *his* heart, have you?" Eve asked softly.

Maddy blinked at her. "Huh?"

"You said he thinks he doesn't have a heart anymore, so give him one."

"But how?"

When Eve merely shrugged, Maddy jumped off her stool, grabbed her purse, and started to leave.

Eve ran around the counter and dragged her to a stop. "You can do this," she said sternly. "You just have to think like the man. And you have your residents. If he can enlist their help, why can't you? And don't forget Sarah; you can't tell me William isn't already in love with her, too, and that he doesn't already care for your mom and Rick. You sort of all come as a package, Maddy. The family he lost can't ever be replaced, but there's no reason all of you can't become his new family."

"But what if that only scares him even more?" Maddy

whispered, clutching her purse to her chest. "He's having a hard time believing he loves *me*. What will happen if he starts feeling responsible for everyone else's happiness as well?"

"Maybe he'll find out he's got so much heart that his chest just might burst."

"Or he might run off and marry Carolina Oceanus."

"William Killkenny is a lot of things, but he's not a chicken," Eve said. "I believe he is in love with you, and I'm confident you'll find a way to prove it to him." She nodded at Maddy's purse. "Just point your gun at him, and make him admit he loves you."

"I can't. Mac turned it into tiger fur."

"He what?"

"Speaking of turning things into something, how is Fiona doing?" Maddy asked softly. "What little bit I saw of her . . . well, she looked terrified. William told me some guy had raped her in the eleventh century, but then she died giving birth to her son and came to this century as a hawk. He said Fiona hates men and was quite happy as a hawk, and now everyone is upset that Mac made her human again."

"I don't think Kenzie's all that upset to have his sister back. And Matt arrived at our house around midnight last night, and he was so overjoyed that he couldn't stop hugging her." Eve's eyes turned pained. "It's just that they can't stand seeing her so distressed. I don't think Fiona hates men anywhere near as much as she's afraid of them. She felt safe being a hawk, but now that she's a young woman again . . . well, last night she acted sort of . . . ashamed in front of them."

"Ashamed? But being raped wasn't her fault!"

Eve shrugged. "I know that, and you know that, but you have to remember what century she's from. Back then, a woman's chastity was a strong part of her identity." She shook her head. "Nobody knows exactly what happened to her. Both

Matt and Kenzie had already left home, and when they finally returned their mother and sister and nephew were dead, and their father had gone quite mad. And Fiona certainly isn't going to tell them any of the details. Personally, I think the guy did more than rape her."

"Maybe being thrust into this century is as overwhelming for her as being alive again is," Maddy suggested. "And once she gets used to everything, she might confide in you or her other sister-in-law, Winter."

"That's our hope. And being around modern women should help." Eve smiled. "Fiona did perk up when she realized that she was going to meet her niece and namesake. Remember, Winter and Matt named their new baby after her."

"Oh, that's right! And there's nothing like a newborn to get a person's mind off their own problems."

"So, did I hear that your cousin wasn't interested in having a drùidh for a brother-in-law?" Eve asked.

"Omigod, are you kidding?" Maddy said with a laugh. "I honestly thought Trace was going to faint when Carolina said she intended to marry him and have lots and lots of babies, and they would live happily ever after for a thousand years." She sobered. "I'm afraid Trace might be just as bad as William when it comes to matters of the heart, and that like Fiona, he has a few secrets of his own he's hiding." She gave Eve a hug. "Okay, I really have to get back to work now."

"But how are you going to make William realize he loves you before you two get married?"

Maddy opened the door and looked at her. "I'm sure as hell not waiting for him to say it *before* we get married, or I'll be rolling down the aisle in a wheelchair. They're just words, Eve, and I don't care if I ever hear them. It took more courage than I knew I had, but I gave William my heart with no conditions attached." She smiled. "And I happen to have a friend who just

312 Janet Chapman

happens to be a powerful drùidh, and if William Killkenny starts giving me too much grief, I'll sic Mac on him."

"I don't think drùidhs are allowed to interfere in people's lives like that."

Maddy laughed at that. "Mac doesn't seem all that worried about playing by the rules—look what he did to Fiona. And William said we don't have to worry about those wolves coming back, because Mac's going to make sure the guy who sent them will be too busy looking over his shoulder to cause any more trouble."

Maddy suddenly ran her gaze up and down Eve and frowned.

"What?" Eve said, looking down at herself.

"I'm trying to picture how big your belly's going to be in October."

"Why?"

"So I can pick out a really nice dress for you." She chuckled. "It'll be refreshing to have the bridesmaid pregnant instead of the bride."

"Maddy, he hasn't even *asked* you yet."

"I was thinking Columbus Day. Um . . . you'll understand if I don't ask you to be my maid of honor, won't you? I'd like to give Sarah that honor."

"Of course Sarah should stand up with you!"

"And what do you think about my having the wedding at River Run? We have that beautiful gazebo, and the maple trees will be in full color. It shouldn't be too cold for an outdoor wedding in October, should it?"

"You think you can plan the wedding of your dreams in six weeks?"

"No. But I can plan the wedding I really want—one that's intimate and personal, with all the people I care about in attendance." She grinned. "Maybe I'll invite Mac."

Eve laughed. "I'm sure William would love to have the man who tried to buy you come to your wedding. You're not afraid when the preacher asks if anyone has any objections that Mac might raise one or two?"

"Naw, I think he's actually happy for William. Although it sure was fun having two men haggle over me." She started walking backward down the sidewalk. "I'll call you tonight. Maybe we can get together and go over my wedding plans."

"You need a proposal first!"

"I'll give him a week, and then *I'm* going to propose to *him*," she said with a laugh, giving a wave and spinning around to head toward the side street.

Maddy smiled to herself as she marveled at how *not* scared she was. William was right; sometimes fate did give second chances, and she wasn't about to blow this one. She was marrying the man of her dreams, and they were going to live happily ever after for forever—because she sure as hell wasn't going to let William blow his second chance, either. He'd fought too hard to become human again to settle for anything less than full-blown love.

Maddy suddenly stopped walking. When William had entrusted her with the box containing his dragon claw, he *had* handed her his heart!

Which meant she *could* give it back to him.

Only not the way it was now—representing his years of anger and despair—but somehow reshaped into a symbol of his love.

When she got home, she had to find that claw, and then use it to show William that six years of being a dragon hadn't stolen his heart but had, in fact, made it stronger.

Chapter Twenty-six

*H*e asked for her hand in marriage three days later; during a candlelight dinner, surrounded by enough flowers to make a bee sneeze, and he even got down on *both* knees. A table had been set up in the center of the large gazebo overlooking the river, little white lights had been hung from the rafters, rose petals had been strewn over the floor, and every window of the nursing home had faces peeking out of them.

William had been dressed in a perfectly tailored suit—although just before getting down on his knees, he'd taken off the jacket, given her a wink, and rolled up his cuffs.

Maddy had been wearing her scrubs.

His proposal had been practically verbatim to what she'd written in her diary, except the word *cherished* had replaced love. And the diamond ring he'd held out to her was absolutely beautiful; the stone tastefully sized instead of garishly large, two shiny pink tourmalines nestled on either side of it.

That was why Maddy was sitting on Sarah's bed right now, staring down at her empty left ring finger as she waited for her daughter to finish brushing her teeth. God, she hoped she'd done the right thing. She hadn't said yes when William had asked her to marry him; she'd said . . . maybe.

Maddy took a shuddering breath, remembering how shocked he'd been—that is until she'd reminded him that she came with a daughter who would also be affected by her decision, and that he needed to ask Sarah, too.

William's beautiful marine-blue eyes had turned downright pained; obviously appalled that he hadn't thought to include the girl. Rick had already given his blessing, William had told her, since of course he'd had to ask the man of the house for her hand. Then he'd felt honor-bound to ask Patricia, and the woman had hugged him and kissed him and said yes through a small river of tears.

But when Maddy had only said . . . maybe, William had jumped to his feet, shoved her beautiful ring in his pocket, and grabbed her hand with every intention of driving to her house to ask Sarah immediately.

Maddy had pulled him to a stop, this time reminding him that the girl was only nine and that he couldn't expect a child to make that kind of decision in two minutes. She had instead promised to tell Sarah that night, and then they would give her time to get used to the idea before *he* personally asked if she'd like them to become a family.

"Where's Mr. Killkenny?" Sarah asked, running in and jumping up on the bed. She grabbed the book off her nightstand and slid under the covers. "We still have two chapters left of *The Chronicles of Narnia*. Isn't he staying with us anymore?"

"No, he's camping out on his land on Dragon Cove. He was only staying with us until his arm healed enough that he could take care of himself. Don't worry; you'll finish your story with him. But right now you and I need to have a little mother-daughter talk."

Sarah suddenly took on a mutinous look, her chin lifting defiantly. "I don't care if I am in trouble," she said. "If you make me take it back, I'll just say it to her again."

Maddy arched a brow. "Excuse me? Who is the *her* you said something to, and *what* did you say?"

Sarah blinked in surprise, her cheeks turning pink at the realization she'd just tattled on herself. "Sissy," she said, lifting her chin again. "I told her that if anyone was a gold-digger that *she* was, and that she's also a tight-assed, man-trapping hussy with the brains of a chipmunk, because everyone knows you're supposed to get pregnant *after* you get married, not before."

Maddy didn't know if she was shocked or downright proud of the girl. "Mind telling me what compelled you to say that to Sissy?"

Sarah's mutinous glare turned uncertain. "I was watching TV in the living room Sunday, waiting for Dad to bring me home, when I heard Sissy tell him that everyone in town knows the only reason you're chasing after Mr. Killkenny is because he's rich. But when Daddy said it was about damn time you started dating again and that he was happy for you, Sissy exploded and started shouting at him. She said the only reason you divorced him was because *he* hadn't been getting rich fast enough. Then she said your best friend, Eve, snatched up Mr. Gregor before you could, so you went after Mr. Killkenny before anyone else could get him. But instead of calming down when Dad told her to, Sissy started calling you nasty names and said it was obvious you were jealous of her because Daddy's construction business finally started making money."

Maddy opened her mouth to say something, but Sarah rushed on with her confession. "Sissy said you must really be desperate, since everyone knows Mr. Killkenny is crazy because he drives like a madman and is building a big ugly *castle* down on Dragon Cove."

"Do you think Mr. Killkenny is crazy?" Maddy asked softly.

"No! That's why I ran into the kitchen and told Sissy he wasn't. I told her Mr. Killkenny is smart and nice and polite, and that he doesn't treat me like a baby. But when she called him a caveman, I called her a tight-assed, man-trapping hussy with the brains of a chipmunk," she finished on a whisper, her cheeks bright red.

Maddy tried but couldn't stifle her smile. "And how did that go over?"

"Sissy burst into tears and ran upstairs, and Dad just quietly told me to get my stuff and get in the truck."

"Did he say anything to you on the ride home?"

"He asked me if I felt comfortable around Mr. Killkenny."

"And you said?"

"I told him I like Mr. Killkenny, and I explained how he taught me about using misdirection when somebody says something I don't like." She gave Maddy a sheepish grin. "I guess I should have tried using it on Sissy, but she made me so mad that I just forgot. I told Dad you're not chasing Mr. Killkenny because he's rich; that he's been chasing you because you're so pretty." Her smile broadened. "And Dad agreed with me. He said your new hairdo makes your eyes look as big as saucers and that maybe I should get my hair cut just like it. Can I?"

Maddy arched a brow again. "I thought you wanted to keep it long to bug Sissy because she's been trying to talk you into getting it cut for the last three months?"

Sarah got a mutinous look again. "If I had, everyone would have thought I was trying to be just like *her*. But I only want *one* mom, and . . . and that's you," she said, her eyes welling with tears. "Can you tell Sissy to quit trying to make me call her Mama? It's not disrespectful for me to call her Sissy, is it, if that's her name?"

Maddy pulled her into her embrace. "No, sweetie, you can

call her whatever you want." She chuckled. "Except a tight-assed hussy."

Sarah sighed and wiped her face on Maddy's shirt. "When Sissy has her baby, can I get a puppy?"

Not quite sure if she was being misdirected or simply manipulated, Maddy chuckled again. "I'm afraid that's something you're going to have to ask Mr. Killkenny."

Sarah pulled away in surprise. "What's he got to do with my getting a dog?"

"William has asked me to marry him, Sarah, and if I say yes, that means you and I would be moving in with him."

"We would?" she squeaked, her eyes growing huge. "In his castle on Dragon Cove?" Her huge eyes suddenly turned worried. "Wait, does that mean we'd have to leave Gram?"

"That's how it works, Sarah—children grow up and eventually move away from home. It's what you're going to do someday, too."

"But if Rick moves out, too, she'll be all alone!"

"We'd only be six miles away, not six hundred. You'll still see Gram whenever you want. And you can have sleepovers with her." She brushed back Sarah's hair and tucked it behind her ear. "And we might not be moving at all. I haven't agreed to marry William yet."

"You haven't? But I thought you really liked him."

"I more than really like him, sweetie. I love William. But I also love you. That's why I explained to him that he would have to propose to you, too." She gave her daughter a lopsided grin. "We come as a package, Sarah. If you were two years old, then I would make the decision myself, doing what I thought was best for both of us. But you're almost ten, and you deserve some say."

"Daddy didn't ask me if it was okay for him to marry Sissy."

"The circumstances are different. Your dad has another child on the way, so he's doing what he feels is best for everyone. And you aren't living with him all the time, whereas you would be living with William. That's why I'm asking you to think about how you'd feel if we got married."

Sarah's big brown eyes turned worried again. "But how can I know what I'd feel until it actually happens?" she whispered. "I really like Mr. Killkenny, but what if he's only being nice to me because he likes you?"

"Do you trust me, Sarah?"

"Of course I do. You're my mom!"

"Okay, then, let's make a pact: *we* won't marry William until you are absolutely certain it's the right thing for both of us. And if it takes you two weeks, two months, or two years to get used to the idea of having another man in your life, then that's simply how long it takes. No pressure." She laughed. "Although I imagine you might get a few bribes from William." She gave her daughter a stern look. "But I think you're old enough and wise enough to take them in the spirit they're given—as long as you don't take advantage of the poor sap. Sometimes William gets carried away with his gifts."

That got a smile from Sarah. "You mean like motorcycle rides and a puppy and maybe even a horse of my own?"

Maddy gestured for her to slide down so she could tuck her in. "If I catch you even sitting on that motorcycle I will cut your hair myself, and we both know how lovely you'll look then."

Sarah shuddered. "I still have nightmares from when you cut it two days before my seventh birthday party. I thought Elvira was going to take the clippers to *you* right after she got done fixing it."

Maddy stood up and turned off the bedside lamp.

"Mom? Is Mr. Killkenny really going to ask me if he can marry you?"

"Yes, he is. But you don't have to give him an answer right

away, just like I didn't give him one tonight. You only have to promise that you'll think about it."

"If you do marry him, will he want me to call him Dad?"

"No, sweetie. I think one father is enough for any girl. But you could ask him if it's okay to start calling him William."

"Is he really building a castle?"

"Not a castle like you're picturing. He's building what's called a keep, which is more like a large house with lots of stone and maybe even a small tower."

"It sounds big enough for Gram to come live with us."

"You can't put conditions on your saying yes to William, Sarah. Besides, did it ever occur to you that maybe Gram might like to have her house all to herself again? Living alone isn't a punishment, sweetie; sometimes it's a blessing to have your own space and then have everyone come visit. Gram has slowly been building a new life for herself since Grampy died and has even gone on a few dates. Maybe our leaving will open up room in her life for someone new."

Sarah's eyes widened. "I hadn't thought about that." She grinned. "Imagine Gram with a boyfriend."

Maddy walked to the door and shut off the overhead light, then looked back. "Your little extended family is growing in leaps and bounds, isn't it, baby? But let's keep William's marriage proposal just between you, me, Gram, and Rick, okay? Nobody needs to know about it until we decide if there even will be a wedding."

"Does Mr. . . . does William love you, Mama?"

"Yes, he does. And I believe he loves you, too. But he has a hard time saying what he feels, so that's why it's so important that you listen with your heart. People's actions speak louder than their words. You pay attention not only to how William treats you but to how he treats everyone else, okay? And Sarah?"

"Yeah?"

"You have to consider your father's feelings, too. Don't make him feel as if he has to compete with William for your affection. There's enough room in your heart for both men, and it's going to fall on your shoulders to reassure them of that."

"How do I do that?"

"By just being yourself." She grinned. "And using a bit of misdirection when you have to. When you're with your dad, don't talk about William all the time, and when you're with William, don't talk constantly about your dad. Just *be* with them. I promise, if you take this one day at a time, everything will work out for the best, so try not to stay awake half the night thinking too hard, okay?"

Sarah settled down into her pillow with a sigh. "I won't. Maybe I'll dream about living in a castle with my new puppy and pony. 'Night, Mom."

"Good night, baby," Maddy said softly, closing the bedroom door all but a crack.

She walked to her bedroom, sat down on the bed, and let out a deep sigh, still smiling. Poor William. He didn't have a clue what he was in for. Sarah Jane was going to give his big, sappy heart a real workout in the coming weeks, because that little girl was definitely her mother's daughter.

Maddy pulled the small wooden box he'd given her from under her pillow and lifted out the dragon claw to study it.

And then she suddenly smiled again.

She went to her vanity and sat down, picked up her emery board, and carefully slid it across the claw's razor-sharp point. When it didn't even leave a mark in the amazingly hard keratin, she turned the board over to the grittier side and tried again. But when that didn't do much of anything, either, she picked up her metal fingernail file and tried that.

"Okay, I guess you really were a badass dragon," she

muttered when the metal file did little more than scratch it. "Let's try the nail clippers."

But Maddy sighed in defeat ten minutes later, setting the claw down beside the broken clippers and the file she had snapped in half, and sucked on her bleeding thumb. Tomorrow on her lunch break she'd have to go to the hardware store and get something a little more lethal.

She put on her pajamas, shut off the overhead light, and walked over to the window. Lifting the shade, Maddy peered up at the knoll and then gave a small wave. "Good night, Mr. Bogeyman," she whispered.

She climbed into bed with a smile and dreamed of being curled up in William's arms, the strong, steady beat of his magnificent dragon heart lulling her to sleep.

Chapter Twenty-seven

*W*earing her mother's beautiful wedding gown and surrounded by everyone she loved, Maddy stood beside William
in the center of River Run's large gazebo, the two of them facing
Father Daar. Sarah stood next to her, looking like a miniature
bride herself in a re-creation of her grandmother's gown, sport-
ing a spray of flowers in her hair, cut almost identically to
Maddy's. Eve stood beside Sarah, her blossoming belly lost in
the gathered waist of her muted rose dress.

Kenzie stood beside William, and Trace beside him. Rick
had joined his mother after giving her away, and the fifty or so
chairs surrounding the gazebo were filled with everyone dear
to Maddy's heart. Even the weather was cooperating; the mid-
October sun all but setting the trees on fire with color, the warm
air being stirred by a gentle breeze wafting up the river from the
bay.

Her sweet, darling daughter hadn't held out even two minutes against William, much less two days or two weeks or two
years—thank God. When William had walked into the Lane

kitchen and gotten down on one knee to ask Sarah for her mother's hand in marriage, Maddy had discovered she was worth exactly one dog and a white four-poster bed. As soon as he had finished his awkward though heartfelt speech, Sarah had squealed in delight, thrown her arms around William and kissed him right on his cheek. She had then grabbed the leash attached to the puppy he had deviously brought as a bribe and run outside with her new very best friend.

William, still on one knee, had then held out his ring to Maddy once again. Only this time instead of reciting what she'd written in her diary all those years ago, the romantic sap had simply asked if she would please be *his; until the end of time.*

Immensely glad that Mac had been bartering with William for her instead of with Sarah, Maddy had let him slip the ring on her trembling finger, then thrown her arms around him and kissed him quite passionately.

And despite knowing better than to give them free rein, she had nonetheless relinquished control of the wedding reception to the residents, and for the last five weeks her herd of turtles had been keeping secrets to themselves, and the sitting room off limits to her. And although she hadn't been allowed to peek for the last two days, Maddy suspected the River Run cafeteria had been transformed into the main hall of an Irish keep; complete with wildflowers, wooden bowls, metal tankards, and honest to God live doves. She also suspected that there was a warhorse hidden somewhere, waiting for Prince Charming to carry her off into the sunset after the reception.

She was so excited she couldn't stop trembling, and so damn happy she couldn't stop smiling to *finally* be pledging her troth to the man of her childhood dreams.

Or at least, that's what she hoped she was doing. Father Daar was speaking Gaelic, and as near as she could tell, only Kenzie and William knew what he was saying. The old priest suddenly stopped in what seemed like mid-sentence and pointedly glared at everyone sitting around the gazebo. Maddy assumed this was the part where he was checking to see if anyone objected to their getting married, and she was suddenly glad she hadn't invited Mac.

"I object," someone said from somewhere behind her.

Maddy turned with a gasp—though it was lost in the collective gasp of the audience. Only instead of also turning to look, William just closed his eyes on a groan.

"Who said that?" Father Daar demanded.

A man in his mid-thirties, with shoulder-length blond hair, ruggedly handsome features, and piercing green eyes walked up to the gazebo and stopped at the bottom step. "I did."

"And just who would you be?" Daar asked.

The man gave a slight bow. "Maximilian Oceanus."

"Nay!" the old priest cried, taking a step back. "Ye're not!"

"I'm afraid he is, Father," William said quietly.

Maddy blinked at the man—who didn't at all look like the Mac she remembered—and then she blinked at William. "Did you invite him?" she whispered.

William arched a brow. "You mean you didn't?"

"I guess my invitation got lost in the mail," Mac drawled, walking up the steps. He stopped and looked down at Sarah, and extended his hand to her with a warm smile. "Sarah, isn't it? I'm Mac, a good friend of William and your mother."

After an uncertain glance at Maddy, Sarah transferred her bouquet of white roses to her left hand and took his even as she eyed him suspiciously. "If you're their friend, then how come you object to them getting married?" she asked bluntly.

It appeared that Father Daar had finally regained his wits. "Yes, Oceanus, on what grounds are you objecting?" he echoed.

Mac turned his attention to Daar. "On the grounds that Ms. Kimble is marrying Mr. Killkenny because she believes he loves her, when I happen to know that is impossible."

Maddy barely refrained from snorting, but her sweet little daughter was nowhere near as circumspect and snorted quite loudly. "Of course he loves her," the girl said, drawing Mac's attention again. She thrust her chin out defiantly. "And he loves me, too."

Mac arched an inquiring brow. "Are you sure about that, little one? Because it's been my experience that a person needs a *heart* in order to love, and William Killkenny doesn't have one."

"He does, too!" Sarah all but shouted, her face turning red with anger.

"Sarah," Maddy whispered, reaching for her.

"No, let her speak," Mac said. He folded his arms over his chest and smiled down at the girl. "She seems so confident, I find myself curious as to why. So, young Miss Kimble, what makes you so sure William Killkenny has a heart?"

"I know he has one because I heard it pounding so hard I thought it was going to burst out of his chest. And then I felt it thumping against my ear when he was hugging me so tight I couldn't breathe." She lifted her chin higher. "And he kept saying over and over that he'd die before he'd ever let anything bad happen to me. So he *does* have a heart, and he *does* love Mama and me."

"What are you talking about, Sarah?" Maddy asked, turning her daughter to face her. "When did William say that to you?"

But Sarah looked past her at William, her eyes suddenly uncertain.

Maddy also looked at William, only to find him standing stone-still, his deep blue eyes guardedly haunted.

"It was my fault!" Sarah cried, pulling Maddy around to face her. "He told me not to go that far out on the point, but I went anyway. And then a big wave suddenly came and knocked me over and sucked me into the water."

"Into the *ocean*?" Maddy gasped, dropping her bouquet to

grab Sarah's shoulders. "When I left you with William yesterday while I went into Ellsworth, you fell in the ocean? And
you didn't tell me? Sarah!" she cried, twisting to glare up at
William.

"I promised William I'd tell you," Sarah said. "Only I had to
beg him to let me wait until after the wedding."

"But why?"

The girl dropped her gaze, her lower lip quivering. "Because
I was afraid you would think he was irresponsible," she whispered, "and then you wouldn't marry him." She looked up, her
big brown eyes welling with tears. "But you just gotta marry
him, Mom. You'll break his heart if you don't."

"Sarah," William said on a strangled whisper, dropping to
his knees.

"You do too have a heart!" the girl cried, throwing herself at
him. She wrapped her arms around him and pressed her ear to
his chest. "I can hear it, and it's beating just as hard as it was
yesterday." She lifted her head and clasped his face between her
small hands, looking him directly in the eyes. "You don't listen
to that man, William. He isn't your friend, or he'd *know* you
have a heart and that you gave it to Mom and me."

Sarah turned fierce brown eyes up to Maddy and then
looked back at William. "You remember what you told me yesterday when I didn't want Mom to know I fell in the ocean? You
said I never, ever have to be afraid of telling the truth. And *you*
don't have to be afraid, either. It's okay for you to tell Mom and
me you love us," she whispered, her tiny little nose only inches
from his. "But if you can't say it out loud, then that's okay, too,
because we already know you do. Everyone might think I'm
just a kid, but I'm old enough to know love when I *feel* it." She
dropped her hands, but her eyes continued boring into his, her
voice rising with the power of her conviction. "Mom told me
that a person's actions speak louder than his words, and you

practically *shout* you love us a hundred times a day in a hundred different ways."

Maddy could see that William was visibly shaking now, and for the first time since she'd met him, the pleading eyes he lifted to hers were filled with uncertainty.

"He's been shouting his love to me, too," Lois suddenly said, standing up.

"And me," Charlotte said, vaulting out of her wheelchair. "Every day, in a hundred different ways."

Samuel also stood up. "Even I can hear him, even without my hearing aids. Hell, they can probably hear him all the way to Oak Harbor."

"Any fool can see the man's got a heart as big as the ocean," Janice said, clutching the back of Mem's wheelchair.

"Because it takes a *huge* heart to love the bunch of us," Mem added, her frail chin lifting defiantly as she glared at Mac.

"It's more likely *you're* the one lacking a heart," Elvira growled at Mac.

"What we're saying, Mr. Oceanus," Elbridge said, walking to the bottom step of the gazebo, "is that everyone here, from nine to ninety years old, *objects* to your objection that these two big-hearted, loving people should get married. Now, can you find your own way out, or do you need me to show you to the door?"

Utterly confounded as he faced the residents, Mac suddenly gave them a bow. "Forgive me, please," he said softly. "It seems I've made an egregious error." He turned and held out his hand. "I'm sorry, William, for mistaking you for someone I knew . . . a very long, long time ago."

It took him a moment, but William finally shook Mac's hand.

"And Madeline," Mac said, turning to her, "I wouldn't have returned you within a week, because I would have stopped time itself in order to keep you." His eyes crinkled in amusement. "I believe you'll be needing a godfather in . . . oh, seven and a half months, so just tuck my invitation into a bottle and toss it in the sea, and I promise to be here for the baptism."

Maddy gasped, grabbing William for support. "I am *not* pregnant," she hissed.

Mac glanced briefly at her belly before lifting laughing eyes back to hers. "Really, Madeline, you think some flimsy scrap of plastic is going to stop a soul that's wanting to be born?" He chuckled softly. "He'll be quite an interesting young man, I'm guessing, considering his parentage."

Since all Maddy could do was gape at him, Mac turned his attention to Sarah. "And you, young Miss Kimble—thank you for pointing out how a person might recognize love, for I confess it's always been a mystery to me." He touched one of her soft curls. "You are a very wise young lady, and although she's a few years older than you, I believe you'll be a great help to your new aunt in the coming months."

Maddy felt William stiffen on a sharp breath. "What have ye done, Oceanus?"

Mac turned to him. "She's my wedding present to you, William." He shrugged. "I'd planned to bring her with me today, but the little magpie told me to tell you she'd get here just as soon as she finds her basket of ribbons." He sighed. "What is it with little sisters, Killkenny? Do they think it's their *duty* to drive their big brothers insane?"

"Are we having a wedding or not?" Charlotte called out. "Because that ice sculpture is going to look more like a frog than a dragon if it sits out much longer."

Elbridge started to climb the steps of the gazebo, but Mac held up his hands. "I'm going, I'm going," he said with a chuckle, backing toward the opposite staircase. He stopped and gave a deep bow to everyone, then straightened with a wink at Maddy. "You know how to reach me, Madeline, if this *big-hearted* Irishman becomes too much of a handful," he said, nodding toward William. He held his arms wide. "So I believe I *will* give my blessing to this union, as well as my hope that you all live happily ever after for—" He grinned. "For a very, very long time."

A stiff breeze suddenly swirled up the river from the ocean, engulfing the gazebo and all of the wedding guests in a blanket of blinding white fog. And when it just as suddenly cleared not a minute later, Maximilian Oceanus was gone—a cacophony of channel buoys tolling like laughter behind him.

Chapter Twenty-eight

$\mathcal{M}$addy leaned back against William's chest, smiling at the rhythmic *clip-clop* of Rose's hooves on the pavement as they exited the River Run parking lot and started down the moonlit street. "Did we just get married, Mr. Killkenny?" she asked, her smile widening when she heard him sigh.

"I'm afraid we did, lass."

"So . . . do you feel like a husband?"

That got her a chuckle. "I'll let ye know in the morning when I wake up and realize I no longer have to sneak out your bedroom window before your mother or daughter walk in on us."

"Isn't it funny," she murmured, snuggling deeper into the warmth of his embrace, "how one minute it's scandalous for two consenting adults to have sex, but after standing in front of a bunch of people and *announcing* their intention to sleep together, it's suddenly okay?"

"'Tis obvious marriage was invented by a woman."

Maddy canted her head back to grin up at him. "You missed that one by a mile, Willy. Marriage was invented by some poor, haggard *father*." She faced forward again. "Is Mac really bringing Gabriella to this century, like he brought Fiona?"

William's arms tightened around her. "It would appear that's his intention."

"But what did he mean when he said she wouldn't come until she found her box of ribbons?" She looked up at him again. "Hiram told me you asked him to give your sister a message that had something to do with ribbons. Is Gabriella using them as an excuse to put off coming here for some reason?"

William kissed her forehead. "It's more likely Gabby is planning a reunion that will involve my being the brunt of a devious stunt." He both shuddered and chuckled. "God save us—the girl's had·a thousand years to plot her revenge."

"Revenge for what? Did you steal her box of ribbons or something?"

"Oh, no, ye don't," he said, nudging her around to face forward. "I'm not about to tattle on myself—especially considering I'll soon be the only male living in a house with *three* frightening females."

Maddy pulled his hand down to her belly. "According to Mac, you won't be the only male in seven and a half months." She snorted. "Apparently you knocked me up, Mr. Killkenny, *before* you made an honest woman of me." But then she sighed. "After the lecture I gave Sarah on the proper order of marriage and babies, now how in hell am I supposed to persuade her to do as I say, not as I do?"

"Do not worry yourself; I will make sure the girl is wedded and bedded in the proper order, even if it means locking her in our tower until she's thirty."

Maddy smiled into the night again. "Have I ever told you I love you?"

He squeezed her so tightly that she squeaked. "A hundred times a day, lass, in a hundred different ways."

"Oh! Now that we're finally alone, I have something to give you," she said, sitting up to reach under the high collar of her mother's wedding gown. She'd wanted to change into more comfortable clothes after the reception, but the women had all ganged up on her, complaining that she would positively ruin her fairy-tale wedding if she didn't ride off into the sunset wearing her beautiful gown. "Damn," she muttered. "Would you unbutton the collar of my dress?"

He gave a hearty chuckle. "An eager bride, are ye?" he whispered against her ear—which made her shudder sensuously. "I believe I was fourteen the last time I tried to *go parking* on a horse," he continued as he attempted to undo the buttons. "But if ye can't wait until we get home, then I'll see if I can remember how it's done."

Maddy turned to blink at him. "You actually did it on horseback?" She eyed him suspiciously, even as her hormones—the same ones that had gotten her pregnant before her wedding—started doing their infamous little happy dance. "How?"

William suddenly draped her over one of his arms, lifted one of her legs across his chest, and spun her around before she could even squeak in surprise. And damn if her hormones didn't go into full riot when she found herself clutching his shoulders, facing him, intimately straddling his thighs.

"Well, now," he whispered, his hands gathering up the hem of her long dress, "I believe it involves one of us having a nimble body, the other good balance, and an obliging horse."

Maddy glanced over her shoulder, wondering who was driving Rose. "Um . . . William," she said, although it came out as a squeak when his wandering hands stopped on her hips.

Which were naked, since she wasn't wearing panties.

Well, she *was* an eager bride, and having planned to pounce on her groom the moment they reached Dragon Cove, she wasn't risking another lovemaking debacle like the first time she'd attacked him.

"Wait. No. Stop!" she squealed when he pulled her even more intimately against him—revealing exactly how eager *he* was.

Her petition was answered by a groan. "Ye can't let me know you're not wearing underpants and then ask me to stop." He rested his forehead against hers. "Even if someone should see us, your dress will shield the fact that I married a wanton woman. You're already with child, and we announced our intentions in front of a priest, so there's no reason for us to stop. And ye needn't worry about Rose, either; she's not one to carry tales back to her stall mates. Now, do ye have any other concerns?" he growled, pulling her against him again.

She cupped his handsome face between her hands but stopped short of kissing him, because she really, really wanted to give him her gift before they made love the first time as husband and wife. "Don't worry, Mr. Killkenny," she whispered, her lips brushing provocatively against his—making *him* shudder. "I have every intention of going parking on this horse, if for no other reason than to see if it really is possible. But I want to give you my wedding present first."

"I believe I've been trying to let you give it to me for the last five minutes."

That made her laugh, and she reached up to undo the buttons at the nape of her neck. "No, I have something else I want to give you first."

Only he lifted his hands to catch her when she started to lose her balance.

Which also lifted her dress.

Which in turn exposed her naked bottom to the cool night air.

Maddy threw herself forward with a gasp, trying to push her dress back down.

They might have been okay if Rose hadn't suddenly stopped walking.

Maddy grabbed William's shoulders to right herself just as he lunged forward in an attempt to catch her. "Christ almighty, will ye quit your squirming."

"William, we're falling!"

Stating the obvious did not keep it from happening, however. William wrapped his arms around her as they went tumbling off Rose, twisting so that he took the brunt of their fall as they landed on the library lawn.

Hearing his grunt come out as a *whoosh*, Maddy scrambled off him, only to hear him grunt again, this time several decibels louder and quite a few octaves higher.

"Omigod, William!" she cried, reaching for him. "I'm sorry!"

Apparently thinking that she was attacking him again when her feet got tangled up in the train of her dress, William caught hold of her shoulders to guide her fall, spun her around, and pinned her to the ground. "Maddy, darling," he growled. "Let's say we just lie here for a while and enjoy the evening air."

"I'm sorry, William," she whispered. "Are you in much pain?"

He lifted his head. "I don't suppose they taught you what to do for such injuries in nursing school, did they?"

She grinned up at him. "Actually, they did." She cupped his cheeks. "First, we're supposed to give the patient mouth-to-mouth resuscitation, and then, once we're confident that he's breathing heavily and his heart is racing, we're supposed to . . . um . . . examine the wound and decide if further action is necessary."

"And if it is? What sort of action would ye take?"

She traced his perfectly groomed goatee with her thumb. "If I remember correctly, the textbook said we should surround the injury with lots and lots of heat."

"And just how would ye go about doing that?"

"Well, the prescribed method would be to get the patient into bed, but in this case, I believe a horse would work equally well. Then the textbook said we should use our own body to surround the injury and apply just the right amount of pressure, and then slowly—very, very slowly, it said—start moving up and down the injury until we feel the patient is recovered enough to take over from there."

William lifted his head and looked up and down the lawn.

"What are you looking for?"

He smiled, even as he continued looking around. "A nurse."

She gave his shoulder a shove, pushing him off her so she could sit up. "You are *married* to a nurse," she sputtered in laughter, reaching up to undo her collar. "And I intend to administer *intensive* care just as soon as I give you my gift."

But upon getting the collar open and not finding the chain that should be hanging around her neck, Maddy scrambled to her feet. "Oh, no, I can't find it!" She contorted her arms and unzipped the back of her dress, pulling it down off her shoulders. "The chain must have broken," she muttered, sliding her arms out of the sleeves so she could pull her slip away from her bra.

A car drove down Main Street, and its windows suddenly lowered, and several teenagers—male and female—stuck their heads out, their whistles and catcalls lost in the sound of the car's honking horn.

"Madeline, you are undressing in the town square," William growled, slipping out of his jacket and tossing it over her shoulders.

"I don't care!" she cried when she didn't find the chain inside her bra. She shoved her slip down over her hips along with her gown, stepped out of them, and got down on her knees to start searching through the material. "I have to find it, William." She stopped only long enough to lift pleading eyes to his. "I broke three grinders and spent weeks making it for you." She held up her hand to show him the bandages on her fingers. "I know I told you that I cut my fingers pruning my rose bushes, but I really cut them making your gift."

She started searching again.

William took hold of her shoulders and lifted Maddy to her feet, tucked her arms into the sleeves of his jacket, then raised his finger to cover her lips when she started to protest. "Hush, lass. Is this what you're looking for?" he asked soothingly, reaching into his pants pocket. He held his hand up between them and opened his fingers to let a thin chain drop out, his dragon claw dangling from it.

"How did you get it?" she asked with a gasp.

"When Mac shook my hand before he disappeared, he pressed it into my palm."

"But it was around my neck then, so how did Mac get hold of it?"

William arched a brow. "Only one of two ways that I know of; the first being that he reached down your dress and dug it out of your bosom."

"He did not!"

William flipped his hand to toss the chain into his palm. "Then I guess he must have gotten it by magic."

"But why?" Maddy whispered, lifting her gaze to his, a lump rising in her throat. "I . . . I was supposed to give it to you, William. It was my wedding present to you."

He looked down at what was left of his old dragon claw. "You're returning my gift?" he asked, not looking at her.

"No. No!" she cried, clutching his hand that was holding the claw. "I'm *never* giving it back. I only intended to show you what I did with it, so you would understand how I see you." She let go of him and held out her hand, palm up. "I intend to wear it forever and ever, William, as . . ." She felt her cheeks heat up and looked down at her gift to him through suddenly blurry eyes. "As a token of your love," she finished on a whisper.

He lifted her chin with his finger. "Ye spent the last few weeks filing my claw into the shape of a heart," he asked softly, "to show me how you see me?"

All she could do was nod.

"And now you're wondering why Mac ruined your surprise by taking it from you and giving it back to me?"

Maddy threw herself at William and wrapped her arms around him so tightly she made him grunt. "I don't care if you don't ever say you love me," she said, nearly sobbing. "And I don't need some stupid old token to remind me, either. Mac's wrong, William; you do have a heart, and it belongs to *me*." She leaned back to glare up at him. "You were only a bogeyman, you big sap," she said softly, breaking into a smile. "And not a very good one, seeing how you couldn't even scare me away. Real monsters *enjoy* scaring the bejeezus out of people, and I happen to know that you didn't enjoy one minute of your life as a dragon."

"I enjoyed flying."

She went back to glaring at him. "Oh, William, just let me love you, will you?" she whispered, dropping her forehead to his chest.

He nudged her upright in order to slip the chain over her head, and then leaned her away in order to settle his heart-shaped claw between her breasts. "Mac gave it to me so that I could give it to you again," he said, running his fingers through her hair to hold her as she looked at him. "*After* he made one small alteration to it. You may have shaped the claw into a heart, but you forgot to include the symbol of a strong arm."

"But that's the symbol on *your* medal. Why would I need it on mine?"

"Because men need a strong arm sometimes, too, and I believe Mac wished to point out to both of us that you are mine."

"I'm a strong arm?"

"You rescued me, didn't you? And gave me back my heart so I can love you."

Maddy sighed, even as she smiled. "You never lost your heart, William."

He sighed right back at her, but he didn't smile. "Did I just acquire a wife who intends to spend the next fifty years contradicting her husband?"

She reached up to toy with the heart-shaped claw hanging around her neck. "And if you did, just what is my big, bad bogeyman husband going to do about it?"

Still holding her face in his hands, he finally smiled, and it was tender and sweet and held only a hint of mischief. "I imagine that just before I dig out my knife and cut off yet another one of those offending bras ye insist on wearing, I will likely tell you that I love you a thousand times *more* than a hundred times a day, in many more ways than I can count."

Maddy's heart started thumping so hard it actually hurt.

He brushed his thumbs across her cheeks. "Please don't cry, Madeline. I promise I'm not just saying the words, I'm meaning them. I love you more than life itself, wife, and am giving you my heart to hold in your strong arms forever and ever, as I vow to hold yours in mine."

He had to prop her up in order to kiss her then, as she'd gone quite weak in the knees, and Maddy didn't think she'd ever breathe properly again.

The romantic sap.

Who knew that when a scary-looking, buck-naked caveman had walked out of the library and kissed her in front of half the town in the pouring rain, they'd be standing in the very same spot as husband and wife not three months later?

When he finally let her come up for air, Maddy slowly looked around to make sure they didn't have an audience. Then she smiled at his expectant look as she placed her hands on his chest, surreptitiously moved her foot just beside his as she leaned against him, and shoved him into the small grove of young junipers not three feet away.

His yelp of surprise was lost in her laughter as she straddled his hips and held his hands down on either side of his head.

"William," she said very, very softly.

"Yes, Madeline?"

"Boo."

Turn the page

for a special look at

MYSTICAL WARRIOR,

the final book in

the Midnight Bay trilogy

by *New York Times* bestselling author

Janet Chapman

Coming soon from Pocket Books

"Goddamn it, Gregor, I am *serious*. You have one week to find Fiona a new place to live," Trace growled into his cell phone as he stood in the middle of his neatly organized, cobweb-free barn. "Because if you don't, I swear the next time she goes into town I will torch my own damn house to get her out of here."

"What's the matter, Huntsman, do ye not like having fresh eggs for breakfast?"

"Eggs? You think this is about the chickens? Or the goat? Or the goddamned horse the size of an elephant? It's about your sister cleaning and rearranging every square inch of my barn. She organized my *tools*, Gregor. And she found an old scythe and leveled every damned last weed all the way to the street!"

"Aye," Kenzie said on a sigh. "Women do have a tendency to nest."

"Nest?" Trace repeated through gritted teeth. He walked over to look out the side window, only to scowl again when he saw Fiona—wearing *his* tool belt around the waist of her long coat—nailing a board she'd obviously found during her cleaning spree to one of the rotten paddock posts. "Damn it, Gregor, if she keeps fixing up this place they're going to raise my taxes."

The horse and goat were in the paddock; the horse nuzzling Fiona's shoulder, and the goat, its neck stretched through the fence, trying to reach the leather pouch on her tool belt. Her dog, Misneach, was standing in a small water trough that Trace had never seen before, and the pup kept driving his head under the water, only to surface with a rock in his mouth, which he would then drop in the water again.

Trace's mood darkened even more when he caught himself noticing how the low-hanging November sun made Fiona's hair look like spun gold—especially the tendrils framing her flawless face—and how graceful and efficiently she moved. And he sure as hell didn't like that he *liked* coming home to a house that wasn't empty, with the smell of wood smoke and the aroma of fresh baked bread assaulting him the moment he stepped out of his truck.

Thank God he kept his door locked; if she ever saw his living quarters, she'd probably have a field day—or more likely a month of field days—cleaning the kitchen and organizing his sock drawer.

"Don't ye see," Kenzie said, turning serious. "Fiona's nesting must mean she's grown comfortable with you. That's amazing progress in only two weeks, considering Killkenny got nothing but grief from her."

"When he was a *dragon* and she was a *hawk*," Trace growled. "But whenever William or any other man stops by, she still vanishes and doesn't reappear until they're gone. And," he continued when Kenzie tried to say something, "she can't be comfortable with me, as we haven't spoken two entire sentences to each other since I agreed to let her keep that puppy. Which," he went on hotly, glaring at the chickens scattered throughout the yard, "has turned into twelve hens, a goat, and a horse. And when I stopped in just now to pick up some tools, I found two skunks curled up in some rags in a box on my workbench."

"They're orphans," Kenzie said, the amusement back in his voice. "Fiona called this morning and asked me to go over there to check them out, and they told me they hadn't seen their mama for many, many days."

"They told you they're orphans," Trace repeated, deadpan, remembering this was the man he had seen transform into a panther.

"Aye," Kenzie said. "And they gave me their word they won't spray anyone not directly threatening them."

Trace closed his eyes on a silent groan.

Great. Wonderful. How friggin' fantastic *nice* of them.

"Ye needn't worry; they'll be taking their winter sleep soon, and Fiona offered to let them stay in the barn only until spring."

Trace snapped his eyes open. "Can *she* talk to animals?"

Kenzie chuckled at his alarm. "Nay, but she does have a certain . . . empathy for creatures. Ye might remember she was a red-tailed hawk for several centuries."

What he remembered was that he was dealing with a clan of *magic makers*.

One of whom could turn him into a toad.

Trace scowled out the window again when he saw Fiona wrestling another board into place, two nails held between her pursed lips and a fine sheen of perspiration making her hair cling to her flushed cheeks. "One week," he snapped, not caring if Matt turned him into a goddamned slug. "You get your sister and her zoo off my property by next Tuesday, or I swear this place is going up like a rocket on the Fourth of July."

A loud sigh came over the phone. "Can ye not give this arrangement more of a chance? It means a lot to me, Trace," Kenzie said, his voice growing thick. "When I brought the mare to her, I saw a hint of the woman Fiona was becoming before that bastard assaulted her. Just give me enough time to explain to her that she can't take over your home, and I'll persuade her to turn her energies toward pleasing *herself* instead of you."

Trace suddenly stiffened, not knowing which shocked him more: that Fiona was working her pretty little ass off making sure he liked her, or that *he* hadn't realized what she was doing. The eggs and fresh baked bread he kept finding on his doorstep, the boughs she had tucked along the house before he could do it himself, the barn swept clean of every damn last cobweb, his tools organized, her living in virtual darkness every evening—she'd been building brownie points against his ever getting angry at her.

How in hell had he missed that?

For chrissakes, he was *trained* to read people.

Which is why, when he had seen it was taking every ounce of courage she possessed just to ask him if she could keep Misneach, he'd folded like a house of cards. And going against his own better judgment, he'd conned her into helping him bank the house, hoping she would see that he wasn't anyone to be afraid of.

Only he'd nearly blown it when she'd dropped that pail of nails.

Christ, he'd wanted ten minutes alone with the bastard that had caused the terror he'd heard in her screams.

And when he'd continued having her help him as if nothing had happened, she'd become no better than her clueless puppy, eagerly pitching in and even appearing disappointed when he'd sent her inside. And then she'd worked nonstop for the next six days, turning his house into a goddamned *home*.

"Your sister's demons are not my problem, Gregor. And if *you* can't deal with them, then move her in with some little old lady who needs mothering." Remembering the flood of inquires he'd gotten down at the docks about his pretty new tenant, Trace snorted. "Just make sure you find one who owns a shotgun, because some of the idiots around here have the finesse of a bull moose when it comes to courting women."

"This is why it's important that Fiona live over you."

"Dammit, Gregor; I am the *last* person you want around her."

Trace immediately realized his mistake, and the prolonged silence on the other end of the phone told him that Kenzie hadn't missed it, either.

"You're attracted to her," the highlander said quietly.

"Goddamn it!" Trace growled, kicking the wooden barrel he was standing beside as hard as he could. "I am—"

Trace snapped his mouth shut when the air compressor sitting on top of the barrel rolled off and slammed down onto his workbench.

Or more alarmingly, it slammed into the box holding the skunks—the startled screams of its occupants mixing with his own panicked shout. Trace dropped the phone to catch the box, at the same time trying to turn the opening away from himself.

He'd have succeeded, too, if the heavy compressor hadn't continued its descent and slammed into his knee. Trace fell with a shouted curse, shoving at the box as he tried to scramble away. And that's when that damned compressor struck his head, just as the skunks tumbled onto the floor beside him.

Apparently believing this was well within the bounds of being directly threatened, both skunks let loose everything they had, hitting him point blank.

Trace's roar ended on a choked gag when a cloud of putrid musk enveloped him. He blindly rolled in the direction of the door, his eyes burning like they'd been doused with acid, his mouth and throat on fire as he held his breath, while fighting the urge to vomit. But finding he couldn't crawl on his right knee, he ended up dragging himself from the barn even as he scrambled out of his jacket and ripped off his shirt. He tried getting to his feet then, only his knee gave out and he fell to the ground.

He threw up, and lay there gagging, gasping for breath.

"I've got you," he barely heard over the roaring in his head.

"No, get away," he choked on a series of convulsing heaves. He blindly swatted at her, but still she managed to manacle his wrist in a surprisingly strong grip, and then wedge her shoulder under his armpit as she straightened to lift him up.

They stumbled toward the house. "Water. Outside faucet," he rasped, fumbling with his belt buckle with his free hand.

Christ, he couldn't breathe!

He slammed against the granite foundation as he felt for the faucet, and gave a shout of relief when the deluge of water gushed over his head. He lay on his side not caring if he drowned in the icy water, because it sure as hell was better than drowning in skunk piss and vomit.

Trace felt something tugging at his feet and realized Fiona was taking off his boots. He unfastened his jeans and then gritted his teeth against the pain in his knee when she pulled them off. He dragged himself back under the spigot again, and let the water continue to flush his eyes and pummel his body.

Misneach, who'd been barking incessantly this whole time, jumped at him but gave a strangled yelp and ran away in a fit of sneezes.

Trace didn't know how long he lay there, and didn't even care that he was naked; he only knew that whenever he moved from under the water, he started gagging again.

The water suddenly shut off, and his protest got lost inside the heavy material that enveloped him. "Go away," he shouted, blindly feeling for the spigot as he tossed the material away and turned the water back on.

"Oh, thank God you stopped by!" Trace heard Fiona cry as she was moving away. "You have to help me get him in the house. He hurt his knee and can't walk."

The water shut off again and the material returned; this time wrapping around him like a straitjacket just before he was hauled to his feet.

"Christ, Huntsman, did ye kiss their asses?" Kenzie growled. "Fiona, grab that jug of vinegar I brought."

When Trace's knee gave out on him again, the highlander hefted him over his shoulder with a muttered curse, and started off.

"Not the house!"

"Nay, I'm taking you down to the salt marsh. Fiona, go get a blanket and then bring it and the vinegar down to us."

Great. Wonderful. Friggin' fantastic. A swim in the freezing ocean is exactly what he needed. Trace vomited again—which started his nose and throat burning all over again. "Forget the week," he ground out, wiping his face on the back of Kenzie's jacket. "I'm torching the house *today*."

Kenzie chuckled. "You'll likely want to burn the barn at least, along with your clothes and my sister's coat."

After wiping the tears pouring from his eyes, Trace held his head to keep it from bobbing with Kenzie's strides. "My face is numb," he muttered. "I swear skunk piss is worse than pepper spray. The military should bomb the bastards out of those Afghan tunnels with this shit."

"Aye, I've seen the little buggers send warriors scattering right in the middle of battle. Here we go," Kenzie said with a grunt, shrugging Trace off his shoulder and dropping him next to a tidal pool. "Hell, Huntsman, couldn't ye have left your shorts on, at least?"

Trace leaned over to splash some seawater on his face, and gave a snort. "Apparently your sister isn't so shy that she wasn't afraid to strip me naked in a matter of seconds." He looked toward the house and saw the blurry figure of Fiona racing down the path along the paddock fence, a blanket in one hand and a jug in the other. He glared up at Kenzie. "She goes home with you *today*."

The highlander bent over and gave the coat Trace was sitting on a sharp tug, rolling him into the pool—his roar of outrage turning to curses when he landed in freezing water up to his chest.

Kenzie turned to block Fiona's view as she approached them. "Just leave the blanket and vinegar," he told her. "And go put Trace's clothes in a pile in the middle of the driveway, along with your coat," he instructed, handing it to her, "and light them on fire. Then go change your own clothes," he continued, moving slightly when she tried to see past him. "And after ye do, go in his home, fill his bathtub with hot water, and put a kettle on to boil."

"No!" Trace shouted, making the highlander turn to look at

him. His vision might be blurry, but he could see the amusement on the bastard's face. "I can run my own bath. And besides, the door is locked." He splashed more seawater on his face and then screwed his fists into his eyes, trying to clear them. But when he leaned around Kenzie to look at Fiona and saw her own eyes were puffy with skunk fumes and filled with concern, he blew out a deep sigh. "Just don't burn my clothes without taking my wallet out of my pants first, okay?" he said calmly.

She nodded, and holding her coat away from herself, turned and started back toward the barn at a run.

"His house key is likely on the key ring in his truck," Kenzie called after her. "Ye run a bath and put the kettle on."

"Damn it, Gregor. I don't want her in my house."

"Why? Are ye keeping a naked woman tied to your bed?" Kenzie drawled, unscrewing the cap on the vinegar. "Close your eyes; this may sting."

Trace snorted, which ended on a sputter when the vinegar cascaded down over his head and into his mouth. He gargled, then spit it out and ran his hands over his face and through his hair. "How did you get here so fast?" he asked, shuddering against the cold as he rubbed the steady stream of vinegar over his chest and arms.

"I was in town, at Eve's store. Lucky for you she uses vinegar to wash the windows," Kenzie said, directing the stream over his back. "Mind telling me what possessed you to disturb those skunks?"

Trace stopped washing to glare up at him. "I didn't; my air compressor did. Apparently your sister thought it belonged on top of a barrel beside my workbench, and when I kicked the barrel, the compressor fell on the box of skunks. Then it hit my knee just before it smashed into my head." He touched the stinging lump on his forehead, and finding his fingers covered in blood, he glared up at Kenzie again. "That compressor must weigh as much as she does, so not only *why* did she think it belonged up on the barrel but *how* did she get it up there?"

Kenzie shrugged, and poured the last of the vinegar down over him. "That will have to do for now," he said, picking up the blanket. "We better get you into a hot bath before the cold takes your strength." He laid the blanket out on the grass, and reached out to Trace. "If ye have scotch, I'll dose your tea with it for you to sip while ye soak."

"Not that I'll taste it," he said, giving a grunt when Kenzie hauled him out of the tidal pool and dropped him onto the blanket. "I'll be lucky if I ever get the smell of skunk piss out of my nose hairs, much less taste anything again." He pulled the blanket around himself and dropped his throbbing head in his hands with a groan.

Kenzie squatted down in front of him. "I'm asking as a friend, Trace, that ye please let Fiona stay," he said quietly.

Trace lifted his head to look the highlander in the eyes. "I came within one blow of killing a man the last time I got between a woman and her demons—now she's dead, the guy who killed her is serving five years for manslaughter, and I got kicked out of the military." He dropped his head back in his hands. "As much as I'd like to help you, I've got my own demons to fight."

"What stopped you from killing him?"

He looked up again. "Only the knowledge that I was as much to blame for her death as he was."

"It's been my experience that intelligent men learn from their mistakes, my friend, and I have every reason to believe you won't make that particular mistake again."

"Oh, I won't. I have no intention of ever getting involved with another woman."

Kenzie chuckled at that, and lifted Trace with him as he stood up. "No offense, Huntsman," he said, hefting him over his shoulder. "But with your stones—even shriveled as they are from the cold—I can't quite see you becoming a monk."

"Lovely, Gregor," Trace muttered, gritting his teeth at being carried like a stinking sack of grain. "How friggin' *nice* of you to notice."

Passion is stronger *after dark.*

Bestselling Paranormal Romance from Pocket Books!